The Harris Cc

Mad

The truth, the whole tru⌣
well, that depends on who you are asking.

The Harris Connection is a series of novels continuing on from each other, but from a different character's point of view.

In book 1, **Christie & Co**, we see the world through Christie's eyes. We discover how she juggles the changes in her life after her mother is revealed to be a world-famous actress. In the rollercoaster of events which follow, every truth she reveals is the truth.

Well, it's Christie's truth – and I still believe her.

In book 2, **Maddie's Men**, we see the world through a mother's eyes, the fame, the fortune, the failures. Every sacrifice she has made comes back to taunt her as her secrets are paraded in the press. Every truth she reveals is the truth.

Well, it's Maddie's truth – and I believe her too.

In book 3, **Trudy's Tryst**, we see the world through the eyes of one blessed with beauty, poise, status and wealth. Trudy's life spirals into a new realm of reality with the unexpected bonus of a roommate. Every truth she reveals is the truth.

Well, again, it's Trudy's truth – and, honestly, I believe her too.

About the Author

Kathleen Clunan was raised on a farm in Lancashire. Being the middle child of six gave her lots of freedom and opportunity for mischief making. Helping out on the farm, climbing trees, ditch dodging and hanging from zip lines were a big part of her childhood. Piano lessons – not so much!

But then she had to grow up. Kathleen played a major role in running the family business whilst bringing up her own family in the same farmhouse she's been raised in. After a significant brush with illness, she decided to pursue her real passion, writing. Her first book was published in 2019, *The Evolution of Christie Harris* (now re-released under the title: *Christie & Co*), and she had intended it to be a stand-alone novel. However, due to the popularity of the characters, she was inundated with requests to continue the story, which she did. *Maddie's Men* was published in 2023.

Kathleen is currently extending the characters further in her third novel, *Trudy's Tryst*, whilst still continuing to run the family business.

Follow her on Facebook

 Kathleen Clunan

www.KathleenClunan.com

The Harris Connection
Book 2

Maddie's Men

Kathleen Clunan

Maddie's Men
Kathleen Clunan

Published in the UK by Eagle Eye Books

Revision 1 2 3 4 5 6 7 8 9 26.08

Printed and bound by Cloc Books Print, UK

ISBN: 978-0-9931860-8-0
A CIP catalogue record for this title is available from the
British Library

Dedicated to Jakson, Lola and Izzie.

My joy.

Developments

- Old Flame
- Remembering the Abyss
- Impressions
- United Front
- Baby Steps
- Standoff
- Rules, Regs and Revelations
- Suits
- Honey Buns
- An Easy Ride
- Addiction
- Pauletta
- Marshmallows
- Connections
- Shot
- The Tour
- Wriggle Room
- A Storm and a Teacup
- A Hit from the Past
- In the Zone
- After the Storm
- And Again
- The Truth of Tears
- Hankering for Change
- The Gift
- The Dream Team
- Backstory
- Terry's Torment
- Undertones
- Release
- Loyalties
- Repercussions
- Threads
- Setups and Upsets
- In the Nick of Time
- Home
- Safe Hands
- Butterflies
- Encore

Dear
Auntie Maddie/
Maddie Harris/
Madeline De-Muir,

As you can see, I'm struggling deciding who you are in my life.

For so many years, you have been my lovely Auntie Maddie, held close by happy childhood memories, letters of advice and challenges. You encouraged me to follow my dreams.

My life was settled. I loved my career. And living here with my BFFs – Trudy and Suzi – meant life was never dull. Especially with Trudy and her champagne lifestyle and droll sense of entitlement. Then all of a sudden – BAM – Mum and Dad break the news of my true identity – they are actually YOUR parents, and you are my mother not my Auntie Maddie.

But there's more... You are also the famous actress Madeline De-Muir...

Really? And I was just about, almost, nearly figuring out how to get my head around the whole thing, when – BAM – without my knowledge or consent you launch

Evolution, an exhibition of all the artwork I've done for you over the years. My whole childhood and adolescence on display, for the whole world to see.

Maybe you can understand why I have trust issues with you?

But, you know, Miles confided in me about his life on the streets. His life transformed with you taking him in, educating him and making him your PA. I feel proud of you for taking the risk. Certainly, prouder of that than any of your grand awards, because at the end of the day, it's relationships that count.

Your charity – the Keep-a-Key kids – how you change their lives, and always have time for them. I'm not jealous or resentful, but I can't help feeling you should have made more of an effort for me, when you came back.

I want you to know, I am trying, I am. But I need time because I have so much to come to terms with. I wake up every morning wondering whatever is going to happen next.

I really want to love you as much as I have always loved Auntie Maddie, with her crazy stories and invaluable support. But how?

Christie
              X

Maddie's Men

Old Flame

Devour every single inch of your body

He shifts his weight from one foot to the other, folds his arms across his chest. 'So?' he demands.

'You found me.' My voice is hushed, breathy. I rest forward. 'Why don't you sit here, Scott? I could make us a nice cup of tea.'

'I haven't travelled five thousand miles to drink tea, Maddie, and I think you know it.'

I nod, pat the sofa. 'But you could sit, I feel ill at ease with you towering over me like—'

'You're ill at ease, Maddie! You feel ill at ease, do you?' Scott lets out a mirthless laugh, turns and walks to the window, rests his hands on the sill and drops his head. 'I can barely bring myself to look at you.'

Cowboy boots and faded jeans. Shirt sleeves rolled up showing off strong, tanned forearms. Open collar, no tie and about two days' worth of stubble.

I feel the old familiar sensations returning, gently, I stroke my clammy hands together. Hold the panic deep inside, kept in check, acknowledged. I try to control the palpitations sparring to control me.

'I know it must have been a shock—'

'A shock! I'd say so.' He turns to look at me.

There's no need for any level of pretence with this man. I can feel his scrutiny stripping away my years of carefully constructed defence. I have no defence; none that will appease him anyway. The set of his jaw and

1

steel eyes are more menacing than I could ever imagine they'd be.

A silent sigh escapes me. 'I never intended you to find out like this, it's all happened so quickly.'

His body, set like stone, except for the barest shake of his head, blocks out the light from my window. 'I don't know how you can sit there and say that, Maddie.' He continues to studies me. 'How could you do that to me?'

I look away from him, the pain is too raw. 'I was young…' I look back up at his face, still handsome after all these years. More so. The urge to cup his face in my hands and kiss away the hurt so brutally exposed in his eyes, draws me back. Precious images, protected from distortion, leap seamlessly into my mind's eye.

*

'I'm out of breath, Scott!' I pant.

'Then stop running! You know I'm going to catch you anyway.'

Sinking against the trunk of an ancient oak, I cherish the bite of its bark, sure it will last only seconds. Throwing my head back as his arms encircle my waist, scooping me off my feet, I let out a squeal of laughter. Half-heartedly try to wriggle out of his grasp, loving the strength of his arms around me.

My breath is fast and shallow, the buzz of anticipation fizzes through my body. I twist and gaze up into his sure face. 'And what do you plan to do now you've caught me?'

Laughter and passion dance in his eyes. 'The same thing I've done every day of this summer.'

The briefest of kisses tempts my lips. 'I can't remember, remind me.'

He lowers me to the ground, kneels beside me, leans close and whispers, 'I'm going to devour every single inch of your body—'

I giggle. 'You think?'

'Oh, Maddie, I know it. Starting with your... EAR.'

Shrieks of youthful abandon are lost in the centuries-old woodlands.

*

'I find out, by pure chance, Maddie, that I've got a fully-grown daughter. An artist, like myself, no less! And you sit there and tell me it happened quickly! I'd like to say I'm impressed by the face of you.' Scott draws his hands over his stubble and sets his eyes on mine.

'I'd moved away with Mum and Dad before I had time to tell—'

'Twenty-five years ago!'

Looking down at my hands resting palms up, I notice the beginnings of calluses caused by my crutches. 'I was sixteen and pregnant,' I say gently. 'I had little choice but to let my parents take care of me.' I raise my eyes back to his. 'You were full of your big plans. Finish college and off to America to seek your fortune. Not once did you say your plans involved raising a child.'

He turns and looks out of the window. 'They were our plans, plans for us.'

'No, I was just tagging on to your dream. Swept along by the romance of running away to the US of A. How could I steal that dream from you?'

'You stole my chance to raise my daughter, our daughter.' He turns back to me. 'I'd have looked after us, Maddie, somehow.'

Looking at him now, it's hard to believe otherwise. But back then? I shake my head. 'I wish it were true, but I think we both would have sacrificed our dreams. Yours, at least, came true.'

'Says you. The number of times I tried to reach you. It was impossible.'

'I wrote.'

'Three letters! Three letters, and not one of them mentioned *us* having a child.'

'I'm sorry. I really didn't think.' I look away, the intensity of his scrutiny, sears the sham of self-control I'm clinging onto.

'You didn't think. And then, all these years later, a quaint interview with an up-and-coming artist, reveals she's the daughter of the adored actress, Madeline De-Muir... I only had to see her face to know she was mine. The way she moves, the tilt of her head, how she holds her pencil – poised like a spear. The only mystery, is that nobody else has made the connection.'

'Why would they? Like you said, five thousand miles away. People are too busy analysing my reputation, delving into my past, my charities. All the added drama about the fire at the gallery. My concern for Miles has, until now, been my primary focus.'

The door swings open. 'Another man stamping on my clean carpets!' Pauletta stands defiantly glaring at Scott. She has a duster tucked into her waistband, and a utility belt housing a selection of cleaning products slung low on her hips like a domestic gunslinger.

'Pauletta, I'm just trying to have a quiet meeting here—'

'Is not, sorry to say, quiet meeting, madam! I hear him shout.' She points an accusing finger at Scott. 'Is like, what you English say, ́spaghetti bolognaise in here. Is not what I used to. I do not like it, and not put up with it.' She glowers at him. 'And now, to make more mess is your keepies!'

Pauletta all but drags Frankie and Mickey through the door. Both teens are bereft of their new trainers and sporting threadbare socks. 'You keepies be nice, yes? I put goodies in bag for home,' she says, spinning round and slamming the door as she leaves.

They both look down at their feet, Frankie shrugs and then eyes Scott suspiciously. 'Sorry, Maddie, we didn't know you already had someone here.'

'It's not a problem.' It's a welcome relief to see two of my success stories! 'Come on, sit yourselves down, and tell me how I can help.'

Mickey offers a shrug of thanks. She shuffles to the corner of the room, disappearing down onto a small, padded stool, her knees bent somewhere up about her ears.

Frankie sits beside me in the place I'd offered Scott earlier, and frowns. 'We haven't nowhere to go, now the gallery's, y' know. And you and Miles always said we'd have a place, no matter what happened with the gallery.'

I nod and make eye contact. 'Yes, we did. However, Frankie, none of us anticipated the gallery fire—'

'Yeah, but—'

'Frankie!' I use my no-nonsense tone. 'Things are tricky at the moment. But I hope you and the crew have enough confidence in the *Keep-a-Key* team, to know we are working something out.'

'Yeah, Mrs Price is doing her best, but she's no Miles, he's the deal, yeah?'

'Yes, he's the deal. He'll be out of hospital soon, and no doubt back at it, in no time at all.'

Frankie leans in close, and glances meaningfully at Scott. 'Thought he was going to be his replacement,' he barely whispers.

'No,' I whisper back. 'There will never be a replacement for Miles.'

Frankie nods, reassured. 'Okay, thanks. Come on, Mickey, can't you see Maddie's busy here. And I'm starving.'

Mickey uncurls herself into an almost upright stance, and trudges wordlessly after Frankie. At the door, she turns, a shy smile plays on her lips. 'See you.'

'Don't forget to see Pauletta for your goodie bags.' I massage my forehead. 'Sorry about that, where was I?'

'You were just explaining, how you haven't given me a second thought when that *woman* barged in.'

'Oh, ignore Pauletta. She's just a bit temperamental.'

'Yeah? Sounds like you'd do well to be shot of her. And those kids! What are you, their keeper?'

I roll my eyes, Pauletta threatens to leave at least twice a month, I don't need the drama… And I suppose I am their keeper. It has a nice ring, the keepies keeper. I doubt Scott would understand. I sigh. 'Look, Scott, I *have* told Christie about you… Not who you are, but who you were to me.'

'So, when do I get to meet her?'

Suddenly the stress of the last few days swamps me, and the enormity of what lies ahead threatens to drag me back to a place I'd rather not return to. I push myself up, reach for my crutches and stand, managing to address the imbalance caused by my plaster cast.

Scott steps forward. 'Where are you going?' He reaches out, but stops short of actually touching me.

I'm not sure if his intention is to help me or stop me. 'You might not want a cup of tea, but I do. I've had no lunch, been at the hospital with Miles all afternoon. You do know that when my gallery went up in flames, my PA was inside. And as soon as I get home from visiting him, I'm ambushed by you!' I raise myself up to my full 5ft 4, and head for the door. 'I need to get a drink.'

Scott looks down at my cast. 'Here, let me.' He steps in front of me and opens the door.

'Thank you, I can manage from here.' So glad I made sure my toenails match my pink, plaster cast. I swing myself through the tiled hallway towards the kitchen. Thankfully, my body is just about used to this. The first few days of using crutches was agony! I found muscles I didn't even know existed.

'Let me.' Again, Scott steps in front of me, reaches his hand out. 'Is the kitchen through—'

'No! Don't open—'

Terry launches himself fully at the intruder, attaching himself valiantly to the hem of Scott's trouser leg.

'Arh… Get it off me!' Scott shakes his leg.

'Terry!' I holler.

My crutches clatter on the tiles, Terry briefly loosens his grip on Scott's jeans. I scoop the tenacious terrier up. Resting my weight against the wall, I gently scrunch my fingers through his scraggy fur. 'Shh, shh, shh. It's okay,' I soothe. I feel Terry's taut body begin to relax. 'Come on, that's better, no need to get yourself all worked up.'

I watch Scott shuffle away from us rubbing his ankle. 'Sorry about Terry, he'll be okay once you've been formally introduced.'

'That dog should be locked up.'

'He was!' I tut, and nod towards the door. 'He was in the boot room… A room he feels safe in.' I bob my head down, lift Terry level with my face. 'Hey, Terry, this is Scott. No need to get all upset.'

I tuck Terry under my arm. 'Scott, would you like to say hello?' I raise my eyebrows. I'm still resting awkwardly against the wall, and my weight is mainly on my healthy leg.

'Are you sure he's safe?'

I hold out my hand to Scott. 'Let him have a sniff of you.'

'Why not? He's already had a taste.' He offers his left hand, and taking hold of it, I guide it to Terry's nose. Terry has a good old sniff, then he starts to nuzzle at Scott's palm. Before I can stop him, he wriggles out of my grasp, and is clambering up Scott's chest… And decides to settle with his head and paws resting on Scott's shoulder, his bum supported in the crook of Scott's arm.

'There you are, you've passed the test. He likes you.'

'Pleased to hear it.' Scott absently strokes the scrag of Terry's neck. 'Dare I ask what would have happened if I hadn't passed?'

I can't help smiling. 'Really, you don't want to know, suffice to say, he'd have gone in the other direction.'

'Thanks for the warning!' He grimaces and looks down, then back at me.

'I was fairly sure you'd pass.'

'How sure?'

'I'd say, maybe 90%.' I smile, in what I hope is a reassuring way. I take in the slow nod Scott offers and my hand automatically reaches out to Terry. 'So, Scott,

I'd like to formally introduce you to Terry the Terrier, guardian of the garden and friend filterer...' My eyes lock with Scott's, and for the first time, I notice that old glimmer of humour.

'Friend filterer, as in, if they live, they can be your friend?'

'As in, if he lets them live today, they can be my friend today and probably tomorrow, but they'd better not push their luck too soon. After a few weeks, maybe they'll be safe to roam freely about my home.' I bend and pick up my crutches. 'Follow me, the kitchen is through here.'

I push through the double, swing doors into the dining room. 'I try to keep Terry with me, otherwise he's all over the house causing chaos.' I nod towards the window seat with its beautifully balanced scatter cushions. 'He especially likes worrying cushions, and thoroughly enjoys rummaging through the washing basket.'

Scott follows me to the far end of the room. I push down the kitchen door handle with my elbow, a skill I've now mastered, and lead the way in.

Late-spring sun floods the room with gentle warmth and mellow lighting, a perfect foil for the cool of the duck-egg blue units. There is no sign of Frankie and Mickey, they must have grabbed their goodie bags and escaped before Pauletta could interrogate them.

'Take a seat.' I nod towards the breakfast bar overlooking the garden. 'Will you have a drink?'

'Think I need one, coffee, strong and black.' Scott is across the kitchen in a matter of strides. 'What shall I do with this little fella?'

'Do you want to go outside?' Terry's head shoots up from its resting place. 'Just pop him down and open the back door, he can have a mooch outside while we have our drinks.'

I turn and busy myself. I hear Terry scamper to the door, then Scott follow, the door opens and gently closes. As the kettle clicks, the sound of a breakfast stool swivelling and the sigh that follows, confirms Scott is sitting at the breakfast bar.

The knowing someone is waiting, watching, listening, without the visual confirmation, is very empowering. I feel the tug of a smile, and for the first time since Scott turned up on my doorstep, the tummy tremble eases.

Slowly, as I methodically stir my tea, serenity settles. The steady glug of the coffee machine adds to my sense of wellbeing. I add sugar and milk to my tea.

I turn and look at Scott sprawled on the stool, incline my head, hope to appeal to his softer side. 'Would you mind? If I try, I'll slosh most of our drinks all over the floor.'

'Sure.'

I tap my way over, perch on a stool and prop my crutches beside me, as Scott carries our drinks, and places them on the breakfast bar. I hug my oversized mug between my hands, lower my head and take a satisfying sip of the hot, sweet brew.

'Thank you,' I say. 'I needed this.' I look out at Terry tossing a ball up in the air, quite happy to amuse himself.

'Doesn't exactly go with your image.'

'I think we can both safely assume, that my image has been all but dismantled.' I turn to look at Scott. 'And it's very much up to you if it'll ever recover.'

Scott raises his chin, folds his arms over his chest. 'Good try, Maddie. But I know you better than that… and, more importantly, you know me better than that.'

'It would only take a few words from you, and I'd be…' I look away from him. The damage he could cause, would go way beyond my reputation.

'I'm not here for you, Maddie. And I'm sure you've enough influence to turn this around. I'm here for my daughter—'

'Our daughter—'

'The daughter, I have only just found out I even have!'

His words pierce me like daggers, tossed with precision to inflict the most pain. It's a pain I deserve, one I've carried deep inside of me for years. A pain, waiting for this very moment to flourish.

Silent tears make their way down my cheeks. No point in denying them, but then, neither can I embrace the release of them. There is no release, because I cannot go back and change what is.

I turn to Scott, I've no hope of his forgiveness. 'I am truly sorry…' I choke the words out. 'Truly sorry. I was too young to understand the consequences of the choices I made.'

Scott shakes his head. 'You didn't even give me the chance…' His voice is hoarse with emotion. 'I'd have been a good dad…'

I pull my bottom lip between my teeth, taste the salt of my tears. 'I didn't think you'd want us.'

He sighs, shrugs his shoulders. 'You didn't give me the choice. One day we were daydreaming our pretend futures together, the next, you were gone. No warning, just gone.'

'My father didn't get much notice. Just a couple of days me and Mum had to sort out all the packing, and away to a new parish we went.'

'You could have told me. Even later, when you wrote.' Scott's eyes swim with emotion. 'You should have told me, Maddie. I had the right to know.'

'I know, it was easier not to, Scott. I'm sorry, I took the cowards way, but I can't go back in time and change it, or I would.'

Scott sips his coffee, his eyes never leaving my face. I take my mug between my hands again and drink my tea.

'Worse, I can't believe you let your parents bring Christie up after the hellish childhood you endured. They dragged you from town to town, school to school. The horror stories you told me. Where they even true?'

I swallow down the bile. The tautness of my cheeks sending pinnacles of pain to my eyeballs. 'I wish those stories weren't true. You saw them, always on a mission.'

'I would have thought your parents would have been the last people on the planet you'd let bring up our child. Apparently not.'

I put down my drink, push it away, suddenly find its sweetness too sickly. Terry is still bounding about with his ball. I turn to Scott. 'They changed, really changed. I was a mess. Really, a mess. The state I was made them realise what they'd put me through. I made them promise to find somewhere out in the countryside to bring up Christie. Somewhere she could make friends she could keep forever.'

'People like your parents don't just change.'

I shrug, no point in arguing.

Scott stands, strides to the back door, opens it and whistles. Terry scurries in. 'Guess I'll have to see it for myself to believe it. Miracles aren't my thing.'

Remembering the Abyss

I'm good at secrets

My tummy trembles return. The thought of introducing Scott to my parents is terrifying. I let out a deep breath. 'Hold on a minute, Scott! I can't just turn up with you… and say, "Oh, by the way, this is Christie's father.", can I?'

'I don't know why not. I'm sure, even they are well aware it wasn't an immaculate conception.'

I shake my head. 'That's not what I mean, and you know it!' Terry ambles to my side, and sits down looking expectantly at Scott. 'They've had enough stress over the last couple of weeks, without you turning up and giving them more.'

'What do you think I'm going to do, Maddie? All I want, is an introduction to the two people who've had the pleasure of bringing up my daughter!'

'Exactly! Have you any idea how threatening that sounds?' Both Mum and Dad are doing their best, but they're getting on. The last few weeks must've taken their toll, then the fire. And now, keeping both me and Christie calm, visiting Miles, they must be exhausted.

Scott lets out a deep sigh. 'You've got to know, I want to meet Christie as soon as I can, right?'

I nod, look away. Of course, he does. I can almost feel the twist of a knife in my gut, adding torment to my shaken demeanour. My tentative relationship with Christie, already under the media microscope, is likely to be shattered. I brace myself for Scott's response, take a deep breath, turn and look him in the eyes. I have no choice but to tell him the truth. 'Scott, right now, the last thing Christie needs is—'

'Whatever you were going to say, leave it!' He plants his hands low on his hips, and raises his chin a notch. 'She's my daughter, and I want to get to know her, finally.'

'Me too…' I whisper.

Scott steps closer to me. 'What did you say?' His eyes challenge me to repeat the words.

I shake my head. 'I said, *me too*. I want to get to know her too.' I hold his gaze.

'You've been doing that all her life.' Scott tosses the words my way. 'Now it's my turn.' His arms fold across his chest.

If only that were true. 'I think you need to sit, and listen, Scott, because I need to explain a few things.'

Scott looks away from me, then stalks back to the breakfast stool. He sits, legs sprawled, and tilts his head. 'I'm all ears.'

I had hoped to have more time. More time to get the whole thing mapped out in my head. More time to give a confident overview of my actions and reasoning behind them. But Scott is sitting here, his face commanding and his mind closed…

'I need to start right at the start. You'll probably struggle to believe whatever I say, Scott… And I know I've… I've… By omitting to tell you about th—'

'For crying out loud, Maddie! Get on with it!'

I rest my elbows on the breakfast bar, drop my head into my hands, close my eyes. Think Maddie, think…

'And you can spare me the dramatics!'

If that's what he thinks, I keep my eyes closed. 'I didn't have an easy pregnancy... The upset of moving... Losing you... It was... And then, there were complications.' My hand automatically drops to my abdomen. Scott isn't here to learn about me. I trace the translucent scar left by the surgeon. How I love the reminder that Christie grew inside me, came from my belly. 'Christie was a small baby, four pounds six and a half ounces to be precise. I'll get the photos of her, later...'

I hear Scott scrub his hands over his stubble. 'Yeah. Thanks. I was going to ask about seeing them.'

I open my eyes, look at him. I focus on his lips, the barest of smiles is just about making an appearance. His face used to light up with laughter, years ago.

'Christina Ann was taken from me. She was put in an incubator, with monitors stuck all over her pink body, a little knitted cap on her head and a huge nappy wrapped around her... They let me put my hand in, and her tiny fingers clamped around my finger... And I felt...'

Scott's broad smile transforms his face. The tautness of his jaw has relaxed, the frown lines have vanished and his eyes have softened. 'Was she beautiful?'

'She was pink, and scrawny...' I close my eyes, try to bring back the image of her. In truth, I only remember the image in the photo... It's the emotions that swamp my brain. 'She cried, her face, all of her was wrinkly. No, not beautiful to look at, but to my eyes, she was... She was perfect. Just incredibly perfect... I couldn't believe how perfect.'

Scott nods. The unshed tears swimming in his eyes make their midnight blue, as clear as tropical lagoons. 'I wish I'd seen her, Maddie.' He looks at the span of his hands. 'Felt her fingers grasp one of mine.'

The stab of pain in my throat as I hold back my own tears, forces me to look away. I've no right to feel this pain with him, I caused it. And he's got every right to hate me for it. 'I'm sorry, Scott.' My voice breaks. 'I never intended to hurt you, to hurt anyone…'

'Did you not think I deserved to know… Had the right to know?'

I shake my head. 'I didn't think anything, Scott. I looked at her, heard her mew-like cry, and I felt… I felt numb with terror… I knew, I knew there was no way I could give her the life she deserved.'

'You could have got in touch with me, I'd have helped… We could have sorted something out, between us.'

I half cover my mouth with my hand. 'No, Scott.' I shake my head at the naivety of his statement. 'I was a mess. Physically, mentally… I could scarcely cope, even with the help of both my parents. If you'd been there—'

'I would have helped!'

I can see the fierce belief in his face. But I know, he would only have made things worse for us. And how much of those awful first few months dare I share with him? Does he really want to know? I've tried to block them from my mind.

The weeks of lying in bed, despondent and unwashed. Staring at the walls, each in turn, as Christie was tended and cooed to by my mother. Turning away, as Mum tried desperately to help me bond with my baby. Half-listening to the hushed conversations taking place outside my room.

I slept, or didn't. Days passed without being lived. Plates of food were placed at my bedside, to be taken away hours later, sometimes picked at, sometimes not.

Eventually, a name was given to my despair. Post-natal depression. Not uncommon. And given my age, the trauma of the birth, and my unpreparedness, not unexpected, declared the professionals.

Slowly, slowly, my guilt started to ease... Looking back, my parents were, quite frankly, amazing. I started to come back to the real world. I started eating again, taking long hot showers, reading magazines... I even pushed Christie out in the buggy with Mum a couple of times.

But still, the long slog of motherhood hung over me, a suffocating blanket snuffing out my identity. Before Christie was conceived, I'd thought I was the only unique person on the planet. I'd cherished my individuality. Having a baby, alone, categorised me. I was a single mum. I had seven average GCSEs, no job and little desire to get one. Some days, it'd take me until dinner time to mask the puffiness of my eyes.

'Scott, it was a very dark time. Not just for me, but for my parents too, and—'

'Oh, I'm sure it looked bad for them! With your dad being a vicar, such a perfect example to us all!'

'You see, Scott! How can I let you meet my parents again, after all these years, when you have so little respect for them?'

Scott looks out of the window, then down at Terry. 'Come on, Terry, do you want to go back out?'

Terry – the traitor – trots over to the door and Scott lets him out.

Scott remains standing. 'I used to think your parents were freaking awesome. I can't believe they didn't try harder to find me… They must have known I was Christie's father… Every day, every day they saw me skulking about waiting for you…' Scott scoops a wayward curl, secures it back behind his ear. 'I even joined the "Chalk 'n' Talk" gang your dad ran!'

Ah, yes, one of Dad's famous youth programmes – this one aimed at stopping spray-can graffiti all over the town. 'But you chalked and didn't talk.' I remember Dad telling me.

'What was I supposed to say? "Rev. Harris, me and your daughter make out every day in the wood.", that would've gone down well.'

I shrug. 'You could have told him about your plans to be a grand artist and make your fortune in America.' I'm tempted to add, as you told me. 'You could have told him we hung out.' I raise both brows and offer a brief smile.

'So could you, Maddie, but you didn't.'

'I wanted to keep you a secret—'

'Because you were ashamed of—'

'No, Scott!' I say in a raised voice. 'Because you were the only one in my life who gave a damn about—'

'And you repay me by running out on me! Hard to believe.'

'I repay you by protecting you from my shipwreck of a life.'

Scott steps close to me. Levels his eyes to mine. 'Your shipwreck of a life? Really?'

I feel him searching the depths of my soul, our eyes locked. Neither of us prepared to be the first to break the bond. 'I was a nightmare… You were the only one I felt understood me… The only one who actually liked me.'

Scott spins away from me, turns back, a scowl gnawing at his brow. 'Liked you? Maddie, I would've done anything for you… Surely you knew…'

'All I knew, was that with you, I felt alive. All you ever talked about was your art, and going away. We never talked about "us". The "us" just happened, unplanned…' I almost add, like Christie.

His face softens. He reaches out his hand, rests it on the cool marble of the breakfast bar close to mine. 'I thought you knew. You were so confident, carefree… I thought you must know how I felt about you.'

I nod. 'Perhaps, deep down I did… It was a long time ago.' Terry is back tossing his ball. 'Mum and Dad knew I was no way able to commit to looking after Christie. They gave me the chance of a lifetime, the opportunity to go to drama school, if I could get in… And I took it… For the first time ever, I worked my socks off. Earned myself a place.'

'The first time you wrote.'

I nod. 'Yep, I was so nervous, excited… I wanted you to share it with me…'

'It was a whole year after you'd left me… You didn't even say where you'd gone, where you'd been. And all you gave me was the poxy address for your digs in London—'

'You didn't reply.'

'It was like a slap in the face! Not even an explanation.'

'And still, I wrote again when I got my first part… At least you replied, but after your obligatory congratulations—' I kept the letter. 'It was like, I was just some random girl you once knew.'

'What did you expect, Maddie? You'd been gone over a year, it'd taken me that long to get you outa my head… Jeez, no way did I want to go down that route again.' Scott drags his hand through his hair.

He used to do it all the time. I look away, tap my fingers on the counter. 'After I got the lead part in *The Fallen*…'

*

I drag my feet following Mr Boswell to his office – if you can call a caravan, no matter how grand, an office. On set, for the second day, and already I'm in trouble – a failure.

He points to a sofa across from his leather, swivel chair. 'Have a seat, Madeline.'

I fold myself into the corner of the sofa, arms clamped over my chest, legs double crossed with my toes wedged at the back of my supporting ankle, and my head hung low. I peer out from under my fringe. 'Thank you, Mr Boswell.'

He leans forward in his chair, brings his head down level with mine. His piercing eyes bore into me. 'If you and me are going to work together at close quarters, Madeline, I think you should call me Tim. Yeah?'

I nod.

'Right.' He rests back in his chair and lets out a loud sigh. 'So, show me.' His face is void of emotion.

Keeping my eyes locked with his, I stand. I unbutton my jeans, unzip them and slide them over my hip bones, feel them slither down my legs.

His eyes dip and he leans forward. 'You know what I want to see.'

I hook my thumbs inside my knickers and begin to ease them down. I stand motionless as he inspects me. The cool air prompting goosebumps to invade my exposed skin, and beyond. Looking away, I fold my arms tight over my chest again.

*

'Playing "Lucy" in *The Fallen,* changed my life forever. It changed *me* forever.' I shrug. 'Mum and Dad looked after Christie as their own child. If the press had discovered I had a daughter, they'd have gone to town.'

'I could have kept our secret, I'm good at secrets. You of all people should know that.'

'I know, Scott, and I've always been grateful for your consideration.' I remember lying naked and totally at ease on a bed of leaves. Unashamedly absorbing the gentle heat as dappled sunlight filtered through the canopy of our tree. Scott's easel propped by twigs at one corner to keep it level, as he painted.

A natural talent, he captured the radiance of love emanating from me, I practically glowed... The portrait of a naked Madeline De-Muir at age sixteen, would have sold for a small fortune back in the day... And Scott would have absolutely needed the money, just starting out as he was. The instant notoriety would have kickstarted his career.

He shrugs. 'I could never sell it, Maddie. It'd be like selling my soul.'

'Thank you, it's... I know you could have made a lot of money. It's very noble of you...'

Scott laughs, his eyes alight with mischief. 'Not that noble, Maddie! I have the pleasure of looking at you whenever I please.'

I feel my cheeks flush, the thought of Scott seeing me now... I clear my throat. 'I let you know about playing Rose in *An English Rose*, then I went off to Hollywood for a glittering lifestyle, as scripts dropped into my hands at an alarming rate. As you know, it didn't take long for the shine of the film industry to wear off.'

I fold my arms across my midriff, hugging myself as the embers of loneliness are fanned by those long-ago memories. The yearning to be home and hug my little angel overpowered me.

Scott steeples his fingers, just as my dad does when he's about to voice an observation. 'All that glitters, is not golden,' says Scott.

I smile. 'Yep, I know that now… It took me a time. In the meanwhile, Mum and Dad became Christie's Mum and Dad. They'd moved to a country parish, thrown themselves into the community. By the time I came home, Christie had started school and made friends and was living the dream childhood… I couldn't take her away from that.'

Scott stands. 'What! You just left her again!'

'She didn't know me, Scott…' My voice is hushed. 'The press was all over my every move, and I couldn't chance Christie being exposed to all that… Mum came up with a plan, and I went with it.'

Scott strides to the backdoor, opens it and Terry falls in. He closes the door. 'And what was this plan you went with?'

'I dressed up as an elderly Aunt, Auntie Maddie. The press never found out, and for a few years, I got to see Christie as often as I wanted… But then, as time went by, Christie became more astute, I had to stop. It was too risky.'

'But you're back seeing each other now. And you've chosen a very public way to reveal you're her mother. Christie's idea to promote her art exhibition?'

I shuffle off the stool. Squat down next to Terry, chuckle his chin. Safer to look at Terry than Scott. 'Not Christie's idea. She didn't know anything about the exhibition, or who Auntie Maddie really was, until it opened—'

'But that was only—'

'I know!' I raise myself up, perch back on the stool. Look him in the eyes. 'I know… Three weeks ago.'

'Jeez, Maddie! What were you thinking?'

'Exactly the same as you. I want to meet my daughter.'

Scott tilts his head to one side and looks up. 'Is she up there?'

'No, that's Pauletta.' Pauletta will be keeping her ears open, ready to pounce, if she thinks Scott has overstepped the mark. I smile, her people skills may be lacking, but her mother bear instincts are honed to perfection.

Scott lets out a breath and looks away. 'Anyhow, it isn't surprising, the kid's going to need some time.' He looks back at me. 'Why'd you have to make it so darn public, Maddie? You could of just sat her down with the Rev and Mrs Harris, and spat out the truth… Like you've just gone and done with me.'

I pass my hands over my face, rest them back on my lap. 'Yes, I could have done that, except… Have you seen any of her artwork?'

'Yeah. It's good. I only saw what they previewed on the TV.'

I nod. 'It's better in real life. She's a natural… Like you, Scott. And she's been beavering away teaching… No intention of ever exhibiting her work.'

'Okay. So, you being the marvellous Madeline De-Muir thrust her into the limelight…' Scott raises his eyebrows. 'Without even asking her.'

'If everyone knew Christie was my daughter before the *Evolution* exhibition, she would have been accused of using my name for gain. By the exhibition being launched by an unknown, the excellent reviews she received are based on merit alone.'

He can't argue with my logic, or my motive, but he can, probably will argue with my method. I need to get Scott on side. And the only way I can do that is by… I balance myself between my crutches. 'Follow me, Scott, I need to show you something before you leave.'

Impressions

The urge to physically shake him

Terry scurries ahead of me, waiting for me to open doors. Scott follows, I imagine not too keen on opening doors after his first encounter with Terry. I lead us into the front lounge.

Scott, in the middle of the room, lets out a long whistle and does a slow three-sixty-degree turn. 'Is this the same room your interview was shot in?'

I move to the same chair I sat in for my now infamous interview, and settle myself in for another spat. 'It is. Are you going to take a seat?'

Scott makes himself comfortable on the sofa opposite me. 'I'll say one thing for you, Maddie, you sure do have a beautiful home... Very English.' He points to the original, intricate, hand-painted architraves. 'Timeless elegance. The kinda house I've always imagined you in.'

'Thank you.' I reach down beside my chair, pick up the brown paper package, and lie it on my lap. It has remained untouched since the evening of my interview – the night of the fire.

'Ah, you want to show me Christie's painting. The one too precious to share with the rest of the world... Trying to soften me up, eh Maddie?'

I laugh. I'm surprised at how girlish I sound. 'No, Scott. I want you to see first-hand how incredibly talented our daughter is... And also, I want you to understand why my PA launched himself into a burning building, to rescue the contents.'

'Okay, I can go with that.'

I rest forward in my chair. 'Do you want to watch me unwrap it?'

Scott gets up and stands by the side of my chair, towering above me. I carefully untie the jute string, run a hand under each side of the paper and reveal the masterpiece beneath.

I feel tears welling in my eyes, and catch my breath at the exquisite beauty of the face before me. I'm filled with the same abundance of sheer joy and awe as the first time I saw it.

Scott drops to one knee to get a closer look. He holds out his hand. 'May I?'

I nod, unable to speak.

Scott lifts the portrait from me and tilts it at various angles. He nods, stalks over to the window and holds it in the daylight. As one would delicately cradle a baby, he rests the painting on one arm. Then as a mother would run her finger over the velvety skin of a new-born, he traces the brush strokes with his forefinger.

I take in his every move, trying to glean if Scott sees in this painting the same as I. Slowly, the inkling of a smile emerges on his face. Scott's head begins to rock gently back and forth. He continues to scrutinise the image before him.

The urge to physically shake him to get a verbal response, makes me tether my fingers together in frustration. Say something, anything! Don't make me ask!

Finally, Scott raises his head, his eyes meet mine. 'She's got it.' He nods.

I let out a laugh of relief. 'Phew, I'm glad *you* think so.'

The smile has transformed his face. 'And here's a man who's been stripped and branded, if ever I saw one!'

'I've not heard that one before. What do you mean?'

Scott brings the portrait back to me and holds it up. 'This guy, whoever he is, he's got no chance! His defences have been stripped back, exposing his weaknesses, and he's been branded by his woman. He isn't going nowhere!'

'I see…' Well, that just about sums up Miles. He'd do anything for Christie. And to think they both almost blew it. 'You're right. He isn't going anywhere.'

'If the quality of the work in the gallery is anywhere near this mark, it's no wonder your PA went in to rescue it.'

'It is this good. But obviously, it has sentimental value too.'

'I'll tell you, Maddie, you're lucky to have that level of commitment from your PA.'

I take the painting from him. 'I know it. But Miles is like one of the family. He's worked with me for eons, knows Mum and Dad. Recently he's been working closely with Christie, too.'

'Sounds like the kinda guy you'd want around.' Scott's tone is flat, it's lost some of the lustre from his glowing reaction to Christie's portrait of Miles.

'He is, but enough about Miles. Now you've seen how good Christie is, maybe that will help you understand why I wanted her to have her art out there, before our relationship was exposed.'

'I get it, just wish I'd been in the loop years ago.' His face is like stone.

'Right, well, I'll sort out for you to meet with Mum and Dad ASAP. Get things moving.'

'Appreciate that, Maddie.' His face says otherwise. He walks over to the door. 'I'll see myself out.'

'I'll—'

'No, you've done enough.' Scott opens the door, looks back at me. 'Out of interest, Maddie, who is the guy in the portrait?'

I smile. 'Oh, I thought you knew. It's Miles, my PA. He'd do anything for—'

'I should a known!'

'Oh, no, it's—'

'Let's face it, Maddie, you've still got all your assets, and you wear them well. So why not? Why not, screw your *PA*?'

Scott slams the door behind him with enough force to rattle the chandelier.

United Front?

I had more balls at sixteen

I think Scott must have hired the biggest MPV the company had. I don't want to sound ungrateful but the door handle is about level with my chin! 'Scott, thanks for the offer, but how do you expect me to get up there?'

He steps forward, and swings the door open. 'Put one foot on the step, grab the hand bar and pull.'

I prop one crutch, keep the other for balance—

'For crying out loud, Maddie, let me!' Scott's hands clamp around my waist and he launches me into the passenger seat.

My whole body is electric. A flutter of familiarity feathers through me. Goosebumps tingle at the base of my spine, the nape of my neck and everywhere in-between, tempting me, reminding me of sensations buried long ago. The whoosh of air escaping me, sounds less an expression of shock, more a release of pent-up desire. Irritation flits to the surface. 'Was that necessary, Scott? Really?'

He thrusts the abandoned crutch at me. 'Here.' He swings the door closed.

Looking back at the house, I notice the front-lounge curtain twitch. Pauletta has been bombarding me with her cast-iron opinions of Scott since she arrived this morning. It's a relief to escape. Letting out a calming breath, I readjust myself, and click on my seatbelt. The car lurches as Scott hauls himself into the driving seat. I close my eyes briefly, try to compose my thoughts and turn to look at him. 'A bit of warning, would have been nice.'

'Why? You'd only have bellyached about it.' He starts up the engine. 'And you've got to know, Maddie, I'm in no mood for your dramatics. Not today.'

'A little courtesy goes a long—'

'I'll stop you right there!' Scott scowls at me. 'I've agreed to meet *your* parents, before I get to meet *my own* daughter. I'm doing things your way, even though... Even though it's killing me inside.'

'And I appreciate it, but a bit of propriety—'

The roar of the engine cuts into my words. I'm sure Scott has no idea how difficult today is going to be for my parents, or me for that matter. The conversation with them yesterday about Scott didn't go to plan... In fact, it wasn't even a conversation. I only explained who he was, and waited for a response.

It wasn't worth the wait. They simply agreed to meet Scott today, but made no other comment... This from parents who've clawed me back from the jaws of depression, and helped me through the various consequences of my many flawed life choices. To say I'm concerned, is putting it mildly.

Oh, yes, they've helped me beyond measure. Have never used my mistakes as a weapon, more as a tool to teach and explain. I've always been grateful, because above everyone else, they have more reasons to feel let down by me.

They've helped me see a way forward, when I thought I'd nothing to live for. Carried me when I hadn't even the strength to raise my head. Encouraged me to forge a life to be proud of.

I look at Scott. And here again, I'm bringing trouble to their door. 'It's not going to be easy for Mum and Dad.'

'Tell you what, Maddie, just keep reminding yourself who wangled this mess in the first place. It wasn't me.' Scott waits for the gates to open, eases the car forward. 'You going to tell me the zip code, or tap it in yourself?'

I stretch forward and enter the postcode. The satnav plots a route skirting around Chippington, over the river then on towards Clover Beck. Expected time of arrival 15:22. Twelve minutes, it stretches out before us like a prison sentence…

Despite the initial revving, Scott drives with care, and much slower than I imagined. The afternoon traffic is fairly light. Chippington isn't exactly buzzing with industry or commerce, but because the only way south out of town is over the river – school pick-up time is a pain.

'How close are we to the gallery?'

'It's way over the other side of town, Scott… We're not allowed inside yet; it's held up by scaffolding.' I close my eyes, tilt my chin up to allow the heat of the sun to wash over me. 'I'm dreading all the hassle ahead with the insurance company. I'm hoping Miles is going to be up to sorting it all out.'

'I'm sure he'll do it, even if he's not.'

'Yes, he'll try…' I open my eyes, look at Scott's stony expression. 'I don't need to worry about that now, do I? Today is much more important.'

'It is.' Scott briefly glances my way. 'Get today out of the way, and then I get to meet my daughter.'

'Yes, but today's a big day, Scott. Mum and Dad want to—'

'What? See if I'm a suitable person to be Christie's dad?' he snaps.

'They just want to get to know you... About you. I've already told them how successful you are in America.'

'Yeah, yeah.'

My skin prickles with frustration. 'What does that mean? I'm doing my best to smooth the way—'

'Smooth the way! Can you hear yourself?'

I take a deep breath. 'All I want is for everyone to get along. And this attitude of yours—'

'You really think my attitude is the biggest issue at stake here?'

'One way or another, we've all got to sort this out, and...' I sigh. 'I just want you to be nice to my parents, they're getting old.' Chippington is behind us now, the satnav says ETA 5 minutes. We'll soon be at Clover Beck, and I'd rather not be at loggerheads with Scott.

'Fine, I'll be nice. But don't expect me to take any flack. You left me, remember.'

'Let's not even go there. We are just going to have afternoon tea, and a "getting to know you" session.'

Scott indicates right, and follows the lane a way down. He indicates again and draws to a halt at the roadside. The engine turns off and Scott turns to me. 'Jeez, Maddie, afternoon tea?' He holds out his hands. 'How'd you expect me to fair with teacups and saucers? I'm not built for dinky little fairy cakes.'

'Butterfly.'

'Pardon?'

'Butterfly cakes, not fairy cakes, and you'll be fine. There's always Battenburg, and probably scones too...'

'Whatever they are, I'm just not... I'm not delicate enough.'

'You are with a paintbrush.' And other things too, if I dare to remember. I feel a blush creep up my neck. Irritated, I say, 'Scott, stop fussing! You'll be fine.'

I hear his grunt of acceptance, and again we are on our way. The fields at either side of the lane are mostly lush with a variety of neat crops. We pass *The Rose and Crown* public house, apparently in the middle of nowhere... but then, after a few sparse farmhouses, the lane makes way for the village.

Centred around an impeccable village green, Clover Beck boasts a corner shop, a part-time Post Office and a church, with a gentle walk to the pub. Everything a recently retired vicar could wish for.

Scott stops at the roadside by Mum and Dad's house, and looks down the drive. 'Is this it? I was expecting something more in keeping with a humble vicar, not an *X Factor* pad.'

'Yes, it's okay to pull into the drive.' I can tell he's taken aback by the house; I really do hope he doesn't make a thing about it.

Scott draws past the gateway, swings his left arm over the back of my seat, turns and reverses into the drive. I tap the screen with the rear-view camera image. He turns, drops his arm and shrugs. 'Old habits...' He smiles and nods back towards the house. 'Looks like they've been waiting for us.'

Mum and Dad are standing side by side on the portico step. Mum's hands hang casually by her sides, Dad's are clasped behind his back. I turn to open my door.

'Hold on.' Scott catches my arm. 'Let me go round and get the door. I don't want them thinking I'm a complete…' His eyes hold mine. 'I know it's going to be no walk in the park, but I want to make a good impression, okay?'

'I know, none of us are going to find this easy, just…' I shrug. 'Be yourself.'

Scott hops down, and strides round the front of the car and opens the door for me, and takes my crutches. 'Can I help you down, Maddie?'

'Please.' As I place my hands on his shoulders our eyes meet. His hands circle my waist, he lifts me to the ground carefully without breaking eye contact. Again, my senses are hyperalert. I can feel the heat emitting from his hands through the thin cotton of my blouse, searing my skin. He continues to hold me steady while I balance my weight between my crutches.

'Feels like old times,' he whispers.

I hope the smile I'm wearing looks serene, that reference to our past hasn't helped one little bit. Something about this man pulls at the very chords of my core, is impossible to ignore, too crazy to conceive.

As I steadily make my way towards my parents, Scott keeps pace with me. I'm gripping my hands so tightly my knuckles are white, ridiculously on edge for a meeting twenty-five years after the event. I had more balls at sixteen telling them I was pregnant!

'Mum, Dad, this is Scott.' I feel all the uncertainty and apprehension I should have felt all those years ago.

Scott reaches out his hand to my father. 'Good afternoon, sir. Thank you for agreeing to meet me. Mrs Harris.' Scott shakes their hands in turn. 'It's good to see you again.'

I'm pleased Scott has toned down his lazy American accent. He appears confident and at ease, and I can tell Dad is scrutinising him.

Dad nods. 'Pleased to meet you, Scott...' For a split second, I think he's tempted to add "At long last." But the moment passes. 'Come on in.'

Mum pats Scott's arm. 'We are both very pleased to be meeting you.'

The smile that captured my heart, Scott now bestows on my mum. He links her hand through his arm as if he's known her a lifetime, turns to me and winks. 'You've a remarkable home here, Mrs Harris.'

'Thank you, Scott. Call me Anne, Mrs Harris sounds so formal. And really, we can't take full credit for the house, Maddie found—'

'Mum! I'm sure Scott isn't interested in the details.' The last thing I need is Scott knowing all my financial dealings.

'Oh, okay, love. I just thought...' She turns and smiles at Scott. 'She's very modest.'

I shake my head in disbelief. It looks like he's already won her round to the extent of revealing all my secrets. Not sure Dad is going to be as easy. I follow the trio into the sitting room.

Scott walks over to the portrait of my parents hanging above the mantlepiece. 'Is this one of Christie's?' he asks.

Mum nods. 'Yes, it's one she did just after she finished her PGSE, that's the teaching qualification.'

'Aha, got it. It really is quite impressive, the way she uses light and shade is very sophisticated... And her brushstrokes...' Scott turns and looks at me. 'Yes, she's a fine artist.'

The coffee table is set impeccably. Mum's three-tiered stand displays tempting delights. Mini savouries occupy the bottom tier, the second holds butterfly cakes, evenly sliced Battenburg and scones with jam and clotted cream, the top tier holds a selection of petit fours. Mum's best china teapot is steaming and the matching crockery await our attention.

Scott turns and eyes the contents of the table. 'You've gone to a good deal of trouble there, Anne.' He holds up his hands. 'I'll apologise in advance, if my manners don't match up to your generous hospitality.'

'I'll hear nothing of the kind, Scott,' Mum gushes. 'We're just happy to be getting to know you.'

'And me you,' he replies.

Dad clears his throat. 'Well, shall we get settled then? Anne, are you going to pour the tea?'

Mum busies herself. Scott folds himself into an armchair, I sit opposite him in the other armchair. Dad sits on the sofa between us, like a tennis referee, one hand on each of his knees.

My stomach is churning while I wait until Mum has finished pouring and passing out drinks. I know I've got to take the lead with this. 'Mum, Dad, I'd like to properly introduce you to Scott Scobie. Christie's… biological father.'

My dad nods at Scott, Mum maintains her pleasant smile. Scott looks to me to carry on.

My stomach lurches again. I try to expand my diaphragm with each of my breaths… one of the techniques I have used since my drama school days. Keeps the belly from splurging out, and the lungs well supplied. Unfortunately, today my breath is too shallow. 'I know it's late in the day—'

Dad muffles his splutter with a cough.

'... but, strange as it may sound... As more time has passed by, the more anxious I've become about telling you.' I fold my hands on my lap. Now, the bit none of them will be pleased to hear. First, I look Scott in the eyes, next my father and finally I lock eyes with Mum. 'But since neither of you actually asked who...'

Mum holds my gaze. 'Maddie, love, you were in no fit state.' Mum glances at Scott.

I nod. 'He knows. I told him.'

Dad nods slowly. 'Fair enough. Then I'm sure you'll both appreciate that your mother and I didn't want to cause you further distress.'

I can feel the tension starting to ease. 'I know Dad, but all these years...' I look at Scott. 'I thought you didn't ask, because you thought I wouldn't know.'

Scott raises a brow, looks away from me, mutters something and shakes his head. I hope he knows how impossible that would be.

Dad taps his knees. 'To be truthful, and you know I am, I always hoped it was this young man here... But Maddie, you were just so...' Dad looks to Mum.

'Wild, Maddie. You were out of control,' says Mum. 'We didn't know where you were most of the time. We spent hours trekking the streets looking for you.'

Scott rests forward out of his chair. 'She was with me... Always with me.'

Dad fixes me with his piercing blue eyes, and raises both brows. 'The worry you could have saved us... But it's in the past. It doesn't matter now.'

I look down at my hands folded on my lap. I'm sure I look calm and relaxed, but the reminder of my rebellion always fills me with shame. It's the reason I help troubled teens, hopefully before they go off the rails like I did.

Dad takes a leisurely sip of his tea. He places the cup and saucer back on the table, steeples his fingers. 'What we need to decide, today, between us, is what's the best course of action to take with Christie.'

'I would think that's obvious,' says Scott. 'She needs to meet me.'

Dad taps his steepled fingers. 'I'm not so sure.'

Scott closes his grip on each of the chair arms, his knuckles white. 'And what do you mean by that?'

I know.

Trouble!

Baby Steps

Scott must be seen as one of us

Dad threads his fingers together and rests them on his lap. He's probably asking for divine help to get us through this awkward encounter. 'I think we can agree, we all love Christie… And, it follows, we all want what is best for her.'

Scott looks fit to explode. 'Reverend Harris, I can assure you, I have no intention of causing Christie any problems. I just want to get to know her.'

Dad nods, and looks at Scott. 'I know you have no *intention* to cause any problems for Christie… Just as you had no *intention* to get my sixteen-year-old daughter pregna—'

'Dad!'

'So, you want to punish me twenty-five years later!' Scott gets up and walks over to the mantlepiece. He stands with his back to my parents, but I can make out the torment on his face. For a brief moment he glances my way. 'If I'd known Maddie was carrying my child, I'd have tracked her down.'

'Yes,' Dad says in a reasonable tone. 'I can see you believe that, Scott, but—'

Scott spins round. 'She… Left… Me!' He grinds the words out slowly. 'We spent every second we could together, and then you all up and move! She didn't even tell me she was leaving.' Scott turns his attention to me.

I look away, can't bear to see the raw emotions in his eyes. 'I'm sorry, Scott. I was scared.'

Mum clasps her hands. 'I think we need to stay with the here and now. We can't change the past.' She offers Scott a passive smile. 'Come on, please sit back down and let's try and sort this out.'

'Okay, but I'm not the bad guy, here. I'm doing my best to get my head round having a grown-up daughter I've never been told about.' Scott sits back in the armchair opposite me.

Dad unfolds, then refolds his hands. 'We understand that. But we've also got to think about what's going on in Christie's life. She's already got a lot of adjusting to do.'

Mum smiles at Scott. 'It's only natural you want to meet her as soon as you can. But she's only just learned about Maddie. And, all the publicity… Well, that went off the scale after the fire at the gallery…'

'So,' Dad starts, 'you can understand, we want to cushion her from any more unsettling situations.'

'And, especially remembering what happened to Miles,' I say in a hushed voice.

Mum nods. 'He'll be out of hospital tomorrow, Maddie, love.' She looks at Scott. 'We were all so relieved he got out safely. He's such a lovely, young man, and we're all looking forward—'

'Mum, one step at a time.' Surely Mum understands, he hasn't even met his daughter, never mind a potential son-in-law.

'Yeah, let's leave him out of it.' Scott's American drawl makes a return. 'I kind of think, no matter when Christie finds out about me, she's going to freak.'

Dad rests back in the sofa, looks for all the world like this is just a quaint chat with old friends. He smiles.

'Oh, she'll have a bit of a meltdown. It won't last long... If truth be known, she's probably tougher than the rest of us put together—'

Oh, yes.

'...but she's young, so hasn't figured it out yet.'

Scott leans forward in his seat. 'So, what's the big deal then?'

Dad smiles. 'Well, on the face of it, everything should be hunky-dory. She's got a world-famous movie star for a mother. She has her own art exhibition, albeit pending an urgent new venue... And then she discovers her biological father is an incredibly successful Los Angeles artist himself.'

'Exactly,' says Scott. 'So, what's the problem here? I can open doors for her that other people don't even know exist.'

'The problem is, and please understand, for my wife and I it's crucially important... How long are you planning to stick around for, Scott? Christie is more than capable of readjusting to have you as part of her life... But if this is just a whim of yours, and you're going to swan in and out of her life whenever it suits you, I think you need to seriously consider if that's the best for Christie.'

Scott is up and pacing. 'I flew in from Los Angeles, just as soon as I found out about Christie... I have left the handover of a very lucrative commission to my creative manager at the main Scobie gallery... And believe me, that is not the way to endear yourself to wealthy tycoons. All my upcoming engagements for the next week have been cancelled... Does that sound like a whim?'

'A whole week!' Dad notes.

Oh, Scott! Big mistake, a whole week. Dad sacrificed his career to bring up Christie. He was being fast tracked to become the youngest bishop the C of E had in England. Gave it up for a tiny parish in the middle of nowhere, to be a humble vicar on a humbler salary. And Mum sentenced to twenty years hard labour, keeping the choir and flower ladies from open warfare.

I try to catch Scott's eye, but he's too busy re-examining Christie's artwork. 'You see,' he says, 'I can introduce Christie to all the right people.' He turns, and looks at my parents.

'Ah…' says Dad, his eyes crinkle at the corners as he offers Scott a smile. 'And, for the record, where are all the right people?'

'Well… LA, of course… You're never out of new clientele, always a fresh wannabe with a sponsor eager to commission a piece.'

Mum nods. 'We looked you up on Google,' she confesses. 'The amount of work you've exhibited is quite something… And then the private commissions as well… You must be working all the time.'

Scott laughs, and instantly looks years younger. 'No, Anne… The trick is to look busy. I tend to paint frantically, producing quantity… Then go back and add finesse as and when I can. So, then when I'm asked to do a specific piece, I can legitimately profess how busy I am… It gives me the option to turn down work, without offending.'

Dad steeples his fingers again, and rests his chin on them. 'I'm sure you're able to, let's say, negotiate a fair price if there's the chance you could make yourself available.'

Scott shrugs and looks slightly put out. 'It might appear like a ploy, Reverend Harris, but no. There are commissions I would never take, regardless of the benefit, be it financial or by increasing my profile...'

'We did notice,' Mum starts, 'that most of your portraits are of young women.'

Again, Scott is up on his feet, pacing, looking furious. 'You know, I don't have-ta defend myself to you guys. But anyways, yeah, the vast majority of my paintings are pretty young things... Most of them commissioned by their pushy Mammas and Papas. Most of them desperate for some exposure, wanting to catch some producer's eye...'

'Oh, I wasn't suggest—'

'Oh, I think you were, and I suppose I should have expected it from you guys.'

'No, Scott,' Mum says quietly. 'I'm sorry you think that of me. I was just wondering if that's the sort of work Christie would be interested in, and I really don't think it would be.'

Scott mutters to himself, drags his hand through his hair then drops back into his armchair. 'Okay. I'm sorry, Anne. I've got all defensive here. My therapist is going to have to work through this with me back home.'

I notice my parents exchange glances. 'Everyone has a therapist in America,' I say.

'Oh, yes, dear,' says Mum. 'So, Scott, how often do you meet with your umm... therapist?'

'I suppose every couple of weeks, keeps me on track. I'm not one of those wackos who goes every other day if that's what you're thinking.'

Mum smiles at Scott. 'Of course not. It's just less common to be seeing one's therapist in the UK. But then, we should be more open about our mental health. The British "stiff upper lip" has a lot to answer for.'

Dad huffs. 'If people bothered to talk to their local priest about their problems—'

'Not now, Dad!' I shake my head. I can't cope with one of his "back in my day" chats.

'Only saying. But point taken, Maddie.' Dad rubs his hands together. 'So, back to the here and now. Well, Scott, you've a whole week to get to know Christie. And then, what? Are you going back to LA?'

'Sure, I've time enough to get acquainted with my daughter. But for sure, I've commitments over the pond I need to fulfil.'

Dad nods his head slowly, Mum shoots me an anxious look. I take up the gauntlet. 'Scott, I'm only just getting to know Christie, and it's not as straightforward as you seem to think.'

Scott lets out an extended sigh. He drags both his hands through his hair, settles with his fingers locked behind his head and elbows splayed. 'Do you not think, that'll be because you kept her true identity from her?'

I look away from him, down at my hands still resting sedately together on my lap. My heart is beating so fast, it feels like it's going to bound right through my ribcage, and end up laying exposed and alone before them. A bloody mess, just like this. I can feel the hostility of his glower, eating away at my demeanour, threatening to uncover my true emotions.

My parents and Scott, between them have shaped my entire existence. Yet, I've managed to cause havoc for each of them. And while I can bask in the forgiveness of my parents, albeit with my own self-imposed remorse, I doubt I'll ever have that luxury with Scott. It would at least be nice if we could get along.

I raise my eyes to his, hope he can decipher my plea for understanding. 'Yes, Scott. I'm sure you are right. And if it had been as easy as walking into her life, without any thought of the consequences—'

'Oh, is that what you're accusing me of?' derides Scott.

'No. I'm in no position to accuse you of anything.' I hold his gaze.

'Darn right!'

'All I'm saying, is we need to go about this gently, baby steps.'

'Baby steps,' he repeats. 'You mean like the ones I missed.'

Silence hangs between us, a suffocating vacuum. I close my eyes for a second, hope this day will get no worse.

Mum stands up, and passes me my cup of tepid tea. Then she holds out Scott's for him. 'Here you are.' She gives us each a reassuring look. 'We all want what is best, so let's work towards that.'

Scott lets his hands drop from the back of his head, he steadies the cup with one hand and holds the saucer with the other. 'Thank you.'

'You are more than welcome, Scott.' Mum nods towards the untouched food. 'None of us are feeling much like nibbles. I'd thought it would help if we had lovely food. Oh well.'

Dad rests forward out of his seat as Mum sits back down on the sofa. He clears his throat. 'I think, we all need to be brutally honest, and say what we're thinking. We can't just skirt around the issues all afternoon.'

'I'll make it easy,' says Scott. 'I want to have a respectable introduction to Christie within the next twenty-four hours. It's imperative for you guys to make it plain, I only learned about her a couple of days back, and I've gone to a lotta trouble to find her. I'm not budging from that.'

I nod slowly, no one can blame him. 'Well, Scott, I agree, you need to meet Christie sooner rather than later. I'm happy to be involved in your meeting, but I think it would be prudent to forewarn Christie. She's had enough surprises lately.'

'None of them down to me!' growls Scott.

'No,' I whisper. 'I take full responsibility, it's all down to me.'

Dad nods. 'Yes, Maddie, it is. But your mother and I are here to help. We don't want you to forfeit your relationship with Christie. You've waited so long, and now...'

My throat tightens, and I purse my lips to stop the quiver of emotion being visible. All these years, standing on the sidelines just waiting to have a conversation with my daughter. 'I know, Dad. But Scott's right. None of this is his doing.'

Scott's expression softens. 'So, how we going to play this?'

I stroke my hands downwards over my face, smoothing my fingers over my eyelids then across to massage my temples, leaving my eyes closed for a moment or two.

I look at my parents. 'I think it would be better here than at my place, if you're okay with that?'

Mum nods. 'I can make up an afternoon tea, if you like.' She looks at the food before us.

Scott leans out of his armchair, takes a plate and selects one item off each of the tiers before us. 'That would be incredibly kind of you, Anne.' He bites into his dainty sandwich and nods. 'Very nice.'

Dad picks up a plate, and starts adding savouries. 'Good idea, Maddie. Christie will be more relaxed coming here. And your mother always does us proud.' He looks at Mum. 'Thank you, Anne. I doubt any of us say it often enough.'

Mum flaps her hand, and the start of a blush creeps up her cheeks. 'It's no trouble. Oh bother, you silly old fool... I'm all embarrassed now!'

Dad pats her knee. 'I know.' He grins.

I can't help smiling. Scott catches my eye. I can see he's touched and slightly amused by my parents' obvious love for each other.

A lump the size of *Snow White's* poison apple forms in my throat. I drag my eyes away from Scott, I'll never have that kind of long-lasting love my parents share.

I sigh. 'So, I'll phone Christie as soon as I get back home. I'll arrange to meet her after I've met with the insurance chappies tomorrow morning.'

Scott frowns. 'Can't they wait? Surely this is more important.'

I nod. 'Oh, this is most definitely more important. But some "clipboards" from the claim's assessment department want to check over the gallery site. I told them, nobody is allowed to go inside. Miles usually sorts out all this sort of thing.'

Scott lets out a breath. 'I'd like to get a chance to see this gallery of yours. If I come with you, it will kill two birds with one stone.' Scott's eyes lock with mine.

'Meaning?' I say.

'Meaning, Maddie, I'll ride shotgun, they'll not mess with me.'

I shake my head and look heavenwards. 'Scott, I am quite capable of dealing with these men.'

Dad purses his lips. 'He's got a point, Maddie. The reason Miles always sorts these things for you, is to protect your reputation. And, at the moment your reputation needs as much protection as it can get.'

I raise both my hands in surrender. 'Fine. Scott, you can come with me.'

Dad nods. 'And, Maddie, try to be in *Madeline* mode!'

'I don't know what you mean,' I huff.

'Yes, you do,' says Dad, he looks at Scott. 'We all know the real Maddie. And, sorry, but we all know how magnificently you can mess up. Now, is not the time to mess up, Maddie. Okay, love?'

'Thanks, Dad. Tell me straight, why don't you.'

Mum tilts her head. 'Maddie, love, you know he's right.'

'Fine,' I say. There's no point arguing. I heave a sigh. 'So, Scott and I will go to the gallery—'

'Let me know what time to pick you up, Maddie.'

'Ob-vi-ous-ly, Scott.'

Dad frowns.

I ignore him. 'If I bring Scott here, then go and talk to Christie.' My stomach spasms at the thought of it. 'Explain how eager Scott is to meet her. Knowing Scott is here with you two, should reassure her.' I look at each of them.

Mum nods. 'Oh, I'm sure it will. And let her know we've had this little get together today. And how eager we are for Scott to join the family—'

'Steady on, Mum!' I shake my head. 'Scott's here for Christie, not the rest of us.'

'Nevertheless,' says Dad, nodding sagely. 'We are Christie's family; we are a family unit. And so, it follows, Scott must be seen as one of us.'

'Thank you, Reverend Harris. It means a lot to me to hear you say that.'

It's like a sodding "love in", all of a sudden! Scott has clearly passed the "Dad test", for the time being, anyway. I swizzle my forefingers, eager to finalise the plans. 'Then I'll come back here with Christie, and make a proper introduction.'

Mum does one of her excited little smiles. 'Oh, it's going to work out fine, I can just tell. Maddie, get something to eat, you're thin as can be.'

I shrug. 'Mum, I'm the same weight I've always been.' But still, I get a plate, add a couple of sandwiches and one of her home-made, mini sausage rolls.

Mum gets a plate herself, and selects a cream scone. 'So, Scott, what would you like me to make up for tomorrow's special gathering?'

Scott smiles. 'I'll leave that entirely up to you, Anne. This *is* delicious, but how about making Christie's favourites?'

'Splendid idea, Scott.' Mum nibbles gracefully at her scone, even so, managing to get a cream moustache.

Regardless of feeling like I've got spinning swords in my stomach, I'm glad everything is sorted between us. Mum and Dad seem pleased with the arrangements, especially as they'll, once again, be the ones supporting Christie through her crisis.

And Scott is going to have so much in common with Christie, with them both being artists. No doubt they'll hit it off right away. He'll probably try to lure her away, to the US of A. Not to mention them both hating me for keeping them apart for ever.

There is the other scenario. The one that's making the mini nibbles of food I'm managing, stick in my throat. The one where Christie refuses to meet Scott at all. None of them seem to have thought of that, but it's the one that's gnawing away at my resolve. It was an ordeal enough for her to meet me.

I push the untouched sausage roll under the remainder of my sandwich, hoping Mum won't investigate too much.

Scott's on his feet, looking at the portrait of Mum and Dad again. 'It really is incredibly good. I was nowhere near this good at her age.'

'Oh,' says Mum. 'Christie used to have us sitting for hours. Always painting.'

The door swings open. 'What's going on?' demands Christie, her face ablaze.

She remains frozen in the doorway with one hand still holding the handle as Scott spins round. Their identical eyes lock in astonishment. Father and daughter, their profiles silhouetted, mirror each other. The certainty of their shared DNA is without doubt. Neither of them appears willing to break the bond of recognition.

Mum is on her feet walking towards her. 'Christie, love, we weren't expecting you…'

'You've *all* betrayed me, AGAIN!' yells Christie. She turns to me, her eyes crammed with contempt. 'Another little surprise for me, Maddie?' She does nothing to disguise the level of her disgust.

I try to moisten my lips, though my mouth is dry. 'I wanted to tell you about—'

'Too late, Maddie. Too late.' Christie looks briefly in Scott's direction. 'I was wondering who the ridiculous monster truck belonged to!' she hisses. Shaking her head as she leaves, she slams the door behind her.

I'm gripped by nausea as I scramble to my feet. 'Christie! Come back, it's not like that…' I cover my mouth to hold in the howl of despair, close my eyes and drop back into the chair.

Another magnificent Maddie mess-up.

She's never going to forgive me. Not now.

Standoff

I'm tempted to say more

Scott strides towards the door and yanks it open.

Dad is up on his feet. 'Leave her!'

'No chance!' Scott tosses me a loathsome look. 'I've let you guys run the show 'til now, and look where it's got me!' Scott is off after Christie. 'Hey! Christie, just wait up a minute, will you?'

Dad shrugs, and turns to Mum. He holds out his hand and helps her to her feet. 'Let's see if we can sort it out.' He looks at me. 'You too, Maddie.'

Shuffling forwards in my chair, I grope for my crutches; I'm going to need something to keep me upright. I feel like my body has been crumpled like a brown paper bag, just waiting for someone to throw me into the recycling bin. If only I could recycle my life… I'd settle for the last couple of days.

I doubt I'll help the situation. Dad was right. Christie is better left, at least until she's had chance to think this out for herself. I had tried to prepare her for Scott turning up, but she'd shut me down. I knew it wouldn't take him long to hear about Madeline De-Muir's love child. It took even less time than even I thought, thanks to the gallery fire.

And since the only thing Christie has been bothered about has been Miles, I've not pushed it. Well, I have, I've pushed it to the back of my mind.

Following behind them, already I know we're too late. Christie is not going to hang about for an explanation, of that I'm certain.

Sure enough, Scott, with his arms folded, is stood in front of Christie's car.

She inches forward, then revs the engine.

Scott stands, unflinching.

Dad pats Mum's hand. 'Wait here with Maddie. I'll go and try to talk some sense into the lad.' – I don't rate his chances – 'But Christie first, she needs to get away.'

Scott stares at Christie in the car. 'I'm not budging from here! Not until you speak to me.'

Dad is level with Christie, he bends forward and is talking to her. No idea what he's saying, though Dad is Christie's "go to" ally. There's a lot of head bobbing going on.

'Can you tell what he's saying?' I ask.

Mum shakes her head. 'No, but it will be his usual win-win strategy.' – He should have been a Brexit negotiator. – 'It hasn't failed him yet.'

'There's always a first time,' I mutter.

Mum looks at me. 'Don't even joke about it.'

Dad turns to look at us. 'Maddie, Christie wants a word. Come on, love.'

This will be fun. I hobble over. If ever there was a time for my crutches to fail, this is it! But no, they continue to hold my weight. I look at Scott, still standing there, all macho. He's going to struggle to back down, but, really, he has no choice.

Dad offers me a lopsided smile. 'You need to reassure her, Maddie, after last time.'

I nod. 'Okay, Dad. I'll try.' I shrug. 'What about Scott?'

'Leave Scott to me. You just concentrate on Christie.' He pats my arm. 'We've muddled through worse, Maddie. Chin up.'

Dad moves away from the car. He stands facing Scott, blocking our view of him.

I step forward and bend to look at Christie. She is staring resolutely ahead. The window is open about an inch, her only concession.

I take it as a positive. 'Can we talk, Christie?'

'Go ahead. Doesn't look like anyone's going anywhere, anytime soon.'

'Sure. So, about Scott. I didn't invite him to come—'

'Huh, looked like you all were having a fab time. Mum doesn't get the three-tiered stand out every day!'

I sigh. 'We were just trying to—'

'All the usual suspects, plotting and planning behind my back… Do you have any idea how that makes me feel? Again!'

I readjust my weight. 'Honestly, I've no idea how you must feel. I'd imagine, pretty raw.'

She turns to look at me for the first time. 'Darn right.'

'He saw our interviews, put two and two together… Let's face it, Christie, it doesn't take a rocket scientist to see you're his.'

'So, you thought, "Hey, why not invite him round for a cosy little chat". I can't believe you'd do it again. All of you.'

'It wasn't like that. Scott turned up on my doorstep, demanding to see you. I really didn't want to spring another surprise on you, honestly, Christie. That's why we met up today.'

'You could have told him to get lost.'

I shake my head and look up at the never-ending blue sky. 'It's not that simple. Scott's travelled over five thousand miles to meet you, Christie.'

'Nobody asked him to.'

I look back at her, the daughter I left behind. I can't blame her for being filled with resentment towards me, but Scott didn't even know she existed. 'No, nobody asked him to. Yet, still he came.'

'Well, I wish he hadn't. It's complicated enough with you!'

'Look, Christie, you've every right to be angry with me. But Scott didn't know anything about you… And as soon as he did, he came to find you. He knew it wouldn't be an easy ride, but still he came. I think that goes some way to demonstrate the calibre of the man he is.'

Christie looks away from me, towards Dad and Scott. 'They seem to be getting along just fine.'

I can make out the top of Scott's bowed head. Dad has one hand on each of Scott's shoulders, and is looking directly at him. One of Dad's tried and tested methods, give a hundred percent attention if you want a hundred percent success.

I sigh. 'They've only just met, Christie. You know Dad, he's trying to sort it all out. He'll be talking a good talk, making everything seem reasonable, manageable, doable. And, when he's done that, he'll leave us to it, and trust us to work it out.' She continues to watch Dad and Scott. 'And, Christie, we will, we will work it out… Because we have to… Because neither of those two men you are looking at, deserve the anguish of another age of aggro. It's not their fault.'

She looks at me. 'It's not mine either.'

I nod. 'You're right, it's not your fault either. But it's in your gift to offer some hope of a resolution.'

'Thought that was your speciality, gliding over glitches.'

I snort. 'It might seem that way. But gliding over those glitches doesn't work, it allows molehills to grow into mountains.' I nod towards Scott. 'And that mountain looks suspiciously like a volcano about to erupt.' I straighten up and roll my shoulders, easing the crick in my neck. 'Please, Christie, just give him a chance. And Dad.'

Christie irritably taps the steering wheel, and lets out a deep huff. 'Whatever… Fine, but not now! You can go and sort something out with him, and I'll just go along with it, as usual.'

'Thank you, Christie.' Relief washes over me. I'm tempted to say more, but daren't risk blowing it.

'I'm not doing it for you, Maddie. I'm doing it for them.' She stares doggedly ahead.

Her words hit their mark. The relief inside me withers. 'You won't regret it, he's … I'll let you decide for yourself what he is.' My sweaty hands are making me lose my grip on my crutches. I discreetly wipe each of my palms in turn on my linen trousers. 'I'll get them to move so you can get off home.'

'I came here to talk to Mum about something…' Christie shrugs and looks at me. 'Not that any of you bothered to ask…'

I inwardly sigh. 'I'll go and talk to Scott to sort out a meeting—'

'Not tomorrow! Miles is coming home tomorrow. And I've got to sort everything out for him.'

Another rejection, I'd hoped he'd be staying with me. Then again, I'm hardly *Miss Mobility* myself. I nod slowly. 'Not tomorrow, I understand. I'll try for the next day, but Scott's only here for one week and that's—'

'Not my problem.' Christie glances over her shoulder. 'Will you ask Mum to come over here before you go off talking to the men?'

I gesture to Mum for her to join us. 'Mum, Christie wants a word.' I turn and look back at Christie. 'I'll be in touch.'

She nods. 'Bye, then…'

Hardly inspiring words to part on, but better than they could have been. 'Bye, love.'

I swing my crutches into action and head over to Dad and Scott. They both look to me as I make steady progress. Dad wears a smile, Scott a scowl.

'Any joy, love?'

'Yes.' I look at Scott. 'Christie has agreed to meet you. Okay?'

Scott's face relaxes. 'Thanks, Maddie. I'll go over and—'

'Not now, Scott. She needs to get her head around it first.' Scott shuffles. 'I know you're eager, but give her time.'

Scott shrugs Dad's hands off his shoulders, clamps his hands low on his hips, and scowls down at me. 'Jeez, so I've got to wait until tomorrow then! When she's right there, in front of me!'

My heart is back pounding in my chest. I moisten my lips as best I can. I can tell, he's not going to take this well. 'The day after,' I mutter.

'Excuse me! You've got to be kidding, yeah?'

'Miles is out of hospital tomorrow. Christie wants—'

'So, I see,' rumbles Scott. 'I'm playing second fiddle to *your Personal Assistant*!' He shakes his head and strides towards his car. 'Unbelievable, Maddie. Unbelievable.'

Rules, Regs and Revelations

Forget the tutu

'I'll have to drop you here, love. Hospital regs, only ambulances can get closer.'

I look across the car park. Could the taxi drop-off point be any further away from the main entrance? 'Here's fine, thank you.'

He nods towards the meter, taps it with a porky finger, manoeuvres his belly past the steering wheel and looks at me. 'Eighteen-seventy, love.' He thrusts his hefty hand through the open partition.

I pass him a crisp, new twenty-pound note.

He hesitates before taking it, and casts his gaze over me – that's right, chum, only a slither of a tip – he shuffles to face forward. He clicks the meter, and the door unlocks. 'You'll manage yourself, then.' He forces the last of his pie into his mouth, and tosses the wrapper into the footwell beside him.

'Thank you.' Irritation pulses through my body, erratic and irresponsible. His lack of concern, rakes at my reservoir of unfiltered respect for others, at a time when I need evidence that people are, on the whole, kind.

Pushing open the door, I balance myself ready for the gruelling 300 metre trek. Perilous potholes and mounds of moss await. It's nine-fifteen in the morning, and I already feel like the day's defeated me.

I grapple in my bag for the antibac gel Pauletta made me promise to use. Slather it over my hands, and wait for it to dry before gripping my crutches.

After Scott dropped me home yesterday, I'd tried to book a car and driver for today, but no. By the time I'd looked up the number for Elegant Automobiles, it was almost five. The receptionist curtly informed how impossible it would be to provide a car at such short notice, especially since I hadn't an account number to hand.

How I miss Miles, with his easy charm. He would have had that snooty madam eating out of his hand, and I would have had a chauffeur-driven Merc. Would have been helped gracefully out, and certainly not abandoned to navigate my own way to reception.

The two glass doors swish open and I make my way past an orderly queue of people. I notice a couple of middle-aged ladies trying to make eye contact with me, stardom is fickle, but your fans never forget an encounter. Making my way through the corridors, I keep my head down, not wanting anyone to stop me for a selfie. I can feel eyes on me, but today is not the day. The discomfort of overworked, previously unknown muscles, does little to improve my mood.

It would have been better, if I'd been able to come and talk to Miles last night… Before Christie came to see him. Or even the previous night… Before Christie knew anything about Scott.

Before Christie, I knew Miles would back me up in any situation. But that was before.

Now, I'm not so sure. Now, I need to hold back, and see if he steps forward.

Miles is on the second floor, Ward 10, men's surgical, not that he's had any. The couple of nurses in the lift with me are too busy looking at one of their phones, to pay any attention to me beyond a brief smile. They get out on the first floor, leaving me to gather my thoughts before seeing Miles.

The foyer is deserted. I press the buzzer to get into the ward, and squidge some hand sanitizer out of the dispenser on the wall. I rest back as I give my hands a good clean.

'Can I help?' The words echo through the speaker.

I press the green speech button. 'Oh, yes please. I'm here to see Miles Hepworth, he's in the—'

'Visiting time is two 'til eight.'

'Yes, yes, I know but he's in a room alone, so—'

'Visiting times remain the same. This is for the benefit of the patients, and the smooth running of the hospital.' By the tone of her voice, I can tell she isn't used to being challenged.

'I understand, and fully agree. But Miles is being discharged today, and we're having a family crisis.' I bite my lip. 'I don't want him walking into the situation blind, if you know what I mean.'

'It isn't allowed, I'm afraid.'

I slump back against the wall. 'Please, just ten minutes.' Whatever she decides, I'm going to have to get in there to see him somehow. I'd just rather do it legitimately.

'This is very much against my better judgement, but I haven't the time to stand here talking to you.'

I hear a deep sigh, and the extended buzz for the door being released. Swamped with relief, I swing into action, and manage to pull open the heavy door. I sanitize my hands again and traipse over to the nurse's station.

A harried lady in blue scrubs, with the body of a twelve-year-old but the face that has seen it all, nods curtly towards Miles' room. 'Ten minutes.'

'Thank you,' I mutter. His door is closed-to, I give a gentle knock. 'Are you decent, Miles?'

'Yes, Maddie. Come in, I knew you'd get through security somehow.'

I nudge open the door with my shoulder, shuffle in and close it fully with my bum. 'I had to beg.'

'Not one of your strong points.'

'Oh, you'd be surprised,' I mutter.

Even though Miles is sat, it's plain for me to see he's lost weight. He's wearing jeans with the rugby shirt I bought him last Christmas. He pats the chair beside his and shrugs. 'Come on, where do you want to start?'

I sit next to him, put my crutches down and rest my hand on his and shake my head. 'Where? I've no idea. But, how are you, Miles, besides desperate to get out of here?'

'Yes, desperate to get out of here and start unravelling five days' worth of havoc you've managed to muster. I can't even have a near-death experience without...' Miles turns toward me; his face softens but the strain of the last few days is clear. 'So, about Scott?'

I feel a single tear trace a path down the side of my face. 'This is even worse for me than my first meeting with Christie, facing all her resentment.'

Miles rubs his hands over his face, gets up, perches on the side of my chair and slings his arm over my shoulder. He gives me a side-on hug with his head resting on top of mine. 'Maddie, we discussed this. You knew there was a risk Scott would find you before you'd have chance to contact him.'

I shake my head, and stroke the tears out of my eyes before my foundation is totally washed away. Guilt swamps me, I was absolutely depending on Scott finding me. I didn't tell Miles. I'd foolishly thought it would stop Christie blaming me for him turning up. 'I didn't expect him to show up within days, demanding to meet his daughter.'

I can feel Miles nodding his head. 'Christie is… Well, she's not happy, we knew she wouldn't be.'

I pull away from Miles and turn to look at him fully. 'What did she say?'

He blows out a long sigh. 'I'm in a difficult position here, Maddie. What she's told me, she's told me in confidence, as her boyfriend… What I can say, is, she's unhappy—'

'I see! All of a sudden we have secrets!' A fresh batch of tears form, but I still their progress.

Miles pulls my hands down from my face, and looks at me. 'It's not like that at all, Maddie.' He shakes his head. 'Now I'm with Christie, the lines are blurred. But you and me…' He sighs. 'You'll always be part of who I am. And obviously, I know a hell of a lot more about you, than I will ever tell Christie. It's called loyalty, remember? You taught it me.'

I nod in agreement. But my stomach spasms, and the familiar gremlins of doubt, dance to their treacherous tune. 'It's just, I was relying on you to smooth the way, you know, between me and Christie, and Christie and Scott… And even me and Scott. But now, it's all going to be about what Christie wants.'

Miles moves to sit on the edge of the bed. His face still looks haunted by the trauma of the weekend. In truth, he's lucky to be doing so well. 'I thought that was the plan, Maddie. Give Christie's art the exposure it needed. Reveal her true identity, and get to know her. Give Christie the chance to follow whatever path she chooses. It was always going to be about what Christie wants.'

Again, I can only nod in agreement. That is the brief Miles was given. And we stuck to it. But then, as Christie said, it got complicated.

In theory, it should be a dream come true, one great big happy family.

> To-Do-List
>
> Reunite with estranged daughter✓
> Who falls in love with my PA✓
> Who is already like one of the family✓
> Job done.

Except, *I need* Miles. Miles sorts out every aspect of my life, from interviews and press releases, right down to sorting out what day my dry-cleaning is collected. Oh, and let's not forget the simple task of sorting out a car.

It was Miles, who forged a palatable path between me and my parents, when we were at loggerheads about Christie.

In short, he's my fairy godmother, oh, forget the tutu… Suited and booted he's undeniably masculine in an unassuming way. He has that rare quality which oozes charm, yet takes no shit. Men want to be him; women just want him.

I'm immune. I'd somehow assumed Christie would have inherited this immunity. She hasn't. But since Miles is so consumed with his work and has never taken advantage of his unique gift, I'd thought resolving my Christie problem, would be just another job.

How wrong could I be? Their chemistry is palpable. They intrigue each other. And despite the fact Miles is my right-hand man, Christie couldn't stop him from seeping into her heart.

Oh, she tried, boy did she try! She'd thanked him quite curtly for all his help, and sent him on his way. But that same night, the thought of losing him in the fire, proved the depth of their emotional connection. Christie has been practically glued to his side ever since. And I feel shut out from both of their lives. Miles, my prodigy, and Christie, the daughter I've been separated from for a lifetime.

'I know, Miles. I do want Christie to have the freedom to go whichever way she wants, but right now… Right now, I really need your help to sort this out.'

'And you'll get it. But, Maddie, you know me well enough. When my mind is set, it's set. Christie's been on an emotional rollercoaster for weeks now, give her some space, some time to take it all in.'

'I'm doing my best, but Scott is only here for a week, and is short on patience. Thankfully, she's agreed to meet him tomorrow, and I'm just so relieved. But I desperately want them to get along.' I feel my eyes welling up again, and the cool progress of a tear trace the contour of my nose.

Miles shifts back to my side and puts his arm over my shoulder. 'Hey, come on… That's up to the pair of them to sort out. Leave them to it, Maddie. Let's face it, he's going to need to be pretty impressive, to come anywhere near your Dad.'

I nod. 'Oh, he is pretty impressive.' I purse my lips and tilt my head. I feel my face flush under the intensity of Miles's scrutiny.

'Meaning?'

I shrug. 'Oh, you know…' I turn away from him. It's going to be another hot day, not a cloud in the sky. I'd rather not have this conversation now.

'No, I don't know. That's why I asked.' Miles twists his body so he can look at me. 'Maddie?'

'It's complicated.'

Miles nods. 'I'm used to complicated when it comes to you, Maddie. But help me out here… Exactly how complicated is it?'

I let out a deep sigh. 'How long have you got?' I look away from Miles, knowing he can see through the very best of my performances with ease. 'If I close my eyes, I can feel Scott's gaze caressing my body, taste his lips on mine, remember all the details…' I shrug. 'What's the use? It was so long ago, but now he's here, in the flesh…'

'Oh, Maddie, things are going to get messy.'

'Yep… But then, they usually do with me,' I groan. 'I didn't think he'd still entice me the way he used to. Thought I'd be past all that. And, not to make things worse than they already are.' I shake my head. 'Anyway, forget about that, I'm meeting some clipboards at the gallery, who want to assess the extent of the damage.'

Miles stands up and walks over to the window, looks outside, then turns back to face me. 'Maddie, you don't need to be worrying about that. That's my job, I'll sort it. I'm the one who's been working there all these months.'

I link my fingers together, and raise my hands up to my chin, slightly bowing my head. 'Ah…' I lift my eyes to meet his. 'Could be a problem with that.'

'I don't see why. I can't wait to get back to work, I'm sure I'm up to dealing with the admin side of things, at least.'

I take a deep breath. 'But I'm meeting them this morning.'

Miles looks down, shakes his head and drags his hands through his hair. He looks back at me. 'A provisional meeting?'

'They were pretty insistent, wanted to assess the claim. They contacted me three times.'

Miles nods. 'What did you tell them?'

'I told them you were in hospital, and you deal with all the legal stuff. But they wanted to push on they said.'

'Okay, but you did try to put off the meeting until I would be available to help?'

'Yes, obviously!'

'You're absolutely certain?'

'Well, yes. I told them you deal with it all, and that you'd been injured and are in hospital.'

'And they still pushed for a meeting?'

I let out a huff. 'Yes! How many times do I need to say it?'

Miles smiles. 'Exactly.' He sits beside me. 'You told them on more than one occasion, you are not the correct person to oversee this assessment. You told them that the person who is responsible for this, is still recovering in hospital, and would be available in due course. Yet, you were still *pressurised* into a meeting.'

'Well, yes. But it's all sorted now.' I look at my watch. 'I'll be there in 45 minutes having my brains picked, whether I'm the right person or not.'

'Oh, yes, you do need to go to the gallery and meet them.' He smiles. 'But that's it. No more. Tell them you haven't the authority to answer any questions. I will contact them to make a suitable appointment in the coming days.'

I grip my hands tighter. 'But they're travelling miles for this meeting.'

'Good. Perhaps next time they try to browbeat a vulnerable, traumatised client into a premature meeting, they'll think twice.'

I roll my eyes. 'I'm not vulnerable and traumatised! You make me sound like some feebleminded Miss.'

'Trust me, Maddie. Today, that's the part you must play. I know it grates, but just play the part… Otherwise, well, they may contrive a way of not honouring the insurance, if you say one thing wrong. I know how these men work.'

I stroke my hair back off my face and pucker my fringe forward. 'Okay, I'll play the part.' I look heavenward. 'But I'm going to hate it. And Scott is going to think I've lost the plot.'

'What's Scott got to do with any of this?'

'Oh, didn't I mention, Scott's coming with me.'

'No, Maddie, you did not!'

Oops.

Suits

He lets out a slow, tuneless whistle

'The choice is yours. Over my shoulder or a wheelchair.' Scott stares down at me.

I begin to notice people giving us amused looks. I'm sure there weren't this many people milling about the reception area earlier. 'Don't be ridiculous, Scott!' I hiss under my breath.

He takes a step closer. 'I'm not, you are, ma'am. It's not ten-thirty, and you already look like you've battled a bear.' He looks me over. 'I'm happy to make the choice for you.' He moves still closer.

I can tell there's going to be no reasoning with the man. I hold up my hand to halt his progress. 'Fine! Fine, get one of those wheelchairs then!'

He nods slowly, and turns to get one from the aisle by the door. I swear I hear him mutter "Shame", as he walks away. The man is impossible.

A petite brunette, smiles broadly as she approaches me. 'I'd say he's a keeper, Miss De-Muir,' she says, without breaking step.

Almost temped to tell her I missed that boat years ago. But mentally thank her, for not stopping for a photo op.

Scott raises his brows, and inclines his head towards the wheelchair he's pushed to my side. 'You'll have to rest your crutches on the stirrups while I push you.'

I muster as much dignity as I can as Scott guides me into the seat. 'We're not in the wild west now, Scott. They're called footrests,' I mutter.

'Yeah, yeah. Either way, hold on, I think you're in for a bumpy ride.'

I link my right arm around my crutches, and grip the wheelchair arms. Although Scott keeps an easy pace, I list from one side to the other because of the uneven carpark.

'Think I should of strapped you in, like in a buggy… It's kind of unpredictable this chair. How are you doing?'

'I've been better.'

'I'd say so. Nearly there.' Scott stops by his hire car, and comes round to stand in front of me. He holds out his hands. 'Come on, let's do this.'

I accept his offer. Once up, I feel the grip of his hands around my midriff as he scoops me up into the car. I make myself comfortable and watch Scott as he returns the chair to the hospital reception.

He nods politely every time he meets someone coming in the opposite direction, and always offers them right of way. The perfect gentleman. And in fairness, he only threatened to throw me over his shoulder after I'd refused a wheelchair twice. Had it been Miles, I'd have hopped into the wheelchair without a second thought. But with Scott, it just feels wrong to accept his help in any way. In his work, he's surrounded by agile, beautiful young women; by comparison, I'm a middle-aged dear in need of assistance. I'd rather he remembered me as the spirited spark I once was.

The car lurches as he hauls himself into the driver's seat. 'So, to the gallery. I got to say, I'm looking forward to seeing the place.'

'Well, I'm not.' My stomach clenches, as I remember the last time I was there, with Miles missing, and Christie searching the burning building. 'Believe me, it looked better this time last week.'

He taps the steering wheel and turns to look at me. 'Yeah, well… My invitation must of got lost in the mail.'

I inhale sharply and meet his eyes. 'If you're going to be like that, I suggest you drop me off at the gallery and leave. I'll make my own way home.' I raise my chin and maintain eye contact. 'I've enough on my mind concentrating on what I've been instructed to do by Miles, without contending with your jibes, Scott Scobie.'

'Oh, *lover boy* tells *you* what to do, does he?'

'He is not my lover boy! He is my highly proficient Personal Assistant. So therefore, when he advises me about legal things, procedures and documentation, I follow his lead. I'd be a fool not to.'

'Okay, this I got to see! You reeling off a load of legal spiel… Hope your acting skills are up to the challenge.' He starts the car. 'Need the zip code, Maddie.'

I lean across and tap in the postcode. 'When we get there, I'm expecting you to be discreet. The last thing I need is you messing things up.' Scott's slow smile does little to fill me with confidence. 'I mean it, Scott.'

'You know me, Maddie. The soul of discretion.'

I close my eyes. Feeling the heat of the sun wash over me, I try allowing some of the tension I'm hoarding to ebb away. At the gallery, I'll need to appear totally incapable of any independent thought process, and ignorant about all the dealings with the gallery. I'm going to need to smile sweetly, with all the vacant beauty of a mannequin.

And I'm going to need to do it in front of Scott, while his opinion of me is already verging on disdain.

The fact is, the purchase and renovation of the old mill was down to me. Converting it into an art gallery, my vision. And the desire to maintain the authenticity of the building, my mantra, right down to each brick and salvageable floorboard. All this credibility is going to be lost.

That building has the essence of Madeline De-Muir stamped all over it. Oh, yes, Miles did all the chasing, all the paperwork, handled all the nitty-gritty tedious essentials. He dotted the i's and crossed the t's, but I was instrumental in the whole process.

So, acting like a frontman, and nothing more, is going to grate… It's going to grate big style.

I open my eyes, and look toward Scott. 'At the gallery, I'm going to be acting a part, Scott. I need you not to blow it.'

'Dare I ask what part you'll be playing?' He lets out a sigh.

'Well, as Miles set up all the insurance policies, he needs to be the one who handles the claim. Before he does, he wants to go through all the paperwork to check for loopholes.'

'Sounds plausible. Why didn't you just tell the insurance guy that before today?'

I briefly close my eyes. 'I did. But after I was repeatedly contacted to set up a meeting… I caved in, and let it be set up.'

Scott nods. 'I see.' His tone is flat, and his expression unreadable.

'Miles says it's coercive behaviour. I'm going to be playing a part. I've got to come across as six shades short of a suntan, so hopefully the guys will write me off as a waste of time. That should give Miles the opportunity to get up to speed with the paperwork. Then he'll take over from there.'

'I can run with that.'

'Thank you, Scott. The last thing I need at the moment is any more stress. Miles is frustrated at being unable to deal with this first-hand.'

'Uh-hu, I bet he is.' Scott glances at the satnav. 'Almost there.'

I point towards the funnel of the old mill towering beyond the rooftops. 'That's the chimney. It always gives me a buzz of satisfaction that we managed to save it from demolition.'

'Pleased to hear it.' Scott drives into Mill Street. As the gallery comes into view, he pulls over at the side of the road. He looks at the building, the extent of the damage is hidden by a shell of scaffolding. He turns to me. 'Sorry Maddie, got to say, not looking so good.'

'Obviously the fire—'

'Ah, I'm talking about you, not the gallery… Think you could do with touching up your makeup.'

'Right, well…' I feel my face flare with the heat of a blush.

'I don't want you going into battle without your armour.'

I grab my handbag. 'Thanks. I'll just, you know…' I rummage for my concealer and lippy, then flip down the sun visor. As I slide open the mirror, the light flickers on. He's right, I look exactly how I feel, an emotional wreck. My eyes are still slightly puffy, lippy has all but vanished and my foundation has definitely seen better days.

I lean in towards the mirror, and pat under my eyes with my exclusive blend of beauteous blur. I give my lashes a lick of mascara. Brush my brows. Streak a line of passion paradise lippy across each of my cheek bones, and in circular strokes create an illusion of naturally flushed cheeks. I open my mouth with taut lips, finishing off my mini makeover with a generous helping of the same luscious lippy and a pout of my lips.

I sling the makeup back into my handbag, raise my chin feathering my fingers through my hair, and giving my head a gentle shake.

I turn to Scott, tilt my head, give him my statement "take me to bed" eyes, and offer him a lazy smile. 'Is this any better, cowboy?'

'Darn it, Maddie. You sure do know how to turn a guy inside out.'

I allow my lips to curve into a more seductive smile and raise a single brow. 'Thank you, I'll take that as a compliment, Scott Scobie.'

Result.

Confidence restored.

He mutters something under his breath, restarts the engine and drives the last 100 metres to the gallery. He parks behind a silver Volvo estate. 'That'll be your guy.'

'Wish me luck.'

'Yeah, like you're going to need it looking like that.' He lets out a slow, tuneless whistle. 'I'll stick around in the background.'

I unclip my seatbelt. 'I'd appreciate that. Makes me look more dipsy having eye candy by my side.'

Scott rolls his eyes, unbuckles his seatbelt, pops round and opens my door. 'Ready?'

I nod. 'As ready as I'll ever be.' He puts his hands under my ribs, and I rest mine on his shoulder. As he lifts me down, I tuck my lips close to his ear, and whisper seductively, 'Remember, honey, you're only here to look pretty.'

He steadies me and hands me one crutch at a time. Then he winks and slaps my arse. 'Come on then, darlin' let's get this done!' he says loud enough for the two men getting out of the Volvo to hear.

'Sure, Honey Buns.' I tweak his cheek, and I'm rewarded with a look of surprise.

The two suited insurance men exchange unsure glances. The older of the two walks towards us with his hand outstretched. 'Miss De-Muir and Mr Hepworth, I assume,' he says.

Scott gives me a sideward look as I untangle myself to shake the offered hand. 'Well, yes and no,' I say, with a coy smile. I turn to look at Scott and wrinkle up my nose in a cutie way. 'This is my friend Scott. Say "hello" Scott.'

Scott's expression scarcely changes, as his eyes look at the two men in turn. 'Hello,' he says. 'I'm Miss De-Muir's friend.'

I giggle. 'That's enough, Scott, these men are very important; they've come about the fire.'

Scott shrugs and visibly shrinks. Oh, he's good at this!

'Miss De-Muir, I'm Mr Marshall and this is Mr Bainbridge. We're here to set in motion the claim lodged on the 27th of April. I know this must be a difficult time, but we aim to do preliminary overviews as soon as possible in these instances. So, shall we go and do an external inspection of the building?'

'Do a what?' I say frowning.

'Have a look round outside.'

'Oh, yeah! Ha-ha. Just a minute, I wrote down what Mi… Mr Hepworth told me.' I make a show of delving deep inside my handbag. Eventually I come across a crumpled, torn shopping list, written in Pauletta's barely legible handwriting. I pull it out triumphantly. 'Ah-ha, got it!'

'Very good. Does it have vital information?'

I squint down at the scrap of paper in my hand. I take a deep breath. 'It says here, "Please remember, Maddie"…' I look up. 'That's what Mr Hepworth calls me. So… Da-da-da-da-da, "You are not auth-or-ised to make any comments in regards to the gallery or the e-vents surrounding the fire. You have, in all matters per-taining…" Per-taining, don't know what that means, ha-ha. "You have in all matters per-taining to the gallery signed across all pro-fessional responsibility to me, Mr Miles Hepworth. Please make any insurance rep… Rep-res-ent-atives aware of this." So…' I toss the old shopping list back into my handbag. 'Let's go and have a look, then.'

'You have signed over all legal responsibilities to Mr Hepworth?' Mr Marshall questions.

'Oh, yeah. I always do.' I smile sweetly. 'I can't understand all that legal stuff. Mr Hepworth looks after all my assets.'

Scott coughs, and looks away.

'You alright, Honey Buns?'

Scott nods. 'Something just stuck in my throat.'

I pat his back. 'Awww, never mind.' I turn back to the two insurance chappies. 'Ready when you are.'

'Under the circumstances, I think it would be prudent to come back when Mr Hepworth is available, if it's all the same to you.'

'Oh, if you don't mind. Me and my Scotty here, are in need of some alone time, if you know what I mean!'

Honey Buns

I'm a bit of a big deal

'So, how was that for you?'

Scott fastens his seatbelt, but twists to face me. 'Honey Buns? You called me Honey Buns!'

I can't help but grin at his indignation. 'Only after you slapped me on the bum. I wasn't expecting that level of familiarity.'

'I was helping you play the part! I'm sure you could of come up with some other kind of name, you know, like Scott.'

I shrug, surprised at how natural this banter feels. 'Seemed appropriate, you being...' – I really want to say a hunk – 'Let's just say, you fit the role of eye candy, very well.'

I hold his gaze, comfortable under his scrutiny. I know I'm looking good and have put in a blinding performance, so now my self-esteem has been raised no end. The improvisation with Pauletta's shopping list, was spur of the moment, and nothing less than inspired.

And the buzz. The buzz is always the reward. The feeling every actor craves. The applause, the adulation and the kudos all hinge on the integrity of the acting.

I got the impression Scott enjoyed it too... The freedom to play a supporting role to my lead, far easier to act it, than to live it. As teenagers, it was always the reverse. Oh, he was keen, but I was in awe of his talent.

And because of his talent, I was never totally sure if he loved me for myself, or as an ever-eager subject to sketch or paint.

I would always ask, "How shall I pose today?" It was an in-joke between us. Then the sketchbook and pencil would come out. Scott would never show me the end result, the exception being the nude painting in the woods… Scott had planned every last detail of that day.

'Scott, I'll only let you do it, if you'll show it to me.'

'Aw, come on, Maddie, you know it's embarrassing.'

'Embarrassing? It's not going to be your bum and boobs on display for the whole world to see!' I look down and admire my exposed, pale midriff. The need to be constantly smothered in factor 50, means I'm destined to always be the cream rather than the crumble. I don't care, because Scott says I'm beautiful. He says my skin is translucent.

Scott scuffs his foot over some loose leaves. 'The world will never see it, just me… I thought these would be a great contrast.'

'You'll show me, then?' I ask

'One condition.' Scott smiles. The glint of mischief is back, now he knows I'm up for it.

I roll my eyes and sigh deeply. 'I hope this isn't going to be some ridiculous thing, like pick my nose while balancing an apple on my head.'

'I hadn't thought of that!' Scott bends, and rummages his hands through the leaves. He looks back at me. 'I want you to trust me and do exactly as I say.'

My eyes flare. 'Sounds scary.' A shiver of anticipation shimmies through my body.

'Believe me, it'll be worth it.'

I hook my thumbs into the back pockets if my cut-off denims, and smile. 'It had better be, Scott Scobie. I'm putting my reputation on the line here.'

Scott explodes into laughter. 'Think we both know, that boat has already sailed.'

I cock my head, and saunter over to where Scott has started to set up his easel. I turn his head to face me. 'And why do you think that?'

Scott stops what's he's doing, slings an arm over each of my shoulders and pulls me in close. 'Hey, come on. The entire universe knows you are *the danger zone*!'

My face is crumpled into his T-shirt. The fragrant smell of his mum's fabric softener blends seamlessly with his deodorant. I remain rigid in his embrace, thumbs resolutely hooked in my pockets and shake my head. 'But, Scott, you know you are the only one,' I whisper.

'Yes, Maddie. I know.'

Though his face has lost the illusion of innocence, it's the glint in Scott's eyes that reminds me of why I loved him all those years ago. As men do, his lanky, awkward teenage frame, has matured into a strong, defined physique. His eager, boyish desire to please, has been replaced by a confidence, which success and accomplishment bestow.

'You'd describe me as eye candy, would you, Maddie?'

'I would, and I did.' I raise my chin, expecting a witty response. 'Got a problem with that?'

Scott turns to face forward and starts the car. 'Well, considering we share a twenty-four-year-old daughter, I kinda thought I'd rank a bit higher!'

'Oh, come on!' The roar of the engine practically drowns out my words. 'Don't be so silly, Scott. Obviously, you rank higher than eye candy.'

'So, why did you call me it?'

'The same reason you slapped my bum!' I hiss.

'Because I'm cute?'

'Because we were *playing* a part. *Act-ing*, you know, that thing I used to do for a living, to get those insurance blokes off my back. Thought you could handle it, Scott! I've handled more for you.'

'Meaning?'

Images of golden summer days flit for a split second into my mind's eye. 'Forget it, Scott.'

'No, I don't think so. You having a baby all alone, wasn't down to me, and you know it!'

'*That* is not what I'm referring to! Just let it go, okay?'

The car rolls to a halt at red lights. Scott gives me a sideways scowl. 'Don't think I can just let it go, cos I'm at a loss here, Maddie. I was trying to help you out back there, and you totally humiliated me! I'm not used to being treated like that. I don't like it. You hear what I'm saying?'

I let out a snort. 'Can you *hear* yourself, Scott?'

He eases the car away as the lights turn to green. 'I'm used to being treated with a darn sight more respect, Maddie. You handling more for me? What's that about?'

'Like I said, let it go. And for the record, Scott, *I* get treated like that all the time. Women d—'

'Not by me!'

'Maybe not. But, I know, if Miles had been with me, *regardless* of my status, it would have been Miles those two men would have naturally engaged with.'

Scott takes the right turn by the river up towards Ashwood. 'That's the game you play, Maddie. You use the way you look to get your own way, and then complain about it!'

'I'm not complaining about it, far from it; I'm exploiting it! I have no problem letting those two men think they are intellectually superior to me, because clearly, they're not.'

'So, what's your problem?'

'I haven't got a problem! You have! We were acting a part, Scott. And you couldn't cope with being treated like a pretty decoration in my deception.'

'Yeah, well, where I come from, I'm a bit of a big deal… An' here, with you, all I am, is a bit of eye candy.'

My tummy rumbles as we turn the final bend. 'Excuse me! I missed breakfast,' I mutter, placing my hand on my tum. I'd thought we could have grabbed a bite to eat on our way back, but not with Scott in this mood.

Scott looks across at me. 'You got to eat, Maddie. No wonder your mother worries about you.'

'I do eat! I was just behind schedule this morning.'

Scott pulls the car up at the front of *The Manor House*. 'Yeah, sure.'

I fumble for the gate fob and my door keys. 'Thank you, Scott.' – I'm tempted to say it's been a pleasure, but it hasn't – 'You've saved me the trauma of another taxi drive.' I press the fob, and the wrought iron gates swing open.

'Interesting design.'

'Yes… It reminds me of unfurled wings, the way it feathers outward. That's why I chose them.'

'They represent an angel?'

It's what I'm happy to let everyone else believe. I look at Scott; would he understand? 'Actually no. When they open, they symbolise a bird taking flight… They embody freedom. The freedom to be.'

Scott parks the car as close to the front door as possible. He unclicks his seatbelt and turns to look at me. 'The freedom to be what?'

I shrug. 'That's the point, Scott. To be whatever I choose, whenever I choose. Not to be somebody one can pin down or put a label on. Just to be, without having to fit into anyone else's blueprint.'

'Maddie Harris, you are a contradiction.'

'Thank you.'

An Easy Ride?

She lets out a girly laugh

Almost there. Knowing the headrest is perfectly aligned, I close my eyes, rest back and luxuriate in the sumptuous upholstery of the midnight-blue Daimler. A far cry from the taxi yesterday, with its split-leather seats and the sporadic spraying of spittle and pie crumbs. Having Miles back in control of things, even at the very basic level of sorting out my transport, makes all the difference.

So, here I am, enjoying a carefree journey to Little Wilton. Well, not entirely carefree, I'm going to visit Christie, even that, without Miles's help would have been a huge issue. I'm sure Christie would have refused to see me. And obviously, it had to be this morning, before she meets up with Scott.

I raise my left leg and try to definitely not think about the way the arch of my foot is itching. I can't wait to get this cast off! My toes are rocking a lovely shade of purple at the moment, clashing beautifully with the pink plaster.

I'm seriously regretting choosing a pink cast now.

I breathe deeply, and let it go. And again. And again. I have to present an aura of calm, and dispel the desperately-needy persona of the last few days. The gentle undulation of the car helps me focus and relax. All I need to do, is pretend to be myself. Be the Maddie who was "Auntie Maddie", and Christie will love me. I hope.

I open my eyes as the car slows. I can't help but smile at the sight before me. Rose Cottage has the character of a cherished grandpa, a little dishevelled, yet undeniably loved and reliable. The white picket fence is in need of some TLC; dandelions boast, with their yellow heads poking through the slats, and the roses are rioting rather than rambling. It truly is a gloriously under-cultivated paradise.

As soon as the car stops at the kerbside, my driver, "James" – my drivers are always called "James", apparently – gets out, and sweeps open my door, his smile respectful and reassuring. 'Is there anything I can help you with, Miss De-Muir?'

'Thank you, James. If you could just steady my elbow whilst I sort out my crutches.' Oh, how lovely to be lulled into this feeling of being cared for. I'd like to forget I am paying for his undivided attention. Even so, to be cared for, is such a privilege.

James accompanies me to the front door, and raises his hand to ring the bell.

The door is yanked open. 'Oh!' A startled young woman steps back inside the house. 'Sorry, Miss De-Muir… I'm—'

'Miss De-Muir is here at the request of Miss Harris.' James smiles as he smooths over the awkwardness of the situation with finesse. 'If you would be kind enough to enlighten her of Miss De-Muir's arrival?'

'Sure, I mean, yes I will, I mean, shall.'

James nods. 'Thank you, Miss.'

Mouse-like, she scurries off. I recognise Suzi from Christie's paintings, the timid one, bound by convention.

James glances in my direction and nods. 'I shall be waiting in the car to return you home at your request, Miss De-Muir. Is there anything I can assist you with in the meantime?'

'No, thank you, James. You've been most helpful. But please, in the car, feel free to take off your jacket and cap. You must get overheated on a day like today.'

'Thank you, Miss De-Muir, but it's against company policy. The air-conditioning is more than adequate to compensate.' He nods, turns and walks briskly back to the car.

Miles appears, wearing what is commonly referred to as loungewear. His hair is unbrushed, and his face unshaven. 'Morning, Maddie. Come in.'

I raise an eyebrow and look him up and down.

'Don't start, Maddie… We've had a bit of a morning here. *And I am*, let's not forget, still off sick.' He steps back, allowing me to enter.

I edge inside. 'The offer to stay with me still stands… And you do look like you need a hot shower and shave.'

Miles laughs and shakes his head, bends and kisses my cheek. 'Honestly, Maddie! Only you would say that, so soon after I'm out of hospital… Come on.' He puts his lips to my ear. 'Spoiler alert, Suzi is spitting feathers coz she's having to sleep on the sofa so I can have her room,' he whispers.

'She was perfectly lovely with me, and like I said, the offer still stands.'

He leads me into the lounge. The traditional three-piece suite is arranged around a substantial fireplace. Propped up on the high mantle, is a caricature of, I assume the three friends together. In the corner, by the window, is a precariously balanced pile of bedding nestling on a side table.

Miles looks in my direction, and a small smile escapes me. He shakes his head. 'Just sit down, Maddie, and don't make any cocky comments.'

As my bum hits the seat, the unmistakable click of heels sounds from the hallway. A life-sized Barbie strides into the room. She scarcely glances my way, and tosses her deep brunette hair over her shoulders with an unnecessary flick of her manicured fingers. Her lithe body is clad in a polka-dot shift dress that openly advertises what lies beneath. And I doubt very much it'll cover her pert butt when she sits down.

Her skyscraper sandals are to die for.

She sidles over to Miles, runs her finger over his stubble and taps his nose. 'Miles, darling, you look like shit.'

Miles shrugs. 'Thanks. And you look like you should be on the cover of Vogue.'

'I know. But you still look like shit.'

Miles gestures towards me. 'Trudy, I'd like to introduce you to my boss, Madeline De-Muir.'

Trudy steps forward, and has to bend to offer me a limp hand to shake. 'Pleased to meet you,' she says with all the sincerity of a loan shark.

I smile, as I shake her hand. 'The pleasure is all mine. Call me Maddie.'

Trudy removes her hand from mine, but continues to hold it slightly aloof from her body, as if it's been contaminated. 'I'm Christie's friend, and for the record, you're on probation.'

Miles flinches. 'Tru-dy,' he growls.

'Whatev's, Miles. Your boss has turned Christie inside out.' Trudy rolls her eyes. 'Anyway, can't stand about here all day, I've back-to-back clients.' She claps once, and rubs her hands together. 'Laters.' And off she flounces. The door slams with a reverberating bang.

Miles grimaces. 'Sorry.'

'What for? I like her.' I shrug. 'She doesn't like me, but, hey, she's Christie's friend. I wish I'd had a friend like that when I was growing up. I wish I had a friend like that now!'

Miles makes puppy eyes. 'You've got me.'

My sigh escapes unchallenged. If he meant to reassure me, he didn't. 'Miles...' I shake my head. 'Let's leave that for another day, yeah?'

I hear the door open, and look towards the entrance with my smile fixed, ready to meet Christie's disdain.

It isn't Christie.

'Just letting you know, I'm off now. The bathroom is all yours, Miles.'

Miles smiles his most endearing smile. 'Come in, Suzi. I don't think you've been properly introduced to my boss, Madeline De-Muir.' He steps towards Suzi and ushers her before me. 'Suzi, this is Maddie. Maddie, this is Suzi.'

I notice a flare of colour on Suzi's face as she bobs before me – please don't let her curtsy – she hovers with her hand half outstretched.

I smile, need to put her out of her misery. 'Well hello, Suzi.' I take hold of her hand between both of mine. 'How lovely to meet you at long last.'

'Oh, Miss De-Muir—'

'Please call me Maddie.'

'It's such an honour to meet you. I'm such a fan. My Mum says nothing comes close to your "Lucy" in The Fallen…'

'Tell your mother, thank you, that's very kind. It's such a long time ago, but there are some incredibly talented actors about at the moment…' I release Suzi's hand and give her another reassuring smile. 'Jodie Comer is simply exquisite; she can express every possible emotion without uttering a single word.'

Suzi nods. 'Oh, yes…'

Miles looks towards the door and raises his chin. 'Ah, there you are, Christie.'

Hope I manage to continue looking relaxed.

Christie walks over to Miles. 'Good morning to you, too.' She turns to me. 'Maddie…'

'Hello, Christie. Thank you for agreeing to meet me this morning.'

She nods, and looks at Suzi. 'Shouldn't you have left for work?'

'Yep, yeah… I was just leaving when—'

'I'd already been introduced to Trudy,' I say. 'I really wanted to meet Suzi, too… I hope you don't mind?'

Suzi beams. 'Well, I'd best be getting off now.'

'It's been lovely to meet you, Suzi,' I say.

'Bye, then.' She scurries from the room, and I hear the front door close.

Miles grins at Christie. 'After all the fuss about the bathroom rota, I expected to be given the cold shoulder by Suzi.'

'You disrupted the bathroom rota?'

'I needed the *bathroom*, Christie.'

'You should have used the one downstairs. There are few things worse than messing with the bathroom rota, Suzi spent weeks perfecting the timings.'

Miles clasps his hands dramatically and bobs his head down. 'I plead forgiveness, m'lady. I live alone, and am unaccustomed to the ways of the fairer sex.'

Christie sits down in the armchair closest to the window, and plants her hands firmly on her knees. 'I'm sure she'll forgive you… In time…' She looks at the pile of bedding. 'Then again, you *are* sleeping in her bed, too.'

'I haven't eaten her porridge, though!' Miles tilts his head, and sniffs his shoulder. 'And, I might look like shit, as Trudy kindly pointed out, but I smell as fragrant as a summer meadow.' Miles smiles and looks over to me. 'I'll make you both a cup of tea, then leave you to it.'

My stomach flips. 'Oh, I assumed you'd be staying.'

Miles steps closer and ruffles my hair – which took me twenty minutes to get right – and winks. 'No, I think I need a hot shower and a shave.'

Touché.

Christie rests back in her chair, her gaze lingers on Miles as he walks out of the room. As her face softens, her eyes flare. I'm sure she's blissfully unaware of how obvious her feelings for Miles are. As the door closes behind him, she turns to me, the warmth of her expression only a fraction of what it was moments ago. 'So, Maddie, you wanted to see me.'

'Yes, yes, thank you for agreeing.' I moisten my lips. 'I really wanted to clear the air—'

'There's no need. I'm beginning to realise you aren't used to compromising, you like getting your own way… At any cost.' She gives a shrug of dismissal.

I flinch at the bitterness of her response. Looking down at my hands clasped on my lap, I rein in the tears blurring my vision. I look back at Christie. 'I'm sorry you feel that way, Christie.'

'Don't be. If we're going to get along, and I use that in the loosest way, I need to protect myself from the chaos surrounding you, Maddie. I need to toughen up, thanks to you, my life has been thrown into turmoil—'

'I'd hardly say that…' I catch my breath. 'I've opened doors for—'

'I didn't need or want them opening, Maddie. I didn't need the Evolution exhibition. I was happy with my life how it was, before all the family revelations and media attention.'

I look at my daughter. I can hardly blame her, she didn't ask for any of this. 'I'm sorry, Christie… But I'm sure you know the truth would have come out one day… This way, at least, you get your work in the spotlight.'

'And my life. I've spent my entire life trying to blend in! You of all people should know how tough it is being the only daughter of the wonderful, Reverend and Mrs Harris. A lifetime, and now I'm literally frontpage news!'

'It won't take long to settle back down again. Believe me, someone else will be front-page news by next week.'

Christie stands up and walks behind her chair, looks out of the window with her back to me. 'No, Maddie.' She turns to me. 'I think it will still be me. How long before the news breaks that the famous Los Angeles artist, Scott Scobie, is my dad?'

'Yes, Scott *is* big news in LA, but here?' I shake my head. 'I don't think so. And, well, had you heard of him?' I raise my chin, arch my brow and allow the merest of questioning smiles.

Christie runs her hands over her cropped jeans. Her mouth twists briefly downward. 'Suppose not... But that doesn't mean other people don't know who he is.'

I nod, I've prompted enough doubt about Scott's fame to weaken her resolve. I push on. 'But it does mean there is little chance, as in, almost zero chance, of Scott making front-page news here... Or any other page, come to that.'

Christie perches on the chair arm, still keeping a fair distance between us. And from her elevated position, both morally and physically, she looks down on me. 'But regardless of who Scott is in his own right, Maddie, your past relationships are going to be under scrutiny. And Scott crawling out from—'

'You can stop right there!' I snap. Lava-fuelled fury surges through my body. 'Scott didn't *crawl out* from anywhere! He was perfectly settled and getting on with his own life when he—'

'As far as I'm concerned, he should have carried on getting on with his own life! It's all your fault!'

I'm clasping my hands so tightly my fingers are white. And my heart is thumping at my ribs like a battering ram as heat explodes over my chest. 'Yes, yes, it is my fault, and—'

'You could have just met me at Mum and Dad's, if you were so *desperate* to get in touch with me.' Christie stands up and plants her hands on her hips, and leans forward glaring at me. 'But no! You leave it to them to tell me the devastating news... And then, to top it off, you invite the whole world into your seedy past!' she screeches.

She's unleashed the full force of her resentment towards me, and has done the damage that deep down, I knew she would. And I'm in no position to defend my past. I made mistakes, plenty of them.

I could have done as Christie said, met her discreetly at Mum and Dad's, it was my original plan… And if Christie had been making any kind of effort to get her work out there, that's what I'd have done. Instead, she buried herself in school life, pushing her pupils to stretch their skills, and only using her gift as a means of unwinding at the end of the day.

I couldn't let her squander her talent. She has a unique flair, and the ability to see and capture the extraordinary in the mundane. Christie needed a springboard to launch her into the limelight, and that springboard was me…

I knew I'd get trampled on for a while.

I expected the backlash, feared it. Spent many sleepless nights imagining the various scenarios in my head. I knew I'd have to play the long game to gain Christie's respect. I was ready for that, in the scheme of things, it would be a small price to pay. I knew, thought I knew, that in time Christie would thank me for the exposure. So, I was prepared for her initial hostility towards me…

But nothing could have prepared me for this tsunami of venom towards Scott.

I reach for my crutches, and stand up. 'I think it best if I leave,' I say in hushed tones. 'Although I find your description of my past as "seedy", upsetting, I'm prepared to let it pass. But to assume Scott has crawled out from *anywhere*, is simply not acceptable.'

Christie stands. 'I can't believe you're defending him. He got a sixteen-year-old girl pregnant.'

'He was only a couple of months older, Christie.' I start towards the door.

'How many other young girls, I wonder?'

'There are no others.'

'And how would you know?'

I shake my head. 'I just do, okay? I'll see myself out… And when you meet Scott, remember, you are as much of a shock to him, as he is to you.'

Christie folds her arms. 'Really? He managed to track you down in record time. It's almost as if he already knew where to find you.'

I shake my head. 'I'm leaving. I hope you get your questions answered when you see Scott later.'

Miles is making his way down the stairs wearing a white towelling robe, his hair damp and tussled. His relaxed expression changes as he catches sight of me. 'Oh, leaving so soon?'

I nod, my eyes prickle as I feel tears forming. The tightness in my throat makes it difficult to swallow. My mouth is dry. 'Sorry,' I mutter, and put my head down as I head towards the front door.

I hear Miles bounding down the remaining steps. 'Maddie? What's going on?' He rests his hand on my elbow.

I shake my head, and look up at him. His concern, all the justification my tears need to overflow. I bob my nose with the back of my wrist to make sure it's not dribbling, then dab my tears away. 'It was a mistake. I shouldn't have come today,' I croak.

'What do you mean? What's happened?'

'Please, just…' I glance back towards the lounge, then back to Miles. 'Be kind to Scott, yeah?'

'You know me, Maddie, Mr Professional.' Miles nods. 'I'll be kind.'

'Thank you.' My voice cracks.

Miles nods. 'It's okay. You know, you really didn't need to ask.'

'I know. Call me, after...'

'Sure. Sure.' He reaches past me to open the front door, and drops a kiss on the top of my head. 'Don't worry about Christie and Scott, they'll sort it out.'

'Hope so.'

The sunlight is blinding. James steps out of the car and opens the rear passenger door for me. He waits for me to get level with the car and helps me in. I lay down my crutches and James hands me my seatbelt.

Miles has followed me to the car. 'Are you going to be alright?'

I shrug. 'Yeah... I shouldn't have come. Christie needs time.'

Miles nods. 'I'll talk to her.'

'Leave it, Miles. It'll only make matters worse. I can wait.'

'Okay.' He pats the car door and moves away.

'Ma'am.' James steps forward and closes my door, then gets back into the driver's seat and we're off.

I close my eyes and let out a deep sigh. I hope Scott knows what he's going to be walking into. My eyes flick open, I snatch up my mobile, scroll for Scott's number and press dial.

Six rings. 'Come on, Scott, answer.'

'Hi. Can I help ya'?' A Southern Californian accent purrs.

'Oh, sorry. I think I may have the wrong number. Is this Mr Scobie's phone?'

'Yeah, sure is. Scott's just taking a shower.' She lets out a girly laugh. 'I can get a message?'

'No, no message.' I disconnect the call and toss my mobile into my bag.

Addiction

Hysteria crushed my inhibitions

I rest my back against the inside of my front door, not sure if my legs can carry me any further. Despair swamps me. I slither to the ground with my head buried in my hands, shuddering as sobs wrack my body.

From somewhere deep within my chest, I feel like my body is folding in on itself; clawing all the hurts into a tight bundle of agony. Drawing my knees up under my chin, I rest my head down and encircle my legs with my arms. Holding myself rigid, I press my eyes into my knees to stem the flow of tears.

My throat, taut with emotion, traps the explosion of grief from spilling out. Years of suppressed anguish churn and squabble for superiority. Haunted by a past I cannot change, and clamouring for a future just beyond my reach, I'm crushed by a torment of my own creation.

Alone. Always alone.

Until Scott came onto the scene, Christie had been coming round to the idea of having a proper relationship with me. We'd talked a couple of times on the phone, and once, grabbed a snack at Mum and Dad's before she'd rushed off to see Miles.

We'd even made tentative arrangements for me to meet Trudy and Suzi. After this morning, well, I'd have preferred a casual introduction, perhaps in the back garden with a glass or two of wine. But today, while

Suzi was sweet, Trudy was tremendously unyielding and unashamedly cautious. She's the kind of scary friend we all need.

But Christie... I knew the initial shock of learning about me would turn to resentment. I was ready for that, I wasn't ready for the distant appraisal she delivered, it simply isn't her style. I can only think it was a ploy to mask the pain of betrayal she's feeling.

Her volatile tirade about Scott, hit harder than I ever could have imagined. It really was a far different situation than she envisages. Yes, I was only sixteen, but so was he. And I can hardly claim I didn't know what I was doing. I did; I revelled in it.

Scott was the only one who put me at the centre of his world. With him, I was alive and vibrant... And wanted to be.

Like an addiction, I craved being with him every second.

Like an addiction, whatever I got, was never enough.

Like an addiction, all my thoughts focused solely on him.

We stumbled across each other one evening, 25th April. It had been a warm Sunday, which I'd spent mainly in bed listening to music. I was ignoring my parents after yet another house move, not that they'd noticed. I'd snatched up my dinner plate and taken it to my new bedroom, then climbed out of the window to explore the area.

Rain blended with my angry tears. I took shelter in woods next to a park. Taking out a small bottle, I took a swig, scrunching my face at the bitter taste. He came hurtling towards me at such a breakneck speed, I didn't have time to get out of the way. By the time Scott spotted me, it needed his spilt-second reactions to avoid hitting me. He jammed his brakes and swerved his bike off the track.

His landing was softened by a rabble of undergrowth. As he emerged with twigs and brambles clinging at random angles from his clothing, my immediate response was to laugh.

Hysteria crushed my inhibitions.

Stood in a deep, dark wood, with mascara streaked down my face and fighting a fit of giggles, I met the burning light of my life – Scott.

The attraction was palpable from that first moment. At last, my existence felt worthwhile.

But, like an addiction, it didn't end well.

Pauletta

I peep out from between my fingers

'Madam, madam! What you doing on floor? No place for a lady. But you be okay, I have just clean it, but what is matter now?' She rests her hand on my shoulder.

I'd forgotten about Pauletta. With all the kerfuffle earlier this week with Scott, she's been working random hours. She's practically moved in. I raise my head enough to balance my chin on my knees. 'I'm okay. I didn't realise you'd still be here.'

'Is only in morning. I get you up. Make cup of tea.'

Pauletta scoops her wiry arms under mine, and starts to hoist me up. I tilt forward and I'm on my feet. She bends, gets my crutches and holds them out to me. 'Try make no marks on my clean floor with these sticks.'

'Thank you. I'll do my best, Pauletta.'

'Very good, madam. I will bring nice cup of tea, yes?'

I nod. 'That's very kind of you, thank you.' I hobble off to the snug. I can't yet banish memories of the spat with Scott in the lounge. I slump into the well-worn sofa resting my plaster cast along the length of it. I let out a sigh.

I can't believe Scott brought his girlfriend – whoever the latest one is – to the UK. I know he's not married; he has a new *plus one* practically every season. Always some glamour young thing hanging onto his every word, winding her body around his.

Not that I care, I've had long enough to get over him.

And it took time. I'd reached out, in those early letters. I'd wanted to... I don't know what I'd wanted to. But I do know losing Scott felt like I had a gaping hole in my body, a constant ache, a wound that would never be healed. That empty feeling has never fully left. Yes, I had Christie, but every time I looked into her eyes, Scott looked back at me. The shape of her face, the wayward wilderness of curls and the dimples on her shoulders. All Scott. Almost as if she had no connection to me at all. Just a constant reminder of what I'd left behind.

So, for him to bring his girlfriend, after all this time really shouldn't hurt, but a little bit of consideration goes a long way. It's hardly like he needs someone to hold his hand. And as he said, he's only here for a week! I'm sure they could manage to be apart for seven days.

This last couple of days, on the few times we haven't been at each other's throats, the old vibes have skimmed into my consciousness, tempting me with maybe.

I'm being stupid, I shouldn't let him get to me. But whatever he had back then, is ten times more appealing to me now. His stance, raw charisma and the unapologetic intensity of his gaze has all been honed by maturity. He's naturally comfortable in his own skin, unlike the younger Scott who was filled with big dreams and an edge to make them happen.

That stubborn streak, with Christie, might be his undoing. If he doesn't lower his expectations for this first meeting, and Christie doesn't meet him with an open mind, today's meeting between them is going to be carnage. I'm not sure who I feel most sorry for.

Then there's Miles, who sweetly believes everything is going to turn out smelling of roses… The trouble is, for fabulous roses, you need heaps of horse shit.

The door opens, and Pauletta walks in with a tray. 'Here for you madam, one cup of tea and one very nice tasty snack. Is best I can do for you.'

She places the tray on the table in front of me. The bowl of mixed salad, fetta and olives, just the sort of refreshing lunchtime snack I need. 'Thank you. It looks lovely.'

Pauletta nods decisively. 'Then eat!' She takes a cushion and places it on the table. 'I move this lump for you.' She lifts my leg and rests it on the cushion, passes me a fork and the bowl, before I've time to object.

'I can manage, thanks, Pauletta. Really the cup of tea is what I need first.'

She raises her chin. 'Uh-hum.' Sits down beside me. 'I think I stay and keep eye on you, madam. You upset again.'

I stifle a sigh. This is all I need, Pauletta in mothering mode. I have a sip of tea, as always, just as I like it. 'Ahh, lovely. Honestly though, I'm fine.' I stab a chunk of cheese. 'See.' I pop it in, and chew. It feels like churning plumber's putty about my mouth, but I smile reassuringly to convey my enjoyment.

'I stay, just to make sure, yes?' She clasps her hands and sinks further into the sofa, such is her assurance she's the authority to bully me.

I'd like to calmly say, "Get off my sofa, and back to work." But that'll never happen. I nod meekly, fork a random piece of green into my mouth and chew.

'Is that bad man again. I know.' She affirms with confidence.

I chew laboriously and swallow. 'Scott is not a bad man. He's just had a shock to learn about Christie.'

'Huh, I have eyes, I see!' She flutters her arms up and down and shimmies her fingers. 'He has this thing with him. All ladies swoon. Fools!'

My stomach lurches as I force down another leaf. 'You've never even seen him with ladies, Pauletta.'

'Oh, yes. I see him here with you. When dog get him good with teeth!'

I stab a plum tomato, wave it in her general direction. 'You were very rude, when you met him.'

'Ha! I hear him shout at you. But good, he squeal like baby later. I come and see. Think you try kill him.' She shrugs. 'Shame, just dog.'

'Pauletta! Why ever would you think I'd try to kill him.' I stab another tomato as I remember the girly voice answering his mobile.

'Just idea, yes?' She shuffles forward to the edge of the sofa. 'Now, Mr Hepworth, he never shout.'

Here we go again. Miles, the man who can do no wrong in her sight. 'That's because I pay his wages, just like I pay yours.'

'Huh, makes no change in that. Mr Hepworth top man, he no shout.'

'He does shout sometimes, Pauletta. You just choose not to remember, because he's always telling you how wonderful you are.'

She stands up and plants her hands on her hips, giving me a haughty look. 'I am wonderful. I take good care of you, yes?'

If I don't agree, I'll be dealing with mega sulks for weeks. 'Yes, you take good care of me.' I nod towards the remains of the salad. 'As you well know.'

'Yes, I do. And Mr Hepworth. I see to what he need.'

'And Mr Hepworth, too.' Why I'm reduced to grovelling to my housekeeper, I have no idea.

'And why is Mr Hepworth not here for my care, now?' She pulls a face of disgust. 'Is because of that bad man.'

'Pauletta, we've been through this. Mr Hepworth doesn't want to put me out becau—'

'Not put you out, I help!'

'But you aren't here all the time—'

'I happy to move in, for Mr Hepworth,' she huffs. 'I take good care of him, yes?'

'Yes, but he wants to stay with Christie. They are—'

'Not married!' Pauletta spits the words.

'He has his own room.'

'Phuh.' She looks me up and down. 'You believe this? Ha! She take that boy astray.'

I daren't say, he might want leading astray, not the sainted Miles. In Pauletta's eyes, Miles can do no wrong. Her first day working for the famed Madeline De-Muir came as a shock to Pauletta. It was Miles who put her at ease, and charmed her to such an extent, that she's been loyal to him ever since.

Not loyal to me, but Miles.

Before he moved out to get his own place, Miles used to take great pleasure in winding me up about it.

She treated him like her favourite son, and me like his inadequate wife.

'I don't think Christie is going to lead Miles astray, he's far too wise for that, don't you think?'

'All boys get head turned by pretty face.' She takes the abandoned salad from me. 'And that Christie, a spoiled Miss. She take Miles away from your heart. Take him away from my heart also.' She slaps her chest and looks pityingly towards the ceiling.

'I don't think that's going to happen, Pauletta.'

'I do not know why you not take him for yourself, huh? He is good man.'

I roll my eyes; she has no idea how ridiculous it would be. 'Yes, he's a good man. But, how many times? He's like my younger brother and I'm like his big sister.'

'But *not* his sister!'

I'm not going to win this skirmish, and I haven't the strength to reason with her. She comes up with new arguments every time she suggests this fantasy of hers. 'Thank you for the salad, it was very refreshing.' I manage to muster my no-more-questions expression.

She looks into the bowl. 'Is this why you leave half?' She shakes her head and walks out of the room.

I sag with relief, check the time, 11:45. Another couple of hours and Scott will be on his way to meet Christie. Two hours to churn over whether I should warn him about the opinion she has of him. Tell him to be on his best behaviour.

The trouble is, if Christie has done the same web searches as I've done… His ability to attract young female companions is well documented. He is photographed at all the right places, with all the right people.

As he pointed out to my parents, he is well placed in society.

He can open doors.

Christie would be wise to learn from him.

All those pretty young things, and never any adverse publicity. There's usually one ex who's prepared to spill the beans, for the right price, of course. But nothing. Either he is the perfect gentleman, or…

The evidence, getting a sixteen-year-old pregnant, doesn't look good.

And, the more I think about it, the more let down I feel about him bringing his "plus one" along. He hasn't even had the decency to tell me. I don't suppose he thinks it's any of my business. As he pointed out, he's here for Christie not me. In other words, "butt out of my life".

I lift my leg off the table, and back onto the sofa, and bring my other up alongside it. Twisting, I shuffle round and put cushions behind me and lie back, close my eyes. Scott is not my problem, I'll let him deal with Christie himself.

With a bit of luck, Miles will have worked his magic, and Christie will be back to her charming self, not the spoiled Miss, Pauletta has her down as.

I roll my shoulders and relax into the sofa, nothing to do with me. I loll my arm over my eyes to block out the light and sigh. Allow my breathing to slow down, I take deep, calming breaths.

The house is completely still; no hum of the hoover, no stealthy steps in the hallway and no clattering of cutlery. Pauletta must be having a crafty smoke outside, she uses the excuse of poop scooping after Terry. We both know it's a scam, but go along with it to save face. Her contract states "Non-Smoker". Neither of us want the trauma of confronting that truth.

Life's a bit like that, it's easier to overlook imperfections, than state the obvious and cause trouble.

Steady, steady breathing…

'Look who here!' Pauletta's excited voice interrupts my doze.

I hear the snug door open, but don't need to open my eyes to know who's walked in. 'I hope you're bringing me good news.'

'Ah, you were resting, Maddie. Sorry, I had tried to phone, but…'

If I'd bothered to look, I know he'd have shrugged. 'Just resting my eyes, that's all.'

'If you say so.'

'I do.' I draw my hands downward over my face, and stroke my fingers under my eyes a couple of times. Tucking my elbows back, I manoeuvre myself upright, and open my eyes. 'So, good news?'

Miles is perched on the sofa opposite me. 'That depends,' he says.

I look at Pauletta hovering in the doorway. 'I think Miles would like a nice cup of tea, Pauletta. I'll have one too, so you may as well bring the teapot.'

'Yes, madam.' She manages to sound both deferential and insulting at the same time.

Miles smiles. 'Thanks, Pauletta, you're the best.'

'I know, Mr Hepworth, but am happy to hear you say.' She tosses me one of her haughty looks again.

Miles stands and goes over to close the door behind her. 'Have you been upsetting Pauletta?'

'Not any more than usual.' His smirk is a reminder of the years of Pauletta's favour he's lorded over me. I grimace. 'She thinks Scott is a bad man. I've tried to explain about the shock of becoming a father to a twenty-four-year-old. But she won't have it, not one little bit.'

'Ahh, well, that leads nicely to why I'm here.'

My stomach churns. 'Not more problems? I'm still reeling from Christie's onslaught this morning. I was hoping you'd settle her down.' I catch myself biting my lips – old habits die hard – and stop before I draw blood. 'She's not changed her mind, has she?'

'No, not exactly, but she's wanting you there with Scott.'

My heart sinks. Closing my eyes, I let my head flop backwards. 'Great… Just what I need.' I level my gaze at Miles. 'I can't go through another bout like this morning's battle of words. I just can't.'

Miles sits on the sofa's arm by me, and rests his chin on the top of my head. 'She's calmed down. She's willing to meet him halfway, making no reference to your age when she was born. That's a big concession for her, Maddie.'

'Well, I suppose I should be grateful for that. I knew it was going to be tough, Miles. But I didn't think Christie would be this judgemental, I really didn't.'

'Maddie, she's a teacher. She'll have sixteen-year-old girls in her class. She's envisaging a child in her class, yeah?'

'Yes, but I was nothing like a girl in her class. I was wild. I was excluded from all the five schools I went to from being fourteen, all of them… And that took some doing since I hardly ever bothered to go, in the first place. Scott actually rescued me.'

'Maybe she needs to hear that from you.' Miles lifts his chin up and looks towards the door. 'She's on her way,' he whispers.

Miles stands up and opens the door ready for Pauletta. 'Ah, Pauletta, you take so much care of me!'

I try to stop my head from instinctively shaking, and roll my eyes. The tray holds two china mugs, a matching teapot and an array of home-baked delights.

Miles takes the tray from her, and puts it on the table. 'It looks delicious, doesn't it, Maddie?'

'It does, as always, Pauletta, you spoil us.'

'Is a pleasure to look after you.' Pauletta beams. 'Can I help anything else?'

Miles picks up the teapot. 'I'll take it from here, thanks.'

'Thank you, Mr Hepworth.' Pauletta leaves the snug.

I shake my head. 'If I'd said that, she would have glared at me.'

Miles passes my tea. 'I know, but she loves me.' He grins. 'Right, so, back to Christie and Scott. Have you spoken to Scott since this morning, to warn him about Christie?'

I block out the brief conversation with the mystery miss. Telling Miles would feel like a betrayal, I've no idea why. 'No, I've not spoken to him.'

'Good, that's good. So, in theory, you could phone him now, get him to pick you up and come round together.'

I put my drink down, and scoop my hands over my face. Do I really want to phone him again? I shake my head. 'In theory, yes, Miles. But he's going to think I'm meddling, and our relationship, such as it is, is already strained.' I peep out from between my fingers. 'Can you not phone him?'

'He doesn't even know me, Maddie. And as a man, I can tell you, he won't like *me* interfering.'

I groan and cover my eyes again. 'Fine, I'll phone him.'

There's a hurried knock on the snug door, I look up and Pauletta pops her head into the room. 'Big warning! He coming up the drive, in big car!'

I groan. 'Just what I need.'

'I send him away, yes?' she says, unable to keep the glee from her voice.

'No!' Miles and I say in unison.

Miles smiles at her. 'Just show him in, okay?'

Pauletta looks at me and raises her eyebrows. 'Madam?'

Now she asks me! 'Yes, Pauletta, show him in. And be nice!' She stomps off like a petulant teenager in a middle-aged body. 'This is what I have to put up with!' I start to swivel my body round.

'Maddie, stay with your legs up. It gives you the edge, yeah?'

'Because I look so alluring, or because I look so helpless?'

He shrugs. 'Well—'

'In fact, don't bother answering that. My self-worth's already close to the ground.' I loll back and close my eyes. I feel the sofa sag as Miles perches back beside me. 'Don't try and sweet-talk me now.'

'You always look fabulous, to me.' He plants a kiss on the top of my head. I hear the door creek open.

'Got to say, Maddie, you sure do keep us men in line,' growls Scott.

My eyes flick open, and Miles stands up. Scott is stood towering over me, his thumbs hooked into his belt loops, but glaring at Miles.

'Sorry, madam! He rush in.'

'It's okay, Pauletta.' I look at Scott, my heart pounding. 'Thank you for calling, Scott. Would you like a drink? Tea, coffee or a juice?'

Scott glances down at me, then looks at Pauletta. 'I'll have a coffee, strong and black.'

Pauletta remains stock still.

I smile, savouring the silent slur. 'Pauletta, would you please bring Mr Scobie a strong, black coffee.'

'Yes, madam. Is my pleasure.' She turns and leaves the room.

Scott looks fit to explode.

Marshmallows

Tears curl over my lashes

I perch on the edge of the sofa. 'Scott, I'd like you to meet Miles Hepworth, my PA.'

Miles extends his hand; Scott reluctantly shakes it. 'Mr Scobie, it's a pleasure to meet you,' gushes Miles.

'Likewise. I recognise you from Christie's portrait.' He scowls and looks about the room. 'This is a comedown from the rest of the house, Maddie. The room that time forgot.'

I smile, I suppose it would be easier to go along with that idea. 'No, Scott. This is the "me" room. I get to be me in here.'

Miles nods towards the threadbare sofa opposite me. 'Why don't you take a seat?'

Scott nods and sits with his legs outstretched in front of him, ankles crossed. He's wearing the same cowboy boots as the first time he came. He links his fingers at the back of his head as he lounges back. The room feels smaller all of a sudden, such is his impact on my space.

Miles sits at the other side of the sofa to me. 'Actually, Mr Scobie, you've done Maddie a favour.'

'Really?' drawls Scott.

I'm sure Miles can sense the animosity radiating from Scott. I place my hand on the sofa between myself and Miles, signalling I'll take over the conversation. 'Yes, Scott, thank you for calling. Miles mentioned

Christie being a little apprehensive about meeting you. She's asked if I would go along with you, you know, to break the ice, kind of thing.'

Scott nods slowly. 'She didn't seem over bashful when she was acting up at your parent's house.' He looks directly at me, challenging my request through logic.

'Well, yes,' I admit. 'But you need to remember, Christie walked in on the four of us talking about her. No wonder she reacted as she did.'

'At your say-so, Maddie! It was you who arranged that meeting, you and your parents.' Scott hauls his legs back and sits forward, he pulls a face of disgust. 'I should of told you to go jump...' He looks at me. 'I should of said no.'

I sigh, and hold his gaze. 'It was done in good faith, Scott. All of us, wanted to make you meeting Christie, go smoothly. Especially me, because—'

'Yeah, and what happened? It was made ten times worse.' Scott glowers at me and shakes his head. 'And who does Christie blame for this debacle? I'll tell you who, me!'

I pull in my top lip and start to bite down, savouring the discomfort, and deserving the pain. 'Actually, Scott, she blames me.'

'Yeah, whatever you say, Maddie!'

I feel Miles's weight shift on the sofa. I turn and slightly shake my head giving him a glare. I turn back to Scott. 'Look, Scott, Christie blames me. If I'd just made myself known to her, without the fanfare of the Evolution exhibition, you'd be no wiser. And—'

'And that is what she wants! Darn it, Maddie, are you going to expect me to go along with that? Jeez!'

Scott stands, and starts pacing like a party animal in a pandemic. 'You just keep screwing me over.'

I feel Miles's eagerness to intervene. I look at him. 'Miles, do you mind, Scott and I need to do this alone.'

Miles gets to his feet, and gives me a wary look. 'If that's what you want.' He looks at Scott, who's stopped his pacing, then back to me. 'I'll go and keep Pauletta company.'

I smile. 'Thank you, I appreciate it.' I know Pauletta will be close by, keeping a mental record of every word spoken. She's always happy to correct me if I misquote Miles. So, knowing Miles will be close and able to step in if needed, is a relief.

Miles stands and steps towards the door. He looks back at Scott. 'If I don't see you before, Mr Scobie, I'll look forward to seeing you later today.' He closes the door as he leaves.

'You wanna bring your side-kick along? Going to be one hellova private meeting! You and lover boy tagging along to make up the numbers, I don't think so!'

'Christie has only asked for me—'

'So, what makes him think he is going to be with you?'

I draw my hands down over my face. I really don't think now is the best time to tell Scott about the epic, "Christie loves Miles, and Miles loves Christie" sensation. It's not my place to tell him anyway. 'Miles has been resting-up at Christie's since coming out of hospital… I had expected him to stay either here or at my parent's, but…' I shrug, knowing I've boxed myself into a corner. Look down at my hands now resting on my lap.

'But what, Maddie? What's going on that you aren't telling me? Why would he wanna be away from you, and your delightful little helper?'

I can feel Scott staring at me, but daren't look up until I'm totally composed. I raise my chin and hold his stare. 'Look, Scott, Christie has been working very closely with Miles over the last few weeks. Sorting out interviews and meetings and the likes. Thankfully, they get along well—'

'I bet!'

I choose to ignore his jibe. 'And Christie's two friends like him too, Suzi especially, she mothers him. With me being out of action with my ankle, the three girls offered up a bedroom for him there—'

'Happy to take advantage of their hospitality, I wonder why?'

'Because…' I take a calming breath. 'Because, Scott, he could not have been discharged from hospital, unless someone was home to take care of him.'

'Yeah, right, whatever you say.'

'I don't know what your problem is, Scott. Miles will probably be resting after being out this morning. He'll certainly have nothing to do with your meeting with Christie.'

Scott nods slowly. 'Fine, so it will just be the two of us.'

'It will just be us. And I'm going to let you and Christie do all the talking. I suppose… I imagine, Christie is embarrassed meeting you after the stand-off at my parent's house.'

'I should think so! Total lack of respect and—'

I raise my hand. 'Hold on there, she was upset. She still is, and if you go into her home today with this attitude—'

Scott stands. 'I'm not the one with attitude!'

'So why are you raising your voice?' I keep my tone level, appeasing.

Scott turns his back to me, and drops his head. I let the silence hang between us, we both need it. His tense shoulders begin to relax as the seconds pass. He turns and looks at me, his face looks drawn, and his eyes haunted. 'Sorry.'

I can feel the amount of resolve saying that one word took. 'Thank you, Scott. I'm struggling here, myself. I'm not your enemy…'

He gestures to the sofa I'm sat on. 'May I?'

I nod. 'Sure, I won't bite.' The expression on Scott's face makes me regret saying those words as soon as they're out of my mouth. 'Sorry.' A long, long time ago, "I won't bite" had a whole different connotation. The meagre spark in Scott's eyes are a poignant reminder of what we once shared.

Scott sits where Miles sat earlier, close to me, but not too close. He steeples his fingers. 'It's like this, yeah? I need this to be right, Maddie. I want her to get along with me, you know?' He looks directly into my eyes. I nod for him to continue. 'It means a lot to me.'

'Scott, we can all see how much it means to you. It means a lot to me too. I want you to have a normal relationship with your daughter, obviously.'

He shakes his head. 'I guess "normal" is pushing it, Maddie. Do you think you will have a normal relationship with Christie, after all this, coz I don't.'

I look away from him, he's far too perceptive. He could always read my pain. 'Maybe not "normal", but

I'd be happy with a relaxed relationship… If we can get along, you know, go shopping, have afternoon tea, play scrabble… I know I'll never be called, "Mum"…' I turn to him, unashamed of the watery state of my eyes.

He nods. 'And I'll never be called, "Dad". So, we are equal, Maddie.'

I tilt my head. 'You've still every chance to become a dad, Scott. But, it's different for us females… We have a shelf life.' I look away again. The stabbing pain in my chest reminds me I squandered my chance at being a mum. I didn't understand how precious that gift is.

'You never know, Maddie, you just got to meet the right guy.'

I want to say, "I did, it was you.", but I'm not that brave, or stupid. Instead, I pat his hand resting between us. 'And you've just got to find the right young lady.' I look at him and hold his gaze. Give him the opportunity to tell me about the mystery female who answered his mobile, all of two hours ago.

He gives a half-hearted smile. 'I guess, but it isn't easy. The kinda girls I meet at work, they aren't the kind hankering after home and hearth. And work kinda rules my life, yeah? I got to sort it out, coz I got to lot of time to make up for with Christie. I'll be making adjustments. It's real important.'

'That's good to know. It will be good for her to hear that from you, Scott.'

'Yeah.' He rubs his hands over his face and drags his hair back behind his ears. He stands up and tucks his shirt further into his jeans, and strokes it, ironing out imaginary creases. 'How do I look?'

I can't help but smile. His vulnerable expression makes him look ten years younger, and the way his freshly washed hair curls round his ears, is as cute as ever it was. I'm swamped with longing. Sensations from our youth, echo through my thoughts and body, making me yearn for that time of blissful ignorance, when we just loved. 'You look like a nervous teen, getting ready for a first date.'

He similes. 'It feels ten times more daunting than that.' He starts to pace. 'I just want us to get along, and she *is* very opinionated.'

'I know.' The conversation I had with her this morning, springs to mind. 'But it can be a good thing, being opinionated… She knows her mind, and won't be bullied into following the herd.'

Scott stops pacing and looks at me. 'Yeah, but if her opinion of me is already set, I'm going to be just one of the herd, when I want to own the ranch.'

'I understand, Scott, but you're going to need patience. If she's not ready, the best thing you can do is back off—'

'Yeah, I'm sure you did that.'

I edge forward on the sofa; this conversation would be so much easier if I could just wander over and put my hand on his shoulder. 'Please, come and sit down, Scott.'

He does a hangdog expression, but does as I ask.

'Thank you. So, the first time I met Christie – after she knew who I really am – was at my parent's. It hadn't been pre-arranged—'

'Now there's a coincidence. You could of learned from that experience.'

'Yes, I could, but Christie is a grown woman… She goes where she wants, when she wants.' I raise my brows. 'Yes?'

Scott shrugs. 'Yeah.'

'So, Christie was at my parent's. I decided to go round to meet her without her knowing I was on my way – I couldn't wait, didn't want to risk her leaving – she found out. So, she hid outside under a bush—'

'Are you serious?'

'Oh, yes. She hid under a bush and phoned for her friend to collect her—'

'What? No car?' Scott shuffles in his seat.

'She'd had a minor accident—'

'What do you mean "minor accident"? Why do I not know about this?'

'It was just a couple of scrapes and bruises… Nothing to get het up about, Scott. Do you want to know what happened, or not?'

'Yeah, sure I do—'

'Then stop interrupting!' I close my eyes briefly and take a deep breath. 'So, I went round to my parent's expecting to meet Christie. When I arrived, Miles told—'

'You took him with you?'

'Scott! He was already there! Like I've tried to explain before, Miles is like one of the family.'

Scott scowls, but nods for me to continue. 'Go on.'

Every second of that first encounter with Christie, is seared into my brain, eternally eager to be relived at a moment's notice.

I've got sunshine in my pocket sings out from the deep swag of the well-established border.

Miles grins. 'Actually, Madeline, maybe you're in time after all.' He winks, and strides off towards the bushes. 'There you are, Christie. How fortunate…'

Miles disappears into the undergrowth. I can hear muffled voices. Even though I can't make out what he's saying, I can detect the laughter in his tone.

The trolls in my tummy are doing summersaults, the butterflies in my chest are high on nectar, and the thunder of a waterfall in my scull is drowning out my thoughts. Just bring her to me, Miles!

They emerge from the bushes holding hands! My heart skips a beat. 'Christie!' I squeak, grinning uncontrollably. I struggle getting my crutches coordinated, but manage to get closer.

'Hello.' Christie sounds distant, I can tell she'd rather be anywhere else but here.

'I have waited so long! And look at you two, getting along so well already. It's like a dream,' I gush. I drop my crutches and haul Christie into a bear hug.

'So, when Miles coaxed her out of the bushes, I was bubbling with pent-up excitement mingled with fear. I practically threw myself at her.'

'The cool and collected Madeline De-Muir. Now that is one vision, I'd love to see.'

'I'm sure if you trawl your mind of the distant past, you can conjure an image.'

Scott tilts his head, and grins. 'Yeah, I remember this hot chick, Maddie Harris, she used to throw herself at me all the time.'

I feel a blush creeping over my cheeks. 'She must have loved you very much.'

Scott's face becomes stoic. 'I thought she did.' He looks away from me.

I wish I'd kept that thought to myself. 'Anyway, I told Christie how beautiful she was, and she said I looked much younger than she imagined. And then basically told me she needed more time. Didn't want to get swept along with me and my life…'

'Harsh.' He looks at me.

I shrug. 'Harsh, but honest. She was honest, and I suppose that is what I want you to understand about Christie. She might appear all scatty and reactive, but she *is* confident of who she is.'

Scott nods slowly.

'So, Scott, my parents brought her up with a core of steel cushioned by marshmallow. Do not underestimate her.'

He nods, stands up and turns to me. He squats in front of me so we are level, our eyes lock. 'Interesting.' Scott has the essence of a man who has made a profound discovery.

My heart misses a beat. Scott being this close, this intense, catches me off guard. 'How so?' My voice is husky, breathy.

'You and Christie. She is marshmallow with a core of steel – tough, yet presenting a fluffy persona – and you present a façade of steel but actually are a marshmallow, soft, delicious and—'

I place my forefinger on his lip, can't bear to hear the words. Scott is the only one who has ever got me, and I walked away and left him. He continues to hold my gaze as tears curl over my lashes and drop unchallenged to my cheeks. I shake my head. 'Please…'

He reaches out. Runs a thumb gently under each of my eyes. 'But it's true.' Scott continues to hold my eyes captive with the intensity of his insight.

I nod, accept the accuracy of his words. I almost stop breathing as he leans in. My eyes flutter closed automatically, as I savour his lips grazing my cheek with the barest of kisses. I open my eyes and feast on the deep pools of blue staring back at me.

'Maddie Harris, I really need to paint you.'

Connections

I unbutton my jeans

'Gee, I love it. A quaint country cottage, framed by a quintessential, English garden.' Scott turns off the engine and lets out a low whistle. 'You all have taste, you Harris gals.'

The roses haven't been tamed, nor the dandelions beheaded. The picket fence is wonky and still in need of a lick of paint. Everything here is just the same as I left it a few hours ago, shame I can't say the same about my emotional state. However, I hope my own lick of paint will fool everybody.

Until now, Scott has maintained a stony silence throughout our journey.

I think it's fair to say, we had a moment.

I think it's fair to say, it took us both by surprise.

I think it's fair to say, we're both ever so slightly freaked out by it.

And obviously, by "ever so slightly freaked out", I mean we're both having intense, emotional meltdowns, while pretending everything is absolutely FINE.

Seriously!

IT'S FINE.

Before we left, Scott chatted politely with Miles, toning down his American drawl, and attempted the Queen's English, (albeit with a Scottish accent). He even carried the tea tray into the kitchen for Pauletta, and insisted on bringing his car practically through the front door, so I'd hardly any distance to walk.

I'm beginning to feel like a glass virgin, but clearly, I'm not.

And it's all very well, dancing around the elephant in the room with small talk, but when the elephant is sat on your lap, there's not much wriggle room.

I only hope Christie's mood has improved, because my level of trepidation has tripled. But I'll give it a go.

'Yes, Scott, Christie's cottage is picturesque, lovely in the summer months, but draughty in the winter.'

'Small price to pay for a pad like this.'

'Quite.' Now I sound like Queen Victoria! 'Are you ready for this, Scott?'

He looks like a man on the way to the gallows. 'I thought I was, Jeez.'

'Come on, you'll be fine. Remember, she is a teacher, so used to leading, okay?'

'Okay.' Scott nods, gets out of the car, walks round, and holds his arms out to help me down.

As soon as his hands span my midriff, a tremor of awareness rocks through me. It suddenly dawns on me, long ago the intensity of our love, blended to create Christie. Somehow, it's like every fibre of my body identifies the synergy, and wants to relive it.

'Scott, she's our daughter...'

Scott frowns. 'Yeah, I know.' He shrugs and shakes his head. 'It was big news last week, but now, I'm kinda getting to like the idea.'

I shake my head as he passes me my crutches. 'No, what I mean, is, she is *our* daughter. We created her, us, together.'

I scan his face, and savour the transformation from confused to enlightened.

'Uh-hu.' The soppy grin he's wearing is a giveaway to his true thoughts. 'Kinda profound and scary at the same time.'

'It is.' I gesture towards the front door of Rose Cottage. 'Come on, let's get this show on the road.'

Scott holds out his arm, 'After you. You do know it's going to be kind of tough keeping my mind focused on Christie, while I'm remembering...'

The look he gives, scorches my skin, and tells me exactly what he's remembering. The fact I'm remembering too, is neither here nor there. But his ability to ignite all those feelings again is disturbing. I look away and swing into action – I now consider myself something of an expert – and make a hasty retreat towards the front door.

Miles is stood casually leaning on the doorframe, arms folded, ready to welcome us. I'm sure he took in that little exchange between me and Scott, and has noticed how flustered I am. He raises his hand in a half wave. 'Good to see you both, again.'

'Good to see you.' Scott chimes back. 'This sure is a lovely place, Christie has here.'

'It is,' agrees Miles pleasantly. 'Come on in, Christie is waiting in the lounge.'

As I draw level with Miles, he gives me a cheeky wink. 'Interesting times, eh, Maddie,' he whispers.

I narrow my eyes. 'Shh.'

Scott, taking his time, is totally unaware of our exchange. 'Yeah, this is a world away from my pad. Kinda small.'

'Christie seems to like it,' says Miles. 'It's more about the feel of the place, than the floorplan.'

'Oh, for sure. But I guess, yeah, kinda expected it to be all chrome and glass. She's a modern woman.'

I turn and look at Scott. I'm surprised at how mellow his expression is. 'She's a country girl, at heart,' I say.

Scott grins. 'So, not an urban urchin like you.'

'Not at all.'

Christie stands as we enter the room, and turns to greet us with a fixed smile. She gestures towards the sofa. 'Hello, would you like to take a seat?'

I smile. 'Hello, Christie.'

Scott waits for me to sit, then takes my crutches and props them up by the door. He steps towards Christie with his hand outstretched. 'Christie, I just want to say, how pleased I am to meet you.'

Christie accepts his hand. 'Thank you—'

'Scott, call me Scott.'

He holds her hand and her gaze slightly longer than necessary, before he sits down beside me. Christie looks across at Miles, who's hovering in the doorway.

Miles claps his hands once. 'Right then, drinks, what can I get for you.'

I smile, how easily he glides into whatever social situation he finds himself in. 'A cup of tea please, Miles.'

'Yeah, I think I'm going to try a cup of English tea, too. They don't have a clue how to make it in the US.'

'I'll just have Vimto, please Miles.'

'Okay, back in a jiffy.' Miles wanders off into the kitchen.

'Before we start.' Christie's tone is firm and unyielding. 'I want you both to know, my life was remarkably sane and manageable before you two invaded it. I fully understand, you want to get to know me. But, please do not expect me to be falling over myself with gratitude, because you are interfering in my life.'

I feel Scott tense beside me. He rests forward on the edge of the seat, his elbows on his knees, and his hands stretched out. 'I can respect that. I know it must be kinda tough to discover you're not who you think you are—'

'Oh, but I am. I'm exactly who I think I am. That's the whole point. I am Christina Anne Harris, teacher and artist, in that order.'

Scott shuffles back and nods slowly. 'I have the upmost respect for the Rev and Mrs Harris, more so now I've met you. They have raised a fine young woman.'

Miles returns with our drinks, and places the tray on the coffee table.

Christie smiles at him. 'Thank you, Miles. I can take it from here.' Christie stirs the pot. 'How do you like your tea, Scott?'

'I guess strong, with a dash of cream.'

'Cream? Sorry, Scott, no cream, only milk. And any sugar?'

'Milk is, yeah, I mean milk. No sugar.' Scott nods as he watches Christie pour the tea from the pot and add milk.

She passes him the drink. 'Maddie, if I remember correctly, weak, two sugars and lots of milk.'

'Thank you, yes, Christie.' I'm impressed she remembers, though Miles could have reminded her. I take the cup she offers.

'So, Scott.' Christie cradles her juice between her hands. 'Where would you like to start?'

Scott takes a sip of tea, then places the cup onto the coffee table. For a moment he looks unsure, perhaps a little off balance because of Christie's forthright approach. He rests back in the sofa, and scoops his hair behind his ears. 'Well, I'd kind of like to share with you some of what my life is like, Christie. But, you know, first I want to hear all about your accomplishments. I've had the pleasure of seeing some of your work, I'm intrigued with that caricature on the mantle... I'm going to have to see your studio, obviously. Yeah?'

Christie takes a sip of her juice, places it on the table and sits back in her chair. She scoops her hair back behind her ears... Her mannerisms and actions, spookily similar to Scott's. I doubt either of them have even noticed.

She nods. 'Okay, Scott, I'm not sure you've taken in what I said earlier. I don't intend to offend, but actually, my life was really good before all this craziness exploded around me. I had, in fact, still have, a good job at an achieving high school—'

'Yeah, but now—'

Christie raises a pointed forefinger, as she would to a class of teens. 'I haven't finished, Scott. The only pressure with my painting, was Auntie Maddie...' She gives me a pointed look. 'But now, thanks to the power of global media exposure, I have the pressure of public opinion too.'

I'm beginning to think me being here, isn't such a good idea.

Scott shifts forward. 'I disagree entirely. You know, as an artist, unless you have a commission, the only person you need to satisfy, is yourself.'

'People judge, Scott.'

'Let them… But be true to your own vision.'

'Are you?' Christie keeps her eyes trained on him.

'Mostly. I take a select few – and they are select – commissions. Those make it possible for me to choose whatever work I wanna do for the majority of the time. Small price, I say.'

Christie folds her arms, and raises her chin. 'I looked them up. I noticed those select few commissions, are all young women.'

'Sure they are. And their very rich Mammas or Papas pay a mighty fine dollar. What they get in return, is exposure and the kudos of a Scott Scobie hanging in the drawing room. It's all about the image.'

Christie nods. 'I wonder, who is taking advantage of whom?'

Scott waves his hand dismissively. 'It's mutually beneficial. The more well known they become, the more elevated my standing. I've been paramount in launching the careers of…' He shrugs. 'I cannot count how many. This is why, I select carefully.'

'Only the beautiful ones, I assume.'

Scott laughs and swipes his hand over his face. 'You'd think so! But no. I interview the women, some would call it an interrogation. I only accept the ones who will work at it, coz it takes grit and sacrifice to get ahead in LA. If they aren't going to work, there are no picture in the world going to do it for them.'

Christie picks up her juice, and takes a long drink, half draining the glass. 'You make it sound very noble.'

'Not at all, it's just good, sound business sense. You see, in the USA you set your own standard, I set mine high. You got to work hard to get on.'

He makes it sound like a given, it's not. I smile at Christie, and turn to Scott. 'I think that is true of everywhere, Scott. Speaking from my personal experiences, I think you also need to be in the right place at the right time, with the right people and work hard.'

'Oh, yeah, for sure. You got to be in the right place,' gushes Scott.

I nod. 'For me, I just happened to be sent along for the right audition at the right time. I had the right look for the character. I could empathise with the abuse portrayed by the character. They took a chance on me. I was lucky. The production team and everyone connected with the project were focused on it being successful… And I worked hard.'

My stomach reacts to the remembrance of that time, churning and threatening to revolt. I try to keep my expression bland; I can feel Christie watching me. I don't want her knowing how traumatised I still was back then. Leaving her behind. How scared. How lonely. I swallow down the bile at the back of my throat. Take a seemingly dainty sip of my tea, it's all I dare risk.

Scott nods. 'You see, Christie, hard work and being in the right place at the right time.'

I let Scott's words drift over me as I slide back in time.

*

Mr Boswell shuffles forward in his huge leather swivel chair. I train my eyes on the framed photo on his desk, two identically dressed little girls eating ice creams. He drops to his knees in front of me, his eyes fixed and his expression unreadable. 'Am I the first to see this?'

I nod. 'Yes,' I say, clamping my arms tighter over my chest. My skinny, cropped vest top is hardly designed to keep out the chill. I feel sick, and realise

I'm starting to shake. 'I want to go now, Mr Boswell.' I continue focusing on the photo on his desk.

He gets back into his chair. 'Cover yourself up.'

I drag my knickers and jeans back up. 'Can I go now?'

He drags his jacket from the chairback. 'Put this on and sit down.'

I take the jacket from him. 'Thank you,' I mutter. Sitting down, I make myself as small as possible.

'Madeline,' he sighs. 'You know what's at stake here, don't you?'

I nod, eyes wide.

'I, personally took a chance on you playing Lucy. You know, some of the backers thought we'd be better with an older actor.' He shakes his head. 'But as soon as I saw you, I knew I'd found my "Lucy".'

'And I'm very grateful, Mr Boswell, but if—'

'You will be my "Lucy",' he says forcefully. He taps his lips with his forefinger. 'If this gets out, my reputation will be on the line, however, your career will be over. Do you understand, Madeline? Over. Finished.'

With wide eyes I stare at Mr Boswell. I absolutely know I must do whatever I need to do, to get to where I want to be. And this man is my key. I nod. 'I understand.' My voice trembles

He nods slowly. 'Good. So, we understand each other. This is between you and me, not a word to anyone. I have connections, Madeline, and you need them.'

I swallow away the lump forming in my throat. 'Mr Boswell, I'm grateful for your—'

'It's not your gratitude I want. And call me Tim.'

*

'What do you say, Maddie?'

'Sorry, Scott. I was in a world of my own.' My skin feels flushed, but I can still feel the aftershock of the goosebumps crawling over my body all those years ago. I glimpse Christie watching me out of the corner of my eye.

Scott shakes his head. 'Come on, Maddie! You of all people know how important it is, getting a gee up from the right people.'

'Oh, yes.' My face burns.

Shot

In your dreams

Scott stands, and hooks his thumbs through the belt loops on his jeans. He steps up to the mantle and looks at the caricature of Christie with Trudy and Suzi. 'Yeah, this is what I mean about diversity. I love it.'

I know I must be smiling. The intense way Scott is scrutinising the picture is at odds with his casual stance. It was the same perpetual contradiction that used to mesmerise me, way back when. Our passion-fuelled liaisons were interspersed with his cool detachment during our ludicrously professional "sittings", as he liked to call them. He'd grandly announce, "The relationship between an artist and the model must always remain professional.", and I'd giggle and try to lead him astray.

It never worked. He always managed to stay in the zone. His passion wasn't wasted, he channelled it into his work. But once the palette and brushes were away, the model and artist would play...

'I much prefer to paint, especially in oils.' Christie's eyes light up as she starts talking. Her fingers dance to an imaginary melody, twisting, turning, waving through the air. 'It's the texture and richness of colour, and the way it builds.' Her fingers flutter upwards, wispy as dandelion seeds swirling in the breeze.

Scott turns to look at her. 'Yeah, I know.' He grins. 'But you got to have patience, yeah? You have got to have time, and you have got to have money to pay for that time… And that is why commissions are the way to go.'

'I already have a regular income from teaching. Painting is for pleasure, and as soon as I start viewing it as a money-making—'

'Are you good at teaching?'

Christie raises her head defiantly. 'Yes! I trained for four years to become a teacher.'

'I'm sure you are a good teacher.' Scott smiles and sits back next to me. 'Do you enjoy it?'

Christie folds her arms. 'What is this, fifty questions?'

'Just humour me, yeah?'

I know exactly where this is going, and I'm surprised Christie hasn't worked it out yet. And if I'm reading this situation correctly, he's making a bold attempt to steel Christie away to the US of A, right under my nose.

'Christie,' I say. 'A word to the wise, Scott likes to tie people up with their own words.'

I smile, and watch the expression on Christie's face change from confused to enlightened. She lightly threads her fingers together, and rests them on her lap, a graceful poise she's inherited from my mother. It's one I've adopted many times to play for time, and assume the composure of one in control of the situation, while trying to fathom a way forward.

She nods. 'Yes, Scott. I love teaching. I especially love being part of the transformation of my students, knowing I'm making a positive impact on their lives.'

Scott stands. 'And, you've already stated you get remuneration for your trouble. Does it make you love teaching any less?'

'No, I've got to eat.'

Scott grins. 'Yeah, me too. My commissions give me the freedom to eat at the finest establishments, anywhere in LA.' He wafts his hands through the air dramatically. 'How about you, Christie?'

'I don't live in LA; I live in LW – Little Wilton.' She takes a sip of juice. 'And the fare at our local pub is more than adequate for my humble expectations.'

Scott nods, and takes a stroll about the lounge. He stops by the window and looks out at the riotous flowers, flagrantly fraternising with the well-established weeds in the front garden. He turns and rests against the sill. 'You must be doing okay, this place must have cost, being in this location.'

Christie flashes me a look. From Scott's words, she must surely know I haven't told him I bought this place for her. I shake my head enough, I hope, to keep that small detail from him.

She clears her throat, and bathes him in a look of utter bliss. 'Scott, Rose Cottage is a wonderful home, I'm more than happy here.'

I cover my smile with an ineffective cough, which develops into the real thing.

'Are you alright there, Maddie?' Scott gives my back a couple of hearty slaps.

My eyes swim, as I try to control myself. 'Uh-hu,' I manage, and reach for my cup of tepid tea. I take a couple of sips to relieve the tickle in my throat, and massage my neck. 'I'll be okay in a minute,' I croak.

Christie, I notice is valiantly suppressing a fit of the giggles by biting down on her lip. 'I'll get you a glass of water, Maddie.' She all but gallops from the room.

'Christie seems to be warming to me, don't you think?'

I continue stroking my throat. 'I hope so. I really do hope you can have a good relationship with Christie.' She seems to have loosened up a bit, and if he can just keep her talking about her painting, he should be okay. 'She comes alive when she talks about painting,' I prompt.

Scott nods. 'I'd like to see her studio.'

Christie returns, and passes me a glass. 'That should help.'

'Thanks.' I take a few mouthfuls, and savour the feel of ice-cold water tracing its way to my stomach. I close my eyes and nod my appreciation. 'Much better, thank you.'

'I'd love to see your studio, Christie. Would you oblige?'

Christie is caught off guard. Looking awkward, halfway between sitting and standing, she flashes me a look of frustration. She settles for perching on the edge of the sofa. 'It's in the attic, it isn't the grand studio you'll be used to.'

Scott shrugs. 'Yeah, it sounds very idealistic. The young struggling artist cooped up in a dreary attic—'

'I'm hardly struggling!' Christie straightens her spine and sits bolt upright.

'Yeah, yeah, I know, it's a figure of speech.' Scott grins. 'I got to say, it reads like a fairy tale, if you've got those misty-eyed tendencies.'

'How so?' quips Christie.

'Impoverished teacher—'

'Not impoverished!'

'Trying to scrape out a living, beavering away in a draughty, old attic—'

'My attic isn't draughty, much!'

'Has her work thrust into the limelight, by her evil, long-lost, film-icon mother…'

I roll my eyes.

Christie purses her lips, twists them to one side, and lets out a huffy sigh.

'Is discovered as a tempting new talent in her own right.'

Christie shrugs. 'Not really.'

'Yeah, really. And along comes her successful daddy, to show her how the big hitters play, in the US of A.'

Christie makes both her hands into pistols, takes aim at Scott and repeatedly fires. 'She aims, shoots him down in flames, and lives happily ever after! The end.'

Scott slaps both hands on his chest. 'Arrrrhh!' He flops back into the sofa motionless.

I give Scott an enthusiastic prod – get no response – I try a couple more. Christie and I share a rare moment of solidarity, both of us looking in amusement at his ability to stay still. 'Well, now you've done it,' I tease. 'You've killed him.' I tap my plaster. 'And I'm not going to be able to help you bury the body.'

Scott lifts his head slightly and opens one eye. 'What? No attempt to revive me?' He flops back.

A vivid image of me straddling Scott, my lips dipping to his, then my hands pummelling his chest, flits briefly into my mind. I shake my head to lose that picture. 'Be quiet, you're dead.'

Christie grins. 'Do you suppose he's well insured?'

Scott raises his head again. 'You don't need the money, you're a teacher, happy with the cuisine at your local.' He plops back again.

'I could build a proper studio.'

Scott sits bolt upright, sporting a goofy grin. 'Now we're talking. We could work side by side, father and daughter, fuelling artistry through emotion. What d'you say?'

'Unless you'll fit into my studio, I say, in your dreams.'

Scott stands. 'Come on, lead the way.'

The Tour

You've no idea how desperate I am

The invitation to look around Christie's studio, didn't extend to me, so I'm left sat here like a lemon. My cup of tea isn't even tepid. At least the two of them seem to be getting along better than I expected.

Miles appears from behind the kitchen door. 'Is the coast clear?' he stage whispers.

'Yes, come on in. You can keep me company, I've been dumped.'

He sits beside me and gives me a cheesy grin. 'How's it going? I haven't heard any shouts or screams.'

I nod. 'It's going okay, actually. Christie's just showing Scott her studio.'

Miles nudges me. 'Well done, you.'

I snort. 'Not me. Scott has been charming, flattering and generally vomit-makingly attentive!'

Miles laughs.

'It's not funny, Miles! And now he's having a tour of her studio.'

'One can hardly have a tour of an attic. Especially one as rammed as Christie's, you know?'

I fold my arms and let out a deep, heartfelt sigh. 'How would I know? *I've* never had the tour!'

Miles doesn't seem to understand the significance of that. He should.

He came with me on the first viewing. He did all the negotiating, sorted the conveyancing, and all the other legal stuff when I made the cottage over to Christie.

I'd been searching for a property with an outbuilding to convert, but Rose Cottage captured my imagination. And height wise, was more substantial than most.

We could have built in the garden, but the potential to develop the attic into a large space, was obvious. And since the back is south facing, with the row of deluxe, Velux roof windows, the attic is now flooded with natural light.

It may not have the glamour or prestige of a stand-alone studio, but it has its own unique charm. I'm sure Scott will secretly love the space, while at the same time, point out the benefits of a city centre studio.

I'm the only one to never have been invited into her studio. It's ironic, since it was my vision. The last time I was in there, was before Christie even knew it existed.

I look at him. 'The last time I saw the studio, was before Christie got this place, Miles. And since she now knows *who* I am, she hasn't even offered me a peep up there.' I shrug. 'It hurts, okay?'

'Maddie.' Miles rolls his eyes and shakes his head. 'Of course, Christie isn't going to invite you up two flights of stairs, the second of which, is somewhat steeper than is normally allowed. Honestly, come on, you wouldn't manage it.'

'I manage my stairs at home,' I huff

'And how do you manage them?'

'I go up backwards, on my bum. No problem.'

Miles looks thoughtful, nods. 'And that's really the way you want Christie to remember showing you her studio for the first time? On your bum!'

'Obviously, I'd rather be able to walk up there—'

'Then have a bit of patience. When are you getting the cast off?'

I look down at my leg, wiggle my still-bruised toes. 'I'm going back tomorrow, so, hopefully then. They mentioned a boot that could be taken off at night.' I close my eyes briefly, and imagine the luxury of sinking into a hot bubble bath, without having to dangle my leg over the side.

'There you are then, well on the road to recovery. And if you can keep reminding yourself not to fall over Terry-the-terrier, again, problem solved.'

'Ha-ha, very funny! He ran under my feet, as you know. Hardly my fault.'

'Whatever you say, Maddie.' Miles smiles in a patronising way and pats my hand. 'You keep telling yourself that. So, getting your cast off tomorrow.'

'Not a moment too soon! I can hardly wait to slide between those crisp, cool, cotton sheets.' I look at Miles. 'Seriously, Miles, you've no idea how desperate I am!'

I hear a loud cough from the doorway, turn to see Scott scowling at me and Miles. 'Oh, you're back,' I splutter. 'I've just been saying how desperate I am to—'

'I heard!' states Scott. 'To slide between the sheets. Hardly what I expected to hear.'

'I know how she feels,' chirps Miles. 'I feel the same way. Suzi's bed isn't—'

'Spare me the details, yeah!'

Miles grins, clearly amused at Scott's reaction. 'If you're sure, Scott, my man,' he says, in a jaunty style. 'How was the tour?'

Scott shrugs, and turns to look at Christie. 'Yeah, it's a great space. Lots of natural light, maybe too much on a day like today, an' Christie's done well to utilise every square inch of that attic.'

'I'll take that as a compliment,' says Christie.

'Yeah, sure. I'm just not sure how you going to make progress from there. The way I see it—'

Christie raises a pointed forefinger. 'Scott, I'm happy as I am, okay?'

Scott looks bemused. 'Yeah?' He shrugs. 'I kinda got the feeling you had a passion for—'

'Well, that doesn't mean I have to change my whole life to wrap around it.' She raises her chin and folds her arms across her midriff.

Miles shares a smile with me. 'I'll leave you guys to it, then. Maddie, I'll give you a call about a car for tomorrow.' And off he wanders.

Scott gestures for Christie to sit, before he joins me on the sofa. 'The way I see it, is this, if you get the chance to make your passion, your profession, you got to do it. Jeez, how many get that opportunity? I've got gals throwing themselves at me, to get themselves noticed, to give them the edge, to start up in modelling, or the movies.' Scott looks at me. 'Some of them, like Maddie here, have natural talent. Some don't.'

Christie strokes her hands up and down her arms. 'Sorry, Scott. I'm not comfortable with that level of power... In fact, I find it quite disturbing.' She looks away.

He stands, and moves closer to Christie. He squats in front of her, as he did with me earlier. 'Christie?' Their eyes meet. 'Me too. I find it very disturbing, that a man has that much power over who gets the chances.'

'Really? Then why do you do it?' Her gaze doesn't flinch as she challenges Scott.

'Because if I'm doing it, it means they're not going to some sleazeball who's going to do the dirty, yeah?'

Christie nods her acceptance of his words.

'You know, there are *some* good guys in the business. Not many, but some. I'm one of them.'

'Okay.' Christie continues a slow nod, not breaking eye contact.

'Kind of ironic. I used to say, I treat my commissions how I'd want a daughter of mine treating, if I had one. Turns out I had a daughter all along. One who's done fine and dandy, without any of my help at all.'

Christie watches his every gesture, every move. She makes no effort to correct his words, because they are true. She doesn't soften her expression to show compassion or empathy. She makes no attempt to reach out to him in any way at all.

My heart pounds as it breaks a little more. The urge to comfort Scott for all he has missed out on, is making me twitchy. I hold my hands, fingers locked, and hope my state of mind isn't reflected on my face. The seconds pass in an awkward age.

Scott shrugs, looks away from Christie to me. He stands and makes his way back to sit by my side.

The sofa groans under his weight, though he's not fully committed to sitting, more balancing on the edge, ready to pounce at the merest encouragement from our daughter. From experience, I'd say, that's not going to happen.

Seeing him so needy, reduces me to my core value. It's a very low core value. Untangling my fingers, I rest one hand on Scott's arm. He turns to look at me and I add gentle pressure to persuade him to sit back properly. He understands and sits further back in the seat.

I can feel the heat of his body. Electrical tension coiled ready for release, not knowing if for pain, pleasure or a controlled expulsion of useless energy. The author of that, is sat before us, coolly regarding us as a scientist would an ongoing experiment.

Christie hugs herself and looks briefly heavenward. 'As I said earlier, I was happy before either of you sprang into my life. I was happy.' She nods. 'And it's all very well, Scott, you saying you treat all your commissions as you would your own daughter… But there is a huge flaw in that statement, the evidence – as in, *me* – proves otherwise.'

I clamp my hand on Scott's knee to stop him from springing forwards. 'Christie, I was his girlfriend, not his commission. His girlfriend who he used to sketch and paint! And when he did – sketch and paint – he became an artist, distant and totally detached from me emotionally and physically.'

'But still, you ended up pregnant.'

'If Scott had been a mechanic, a milkman or a mountaineer, it would have made no difference to how we felt about each other. We were like magnets, always pulling together—'

'Until *you*, pulled both of you apart.'

'Until I…' I close my eyes briefly and let out a sigh. 'Can you imagine how frightened I was, Christie? I didn't even want to admit it to myself.' I look at Scott. 'I was pregnant, and my boyfriend's head was full of plans and dreams I couldn't destroy. I'd thought, if I left on my own terms, I could limit the pain…' I shake my head. 'Turns out, I was wrong.'

I hope she can accept the sincerity of my words. I hope they both can. I look from Christie to Scott.

Christie stages a slow clap. 'Well done, Maddie. An excellent performance. Not sure how long you've been rehearsing, you've had years, after—'

'Christie,' says Scott. 'I think you know, Maddie is well aware of the repercussions of what she did to us.'

Christie tosses her head defiantly. 'I keep thinking I do, but then she sits here, in front of both of us telling us her sob story.' She looks directly at me. 'It's not just me and Scott, you must have broken Mum and Dad's hearts too.'

I look away, unable to stomach the look of disgust on her face. Her words pickaxes, smashing into the fragile peace I've managed to craft over the years. I'm left squirming with the reality that failure is my legacy. 'If you don't mind, I think I'll go and find Miles.'

Wordlessly, Scott passes me my crutches and I hobble from the room.

'What is it with those two?' I hear Scott ask.

'History, and lots of it,' she hisses.

Wriggle Room

Gentle rotations just beneath my collar bone

'That will be my car, Pauletta. If you just tell the driver I'll be out in due course.' I check my bag to make sure I have everything I need, and start getting up as gracefully as I can from the sofa.

Pauletta wobbles her head. 'Pauletta this, Pauletta that. I am yo-yo. Is no good today when I have that dog to chase all morning while you out having good time!'

'I'd hardly call a hospital appointment, having a good time. Shall I get the door myself?' I watch Pauletta as I busy myself smoothing the collar of my blouse and risk a glance to check my reflection.

Pauletta scurries past me and into the hallway. 'Do not be ridiculous! Is my job. What will people think?' Her soft-soled shoes squeak on the polished floor.

I hide a smile, know full well Pauletta will not relinquish one iota of her responsibilities. She takes great pride in being my first line of defence – she'd be an excellent doctor's receptionist – though she is probably far too nosey!

I listen for the door being opened. 'Miss De-Muir is going out, so is not possible now. Good-y bye.'

'Maddie!' Scott's voice booms from the doorway.

'I said, Miss De-Muir is going out! Good-y bye!'

'Maddie, will you tell Little Miss Mafia to step aside?'

'I am *not* from Italia!'

I step into the hallway. Scott is framed with his arms folded, towering over Pauletta, her hands planted defiantly on her skinny hips, just above her utility belt of cleaning paraphernalia. A modern-day David and Goliath – and we know how that ended.

She turns to me. 'I am sorry, is *this* man again! He will not go away.' She tilts her head way-back to give Scott the benefit of her full up-and-down appraisal. The level of contempt she has for him is etched elegantly on her face. Every nuance of her stance screams, "Back off!".

I clamp my lips together and cough to disguise my laugh. 'Thank you, Pauletta. I'll sort this out.'

Pauletta throws me a surly look and stalks past me, her rebellion diminished somewhat by the squeaks of her shoes.

Scott drags his hand through his hair. 'Thanks, Maddie. Jeez, where'd you find her?'

I smile, and hope the rejection I felt yesterday doesn't show. 'Pauletta found me, Scott. And as she said, I'm going out—'

'Yeah, about that—'

'I can't just drop everything because you turn up on my doorstep unannounced. I have a hospital appointment.' I tap my cast with my crutch.

'You know I'll take you, I'm happy to take you wherever you need to go.'

'Thank you for the offer, but Miles has a car lined up for me. It'll be here any minute.'

'Yeah, about that. I kinda told him to back off—'

'Excuse me!' I raise my eyebrows.

Scott is stood all lean and manly, hands propped low on his hips and a chip balanced squarely on each shoulder. 'Look, I just told him I've got this, yeah? I'm only here a few more days, an' much as it pains me to admit it, I kind of like hanging out with you.' He shrugs. 'It's hardly a date, an' I'll be discreet at the hospital.'

I glance at my watch, and let out a sigh. No time to call a taxi now, and after being left floundering for his support at Christie's yesterday, I'm hardly feeling in the mood for happy chatties with Scott. But the thought of another frantic taxi ride from hell and turning up late for my appointment is even less appealing. 'Fine, but one wrong move, and I'll be getting Miles to sort my journey home.'

Scott performs his duty by hoisting me into the passenger seat, he pulls out the seatbelt for me, and closes the car door. And we are soon on our way.

'For the record, Scott, it's not Miles who needs to back off. As you said, you're only here a few more days, and believe me, I don't need the hassle of sorting all my own logistics when you leave.'

'I'm only giving you a lift to the hospital—'

'I already had one, okay?' I snap.

Scott chuckles. 'Jeez, Maddie, I was wondering where you'd gone. I was beginning to think you'd had a personality transplant.'

I clamp my arms across my midriff, and look resolutely out of the window. If he thinks he can goad me into an argument, he's disregarded the growing up I've done since we parted. 'Whatever you want to think, Scott,' I say calmly. My insides feel like a trillion ants are busy foraging, and every one of them is wearing spikey boots.

Scott switches on the radio, then starts flicking through the channels. He knows darn well how irritating it is. He lingers for a few seconds on a news report, but not long enough for me to take in any details. I tune out, continue looking out of the window. After going through all the channels – twice – he turns the radio off again.

'You know, Maddie, it was that spark that always intrigued me. Shame, you seem to have lost it.'

I turn my head slowly, and look at him. I rub my hands over my arms to try and subdue the army of ants. 'I've left my days of intriguing young men behind. All I'm trying to do, at this moment in time, is forge a relationship with Christie and salvage some scraps of my reputation. I don't need the added drama of a bust-up with my old flame to be public knowledge.'

'Yeah, well, it's the make-ups after the bust-ups that—'

'There'll be no making up between us, Scott Scobie!'

His holler of laughter fills the car. 'Now there's my Maddie Harris, back from the land of pose and poise! I can't tell you how much I've missed you.'

He glances my way and our eyes lock briefly. 'Scott, it was a long time ago that I was *your* Maddie Harris. A long time.'

'You've always been my Maddie Harris, even when you weren't.'

I let it ride. What's the point in correcting him? I'm not the rebellious teen he remembers. Becoming "Madeline De-Muir", allowed me to reinvent myself. I'd recommend it to anyone struggling with being branded by their history. Step out of one life, and into another. It was so liberating. Just to drop all the chaff in my life, and walk away.

Except for Christie.

It always comes back to Christie.

And Scott.

He turns and grins at me. 'And I've always been your Scott Scobie.'

My eyes and nose prickle and my vision blurs with tears. I'm swamped by flashes of bliss from our long-ago time together. Why, after all these years?

Then a stab of jealousy pierces me as I remember the honeyed voice answering his mobile, firming my resolve to keep my emotions in check. I burrow in my handbag for a tissue. 'I think we can safely say, that you, Scott Scobie, have been around the block a few times.'

'You think?' He looks bemused.

'It doesn't really matter what I think.' I dab my nose. 'Hay fever,' I mutter.

Scott parks up the car, his driving fluid and controlled, though I note the set of his shoulders has become rigid. His expression is unreadable as he gets out and comes round to help me down. His hands clamp around my waist, he looks away as I put my hands on his shoulders as he lifts me out.

'Thank you,' I say.

Wordlessly, he passes me my crutches, and presses the fob to lock the car. The short walk to the reception area is slow and awkward. Though Scott is by my side, I feel the distance between us. He steps back as I give my details. I try to ignore the usual titter of interest; it accompanies me everywhere I'm recognised.

As we make our way to the fracture clinic, I smile vaguely, but make no eye contact with those eager for my attention. I know I'm being ungracious. I hope they will forgive me.

Today I feel too fragile. What I have to give, I need to give to myself. Just enough to maintain the pose and poise Scott so eloquently identified. What he's failed to recognise, is that my pose and poise are my safety net, they catch me when I fall.

And I'm slipping through that safety net. I'm clinging onto the cords; I can feel them cutting into my fingers.

And always, always that gnawing fear of letting go; must hold on, must not let anyone close enough to fully see me.

And could anyone understand the real me? Accept I've sunk to the squalid depth of despair, clawed my fingers into the slithery sides of the pit and hauled my way out. I may have scraped off all the visible evidence of the filth, but the stench of my past clings to my memory. Even when I feel the grime of my sullied past swamp me, all the world sees, is the elegant silhouette of my fabulous persona.

But Scott Scobie has already seen the real me, knows which buttons to press to get a response. Knows what makes me sad… What makes me laugh so hard I can hardly catch my breath… What makes my body sing and soar to ecstasy…

Knows me inside and out.

And yet, here we are, in an orange waiting bay, sat on orange plastic chairs, waiting, without a word between us.

A pretty, young nurse with a wonky ponytail, wearing blue scrubs and an expectant expression, smiles at me. 'Miss De-Muir, this way please. I'm Janet, your fracture nurse, today.'

I nod and smile back. 'Thank you.'

I start to stand, and Scott is before me holding me steady, and passing my crutches. Already stepping in to help without any hesitation. Slotting back into my life to make it easier. Picking up on all the loopholes in my wellbeing, and filling them with a Scott Scobie shaped solution.

But only for a few more days. I can't let him into my life again, then be expected to let him walk away. I need to keep reminding myself of how it felt to lose him, I need to strike a distance between us.

'Thank you, Scott,' I say curtly.

He nods. 'Do you want me to come in?'

I shake my head. 'No, I'll be fine on my own, thanks.'

'I don't doubt it, Maddie, but I want you to know, I'm here for you.'

I nod an acceptance of his words, but move away from him. I must stop myself from falling into the tempting trap of Scott's consideration. It would only be a temporary sanctuary, and then trauma would engulf me, again. Better to put up the barriers now, than face that.

'You're only here a few more days, Scott, so let's not play the "Here for you" game. Okay.'

Scott raises his hands in a sign of surrender. 'Whoa! I don't know what's got in to you, Maddie. I'm just trying to help.'

'I don't need it!' I hiss under my breath. 'And I'm sure you'd be much happier back at your hotel with your…' I let the door swing closed behind me, cutting off any response he may have given.

'I'm sure you will find this boot much more comfortable than the plaster cast,' Janet, with the wonky ponytail, assures me. 'Take it off before you go to bed, and do the ten minutes exercises, then do them again in the morning before you put it back on.'

I wiggle my toes. Already the gentle support of the foam boot, feels like heaven compared to the unyielding cast. 'Thank you. I'm looking forward to a long soak in the tub, without having to dangle my leg over the side!'

Janet smiles. 'Sounds like a plan. See how you get on. I've made you an appointment for two weeks' time, but any problems, get in touch.' She passes me a slip of paper with the details, along with a pamphlet with my exercise info, and pushes open the door.

I step out, letting less strain be taken by my crutches, and more weight taken by my ankle. I ignore the dull throb. The sooner I'm back to normal the better.

Scott falls into step beside me. My stomach churns as we walk side by side in silence. I keep my eyes lowered to avoid anyone trying to catch my attention.

At the car, Scott steps in front of me ready to lift me into my seat. He remains stock-still with his arms planted firmly across his chest. 'I got to say, Maddie, you've a strange way of forcing a point.'

I challenge his glare. 'And *you* have a strange way, Scott, of proving to Christie what an exemplary character you have,' I return.

'What do you mean by that? I kinda hope I've validated my intentions, by inviting her to come over an' visit.'

I can feel the heat radiating from my body, searing me from the inside to the out. 'Oh, I'm sure Christie would be delighted by the company you keep,' I all but hiss.

'Well, yeah! I'd expect her to be impressed by the calibre of my clientele.'

I take a deep restraining breath, keeping my lips taught together. I can't help the instinctive shake of my head and the withering look I give. 'Just get me home, please.' I prime myself to smother the sensations I know will consume me as he lifts me into the car.

He clamps his hands around me, all but throws me into my seat and flings the crutches at me. 'Whatever's eating at you, I wish you'd just spit it out.' He stands, one hand holding the car door wide open, the other by my headrest. 'I've done everything I can, to deal with the multitude of glitches fermented by you and your family.'

'Just take me home, Scott,' I mutter, rubbing my forehead to try banishing the headache starting at my temples. 'It's already been a long day, and it's not even noon.'

His hand slips down onto my shoulder, his thumb making gentle rotations just beneath my collarbone. It would be so easy to let my head loll onto his forearm and secure our connection. I sigh, place my hand on top of his for a moment, and savour the familiar feel of it.

I curl my fingers round his, and lifting his hand from my shoulder, I turn to look at him. 'Scott, don't play games. I know you have a lady friend back at the hotel. So just take me home, okay.'

A Storm and a Teacup

We made an excuse and scarpered

Scott closes my car door, and I am bounced out of my seat as the car makes its customary jolt as he pulls himself in. 'I can explain,' he says.

I look away from him and out over the carpark – a jigsaw of vehicles, all shapes and sizes – they blur into a mishmash of disjointed rainbow colours as my eyes tear over. 'Don't. I'd rather you spared me the details.' I dab my nose with a tissue. 'The fact that you brought her is enough.'

He starts the engine, but makes no attempt to drive. The whirr of the aircon is an easy focus for my attention.

He lets out a loud sigh. 'It's not what you think.'

'You don't know what I think, Scott,' I say to the bleary colours swimming in front of my eyes.

'Okay, yeah, but it's not that—'

'Spare me the details, I said! She was familiar enough to answer your mobile. *Your* mobile!'

'She probably thought it was someone from The Scobie Gallery.'

I whip my head round and fix him with a glare. 'What difference does that make? Whoever she thought it was, isn't the issue here, Scott. It doesn't matter! But you brought her with you—'

'Yeah, but she—'

'Scott, you came to England, to meet your daughter for the first time, and you brought a plus one!'

'It isn't how it looks!'

'But it is, what it is,' I say as calmly as I can. 'The fact is, meeting your daughter is compromised by you bringing her along.'

The roar of the engine doesn't quite drown out Scott muttering, 'Bullshit.'. Despite the show of frustration, he drives with care out of the carpark, and joins the steady flow of morning traffic through Chippington.

It won't take much more than ten minutes to be back home to *The Manor House*. I get the exercise pamphlet out of my bag, and stare mindlessly at the diagrams.

'I wanna explain, Maddie. You've gone and got all worked up over something that has nothing to do with you or Christie.' Scott stares resolutely ahead.

I fold the pamphlet slowly and put it back in my bag. 'Fine, Scott. You start your relationship with Christie by keeping a secret. But for the record, that didn't work out for me.'

'She's just a friend, okay? No big deal.'

'Whatever kind of a friend she is, Scott, I'm not being drawn into it. And I'm not going to tell Christie, for obvious reasons. But I will say this, I am not happy about it!'

'Well, what do you know!' Scott lets out a low whistle. 'The high and mighty Madeline De-Muir, isn't happy about it... Well, just *for the record*, Maddie, I don't think you're in a position to judge.'

My chest feels fit to explode as I take a deep breath. 'I am not judging—'

'Sure you are! It's fine and dandy for you to keep my daughter a secret from me for twenty-four years. But hey, I keep one of my friends outa the spotlight, an' I'm accused of jeopardising getting to know my daughter!'

I try to steady my breathing. I know Scott thinks I'm overreacting, maybe I am. I let out a sigh, and earn myself a glower. I don't know if it's my own feelings I'm trying to protect, or Christie's.

I risk a sideways glance in his direction. His shoulders look relaxed, but his grip on the steering wheel is taut. His hair is tucked back over his ears, the length of it just curling up over the collar of his cornflower-blue shirt.

The breadth of his shoulders is more in keeping with those of a lumberjack, than a fine artist. As he manoeuvres the car through the outskirts of Chippington, I can't help imagining the way his muscles must be working beneath his shirt. And how tantalisingly smooth his skin would feel if I ran my fingers over his shoulders, and on down his back.

Closing my eyes, I recall the taste of his lips on mine, the shimmying sensations as he nibbled my neck, the shiver of anticipation as he caressed my body. That feeling of being so bound in the moment, that no other reality exists. Of falling so deeply and completely that my life could only survive if Scott was at the core of it.

I give myself a mental shake, and look again at this man, who was once all I lived for. His hold over me a mystery I have never fathomed. His face is more defined now, astute, and yet more handsome. His wayward, untameable hair, which once marked him as childlike, now preserves his youthful looks. The years have been kind to him, he is a man in his prime. He has an aura of confidence. His easy charm attracts like a magnet, using invisible forces to draw unsuspecting mortals under his spell. Any woman would be a fool to look away from him.

But I do. I look away as my face is scorched by a blush. My watery eyes cured by the remembrance of my misspent youth.

I can't blame him for getting on with his life, we both have. Scott has managed to become successful in his professional life, maintain a healthy social life and cultivate friendships too.

Me?

Yep.

I've managed to screw everything up.

My only success is the Keep-a-Key project, and that is down to Miles. I heave a sigh. 'You're right, Scott. It's nothing to do with me.' I watch the slow nod of his head and try to banish the thought of running my fingers through his hair. 'I overreacted. Sorry.'

His nod is more positive. 'I'm kinda trying to do the right thing here, Maddie, for everyone. An' everywhere I turn I get pushed away.'

I shrug. 'It's not intentional. We're all doing our best in our own way. And whether you know it or not, I'm desperate for you to get to know Christie as much as you can before you go back to your other life.'

Scott lets out a mirthless laugh. 'My other life, I kind of think it's never going to feel complete again, now I know what I'll be missing out on over here.'

'I know exactly how it feels, Scott. But at least you and Christie have a common passion, and through that, the opportunity to have lots of visits back and forth.'

'Yeah, I guess so. But it isn't the same as living on the doorstep like you guys do.' Scott shrugs. He turns off the engine and nods towards my home. 'Back safe and sound without the need to call in the cavalry.' He looks away from me, as if lost in thought. 'You know, it's not only Christie I'm going to miss.'

I let his words envelope my heart for a second or two while I try to conjure up a defence against his charm. A defence about as impenetrable as a breeze on a summer's day. I catch sight of Pauletta practically galloping towards the car, her trusty utility belt stocked and ready for action.

'Ah, I think the cavalry has arrived,' I say, and send up a silent prayer.

'Darn that woman!' Scott shoves open his door, and jumps down. 'You see, Pauletta, I've got her back all safe and sound,' he sings out.

'Is no business of yours! I need to talk to madam.'

Scott slams his door closed as Pauletta yanks mine open. 'Madam. Is those kids again! Here they are, eating me out of hows and home, and will not make any sense to talk to me.'

'Yes, Pauletta, my appointment went well, thank you for asking.' I raise a brow.

Pauletta huffs. 'I got eyes, I can see!' She waves her lime-green Minky cloth at my foam boot. 'This is very trouble to me. Like I say, everyday like spaghetti bolognaise.'

Scott stands, one hand slung low on his hip, the other propped on the top of my car door. 'If you'll allow me, Miss, I'll be helping Maddie outa the car.'

Pauletta spins round to face Scott, the top of her head about level with Scott's left nipple. She takes her time to raise herself up to her full height, then lifts her chin up enough to give him one of her haughty glares. 'You again! You bring more troubles to madam's door. More troubles and more marks on floor for me to scrub!'

'All I'm trying to do, is bring Maddie to her own door. Now if you'll excuse me?' He looks over Pauletta's head. 'Maddie?'

'Pauletta, just let Scott get me down from here. I'm not going to be able to sort anything out stuck in the car.'

She steps aside. 'Then you chase kids out of my kitchen cupboards, yes?'

Scott lifts me down, but leaves his hands resting on my midriff while he balances me. 'The first thing Maddie needs, is a nice cup of English tea. Think you can organise that?'

I open my eyes wide at Scott, tilt my head to see around him and pull an apologetic face at Pauletta. 'I've had a bit of a morning of it. A cup of tea would be lovely,' I coax.

Pauletta gives me a withering look and stomps off towards the house. 'As you say, madam.'

'Make mine a strong black coffee,' Scott chimes after her.

She slams the door.

The chattering stops as I push open the kitchen door. Pauletta was right, the kids have emptied the cupboards. I prop up my crutches, balance myself and thrust my hands on my hips. 'May I ask,' I speak slowly and quietly, 'what exactly, is going on?'

Frankie rolls his head to one side. 'We've all come to see you. Mrs Price is doing our heads in.'

I raise a hand, try not to be distracted by Scott lolling on the doorframe by my side. 'Stop right there, Frankie. We'll come to that in a minute.' I let my eyes follow the trail of discarded crisp packets, biscuit wrappers and selection of various drinks bottles littering every surface of my kitchen. I make a sweeping gesture with my arm. 'Really?'

'Pauletta said we could help ourselves, cos she's busy,' mutters Frankie.

'*That* is not the problem.' I give my head a little shake.

Already Mickey has started ushering the other two to tidy up. 'We're doing it now,' she says.

'Excellent. I'll come back in five minutes.' I shuffle to turn round.

Scott passes me my crutches, and heads back into the dining room. 'I can't believe you let those four kids roam around your home unsupervised,' he says, once the door swings closed behind me.

I sit in the window seat, close my eyes and feel the warmth of the sun wash over me. I try to supress the thousands of niggles vying to claw their way to the surface. Scott has no idea. I'd trust any one of those kids with my life, each one of them has trusted me with their life.

A messy kitchen is the least of my worries, and the least of their offences. 'You know, Scott, those kids have come from the brink of acceptable society, and become ambassadors for my charity. They may not look like the pristine specimens you are used to, but to me they all gleam like diamonds.'

Scott sighs. 'Yeah, yeah. If only your kitchen did, huh.' He shakes his head.

I smile. 'Give it a couple of minutes, and it will.'

He snorts. 'You really think so? I got to hand it to 'em, they've got you wrapped around their little fingers.'

'If that's what you think.' I keep my eyes closed; I don't need to see him to know the look of disapproval he's wearing, but I'm contented to wait. I know what I expect from my kids, and so do they.

I let out a deep sigh, I hope whatever issues Frankie's crew have with Mrs Price haven't gone too far. She can be a bit of a dragon, and since Miles is not about to rein her in…

I hear the door and open my eyes.

Mickey bobs her head round the door. 'It's all sorted, Frankie is just emptying the recycle bin.' She shrugs. 'I did tell 'em not to make a mess, but you know what they're like.'

I think that's the longest she has ever spoken! When Frankie is about, she lets him take charge. 'Thank you, Mickey. I hope they start listening to you.'

She shrugs and disappears back into the kitchen.

I look up at Scott. 'Shall we?'

'Sure.' He passes me my crutches. 'You've got to remember I've seen how your kitchen usually looks.'

I get up and lead the way into the kitchen. The counters are clear, with the exception of two china mugs and my china teapot, which has steam swirling from the spout. 'Ah, this is much more welcoming!'

I can hear Scott shuffling from one foot to another, he lets out a low whistle. Frankie comes in carrying the empty bin, goes into the utility room and returns with a bin liner. The others watch as he puts the bin back where it belongs. He swills his fingers under the tap and looks at me with an apologetic smile. 'Sorry,' he mumbles.

'I should think so too, it looked like a gang of delinquents had raided my cupboards. No wonder Pauletta looked fit to explode.'

'Sorry,' says Frankie. 'I made a pot of tea for you and your… friend.'

'Thank you.' I turn to Scott, raise my brow and tilt my head.

'Yeah, that's real good of you, thanks,' says Scott. He steps past me into the room and thrusts out his hand towards Frankie. 'I'm Scott, by the way. We did meet the other day, but it's good to see you taking care of Maddie.'

Frankie shakes his hand then goes in for a fist bump. 'Yeah, well, what goes around… This is Mickey, Jump an' Baz.'

'Good to make your acquaintance,' gushes Scott, as he shakes each of their hands in turn. 'I hear nothing but good things about you folks.'

'Yeah,' says Frankie. 'We got Maddie's reputation to think of. But it's kinda tough sometimes.'

Scott nods. 'It's always kinda tough, the trick is, to make it look easy.'

I perch on a breakfast bar stool. 'So, about this cup of tea?'

Baz pours out the tea and adds my sugar and milk, leaving Scott to add his own.

I nestle the mug in my hands and take a sip. 'Delicious. Thank you. Right, Mickey, do you want to fill me in on what the problem is?'

Mickey's eyes widen and she quickly looks at Frankie for guidance. 'Mrs Price is good and everything, but she's dead bossy and doesn't tell us what's going on.'

I nod. 'I see, but to be fair, Mrs Price doesn't know herself what is going on. I do understand, she can be a little—'

'She's like Pauletta on steroids!' Frankie chips in. 'And she did know the police were coming this morning to interview her about the fire!'

'Well, that's more than me,' I say. 'Did you talk to them?'

'Naw, we made an excuse and scarpered. They didn't want to talk to us anyhow, just her. But she could of warned us.'

'Maybe she didn't want you worrying.'

Frankie shrugs. 'Anyways, that's not it. We have nowhere to go, and if Miles isn't about…' Frankie looks warily at Scott. 'It just isn't the same.'

I nod. It must be tough for them, the last four months have been packed with activity and deadlines, and now nothing. Just a void filling up with uncertainty. 'Well, for one, Miles is back doing bits and pieces—'

'Yeah! Great, when can we—'

'Hold on, bits and pieces, not full-on projects. I have already seen him a couple of times, but I will be asking him to see if there are any options regarding short term premises… It won't be what you have been used to.'

'We don't care, we just need somewhere to go, or else we'll be on the streets hanging about.'

'I'll get on to Miles. In the meantime, you all owe Pauletta an apology.'

'She said she'll do some cooking with us when she's finished her proper work,' says Mickey. She looks at Scott. 'But we can go if we're in your way.'

'Stay, please. I for one would like to sample some of your cooking.' I turn to Scott. 'Fancy a free lunch?'

'You know me, Maddie, never one to turn down food.'

A Hit from the Past

I don't think so

I lick my forefinger and dab the last of the crumbs from my plate.

'I got to say, Maddie, I'm impressed.'

I grin. 'Yep. Pauletta might have her faults, but she is a superb cook. Better still, she's happy to share her culinary tricks and secrets.' I swirl my finger to collect the final few morsels of pastry. 'And broccoli and stilton quiche is a personal favourite of mine.'

Scott rests back, and eases his chair away from the dining room table. 'So, who made it?' he tilts his head. 'Pauletta or the kids?'

'It will have been a joint venture. Pauletta will have had them all mixing their own batch of pastry. They will each have chosen their own fillings, and she'll have made sure there was enough for them all to take plenty home for their families.'

'And the salad?'

'It takes Pauletta no time at all to whip up an authentic Greek salad. The fridge is her temple.'

Scott nods slowly. 'You like her a lot, don't you?'

I laugh out loud and shake my head. 'She keeps me in my place, but she is… yeah I like her. I don't know what I'd do without her, to be honest. I'm very lucky to have good people around me.'

Scott bristles. 'I guess, by that you mean Miles.'

'Not just Miles, but the whole support team he's assembled. Mrs Price, the one Frankie described as "Pauletta on steroids", she is an absolute gem when it comes down to efficiency. She keeps schedules of her schedules, all up here.' I tap my temple. 'I have no idea where Miles found her, I'm just glad he did.'

'Uh-huh.'

'That reminds me, excuse me while I give her a quick call.'

I scroll down my contacts list and dial. It only takes a couple of rings.

'Miss De-Muir, I was expecting a call, the kids did a bunk as soon as they saw the officers.' She laughs. 'It was only a routine call about the fire.'

'Thank you, Mrs Price. So, no problems?'

'Not at all, I made them a nice cup of tea and went over my statements.'

'Good, the insurance company are eager to get to grips with everything—'

'Surely Miles will be dealing with all of that side of things?'

'Oh, yes, he's keen to get on with it… Mrs Price, there is something I'd like you to look into; I don't want to overload Miles.' I glance at Scott, who's sat with his arms planted across his chest, his face unreadable.

'Anything at all, I'm going stir-crazy, and my lovely hubby has threatened to throw me out at 8.30 every morning so he can have some peace and quiet!'

'Excellent, well not, obviously being thrown out!' I laugh. 'The kids need somewhere to hang out—'

'Say no more. I'm already on it… I've got three possibles, two definite maybes. I'll check them all out tomorrow.'

'Okay, I'll leave you with it then.'

'Rightio. Shall I contact Miles to finalise the details, or…'

'Please, just keep him in the loop. Good luck!'

'Cheerio!'

I look at the blank screen. 'She's gone!' I look up at Scott, the blue of his eyes lock with mine. 'She's already got places lined up ready to be rubber stamped. Impressive, yes?' I stumble.

Scott leans forward and rests his forearms on the table narrowing the distance between us. I can feel him scrutinising me, stripping away my layers of camouflage, seeking out the Maddie who ran out on him. I'm still here.

Still wobbly, still insecure.

Still desperate to be found.

Still hiding behind an image I've created to protect myself.

I look around my grand dining room. The carefully arranged drapes, the elegant furniture, the intricate twin chandeliers, the Turkish rugs, the plush sofas and impressive slate fireplace. All of these, all of these things, buffers and smoke screens and comfortable clichés of a has-been movie star.

I close my eyes and sigh. I do love beauty, but the comfort of my snug with the tatty old sofa and chipped sideboard – where I stash all of Christie's photos in the top four drawers, and my portfolios crammed in the bottom one – is the place I feel most relaxed. Cosseted away, hidden and private, my own world.

And I know exactly where he is, my Scott, the only photo I have of him taken when we were together. Top left drawer, secure in the folds of Christie's birth certificate. A birth certificate with a blank space where the father's name should be. The place where he belongs. The place I denied him.

'Penny for them?'

I open my eyes and look at him. His face is relaxed, playful almost, and I smile. 'Come on, Scott, you don't need to waste your hard-earned money,' I say light-heartedly. 'You've always been able to read my mind.'

'You think?' he purrs. 'You were always an enigma, Maddie, but more so now. You only let me see your soul when I paint you.'

I snort and shake my head. 'That's not true, Scott Scobie, and you know it!'

He smiles his infuriatingly smug smile, revelling in getting a snappy response. 'Gotcha.'

I roll my eyes and look away.

'Seriously, you've changed. The Maddie I knew wouldn't have give up an inch of ground. But here you are, all grown up, an' letting just about everyone…' He waves his arms about. 'You know, encroach on your patch, take over your control of important stuff, the insurance—'

'That's Miles' expertise—'

'Finding a venue for *your* key kids—'

'Mrs Price is more than capable, and—'

'They asked you.' He looks me square in the eye.

It takes all my willpower not to flinch. 'Yes, they did. But Mrs Price is well aware of their requirements. More importantly, she has a greater knowledge of what areas of the town are better at keeping these kids out of harm's way. Like you said, I'm all grown up, and now I know I don't know all the answers.'

I hold his gaze, allowing myself to wallow in what might have been, as I sink deeper into the storm-blue of his eyes.

'All grown up.' He looks away, then back to me. 'But I still see glimmers of the old Maddie, my Maddie.'

'Scott,' I say on a sigh. 'We were kids, and now look at us. Both of us have achieved our dreams. We are so far apart from the kids we used to be. Nobody gave us a second glance back then, no one would recognise me from that time—'

'I would, Maddie. I do. I still see you.'

Agitation darts through my body searching for an escape, like a gazelle being chased by lions. No matter which way I turn, I know I'm doomed, and I don't think I'd survive the fall a second time.

'Scott, please…' I shake my head; I can't let any of those fantasies take hold. 'Let's leave the past in the past.'

Scott shrugs. 'But some things are hard to leave behind. Look, I got to go, I'm seeing Christie, yeah? But like I said, I want to paint you, Maddie. Not for old times sakes, for now, to mark this new chapter—'

'Scott—'

'Hear me out, Maddie. Like it or not, from now on our lives are going to be intertwined, we've got a daughter together. We might as well make the most of it. At least be friends.' He shrugs. 'What do you say?'

'We are friends.'

'So, you'll let me paint you?' He grins, and his eyes light up like the sky on the fourth of July, sending me spinning like a carousel.

'That, Scott Scobie, isn't fair.'

He leaps from his chair and plants a kiss on my cheek. 'Thanks, Maddie! Got to go, don't want to keep Christie waiting. I'm taking her out later!'

'Scott!' I shout after him. 'I haven't said yes!'

'Tomorrow, I'll be here at ten,' he shouts back.

I hear the door slam behind him. With my head resting in my hands, I slump on the table. I should have known there is no point in arguing with Scott. Once his mind is set, he's like a cat on a couch, there's no moving him.

And he knows, darn him, he knows I'm vain!

He knows if it happens, *when* it happens, I'll be a pathetic pushover. I'll be eager for his eye to capture the essence of my former self, the slender waif with the translucent skin.

But he'll do more than that.

He'll expose my secrets, my vulnerabilities, my strengths. He'll delve again into my soul and leave me exposed before all who care to look.

Scott has an impeccable knack, for seeking out what others overlook. When he is in the zone, totally connected and absorbed, there is no hiding from his insight. He paints pure and true.

I let out a groan, he's going to eat me alive.

The squeak of shoes alerts me to Pauletta's approach. I sit up from my slouch and force a smile as she enters the dining room.

'Again, with the shouting! This house, when he comes is like Houston, we got a problem.'

I roll my eyes, frankly Pauletta's grasp of quotes and phrases has not improved over the years. 'Mr Scobie has been complementing your culinary skills, Pauletta. He was impressed.'

'Not impressed enough to come and find me, or offer to do washing-up!'

'Well, I wouldn't expect a guest to offer to do the washing-up! And we do have a dishwasher...'

She shrugs. 'I know my place. But Mr Hepworth, he offers.'

'He used to live here, and if you can remember, made more mess than all the Key kids put together.'

'Is not a problem with Mr Hepworth, he not shout.'

I clasp my hands together. 'So, would you like me to do the washing-up?'

Pauletta glares at me, and starts stacking our plates. 'Do not make crazy fool ideas.' She turns to leave. 'You listen, madam, he is big trouble for you, that man.'

Oh, I hate it when she's right. She lets the door swing shut behind her, before I've time to think of a response.

Miles tucks his head round the snug door. 'Thought I'd find you in here.'

'I'm hiding from Pauletta.'

He fully enters the room. 'She seems in a good mood. She was humming a tune when I arrived.'

'Did you recognise which tune?' I raise a brow, and he shakes his head. '*Hit the road, Jack, and don't you come back no more, no more.*' I sing. 'But I think she's mentally changing Jack for Scott.'

Miles laughs and sits down beside me. 'Take no notice.'

'It's all very well for you, but I feel like a prisoner in my own home. I've been trying to sneak out for a glass of orange juice for the last forty minutes.'

'Leave it to me.' He goes back the way he came and reappears in seconds. He puts his fingers to his lips, signalling for me to stay quiet. 'Pauletta...' he sings out, and grins.

Pauletta is by his side a moment later. 'Mr Hepworth! How happy to see a friendly face...'

– exactly my thoughts – 'How can I help, do you like a cup of tea?'

I smile and sit twiddling my thumbs as she pointedly ignores me.

'Could you bring a pitcher of orange juice and two glasses please.'

She narrows her eyes at me, then smiles at Miles. 'Is my pleasure, Mr Hepworth,' she gushes and darts from the room.

'Well done! So, Miles, is this a social call, or are you here to go over where you are up to with the insurance company?'

'Not the insurance, not yet. And of course,' he bobs down and plants a kiss on the top of my head, 'I am always happy to see you!' – I roll my eyes – 'But I needed to give Christie and Scott some privacy, and I need to talk to you about—'

'One big jug of juice and two glasses for you, Mr Hepworth.'

Miles grins. 'Pauletta, you're a star.'

'I know, but thank you. Is very kind to say. Not everyone notice how good I am.' She sweeps from the room and drags the door closed behind her.

I shake my head. '*Pauletta, you're a star*,' I mimic in hushed tones. 'Thanks for that Miles!'

'You're welcome. I'll pour, shall I?' He doesn't wait for an answer, but fills my glass to the brim and passes it to me. 'Enjoy.'

The bite of cold juice, instantly refreshes my palette and traces a cool path down my throat. 'Mmmmm, delicious. Almost worth the wait.' I take another few sips, trying to savour the rejuvenating nectar, rather than take the gulps I'd like to indulge myself with.

Miles leaves his drink untouched. 'We need to talk about Tim Boswell.'

I place my glass down on a coaster. 'I don't think so,' I say.

'Maddie, that man has contacted the office a dozen times in the last four days. And you know he's a big hitter in the business.'

'I know exactly who he is, and I don't need you reminding me!'

I hug his jacket closer to my body. More than anything, I want to be a star, and Mr Boswell, *Tim* can do it. I know he can. 'Tim, I promise you, I am going to work harder than anybody ever has!' I hope he can't tell I'm shaking beneath the weight of his jacket. 'I'm going to make people cry for Lucy. I'm going to make people believe she is their daughter or sister or cousin. I'm going to make the whole of England want to rescue her.'

He nods. 'You know, I believe you will. But this little scar of yours—'

'It *will* fade, they promised!' I trace over the sensitive area of my scar.

He shakes his head. 'That isn't the issue. Your reputation is...' He picks up the photo of the two little girls eating their ice creams. 'If the press get hold of the fact you have a child, Madeline, I won't be able to protect you.'

'They won't find out.'

'Are you absolutely certain? What about the father?'

I swallow down the bile at the back of my throat. 'I am absolutely certain.' I look away from him. 'And the father doesn't know.'

'A word to the wise, keep it that way, at least for a couple of years.'

'Maddie, he isn't giving up. Now I appreciate some of the details of your early career you have kept deliberately hazy from me, but come on...'

I blow out a lungful of air, and look up towards the ceiling. 'Tim Boswell,' I say in hushed breaths, 'as you probably already know, was the director of my "Lucy". My very first part.'

Miles nods. 'Go on.'

'Over the course of filming, I looked on him as a demigod. Of all the people I've worked with in the industry, Tim is the one whose counsel I most respect.' I look at Miles and shrug. 'You have no idea how close we became.'

'Maddie, I'm not seeing a problem here. If Tim Boswell is one of the good guys, why won't you—'

'*Because* he's one of the good guys! Look Miles, he knows all about Christie. He knew from the second day of filming... he's known for twenty-four years, and not a peep.'

'What? So, you feel like you owe him?'

I feel the familiar tightening in my chest, pulling me in, crushing me with guilt and self-loathing. Year, after year, after year of supressed anxiety weighing down on me; constantly fracturing my belief in myself, undermining every good deed I have ever done with an array of mistakes littering my past.

And still I try. I try to do the right thing, but it's as if I'm hard wired to constantly let down the people I love most, the people I respect most, and the people who believe in me most. Tim is one of those people. 'I don't feel like I owe him. I do owe him. Okay?'

'Why?' Miles shakes his head. 'Fair enough, he kept your secret, but from what I've heard, he's got his own skeletons to keep in the closet.'

I shake my head. 'Not Tim. He's the perfect gentleman. If anyone was in a position ripe for exploitation, it was me. He had every opportunity. But no. Those rumours were totally unfounded, and started by someone he refused to recast because of their drug habit. Had it not been for people aware of the situation, it could have finished him off.' I supress a wry smile. 'That, and the fact that in his office he records every private conversation he has!'

'Is that legal?'

'He has a notice on his door, stating conversations are recorded to capture artistic genius! I always thought it was a bit of a joke…' I shrug. 'But it saved his career, and his reputation.'

'So why do you think you owe him?'

'I was seventeen and he took me under his wing. He's a damn fine director, he taught me the importance of timing, the skill of being motionless and silent, he taught me camera skills, he spent hours standing behind me while I perfected facial expressions in the mirror. How many directors do you think invest that amount of time in their actors?'

'Not many.'

'Correct. Tim Boswell dragged a performance out of me – a rooky wannabe – and set me up to be a movie star. He spotted me for "Lucy", and he demanded me for "Rose" in *An English Rose*. My whole career is down to him—'

'Maddie, I think you're stretching it too far. You do, after all, have the ability to hold an audience spellbound.'

'And Tim Boswell taught me how to do it. He made me a star, and I threw it away. Abandoned my career, the same as I abandoned Christie.'

'He wants to meet up with you.'

I sigh. 'I'm just not ready.'

'I suggest you get ready, because he's travelling up in a couple of days. I can't hold him off any longer.'

I drop my head into my hands. 'Fab, just what I need, another spark near the powder keg.'

In the Zone

Hovers with a Lingering Kiss

Scott looks me up and down, lets out a low whistle. 'I couldn't imagine a more spectacular image.' He props his easel by the door and leans in, brushing a kiss on my cheek.

I smile, breathing in the scent of his aftershave, acknowledging the spark of recognition between us, savouring the sensations. If he had any idea of the amount of planning this moment has taken, he wouldn't be so impressed.

I've let my hair dry naturally, so it feathers over my bare shoulders, with the occasional whisp softening my high cheekbones. My makeup, I've kept to the bare minimum.

My seemingly simple sundress, is anything but. Cut on the bias, the fabric – ice blue, to match my image – moves over my body merely hinting at my flawless curves. The handkerchief hem dances mid-calf teasing my ankles. And the dainty spaghetti straps look scarcely there at all, as the eye of the beholder is drawn to my razor-sharp collarbones, dashed with angelic freckles.

'Good morning, Scott, and thank you.'

'Is the lovely Pauletta having a day off?'

I laugh. 'No, she is having a bit of a strop. Before Miles left yesterday, he gently reminded Pauletta, that *I* employ *her*. It didn't go down too well.'

'Ah.'

'I've asked her to have an early finish today. She must have worked double her usual hours over the last few weeks, with one thing and another.'

Scott waggles his eyebrows, Groucho Marx style. 'Alone at last!'

'Not yet,' I say. 'And she has reliably informed me it's going to rain later – the weather update, courtesy of the gardener.'

Scott pats the easel. 'Better hop to it then, don't wanna waste the light.'

I nod. 'I thought the garden window in the dining room would be good.'

Scott picks up his painting things and wanders off. 'I'll go and have a look outside, since you aren't wanting to search out that tree of ours.'

Like that was ever going to happen! 'Scott!' I grab my crutches and follow as fast as I can. At least with this foam boot I can move better. 'Terry is outside, he'll get in the way, knock things over.'

Scott is already out of the back door. I watch through the window as he bobs down and ruffles Terry's fur behind his ears. Looks like they're friends for life. I prop myself in the doorway, waiting for Scott to come to his senses and realise it's far too hot and bright to paint out there today.

He gestures towards the far hedge. 'Is that a summerhouse hidden at the end of the garden?'

I drop my chin to my chest, darn him, he's spotted it. 'It's a bit tumbled down,' I say, hoping he'll dismiss the idea.

Off he strides. 'I'll take a look-see! Could be just the job.'

Terry bounds ahead of him, then darts off towards the Buddleia bushes. A flutter of butterflies take flight and I hear tell-tale caterwauling as Pixi pounces out, claws flashing at Terry.

'Terry!' I squeal. 'Leave her alone!'

Pixi disappears off behind the summerhouse, presumably through the hedge and on into the fields beyond. Terry has never been brave enough to follow, he just pretends to be top dog.

'Yours?' asks Scott.

I shrug. 'She's a cat, she belongs to herself, but she's happy to honour me with her presence at feeding time.'

Again, accompanied by the low whistle, Scott surveys the summerhouse. 'I like it, Maddie. It's got a kinda ramshackle romantic atmosphere, cool an' shady an' secretive.'

I groan. 'Well, Scott, sounds like you've found your location.'

He turns to me and grins. 'Sure have!' He disappears inside – I hope he likes spiders.

I continue my steady progress to catch up with Scott, hampered by Terry darting back and forth between us. 'Terry! Settle down!' Terry slows his pace, then ambles into the summerhouse ahead of me.

Scott is busy shaking out a patchwork cover for one of the recliners. The space really is a hotchpotch of old garden furniture, random cushions and eclectic patchwork throws.

When I left home for drama school, kitted out for my new life in London, I'd bundled all my old clothes into bin bags and told Mum to burn them – I'd wanted no reminders of my time with Scott, it was too painful. Instead, Mum used up every bit of fabric she could, stitching them all into a selection of multi-coloured patchwork throws.

Years later, she gave them to me. Sometimes I come in here, hold the fabric between my fingers and press it to my face just to be close to the things that were close to Scott. Sometimes, I even think I catch a hint of his aroma, impossible, of course, but I like to pretend.

Scott smooths out another one of the patchworks, and looks about the summerhouse. 'This is all kinda individual and quirky. It is assuredly you, Maddie Harris, and not at all Miss De-Muir.' –Trust Scott to pick out the contrasts – 'Hiding your intensity behind a multitude of haphazard guises.'

The muslin drapes flutter ever so slightly, casting wavering shadows in the cool of the summerhouse. Wavering shadows over my past; wavering shadows over my memories. Being here with Scott is not going to help me dampen my feeling for him, just the opposite. 'Scott, the light isn't that consistent in here, would we not be better inside?'

He starts to arrange a throw over one of the recliners, he ruffles the fabric close to the headrest creating more of a textured impression. 'Nice try, Maddie. In here is just fine and dandy.' He swivels the chair so as to allow maximum light to bathe it. He pats the seat. 'Come on, don't be shy.' He grins.

I prop my crutches in the doorway and hobble across. 'Not shy, Scott...' – More shit-scared – 'Let's face it, nothing here you haven't seen before.'

I perch on the edge of the chair and lean forward to unfasten the Velcro straps on my foam boot.

Scott kneels before me. 'Let me.'

He holds my boot in place, and rips each strap open then eases the boot from my leg. 'I'm going to have some fun trying to match that shade of purple.' He looks into my eyes and gives me a lopsided smile.

'I hope you aren't even going to try! Use your artistic licence and paint it the same colour as my right ankle.'

I automatically raise my leg up off the floor and onto the recliner to protect it from being knocked. Resting back, I leave my right leg dangling, pink toe nails peeping out from my sandals.

'Are you planning on just wearing that one?' asks Scott, gesturing to my foot.

I flick my leg up and slide off the sandal. 'Better?'

'Yeah. So, you just make yourself comfortable while I get myself set up, and then—'

'I have done this before, remember?' Eager to get this preamble over with.

He shrugs and starts setting up his easel, and sets up a makeshift table from the old apple box I usually use to pop my drink on.

I close my eyes and stretch; I know he'll take his time to get everything just as he likes. Once he starts painting, he is totally in the zone, he works fluidly without pausing until he has completed his artwork. He is fuelled by passion and the desire to capture the essence of his study.

I know how consumed he becomes. I tried many times to tease and distract him. It's almost as if his conscious mind gives way to his creative energy. He connects with the psyche of his model and ekes out their personality, transforming it into an image of significance and beauty.

It is Scott's attention to detail and ability to stir an emotional reaction from his paintings, that have elevated his standing in the artworld and with those who want to be thrust into the limelight. And since I want to stay in the shadows, I've got to be brutally honest with myself as to why I've agreed to revisit being Scott's muse. And I'm at a loss.

Is it plain and simple vanity?

Or is it to confirm what I think I already know?

And neither is particularly flattering.

'Almost done setting up here. Just a couple more things.'

I open my eyes. 'I'm ready when you are.'

He sweeps his hair behind his ears. 'Ahhh, no session with you would be complete without these.' He digs out a couple of cans of—

'IRN BRU – Made in Scotland from Girders!' I squeal. 'I haven't had it in years!'

Scott grins. 'Me neither! America isn't ready for it yet!'

'Ha ha, I bet!'

We share a smile of recognition. I can tell by the softening of his expression that he's remembering our many painting sessions accompanied by the blaze of young love, and the epic Scottish soda.

He steps closer and tilts his head. 'It kinda wouldn't of been the same without it.'

'You used to say it let loose your spectrum of vision, you were s-o-o-o high and mighty!' I roll my eyes melodramatically.

He bursts out laughing. 'Sure was, I kind of needed that bluster and arrogance to hoodwink my way in the US.'

'Really?' I tease. 'They didn't take one look at you and think "Gee, this boy's got it all!". I'm surprised.'

He absently starts positioning me on the recliner, as a window dresser would a mannequin. 'If you leave your hand palm up, kind of beseeching, connecting, yeah, that's it.' He lifts my chin with the back of his hand, slowly. 'Find a natural point to hold your gaze… Bingo!'

He readjusts the throw behind me, then he focuses on the handkerchief hem of my dress. 'Great choice.'

Each of his touches is a reminder. As his fingers brush the sensitive skin around my ankles, I feel myself crumbling – he's going to see my very soul.

'I shouldn't of asked.' Scott scrubs both of his hands over his face, tucks a wayward curl behind his ear.

'I shouldn't have said yes.' I sigh. I can tell by his expression that being this intimate, this whole experience has stirred up the past. The easy way we have both slipped back to our old familiar roles, is scary.

Scott smiles. 'You've still got it, darn you, Maddie! How's a man going to resist?'

'You'd be surprised,' I say. 'Can I move?'

'Sure. I'm done.' He relaxes his shoulders, raises his arms, and links his fingers at the back of his head. 'As done as I've ever been.' His attention is fully on me.

I stretch the length of my body out along the recliner and let out a deep sigh. Knowing he's watching my every move, sparks the confidence I always felt when we used to be together. 'It feels good to be able to move. I'd forgotten just how demanding you can be, Scott Scobie.'

Scott's laugh - a rich baritone – is music to my ears. 'You of all people should know, you only get out what you put in.'

'Well, quite! But I never expected to be doing this again, especially not with you.'

'Why not? Like I said, you've still got it.'

I shrug, make no attempt to replace the spaghetti strap as it slips from my shoulder. Scott had wanted to reconstruct the original nude, under the canopy of our tree, if we could have found it. A vision from a time when my body was lithe, alive and free from the grind of time. Painted by a young man madly in love with his muse.

Frankly, not a cat in hells chance! What woman in her right mind would allow that kind of comparison, twenty-five years later?

'You did good.' He leans back and looks at the canvas. 'Like old times, and still incredibly beautiful. Bewitching.'

I shake my head. 'No need to flatter me now! You've got what you wanted.'

'It's the truth. Come and look for yourself. I only paint what I see.'

Tentatively, I feel for the floor with my bare toes. My crutches stand guard by the open summerhouse doors, and my foam boot lays discarded by their side. Throughout my sitting, Terry has laid patiently by Scott's side, now he raises his head, but makes no move towards me. Throughout, I've forced the gentle flutter of the muslin drapes to hold my attention. Had Scott been my focus, I would have melted in a pool at his feet.

I take mini steps towards the easel. Scott stands, and holds me out a steadying hand.

'Thanks,' I say. Our eyes communicate the unspoken words between us – his, the acceptance of my independence, and mine, my appreciation for him not making me feel like an old fuddy-duddy!

Being still and quiet in each other's company has somehow allowed us to relax. The sound of trickling water from the garden pond, the exquisite scent of Dorothy Perkins roses and the occasional buzz of a bumble bee have all added to the tranquil idyl that is my garden. Finally, the pressures of the last few days, weeks, are seeping away, and I can be honest, at least with myself, and admit I've never stopped loving him.

His hands rest on my bare shoulders. 'Close your eyes, I'm going to have you sit where I've been sitting.'

He guides me to the high stool, and positions me in readiness to view his work. His hands are still resting on each of my shoulders, his thumbs grazing my back with gentle rotations.

I can feel the whisper of his breath on the back of my neck feathering sensations of intimacy down my spine, awakening my past. The scent of Scott Scobie fills my airways and I'm lost.

'Okay, you can open your eyes now.'

My eyes flutter open and I gasp. Scott has painted an ethereal vision swathed in mystery and stirring passion. I feel the tears forming in my eyes; know that I am known by this man. 'It's exquisite, Scott.' I whisper. 'Thank you.'

'It's you, Maddie. I can only paint what I see.' He leans forward and brushes a kiss on my cheek. 'Thanks for indulging me. I got to say, I think it's going to be my all-time favourite.'

Pauletta thrusts her head into the summerhouse. 'Is going to be storm, and I am off to home now. Get move on! I not wanting to clean up all muddy mess in morning!'

She's gone before I've time to respond. Terry trundles after her.

'Well, that kinda killed the moment.' Without warning, Scott scoops me up and returns me to the recliner. 'I got to say, her timing sucks.'

I rearrange my dress to cover my bruised ankle. 'But takes nothing away from your achievement.'

He walks over to the easel and turns it to face us. 'Like I said, I only paint what I see.'

I smile. 'I know, but you see more than anyone else.'

He shrugs, and props his hands low on his hips looking at his work. 'I've been gifted a divine subject.' The recliner tilts as he sits down on the edge.

A rumble of thunder threatens the summer sky and I notice an eerie quiet in the garden. 'Sounds like Pauletta was right.' She usually is.

'Yeah, well, she brings out the rebellious teen in me. You've no idea how much pleasure I'd get from stomping muddy footprints all over her squeaky-clean floor.'

'Scott Scobie! I'm shocked. Poor Pauletta working her fingers to the bone—'

'She 'aint no Cinderella!'

His easy humour puts me at ease. 'Maybe not.'

I notice the sky darkening, and smell the tell-tale earthy dampness in the air as rain in the distance is drenching the hungry soil. Another peal of thunder cracks close by, and the sudden heavy patter of rain on the roof takes me by surprise.

'Well either I'm being granted my wish,' says Scott. 'Or we're holed up here for the next few hours.'

I turn to look at him, and am met by the mischievous grin I knew I would be. 'Have you any more Irn Bru?' I raise a brow.

'In the car… If that's what it'll take to keep you here, I'll go get—'

'I'm hungry too.'

Scott shakes his head, stands, and looks at the teeming rain. 'Looks like we'll be makig' a run for it.'

I raise the hem of my dress to reveal my bruised ankle. 'I'll have to make a hobble for it.'

'Better idea.' Scott pulls the throw all around me and scoops me up. 'Brace yourself!' He launches us out into the downpour, and strides towards the house.

I throw my head back and embrace the cool raindrops showering my face, making a mockery of my makeup. They trickle down my neck and my back, rivulets of pure water washing away my resolve. Exactly as it did the very first time we met. I let out a heartfelt laugh at the irony.

Scott's breath is like fire on my neck as he hurries on. 'I hope you're enjoying yourself,' he huffs good-naturedly.

'How could I be anything else, in the arms of my…' I almost say lover.

He sets me down just inside the kitchen. We stand, each looking at the other, a pool of water swelling at our feet. I let the throw drop to the floor, well aware my sundress must be almost transparent.

Scott's eyes flare, he brushes my hair back from my neck. 'You need to get out of those wet clothes before you catch a chill, Maddie.'

I nod. 'I'll go up and change.' Our eyes lock.

'Allow me.' He scoops me up again, leaving a trail of footprints as he heads out of the kitchen, through the dining room and into the hallway. He hesitates at the bottom of the stairs. 'May I?'

I nod my acceptance and he takes the stairs two at a time, as if my weight counts for nothing. At the top, he pauses to take a breath. I gesture towards my bedroom door, reach down and open the door. Scott steps inside.

The intricate baroque fourposter bed stands centre stage cast in the late afternoon shadows.

Scott gently sets me down, hovers with a lingering kiss on the nape of my neck. 'I'd best be leaving you to—'

I shake my head, take his hand and lead him to my bed.

After the Storm

Sink beneath the sheet

Even with my eyes still closed, I can sense light flooding the room with the radiance of a new beginning. I stretch out my body beneath the cool cotton sheet. Arching my back, I point my toes to the far end of the bed. A small moan escapes my lips as my left ankle protests, nothing is going to stop me luxuriating in this feeling.

I extend my arms above my head, splaying my fingers and levelling my palms, then let them flop relaxed on my pillow and let out a deep sigh. At last, my demons are silenced.

For the first time in never, I feel utterly contented. If I could stop time, and repeat one whole day again, it would be the last twenty-four hours.

Every moment, from getting up yesterday and preparing for my sitting with Scott, until waking early this morning has confirmed my suspicions. I still love Scott Scobie. I've never stopped.

Those snatched moments of passion in our youth were nothing compared to our tender love-making throughout the storm and on into the night.

Older, wiser and more in tune with what delights, we explored each other's body with reverence and awe taking no detail for granted and revelling in every sensation. Murmured words of endearment accompanied the pleasures of our bodies, binding our passion and restoring dreams.

A night of tangled sheets and scrambled satisfaction was followed by the gracious gift of forgiveness. Scott traced the silver of my scar with butterfly kisses, easing the ache for the lost chance of motherhood, and the torment of betraying him.

Finally, finally I felt the weight of guilt and shame begin to seep from my soul and I felt whole, restored.

He left at first light, with a promise of later. The scent of him on my body, on the sheets and in this room prove the reality of the night we spent together. Without this lingering proof, I'd struggle to believe it anything but a dream. The magnitude of its impact on me already an astonishing truth.

I trail my fingers over the contours of my naked body, enjoy the fluttering sensations, celebrate the knowledge his hands were there only hours ago. Anticipate the prospect of his return, to my bed, to my life, if only for the next few days.

The thud of the front door being closed brings me back to the reality of the present. I open my eyes.

Pauletta.

I raise my head and take in the state of the room. Scott has laid my sundress over the chaise, the scant slither of my lace panties atop it. Pillows are scattered where they were tossed, and my satin nightdress hangs unworn on the corner of my dressing room door.

I push my feet to the floor, and grimace at the pain in my ankle as I hobble to retrieve my nightdress. I slip it over my head, the cool fabric on my sensitised skin a reminder of the night passion. I skim my panties into the laundry basket. Scoop up the pillows and place them back on the bed. I potter round the room checking for any tell-tale signs that might alert Pauletta to Scott spending the night in this room. Climbing back under the sheet, I smooth it over me as I sit propped up.

Again, I look around the bedroom, all is in its place, there is no visual trace of Scott, but his presence lingers. His scent clings to me, binding like a security blanket round a babe. I reach for the perfume on my bedside table and reluctantly fill the air with one defiant blast from the decorative decanter.

A sharp knock on the door, and Pauletta appears with my breakfast tray in her hands, fresh orange juice and toast. She has a newspaper tucked under her arm and her utility belt is strapped on ready for action.

'Good morning, madam. Is glorious morning with no more storm.' She places my breakfast tray on the bedside table.

'Good morning, Pauletta. Thank you.'

She smiles and tilts her head to one side. 'You are welcome.'

'You sound very happy this morning, Pauletta.'

'Is a very beautiful day, madam.' She walks over to the large, bay windows and draws back the full-length curtains, and the radiance of the day floods in.

'Yes, Pauletta, it is.' I smile, getting more than a customary "Good morning" from Pauletta lifts my spirits further. 'It feels like the kind of day anything is possible.'

She nods. 'Yes, but will not last.' She places the folded newspaper on my lap, and taps the photo of a young woman looking up at me from the tabloid. 'Is very beautiful, yes?'

I lift the paper to get a closer look. Bright eyes and a brighter smile beam back at me, soft golden hair frames a heart-shaped face with a pixie nose and delicate lips. Her long, slender neck hints at long slender limbs and an agile body.

I raise my eyes to Pauletta. 'Yes, she is very beautiful, Pauletta.' I look again at the image. 'I don't recognise her. Should I know her?'

Pauletta shrugs. 'Is not for me to say.' She turns and leaves the room.

I take a sip of juice and lift the tray onto my lap. As usual, she has lavishly buttered the well-done toast, one of her little tricks to help me gain weight. I nibble the toast – know I'm expected to eat all of it.

I absently turn the paper over to read about the mystery beauty Pauletta is keen for me to know. A much smaller grainier photo is further down the page.

Lola-May Gets Back in the Saddle

Everyone's favourite Texan beauty, Lola-May Macaulay, surprises us all by striding out with a new man. Only weeks ago, a heart-broken Lola-May left the sprawling ranch she shared with fiancé, Denver Blake.

It has long been rumoured, that Denver is unhappy with the high-profile nature of Lola-May's modelling career. And now, with her recent network appearances and heightened media attention, Lola-May is poised to land her first prime-time, talk-show slot.

Earlier this week, she was spotted striding across the tarmac at LA International Airport, with none other than celebrated artist, Scott Scobie. Their destination a well-guarded secret. Has Lola-May managed to snare one of California's most eligible bachelors? Or is this

a rouse to spur home-lovin' cowboy, Denver,
to loosen the reins and let Lola-May ride high
in the ratings?

I push the tray from my lap. Trembling, my stomach revolts, and I only just make it to the bathroom before the little amount of toast I've eaten, makes a return. Clutching my chest with one hand, I hold my hair out of the line of fire with the other until the wave after wave of convulsions end.

Still gasping, I fill a glass with water and rinse away the foul taste. I drop to the marble floor, rest my forehead on the washbasin pedestal, and let the stark white column cool me. Taking sharp, shallow breaths, I close my eyes to try and dispel the dizzying, nauseous feeling in the pit of my gut.

The cold floor turns my trembles to uncontrollable shakes. I pull myself up. The glass rattles against my teeth as I take another sip of water. I pull my robe around me and hobble back to my bed.

I sit stoic, upright, clutching my stomach, not sure if holding my pain in diminishes its validity, but knowing I must. My face is set, emotionless.

Terry's pitiful pining at the door snaps me from my paralysis, as ever, he's able to sense my distress. My constant companion in times of need. Mindlessly I let him in. He clambers up beside me on the bed, buries his head into the crook of my neck and nuzzles. I scrunch the fur about his neck. I need this unconditional love, the warmth and compassion – a physical connection with a living being to thaw the halo of ice circling around my heart.

The tears will not come.

The pain will not go.

The pain never goes.

I'm no better able to deal with the consequence of my actions as I was as a teenager. I've learned nothing. Scott will always be my Achilles heel.

I thought I could handle it, the voice on his mobile, the *friend* he brought along... I led him to my bed knowing these things, accepting them. But in the radiant light of day where nothing can hide, the stark truth is, he isn't mine.

I look at the beautiful young woman beaming up from the paper. She has a dance of mischief in her eyes, her smile promises a-devil-may-care attitude to life. By the tilt of her chin, I can tell she's eager to share her enjoyment of life with those who care to tag along. There is no malice, her face is glowing with innocent delight.

Her voice, when she answered Scott's mobile, was easy-going. Her attitude, helpful. She didn't betray any signs of jealousy or threat that another woman was phoning him. Ridiculously, I think I like her.

Last night was a glimpse into what my life could have held, holding up a mirror to my beautiful loveless life.

I told Scott how lucky I am to have good people around me. Mum and Dad, Miles – my prodigy, Pauletta – gate-keeper and protector of my privacy, the almost impeccable Mrs Price, and of course the Keep-a-Key kids. All of them add depth to my life, and collectively make my life worthwhile.

But what I didn't tell him is the truth of how I've longed for his presence in my life. How I've hungered for the passion and tenderness of his embrace. How I've thirsted for his words of devotion. How I've yearned for his beautiful eyes to hold mine and share the invincible bond we once shared. There is no one else who could ever hold that place in my life. The one who my life revolves around and is devoted to, can only be Scott.

Her usual sharp knock at the door, announces Pauletta. Terry darts under the covers.

She steps into the room and looks at the scarcely touched breakfast. She frowns, we both know she is aware Terry has wangled his way into my bed. We both know today is not the day to challenge it. She plants her hands on her hips resting on her utility belt. 'Is not to your liking?'

I try to smile a reassuring smile, but am betrayed by a single tear sliding down the side of my nose. 'Sorry, Pauletta, I'm not very hungry this morning.'

She watches me as she tidies the tray. 'Is not good to miss breakfast.'

'Maybe later.' I pass her the newspaper. 'Thank you… for the warning.'

'Is my job to take care of you, is no trouble, madam.'

'But still…' I cover my face with my hands. The deluge of tears I would have greatly appreciated minutes ago, choose now. 'I'm sorry…' I blubber.

Pauletta thrusts a few tissues into my hand. I hear the tray being put down, and her bony hands gently ease my hands from my face. She looks earnestly into my eyes. 'Is better knowing now, madam.'

'Yes,' I whisper, my throat aching with control. 'Better knowing now.' She nods. 'Is not too late for your heart.'

I cover my face again with my hands as my body convulses with a fresh flood of tears. 'Pauletta,' I splutter – how could she know? 'It was too late the moment I first saw him.' I crumple into a ball, sink beneath the sheet, and embrace the pain.

'I bring Miles.'

And Again

They are sharing a hotel bedroom

The gentle flurry of knocks on the bedroom door can only belong to Miles.

I scrub my hands over my face, push my hair back, dig my elbows back and push myself up into a semi-sitting position. The fitful snatches of sleep I've managed, hardly worth their wasted minutes. 'Come in,' I muster.

The door swishes open, Terry bounds off the bed and Miles dips to stroke his head. 'Pauletta said it was important.' He scans me with eyes that read me well. 'You look dreadful.'

'Thanks.'

Miles closes the door with a soft click, makes his way over to the bed and perches on the edge. 'She showed me the newspaper article.'

I shrug. 'I knew he'd brought a friend with him, she answered his mobile when I called.'

'Ouch!'

'Yep, ouch. She sounds very, sweet.' I nod. 'Sweet.'

Miles nods. 'I take it, you were hoping to—'

'Miles, give it a rest, it's complicated, yeah? Complicated and messy.' I look away from him, he reads me too well.

'So, you've had a lucky escape.'

I turn to him with eyes I know are swollen from my earlier tears. 'I'll never escape Scott Scobie. He's part of who I am. So, no Miles, I haven't had a lucky escape.'

Miles stands and walks over to the large bay window. He looks out towards the front gardens, his hands clasped behind his back. 'He's a fortunate man.' He turns back to me. 'To have captured and kept your heart for all these years.'

'And I'm the fool for letting him.' I snort at my own simplicity.

Miles ambles back to me, and sits down on my bed. He pushes my hair aside and plants a kiss on my head. 'You had Christie. You knew what your love had created, you're no fool, Madeline De-Muir. You're just a soppy old romantic.'

'Same thing,' I retort.

'I'll let that pass, for now. But how do you know he doesn't feel the same?'

'He's a man whose had women throwing themselves at him for years, Miles! Obviously, he's well and truly over me.'

Miles places his hands together as if to pray. 'And you my child, have lived a life of celibacy?'

'More than most.'

'You know, I had Scott checked out when he turned up demanding to meet Christie. And you also know, regardless of his high-profile socialising, his reputation is sound.'

'That doesn't mean he hasn't had a string of well satisfied lovers!' I snap.

Miles shakes his head. 'From what I hear, it does. He's far more discerning than you're giving him credit for.'

'Whatever you think, Miles. But I need to steer clear, and just leave Scott and Christie to forge their own relationship without me. I should never have let him paint me – it was too personal.'

'And by too personal, you mean?'

'I mean, I'm not going to talk about it, okay?'

Now Miles scrubs his face with his hands. 'Oh, Maddie! Are things not tricky enough?'

'Yes, they are! So, leave it, yeah. I already feel like a prize fool, I don't need you rubbing it in.'

Miles gives me an awkward hug. 'What do you want me to do?'

I shrug beneath the comfort of his compassion. 'I don't know, Miles. He'll be going back home in a couple of days, and I don't want to make it any more awkward than it already is with Christie… I'm going to have to have a mystery illness until he leaves.' A mystery illness called a broken heart.

A sharp knock at the door is followed by Pauletta flying into the room. 'Is that man,' she whispers, eyes wide, and face filled with concern. 'He waiting in lounge. I tell him you are in-disposition.' She nods resolutely.

Miles looks heavenward. 'Indisposed, Pauletta.'

'Is what I said. In-disposition.'

Miles looks at me, then back to Pauletta. 'As you can see, Miss De-Muir is unwell, and unable to see anybody today.'

Pauletta nods and taps the side of her nose. 'I tell him.'

'Pauletta,' says Miles firmly. '*Nicely*. Say it nicely.'

Pauletta stands up as straight as she can. 'I do my best, but no promise with that man.' As she leaves the room, she takes on the airs of a Grand Duchess protecting a beloved niece.

I shake my head. 'This, is not going to end well,' I say with feeling. I give Miles a gentle nudge. 'Come on, Miles, let me out. I'm going to have to sort this myself.'

He places a hand on my shoulder. 'Oh, no. Not a chance.'

'Miles! Come on, Pauletta's going to be as tactful as a shovel in surgery.'

'Then I will go. You cannot see Scott looking like that, you have an image to maintain.' Miles stands and strides over to the door.

I snort. 'Scott isn't fooled by my image.'

I hear a door being slammed downstairs and raise my eyebrows at Miles. 'What did I say?'

'Is not possible, Mr Scobie!' roars Pauletta. 'Madam is in-disposition.'

'Yeah, well, why is there a kick-ass car in the driveway? It isn't hers, that's for sure,' hollers Scott.

'Is not my place to say.'

'But you darn well know who it belongs to.'

'Is a very, very, dear friend. Is not my place to say his name,' snaps Pauletta. 'I happy to stand here all day. Save me scrubbing floor after all you men stomping through!'

I hold my head in one hand and point at the door with the other. 'Go, sort it, Miles, before they start a war!'

Miles salutes and gives me a lopsided grin. 'At your service.' He steps out of my bedroom, Terry at his heel. 'Can I be of assistance?' he asks in an overly helpful way.

'Well, I should of guessed!' snarls Scott.

'Is big problem, Mr Hepworth. Mr Scobie, he not listen.'

'I think Miss De-Muir would like one of your lovely pots of tea, Pauletta. Now, Mr Scobie,' booms Miles in a jovial manor. 'I think it's about time you and I had a man-to-man talk.'

'Darn right it is!'

I sink under the sheet as I hear the lounge door click firmly shut.

The pot of tea Pauletta brought remains untouched and is now stone cold. I haven't heard a peep from downstairs, and I'm more than a little disappointed Pauletta hasn't been back to fill me in on what's going on! No doubt she is reluctant to leave her vantage point for fear of missing something spectacular.

Honestly, and I'm gasping for a drink now.

I patter painfully to the bathroom, and run myself a bath. I fill the tumbler from the cabinet with cold water, and gulp it down. I eye up the basket of bath bombs. Can I be bothered? In turn, I lift each, breathe in its scent, then move on to the next. Oooo... Honey I bathed the kids, my fav Lush product of all time! I toss the bath bomb in, and watch it fizz, turning the water an unappealing pee colour – can't have everything.

I scrunch my hair into a topknot, slip off my nightdress and step into the bath, easing myself in. Lying back, I wallow as I'm engulfed in a velvety hug. The sweet aroma filling my head relaxes and comforts me. As the water laps my nape, drawing tendrils of hair loose from my bun, I try to banish the memories of Scott's lovemaking.

The way his hands roamed reverently over my body. The heat of his breath on my neck, the way he nuzzled my ears electrifying my senses, sending pulsing pleasures through every avenue of my body.

The way he cupped my face, ran his fingers to the back of my head, then through the length of my hair letting it cascade to my shoulders… And again…

And again.

I let out a groan. Will I ever be free of that man? Do I even want to be?

I start my morning exercises for my recovering ankle. First pressing the ball of my foot against the end of the bath, adding more pressure, then release… And repeat… And repeat… Again, and again. Next rotations, the water both supporting and adding resistance to my movements. Over and over, and the other way. And finally, the most painful of all, drawing my toes upwards, pushing my heel down and earning a grunt of pain. I manage the 8 out of 10 I'm prescribed to do.

Closing my eyes, I relax. The small achievement of *almost* completing my exercises, a minor victory in a day already feeling like a lost battle.

I hear the sharp knocking on the bedroom door alerting me to Pauletta's presence.

'Madam, madam!' She repeats her knocking on my en-suite door. 'Is development.'

'Is it a fresh pot of tea?' I ask dryly.

'Is not fresh pot of tea! Is more important!' she huffs. 'Like Elvis, he is leaving the building!'

'Mr Scobie is leaving?'

'Is what I said!'

I sit up in the tub, rivulets of water trickle down my body. I'm not sure if the sudden rash of goosebumps is caused by the cooling air, or the fear of never seeing Scott again. To never see him again. I look at the stack of bath bombs, the bottles of potions and the fragrant lotions – all dedicated to my dedication of self-worth. The alure of being worthy to exist in a world deserving of a better version of me.

I press my fingers briefly to my lips. My churning stomach in need of some settling. 'Thank you, Pauletta.'

'I bring more tea now, even though you not kind enough to drink it. And warning to you, they are best of friend now. I do not know what is in possession of Mr Hepworth.'

I hear the door slam, thankful to be left alone. I resist the compelling urge to sink back into the water, and instead pull the plug to force me out.

I buff my skin dry, then slather my body with soothing moisturiser. I wrap up in my dressing gown and start my morning face care routine; a splash of micellar water onto a cotton ball and a gentle swipe all over my face; a dab of moisturiser with sunscreen: done.

And since lover boy has left, no need for perfectly invisible makeup. I hobble into my dressing room, and my eyes instantly fall onto my crutches propped up next to my foam boot – later, much later, Scott went outside to retrieve them, along with his painting gear, from the summerhouse.

One night, and already he is woven into my life, again.

I select comfort clothing and dress, the final thing to go on, the foam boot. I carry the crutches and put them by the bedroom door. I sit on the chaise looking absently out at my beautiful garden – another beautiful day in my seemingly beautiful life.

If only I had a steaming pot of tea, my life would be deemed perfect!

A flurry of knocks on the door can only be Miles – so no tea then – I plaster on as bright a smile as I can muster.

Miles beams and saunters over to me. 'Shuffle up, I have big news.'

'Pauletta already told me you and Scott are best buddies.' I narrow my eyes as I shuffle 'The word traitor, springs to mind.'

Miles laughs. 'Pauletta doesn't know the half of it!'

'Well, I'm waiting—'

Pauletta knocks on the door, entering with a tea tray. 'Is for two.' She puts the tray down on the side table by Miles. She too narrows her eyes at Miles. 'Is not my place to say,' she says, then leaves.

'Looks like you've upset Pauletta, Miles.'

'She'll get over it. So, about Sc—'

'Tea, Miles. I need a cup of tea.'

Miles does the honours, and passes me a hot sweet cup of tea. I take a sip. Bliss. 'Thank you, I needed that. So, about Scott?'

'Firstly, raging with jealousy, seemed to have got it into his head that we are an item—'

'Ridiculous.'

'Exactly. Secondly, he seems to think he's explained about his little friend sharing his hotel suite.'

'Well, he hasn't!'

'Thought not,' says Miles, in an altogether too jolly tone. He grins at me.

'So?' I hiss.

'It appears the lovely, Lola-May Macauley—'

'Spare me the jibes!'

'The lovely, Lola-May Macauley, is one of Scott's little prodigies. A homespun, Texan ranch girl and Rodeo star—'

'Please—' I drop my head into my hands, I can hear the glee in his voice.

'Scott spotted her in a local newssheet—'

'Newspaper, Miles, newspaper! You are not American!'

'Asked if he could do her portrait, and the girl's career exploded.'

I raise my head out of my hands and nod. 'So, yes, I can fully understand why they are sharing a hotel room—'

'Suite.'

'Whatever!'

'Seems our Lola-May has had a bumpy few weeks, and blagged Scott to sneak her out of LA.'

'And Scott was more than happy to oblige.' I nod. 'Well, she's welcome to him.'

Miles laughs. 'Oh, Maddie, this is priceless! Flames of jealousy melt the ice maiden.'

I dig my elbow into his arm. 'It isn't funny, Miles. I can't put myself through all of this with Scott. I just can't. It's a good thing I don't have to see him again before he goes home.'

Miles strokes his non-existent stubble on his chin. 'About that. It seems Lola-May is a huge fan of yours. Scott's bringing her round to meet you this afternoon.'

The Truth of Tears

She blows Scott a kiss

'I do not know what it is you are talking about, madam.'

'This is going to be hard enough, Pauletta,' I say, as sternly as I dare. 'So, please be nice.'

'Is not for me to say. Why that man—'

'*Mr Scobie*, Pauletta.'

'Yes, that Mr Scobie, why he is bringing to this house pretty lady to make you sad.'

'It isn't going to make me sad, she is a long-standing fan—'

Pauletta tuts. 'Is only just out of pram.'

I let her jibe pass unchallenged. 'We are going to share a lovely afternoon tea, probably out on the terrace. And all I'm asking, is that you be on your best behaviour.'

Pauletta wobbles her head from side to side. 'Yes, and Ps and Qs and like a pie!'

'Nice as pie! Yes. Now I'm going to be waiting in the snug. When they arrive just show them into the lounge, and let me know.'

'Yes, madam.'

I hobble through to the snug. Leaving my crutches upstairs might have been a mistake, but I'm not going up for them now. I close the door behind me and sink into the comfort of my threadbare sofa.

I close my eyes and gently run my fingers over them, at least they've lost their puffiness. And the layer of almost invisible makeup has given me a confidence boost – I've gone for natural rather than diva.

And still my stomach is churning! Miles has assured me everything is very above-board and there is nothing but a professional relationship between Scott and Lola-May, but until I see them together…

There are bound to be tell-tale signs if there is something going on between them. And if I don't spot them, Pauletta will ferret them out.

I'd thought my life would be on an even keel once everything was out in the open, how wrong could I be? Scott turning up has turned me inside out, and set back my twenty-five years of recovery.

A sharp knock, and Pauletta appears before me, all fake smiles and even faker humility. 'Madam,' she says, bobbing respectfully. 'I have shown Mr Scobie into the lounge.'

'Thank you, Pauletta. And Miss Macauley?'

'No, madam, is just Mr Scobie.' She shrugs. 'Is not for me to say.'

I roll my eyes. 'But?' I question.

'Is not for me to say.' She bobs her way out of the snug looking more than smug.

I groan and get to my feet, hobble out of the room, cross the hall and on into the lounge.

As I enter, Scott stops pacing. 'Sorry, Maddie.' He raises both hands in mock surrender. 'It was just too much for her to face, meeting you here.' He shakes his head.

'And hello to you too, Scott,' I say pleasantly, and perch on the sofa.

He strides across to me, scarcely brushing my cheek with a kiss. 'Hello, Maddie. I'm sorry. To say I'm hacked off, isn't enough, yeah? Miles was more than accommodating inviting Lola-May here to meet you.' – So, it was Miles's idea, the sneak – 'She's kind of overwhelmed with all this English afternoon tea thing you got going on.'

I try to disguise the relief I'm feeling. 'I suppose it can be a facing if you aren't used to it.'

'Yeah, I kind of thought she had a bit more grit, having been a rodeo gal, and all that.'

I shrug magnanimously. 'Different sort of grit.' The problem is, if I don't get to see them together, I'll never know, and that is going to niggle, bigtime. I sigh. 'So, what's the plan then? Do we just give it up, or shall I meet her at your hotel?'

Scott drags his hand through his hair and raises his brows. 'Would you? She'd be blown away.'

'Of course.' I smile. 'It would get me out from under Pauletta's feet. She's having a bit of a strop.'

He rubs his hands together, scoops me off the sofa and plants a kiss on my lips. 'You're amazing! Well let's get a move on, yeah?'

'One slight problem, I could do with my crutches, they're still upstairs,' I say, with my toes hardly touching the ground.

'Bedroom?'

I nod. 'Yes.'

'I'll go grab them.' He pops me back on the sofa, strides from the room, and I hear him bounding up the stairs.

Pauletta appears in the doorway, her eyes narrowed. 'Mr Scobie, he is upstairs?'

'He's just popped up to get my crutches. We are meeting Miss Macauley at Scott's hotel.'

Pauletta's eyes remain narrowed, and she nods slowly. 'And Mr Scobie, he knows where is your bedroom?' She shrugs. 'Is not my place to say.' She turns on her squeaky heels and leaves, almost colliding with Scott in the doorway.

I close my eyes and thank my lucky stars she didn't take it upon herself to interrogate him. I smooth my fingers over my forehead to erase the frown lines, and open my eyes. I hope my smile looks genuine to Scott.

He passes the crutches to me. 'Here you go.' Scott offers his hand to help me up.

'Thanks. Lead the way.' I follow him out to his car, and prop the crutches just inside.

Scott clamps his hands around my waist and begins to lift me. Awareness sweeps through me. He stops midway, leans toward me, and nuzzles my neck. 'I've been tempted to do that every time,' he murmurs into my ear.

The heat of his breath sends a flurry of sensations cascading through me. I manage to stop the sigh desperate for release, but tilt my chin up to savour the moment. Out of the corner of my eye, I notice the silhouette of Pauletta in the window. I straighten and feel for the seat behind me. 'Pauletta's watching,' I mutter.

Scott shrugs. 'She don't like me much.'

'She doesn't like very many people!'

Scott gets in and takes his time manoeuvring the car into the oncoming traffic. 'She likes Miles well enough.' Scott grins at me. 'He explained, by the way, about you kinda being his replacement mom.'

Really? I clutch my mouth to stop myself spurting out my disbelief. 'I prefer the term "mentor".' I'll kill him, when I get my hands on him – but I try disguising my incredulity. 'But this is the reason Pauletta loves Miles, she only sees him as he was.'

'And how was that?'

I pull a face, not sure I'm ready to tell Scott how the pair of them are woven into my heart. 'Miles was still a student when Pauletta joined me. At first, she was a bit in awe of me, but with Miles, he soon had her eating out of his hand. He managed to relax her into thinking I wasn't quite capable of coping when he was away at university, and gave her the unofficial job of looking out for me.'

'Explains a good deal.'

'But at times, infuriating. So, what about Lola-May?' I say, eager to change the subject. 'She's *your* prodigy, so Miles says.'

'Whoa, hardly that!' He grins and scrubs his chin with his hand. 'I'd like to take the credit, but no. She was raised on a ranch, caught the rodeo bug, and made her name on the circuit. I'd seen a rodeo flyer, she was the main attraction and, yeah, it was crazy – I just happened upon her not quite by chance being tossed to the ground, and almost trampled. She got herself up, dusted herself down and strolled over and said, "Howdy, cowboy.", the biggest smile you ever did see.'

'And the rest is history?' I prompt.

'She kind of disarms everybody she meets. I don't know how she does it, but she does, and that's why I had to have her.'

'You had to have her?'

'In my gallery, I had to capture her. I couldn't resist. She really wasn't up for it at first. As for Denver—'

'Her boyfriend?'

'Fiancé, he insisted on chaperoning her every-where.'

'I wonder why.'

'Come on, Maddie, I'm not like that.'

'But Denver didn't know.'

'Well, he sure as hell does now!'

I laugh, can't help myself.

'It isn't a laughing matter, Maddie! The newssheets are making a deal out of no deal at all.' The frustration is clear in Scott's tone. 'And Denver, he's just not cut out for all this media stuff.'

'I can't imagine him being very happy about the two of you hot footing it to the UK.'

There's a look of exasperation on his face. 'Maddie, it was his idea! That's why Lola-May was so upset, she thought he was breaking up with her. In truth, he just wanted a break from the media circus! I've been playing relationship coach for the last two weeks, trying to patch things up between them.'

A burst of awareness is dashing through my body, re-igniting the smouldering bonfires of passion and understanding from last night. And the dawning realisation that one stolen night, is not going to be enough to satisfy the years of loss.

Loss of the young man buoyed up with big plans and big ideas.

Loss of a soulmate to navigate the years.

Loss of a champion to banish my fears.

Instinctively, my hand reaches out to Scott, is met halfway by his. 'Aw, Maddie, it's good to have you back.'

Anticipation and fear gallop through me, kicking up clods of complications in their wake. But for this moment, I must be satisfied. It might be the only moment I have. 'It's good to be back.'

He squeezes my hand and lets go again to hold the wheel. I draw my hand away, reluctant to suffer this minor rejection, painfully exposing how my fragile composure is easily boosted or bashed by Scott's actions.

'I think I should of called ahead to Lola-May.' He manoeuvres his car into a corner spot of the hotel car park. 'Jeez, not that she's bothered to go beyond the gardens!'

I look out, to where a health spa beckons. The courtyard, with its splendid three-tier fountain gives the hotel an air of grandeur, while the formal gardens cocooned by furtive woodland offer seclusion for lovers seeking privacy, or perhaps children playing hide and seek.

My eyes dart back to Scott. 'Have you offered to take her out and about, show her the sights?'

Scott looks awkward as he gets out of the car. He takes his time coming round to opening my door and lifting me down. No neck nuzzling this time, I notice.

'You know how busy it's been, with Christie, and all.' He passes me my crutches. 'I've kind of left her to stew, hoped she'd get bored and break the deadlock with Denver.'

'And?'

'It's not going to plan.'

I roll my eyes. 'Men,' I mutter under my breath. I force myself into mother-hen mode, try to quash the few remaining embers of jealousy, and determine to get Lola-May's love life back on track. 'Come on, let's see if I can talk some sense into the girl.'

'Good luck with that, she's as bull-headed as a bronco.'

I hobble into reception and Scott leads the way to the old-fashioned, iron-gated lift. He draws back both the gates, and I step into the panelled, dark-wood interior. Scott closes us in and twists the aged dial round to signal the second floor. We chug in elegant fashion to our destination.

Despite the play on tradition, Scott produces a keycard and swipes us into his suite.

'Lola-May, I'm back!' Scott sings out.

I can just about make out slender feet drooping over the arm of a sofa, and a swathe of golden locks tumbling over the opposite end. A hand appears and swishes, as if to ward us away.

'Oh, Denver, honey, I'm missing ya so much. I can't wait to get home…'

Scott plants his arms across his chest and lets out a piercing whistle.

Lola-May's head pops up, and she glares at Scott. Her gaze shifts to me. 'Got to go, hun.' She leaps up, tosses her mobile on the couch and bounds towards me like an exuberant puppy, all eyes and floppy hair. Faded jeans and a vest top do little to diminish the radiance of her lean, bronzed, wholesome body. 'Whoa, it's really you!'

Scott unfolds his arms and gestures towards Lola-May. 'Maddie, I'd like to introduce you to Lola-May. I'd like to say she's usually less excitable, but I'd be lying. Lola-May, the impeccable, Miss Madeline De-Muir.'

I smile and stretch out my hand. 'Call me Maddie. Very pleased to meet you, Lola-May. Scott has been singing your praises all the way here.'

She gives my hand a thorough shake. 'Aw, aren't you so kind, coming all this way ta meet me. I'm just so…' She fans her face with both her hands. 'I can't even say it,' she squeals.

I laugh out loud at her genuine delight. 'That's very sweet of you to say.'

'Come and sit over here. Are you staying for tea? Afternoon tea, English tea… Whatever you guys call it.'

I glance at Scott. 'If that's an invitation, then yes, I'd love to join you.'

She flaps her arms at him. 'Scott, come on, order us something.'

Lola-May guides me to the plush sofa and pats the seat. 'You get an awesome view of the garden from here. Why, Maddie, I'm clean blown away! I musta watched *An English Rose* over a hundred times!'

'You are very generous.' I try to hide the swathes of mixed emotions squabbling for attention as I remember all the truths exposed within me while filming.

Lola-May's hand flutters to her chest, and she looks all teary-eyed. 'The way you took hold of Sienna's chubby little hand…' She swallows, shakes her head and fans her face with her hand. 'You lead her away, without looking back… It broke my heart. And the little mite kept looking over her shoulder.' Lola-May clasps her hand over her mouth.

I remember the hours it took to film those closing few scenes. The young child only had eyes for her mum and kept turning to look at her – Tim had to strategically position the young woman so he could capture Sienna's tear-filled eyes. 'I felt honoured to play Rose, it was a very grown-up script, and challenging.' In oh so many ways. 'And the little girl who played Sienna was a joy.'

'And your single tear, after all you'd overcome…'

I swallow back my own tears now, remember the inspiration for that single tear – if people had known – the thought of my own little girl, who didn't even know my face. The constant reminder, little Sienna always looking for her mommy, her mommy always there, waiting. My little girl, the little girl who I'd abandoned. 'Yes,' I breathe.

Lola-May composes herself. 'It was your elegance and composure. The way you held yourself... I spent hours practicing walking like Rose, like you, I mean! My mama was demented with me!'

'Thank you. I always hoped the character of Rose would be a strong, yet elegant role model for—'

'Oh, she sure was for me! I was torn between being a proper lady an' a rodeo star! At the ranch it was all pitching out the stables an' herding cattle by day, and *An English Rose* by night!'

'And you didn't need to choose, you got to be both.' I lost my chance at motherhood, threw it away.

'I sure do! All cos I practiced all that elegant walking!' Lola-May looks out at the gardens. 'I can't get over how green it is, an 'all.'

I nod. 'It is a lovely view,' I agree. I glance at Scott, who's on the hotel phone, I assume ordering afternoon tea. 'So, Lola-May, Scott tells me you're a rodeo rider, how on earth did you two manage to cross paths?'

Lola-May looks almost coy and cunning at the same time. She has a unique blend of innocence, sass and spark. Just sitting here talking to her makes me feel energised. The well needed ego boost was balanced out by the remembrance of playing Rose – the time I eventually grew up.

'Well, it's kinda funny story! I literally fell outa my saddle and landed yards from his feet. And I thought, he looks kinda friendly, I'll amble over and make small talk to bolster my battered ego and ass.' She laughs and shakes her mane of hair. 'Turns outa be the best career move ever! Denver, my fiancé has been reeling ever since.'

'Is he jealous of Scott?' I ask in a hushed voice.

'Of Scott? No!' She bats her hand in his direction. 'They get on fine enough. He just likes me home, like a good old country girl.'

Again, I nod. 'But what do you want, Lola-May? Scott tells me you have a good chance at a prime-time talk show slot.'

'Yeah.' She rolls her eyes. 'And Denver isn't too keen. But I reckon, I can do a couple of years, bank the money, and we'll be set up. No mortgage on the ranch, and I'll still be young enough to raise a family.'

'Sounds like a solid plan to me,' I say.

'I think so, but Denver wants to be the big man bringing in the bucks, not relying on my money.'

'I think you need to talk it through. You have just as much a right to want your own career, as Denver.'

'Yeah, but I'm kinda happy just doing the round-up on the ranch. It's getting the money to pay off the mortgage, that's problematic.'

Scott sits in the armchair across from us. 'Afternoon tea will be delivered in due course,' he announces grandly.

Lola-May rolls her eyes. 'Scott's come over all lord of the manor since we've been here!' She tosses a cushion at him.

'Hey, cut it out! I'm trying to impress a lady, yeah?'

Lola-May fans her face with two hands. 'Why thank you, kind sir,' she purrs.

'Lola-May, I'm not referring to—'

The second cushion gets him square in the face.

'Can you see what I've got to deal with, Maddie?' He flips the cushion back to the sofa. 'I tell you, Denver is going to have one hell ova life with this one.'

Lola-May beams, her eyes flash and she blows Scott a kiss. 'You betcha, cowboy!'

Scott steeples his fingers under his chin. 'So, you guys back in the saddle?'

'Sure are.'

'Congratulations,' says Scott. 'Maybe I'll get some peace from your incessant bellyaching. I might even get me some time to do a bit of romancing of my own.'

His relaxed gaze settles on me, and I feel the familiar flutter of anticipation feather through me.

Lola-May's mobile pings. 'Pardon me, it might be Denver.' She picks it up and starts to scroll. 'You know, Scott, I don't think there's a woman alive who'd put up with your peculiarities.'

Scott's eyes smoulder as he continues to hold my gaze. He links his hands at the back of his head and smiles. 'Oh, I think you'd be surprised.'

Hankering for Change

The ruthless repercussions of regret

Scott stands patiently holding the car door open. Lola-May insisted on walking us back through the hotel, and called out "good afternoon" to anyone within five feet of us. I can see trying to keep a low profile with her is an impossible task.

She holds me back from the car, eager to keep me for longer. 'Well, thank you kindly for calling round to see me, Maddie. I can scarce believe it.'

'It was entirely my pleasure, and I hope we get chance to meet up again,' I reassure.

'Yeah, looks like I'm gonna to be spending my time between LA and the ranch for the foreseeable. Hey, maybe I could interview you!'

Ah, so that's why she's got me on my own. I glance at Scott, know he's eager to be on his way. I look back to her. 'I leave all my appointments to my PA; I'll pass on his details, though, to be honest, I'm trying to keep a low profile.'

She looks slightly embarrassed. 'Oh, yeah, Scott mentioned—'

I touch her hand. 'It's not a problem, and you know, things have a way of working themselves out.' I offer her an encouraging smile. 'And who knows what exciting things are in store for you and Denver.'

'Yeah, I guess.'

Scott pats the car door. 'Come on, didn't you just say you've been summoned by Miles?'

'Hardly summoned, he just needs to go over a few things, it will save him a journey if we can call in on our way back. Hope to see you soon, Lola-May.'

She pulls me into an awkward hug. 'Be gentle with our lovely Scott,' she whispers. 'He's kinda precious.' She pulls away slightly and looks me earnestly in the eyes.

I nod without breaking eye contact, matching her sincerity. 'I will. It's good to know how much he is cared for.'

Scott pats the car door again. I step away from Lola-May and wave. Scott gets us both into the car and we're off, waving at Lola-May as we go.

'Thanks for that, Maddie, appreciate it. She'll be phoning Denver, telling him all about meeting the famous Madeline De-Muir.'

'She's lovely, and it was my pleasure. I can see why she's such a draw for the networks.'

'Yeah, kind of homespun and sparky all rolled into one.'

I nod. 'I hope it works out for her.'

Scott drives through the country lanes as if he's lived here all his life. The satnav has been put to good use over the last few days. A ribbon of hearts is displayed on his screen from his hotel in Driftwood Sands, through to Little Wilton, then Clover Beck and Chippington and on up to my home in Ashwood, highlighting all Scott's favourite destinations.

'So, what's the story with Miles?'

I sigh, not looking forward to facing the meeting. 'Oh, you know Miles, likes to keep me on my toes.'

'Don't worry, I'll keep my nose out.'

'Sorry, it's not that. Tim Boswell has been in touch with him, trying to set up a meeting between us. You know Tim was my first director, I did all my best work with him. He put a lot into developing my acting, raising my game in the profession. I'm not sure I'm wanting to revisit that time of my life.'

'It could just be for a catch-up.'

'Or, more likely, he wants to use the publicity I've been getting to resurrect my career.'

Scott shrugs. 'You've got to make your own choices. Don't be pushed around.'

I half laugh. 'Oh, I intend to. It would be incredibly tempting, of course…'

'Yeah?' Scott sounds surprised.

'Yes, but then, there's always the dreaded spectre of failure. And I know how vain and fickle I am.'

Scott roars with laughter.

'It's not funny, Scott. Everybody used to love me, and now I'm this baby-abandoning, fame-fuelled fossil.'

'There isn't anything fossil like about you.'

'And if I *do* try to redeem myself in the eyes of the public, I'll be branded a hollow hypocrite, using Christie to get me the limelight.'

Scott stops the car in front of Rose Cottage, and turns to look at me, all the humour vanished. 'You used to be an icon, Maddie. Your ability to spellbind your audience was nothing short of genius. You might be a bit rusty, but talent like that don't just disappear.' He leans in close. 'Promise me, if you really want to do it, and a deal is on the table, promise me you'll do it. Don't let fear stop you.'

His eyes are storm clouds tinged with sunlight; their liquid promises, beg me to cup his face and do everything in my power to fulfil his expectations of me.

An unaccustomed plume of pride dares to poke fun at my self-doubt. I look away, fragments of fretfulness, flit through my body. 'Like you say, it could just be for a catch-up.'

'But if you get a chance, and it's what you want, the Maddie Harris I knew would jump through burning hoops…'

I turn to look at him. 'And the Maddie Harris you knew did jump through burning hoops, and we all got burnt. I can't risk that happening again.'

'It isn't going to happen again. I'm not going to let you disappear out of my life again, no sir.' He shrugs. 'Guess I've just got to keep telling you that, 'til you believe me.'

I smile, but splinters of frozen fear spear my heart, tiny daggers of despair. 'I know, we have Christie now.'

'Darn you, Maddie! If you think that, after last night—'

'Scott, please! Give me chance to work this out.'

The look he gives me could crush a colosseum. 'I thought you had. I thought we did, last night. Seems you're a better actress than even I gave you credit for.'

'Scott—'

The car door slams behind him and he strides round to lift me out. His hands hold me firm, his head is turned away from me and anger oozes from his every pore.

The stark fear of the situation becoming worse forces me to speak. 'Scott, that was unfair—'

'Unfair!' he splutters. 'Just leave it, yeah?' He thrusts my crutches at me, and stalks towards the front door.

'I don't want you to feel trapped,' I blurt out.

He spins round and stands stock-still, glaring. 'I don't feel trapped, Maddie, I feel used. Used, just to give your ego boost before your important meeting with Tim Boswell.'

'That's just not true, Scott. Don't be so ridiculous.'

'Yeah? Sounds to me like you've already decided to go along with whatever he proposes.'

I catch up to him on the driveway, place my hand tentatively on his arm. 'I've made no plans.' My voice is hushed, and hoarse with emotion. 'Yesterday, last night, it was a revelation to me. A view back through the looking glass to what my life could have been.'

He drops his head and briefly closes his eyes. 'It could still be. We can't go back, but I had guessed you'd want to spend time with me, independently of Christie—'

'I do, Scott… I'm just scared to blow it.' I shake my head. 'I'm not taking anything for granted, you have a life in LA, and mine is very much here.'

'And some bright spark invented air travel.'

'But not time travel.' I sigh.

Scott links his thumbs in his belt loops and scuffs his boot along the ground. 'I'm not asking for promises, Maddie, darn it, I can't make any myself. But can we at least be honest about what's going on here, cos for me, this feels seismic.'

I feel a tear snake down the side of my nose and swallow the poison, apple-sized lump in my throat. 'For me too,' I croak.

Scott catches my tear with his thumb.

'Do you two want to pitch a tent or are you coming inside any time soon?' huffs Miles from the doorway.'

I cough. 'On our way, Scott was just helping me, I had something in my eye.'

'On our way,' chimes Scott.

We enter Rose Cottage together. Miles points us in the direction of the front room, then turns to Scott. 'Christie's up in her studio, would you see if she's planning on joining us, Scott?'

'Sure thing. She isn't going to bellyache at me for going up there, is she?'

'No, she wanted me to let her know when you arrived.'

Scott strides from the room. 'I'll remind her not to shoot the messenger.'

I smile at Miles as I settle down on the sofa. 'So, run it by me again, Miles. What exactly did Tim say?'

'First, what exactly was all that about out there?'

'I told you; I had something in my eye.'

'Nice try. I know you better than that. So, is there still trouble in paradise? I thought I straightened it all out this morning.'

I drop my head and give it a shake before looking back at Miles. 'I'm having a wobble. I can't yet take it in that Scott is willing to forgive me, after what I did. Even less believe, that he's seriously contemplating us trying to get back together after all this time.'

'Well, it's a big ask. But let's face it, Maddie, there aren't many men brave enough, and fewer still you've bothered to deem worthy of your time.'

'I don't do dating, it's too scary. I can do the meet-and-greet, but not the getting-to-know-you. It's just too personal.'

Miles shrugs. 'You didn't seem to think it was too personal with Scott yesterday… And it sounded very up-close and personal.'

I drop my head into my hands and let out a deep sigh. 'But you don't understand, that was with Scott, and he's different…'

Miles slings a protective arm over my shoulder and gives me a bit of a squeeze. 'Exactly, he's different. So, what's the problem?'

I let out a heartfelt sigh. 'What am I going to do, Miles? What if I mess it all up again?'

'I can't tell you what to do. But I do know, if you miss this chance, you'll regret it for the rest of your life.'

I let his words sink in. I know the ruthless repercussions of regret. Missed moments. Missed memories. A life of existence rather than exuberance. Only ever touching the surface of reality, rather than diving in and feeling the whole spectrum of emotions, experiences and sensations.

I nod, and wonder who put that wise head on Miles's shoulders, and know instantly, he learned the hard way, like me.

I merely nod, as the clatter of feet on the staircase warn us Christie and Scott will soon be with us.

Christie enters the room first. 'Hi, Maddie, it's good to see you. Has Miles not offered you a drink?'

Miles stands up. 'I was waiting for you guys.' He turns to me. 'Maddie, could I get you a drink?'

I smile. 'Pease, a fruit juice would be lovely. Thank you.'

Miles takes out an imaginary notepad, and licks the lead of a pretend pencil. 'And would sir and madam also like a beverage?'

Christie rolls her eyes. 'Sir and madam are going for a stroll around the village.' She looks at me. 'I'm going to show off the beautiful English countryside.'

'I keep on telling her how awesome it is in the US, but she's not for giving it a chance.'

'Good for you, Christie,' I say. 'I always found it way too hot to be comfortable, when I was working there…'

I regret the words as soon as they are out. The look she gives me is somewhere between hurt and loathing. I can't blame her.

Scott clears his throat. 'Come on, Christie, lead the way.' They both head out towards the front door.

'Orange juice, okay, Maddie?'

'Yes, lovely, and a gag to stop me talking!'

Miles shakes his head, returns a moment later with two glasses of juice. 'So, I've been trying to get to the why and for what purpose, with Tim Boswell.'

'And?'

'And he's perfectly charming while repeating the same mantra, "I need to see Maddie.", so I'm no wiser.'

'It's no good, I'm going to have to meet with him.'

'I'll let him know. He's pushing for tomorrow or the day aft—'

'Tomorrow, I need to get it over and sorted. Scott is leaving the following day…' I shrug. 'I'm hoping he's going to ask me to tag along with Christie to wave him off.'

Miles lets out a deep sigh and stands, he walks over to the window and rests back on the sill. 'I'm not sure that's a good idea.' He scrubs his face with both his hands. 'In fact, as far as your public image is concerned, you absolutely should stay away.'

I flop back in the sofa, allow my head to loll and I groan out loud. I knew I'd have a battle on my hands. 'Miles, please, the last time we parted, I just left. Vanished. Gone. It was like I'd severed my own lifeline. I can't do that again.'

Miles crosses the room, and sits beside me. 'And I'm not asking you to. Just keep it out of the public realm.'

I manage to hold in the prickle of tears, dab under my nose and look away from Miles. I know he's right, but it doesn't change the fact that Scott is leaving, and I have no idea when I'll get to see him again. 'You're right,' I mutter.

He nods. 'I don't think Christie is planning an airport au revoir, she's still coming to terms with…'

I sigh. 'I get it, Miles, she wants to keep Scott under wraps. One less embarrassment to live down.'

He slings an arm around my shoulder. 'Let her do it in her own time. It's been a traumatic couple of months for all of us.'

'And more on the way,' I say shaking my head.

Miles lets out a belly laugh and his face lights up. 'Remember when you packed me off into the big wide world—'

'It was university! Not the big wide world, a campus with lots of students all having a whale of a time.' And it felt like an eternity of time to fill without you, but I smiled, and you never knew how I folded up my heart and put it away until you came back.

'And I was terrified, but off I went with your optimistic words ringing in my ears, "Miles, it's just a huge adventure, have a blast.". So, Maddie, this is just a huge adventure, have a blast!'

'I hate it when you quote me!'

He scrunches his nose and chuckles both my cheeks. 'I know, that's why I do it.'

The Gift

Be charming. I'm always charming

'I haven't done this for years.' Scott brushes his fingers through the grass, and idly plucks a blade, rolling it between his fingers.

I smile. 'I thought alfresco was all the rage in California.'

'I guess. This kinda feels better. A feast of bread an' cheese, washed down with a glass of wine as the sun sets on the horizon.'

'You mean the back of the house.'

'Poetic licence, trying to be romantic here, Maddie.'

I lie back on the picnic rug and stretch my arms above my head. The evening sun has lost its harsh glare, but still holds warmth. My eyes flutter closed and I breathe in the delicate fragrances of the summer garden. The distant hum of a lawnmower is almost drowned out by the frivolous banter of birds all vying for attention as dusk begins to settle. A sense of calm washes over me as I realise, I feel totally content and at ease with the place and time of right now.

I have no idea what my future holds, no guarantee of a happily-ever-after. I'm aware that my budding relationship with Scott is, in essence only just beginning. It feels like invisible, silk-like threads are reaching back through our lifetimes, binding us in ways unknown to humankind.

I'm surprised to discover those old connections still intact. They haven't been eroded and tarnished by time. Their strength, flexibility and subtlety have enabled them to weather the years of separation. And that alone gives me hope. Hope that Scott and I stand a chance at the fabled ending of love stories.

Scott lies by my side, catches my hand in his, our fingers loosely linked, held but not constrained. The rhythm of his breathing adds to my sense of wellbeing. Another moment in time, capturing bliss in a memory molecule.

Scott moves closer. 'This isn't what I had in mind.' He brushes a kiss on the top of my head.

I smile, know he's looking at me. 'What didn't you have in mind, the picnic?'

'No, not that.' He traces the outline of my face. 'When I flew back to the UK, all guns a blazing.' He lets out a sharp, ironic laugh. 'I wanted to wipe the floor with you, *not* lie on the floor with you!'

I open my eyes and prop myself up on my elbow turning to him. 'And I wouldn't have blamed you.' I look away from him. 'It's taken me all these years to come to terms with what I did.' I look into his eyes. 'I'm just thankful, that at least now, you and Christie have got to meet each other.'

Scott nods. 'Yeah, it's going to be interesting times ahead for us. I want to get her to the US. She'll be blown away!'

I can't help but smile at his enthusiasm, but I'm filled with the heavy burden of loss. 'I'm sure Christie will love it, have you introduced her to Lola-May?'

'I hadn't planned on the two of them becoming acquainted.'

'I suspect Christie would be more likely to want to visit if she knew there was somebody her own age to, you know…'

Scott grins and waggles his eyebrows. 'Are you trying to say I'm a boring old man?'

'Perish the thought.'

He moves even closer. 'Cos I'm in the mood to prove you wrong.'

I raise a brow. 'And I'm in the mood to let you.'

It could have been the dawn chorus that woke me, but more likely Scott drawing my body closer to his. Whatever it was, I'm glad I've a few minutes to savour the feeling of being held.

I wonder if the words spoken in passion have any real worth in daylight hours, or if these few days have been only a physical enactment of what could have been. Whatever, I'm happy to take what I can. Scott being here, willing to spend his time with me after what I did is mind-blowing. I deserve only the crumbs of his forgiveness but he's given me a banquet prepared for a goddess.

Regardless of what happens from here, I'll be forever grateful for this blissful time. I trail my hand over the stubble on his jaw, delighting in the coarse bristles sensitising my fingertips. I can't help but smile as he holds my palm to his lips and teases it with a slow kiss. 'Awake at last,' I murmur.

A long sigh escapes him. 'I've had the wildest dream about this gorgeous creature…' He opens his eyes. 'And here you are!'

'Tell me more.'

'I had her in my arms, held her, telling her all my secrets and dreams.'

'That was a very brave thing to do.' I brush a kiss on his neck.

'And she told me her secrets. I think she held back on her dreams.'

'Not as brave as you, Scott. Not yet anyway.'

He rubs his sleepy eyes and props himself up a little. His expression turns from playful to wistful. 'I wish we had more time, Maddie.'

I look into his eyes; deep pools of blue reflect my own feelings. 'When do you leave?'

He drags his hand through his hair and looks away briefly. 'Tomorrow.' He lifts my fingers to his lips and kisses each of them. 'And today, Christie has made plans for us, so…'

I hide my disappointment behind a tranquil smile. 'I understand, Scott. It's Christie you're here to see.' I turn away, I don't want to see the truth of it in his eyes.

'You could tag along,' he says hopefully.

'I think we both know that isn't going to happen. Like you said, you are leaving tomorrow. The two of you have a lot to sort out, and besides, Miles is setting up a meeting with Tim Boswell for today.'

Scott shrugs, pushes a tendril of hair behind my ear and cups my cheek. 'I kinda hoped we'd get some time together today,' he says solemnly.

'We could always have another teatime picnic.'

'Yeah, I was kind of wanting something a bit more classy – for our last night…'

I look away from him and shake my head. 'Don't say that, it sounds so final.'

He turns my face to his. 'Hey, this isn't over, Maddie. It never was.'

I try to swallow the lump in my throat but can't seem to shift it enough to speak. My tongue is clamped to the top of my mouth like a barnacle on a boat's bow. There's a tell-tale prickle in my nose accompanying my blurred vision as my tears form, ready to indulge me in self-pity.

The truth of his words and the sincerity of his embrace are too much. I pull away, swing my legs out of the bed and stand making no attempt to cover my nakedness. I manage to force back the tears as I raise my chin and look at Scott.

His face is filled with confusion, hurt. I offer a weak smile. 'No, Scott, it isn't over, I just don't know if I can last another twenty-four years before we see each other again.'

He lets out a wry laugh and holds out his hand to me. 'Come back to bed, Maddie. How'd you think I'm going to last twenty-four years when I can scarce last twenty-four hours!'

I nod. 'Fair point.' I glance at the bedside clock. 'Pauletta will be here soon.'

Scott makes a move. 'So, you want me gone, I understand.'

'Not gone, but dressed would be more – respect-ful.'

'Sure. You're right. I've got a little something in the car I wanted to get for you anyways.'

My croissant loses its appeal as Pauletta cruises past us, her pursed lips say more than any words – though in my head I hear, 'Is not for me to say.'

Scott brings his glass of orange juice to his lips to cover his grin. I'm tempted to kick him under the table as his eyes light up with juvenile merriment. 'Lovely morning, Pauletta, don't you think?' he chimes, bolstered by boyish bravado.

She turns on her squeaky heels. 'If you say so, *Mr Scobie*. For me is just one more day in life.' She narrows her eyes at me. 'Madam.' She goes into the kitchen, and from the clattering, I suspect she's taking her frustration out on the dishwasher.

'Thanks for that, Scott.'

He grins. 'My pleasure, I kind of want to take her back with me!'

I raise both my hands. 'Feel free, she'll be torturing me for months now!' My mobile pings, a message from Miles – Tim Boswell, 11:30 for an early lunch. Vegetarian, I'm sure Pauletta will rustle up something appropriate. BE CHARMING !!! – I let out a heartfelt sigh.

'Problems?'

'On so many levels.'

'Care to share?'

'One, Tim Boswell at 11:30.' I glance at the clock. 'Ninety minutes to prepare, and for what I don't know. Two, he's expecting an early lunch, so I'll have to grovel to Pauletta. And three, Miles has the cheek to tell me to be charming. I'm always charming!'

'Yes, dear.'

'Not funny.' But my smile gives me away.

Scott pushes back his chair and collects our plates. 'I'll go and cheer Pauletta up for you!'

I roll my eyes and leave him to it. I take the last few sips of juice and try to make out what Scott is saying to Pauletta. Whatever it is, it's unlikely to improve her mood.

The two of them return. 'Pauletta is just giving me a hand hope you don't mind.'

'Not a problem,' I say, as Pauletta scurries behind Scott, head bowed.

'Why don't you make yourself comfortable on the sofa?' says Scott as they leave the room.

I feel an overblown gesture coming on here, and surely Scott remembers how I hate fuss. Always a build-up before disappointment. Flowers from Miles have been the only extravagant gift I've received in years, they're usually to perk me up when I'm down, and certainly not an expression of love.

I hobble over to the sofa, though in truth my ankle is feeling very much better, I still feel a bit unsure without my crutches. I rearrange the cushions and pat them into place, the action confirming my level of unease. I hurriedly shuffle them out of place, don't want to allow the control gremlins back into my life, manipulating my mindset. Having Scott around has reinforced my need to trust my instincts rather than undermine and question everything I do or think.

Scott appears in the doorway. 'I kind of think you should close your eyes.'

'Really?' I cringe. This is going to be painfully excruciating; I just know it.

Scott beams. 'Yeah, really! You're going to love this.'

I try not to feel too sceptical. I close my eyes, the apprehension builds, sending tremors of unease through my belly. All the little memory spikes prodding my conscience, reminding me I don't deserve nice things to happen to me. Images of the times I pretended to be Auntie Maddie, playing with Christie, when I should have been her mum. My teenage screaming rants at my mum. The looks of disappointment in Dad's eyes.

The agony of keeping my eyes closed and letting those thoughts back in is hopefully hidden. I clasp my hands lightly together on my lap, conveying an image of poise and grace.

I doubt Scott and Pauletta will see through the pretence as they'll be busy with their own thoughts. I can hear the two of them shuffling about, but neither of them speaks. The sofa groans as Scott sits beside me, he places a hand on top of mine.

'Is ready now, madam,' says Pauletta, with a degree of pride.

Whatever it is I will be gracious, but I do hope it isn't going to be some ridiculously grand gift of little use and totally embarrassing. I open my eyes, and Pauletta elaborately swishes away a dustsheet.

And there it is.

Tears prick my eyes as I marvel at the exquisite image before me.

Scott squeezes my hand. 'What do you think?'

I cover my mouth, and draw back the tears as best I can. My cheeks hurt as I try to control my instincts. I shake my head. 'Too much,' I mutter. 'Too much.'

Pauletta tosses the sheet to the ground and steps away throwing her arms in the air. 'Madam! Is magnificent! How can you say this?'

I nod, turn to Scott, hook my arm around his neck and rest my forehead on his chin with my eyes closed. 'Pauletta's right,' I whisper. 'It's magnificent, but so humbling. So very humbling.'

Scott raises my chin. 'Look at me, Maddie. It's you, it's you how I see you,' he mutters.

I nod, unable to react fully to the abundance of love I'm being shown. 'Thank you.' I turn to look at the portrait Scott did of me only a couple of days ago, now framed and propped up on the sofa opposite me.

Pauletta is stood, hands resting on the top of her utility belt looking at my image. 'Is splendid, madam.' She turns and gestures towards Scott. 'Mr Scobie, he sees you with true eyes. Not movie star, real lady with kind soul.'

The sincerity of Pauletta's words cloak me in gratitude and I feel all warm and cherished. A tear forms and escapes from my eye. 'Thank you, Pauletta. That is very generous of you to say.'

She pulls a face and shrugs as she starts to leave the room. She stops and turns to me. 'But other things Mr Scobie sees of you with his true eyes, it is not for me to say.'

The Dream Team

I want you back

'Pauletta, he is a *very* important man.'

'Like Mr Scobie,' she all but sneers.

'Not at all like Mr Scobie, Mr Scobie is a *friend*.' Pauletta rolls her eyes. 'Mr Boswell is also a friend, but more importantly an influential film director—'

'So, vegetarian, and with respect. Bring to lounge, then in here to eat in dining room. Keep Terry from biting, I now understand.'

'Thank you.' I stroke my fingers over my brow in the hope of warding off any more frown lines.

'I go and prepare food now.' She squeaks off to the kitchen.

I scan the room. Scott's portrait of me is still propped up on the sofa opposite. I have no intention of trying to move it, I'm hoping it will be a distraction when Tim arrives. I wander across, and stack the cushions at either side of it. The rest of the room is immaculate, as usual.

Pauletta has standards, mine hover more towards the snug and its welcoming comfort.

I decided on wearing a long floaty aqua skirt with a crisp, white, cotton blouse. Neither formal nor casual – today is Pandora's Box, and frankly, anything could spring out.

I doubt Miles has any idea of the significance of this meeting. And certainly not Scott! I'm quite sure they'd both be trying to put it off if they did.

The saying, to have your cake and eat it, is understood by most, but nobody ever explains if you are allowed to just have a taste, then pass it on. Would anyone want a pre-nibbled muffin? Suppose you just have a little nibble, even the tiniest of tastes, is that muffin ruined, unworthy of someone else coming along and savouring every succulent morsel?

Tim is my muffin.

I only had the daintiest crumbs.

But even that was too rich for my palate.

It would have been, could have been a fairy-tale ending.

I trail my fingers over the painting. Tim will love it.

When I first moved to LA it made sense to stay with Tim and his wife, Tilly. Their two girls, Molly and Mia, at eleven and thirteen hooked on to me like a cool, older sister.

Their home was like nothing I'd ever seen, all gleaming, marble pillars, chandeliers and help in black and white uniforms. It was like stepping into another world.

Tilly was more than happy to have me in her home, she saw me as a role model for her girls to follow – had she known what Tim knew, I doubt that would have been the case – I soon became one of her girls. I was one of the family, and unofficial chaperone to Molly and Mia.

Much of the time I was working, a car arriving at five in the morning to whisk me and Tim off to set. Back in time for dinner – at Tilly's command. Exhausted, I'd sit at the table and eat the nutritionally balanced meal prepared for us all.

More often than not, either Molly or Mia would complain about the food. Tilly would nod towards me and say, "Maddie likes it.", and that would be the end of the conversation. We would each discuss the details of our day. For the girls it was the politics of the school social hierarchy; for Tilly, whatever charity lunch date she'd attended; while Tim and I talked unendingly about the details of the day's filming.

It was such a revelation to me how differently Tim viewed the day's events. While I was totally focused on my character, Tim was capable of holding and evolving every nuance of even the smallest of bit parts. He watched the actors intently, and drew from their own development, adding and building depth. Like a sculptor, chiselling away, day after day, consummating his craft, until the completion of his task makes known his talent and a masterpiece is revealed.

The chatter of the family, the easy and open way they bantered and questioned and listened, helped me to adapt to my lush surroundings. The expectation that I'd have food placed in front of me and tidied away after I'd eaten, know my worn clothes would vanish and reappear hanging immaculately in my closet, assume a car would arrive to take me wherever I needed to go – these things became as natural as breathing.

If anything, it was adjusting to a new kind of family life I found challenging. I'd never had the closed family unit the Boswells had. My parents had invited all and everyone into their home, treated them as family, often to the exclusion of me.

Not Tim and Tilly. Like in the film, *Meet the Fockers*, there was a circle and you were either in, or out. I was most definitely in; it was a circle of five. It was not acceptable for the help to be privy to our business. If there was an issue, Tilly resolved it, she may have looked like a laid-back Californian mom, but she ruled her family like a Mother Superior.

Tilly was awesome. Tim's life, all our lives, ran as syrup off a heated spoon – smooth, sweet and satisfying. We were invincible, unbreakable, shatterproof.

For the first time in my life, I belonged.

I belonged to Tim as his prodigy.

I belonged to Molly and Mia as their cool confidant.

But Tilly embraced me as only mothers do, she saw my hurts and insecurities and bathed them in soothing calm and acceptance. Healing the ruptures of my past allowed me to bloom in the eyes of the world, but it also emphasised my own failing as a mother.

I loved Tilly. She was my rock. She was invincible, unbreakable and shatterproof.

Until she died.

I lift my fingers to my cheeks, surprised to feel them wet with tears. I let out a deep sigh. This will never do; I can't be meeting Tim looking like a soggy mess.

But it had been such a shock. Tim and I were busy, immersed in filming *An English Rose* when Tilly's sister came to stay – just to help out, Tilly assured. A couple of months later, Tilly was dead. It was quick. Silent, and quick.

Ovarian cancer is.

She was strong and kind and beautiful. And we needed her, we wept alone, we wept together. Our collective loss, a gaping hole in the midst of the Boswell family – sometimes skirted around, but mostly delved into, allowing our grief to surround and swallow us. We crumbled, were crushed into sparse shadows of ourselves, coerced into a false façade of normality by Tilly's sister.

I'd already decided to return to the UK after filming. Tim knew, but after Tilly, he affirmed that his home would always be mine. I was one of his girls, and he was already tortured by grief – I could see in his eyes he wanted me to stay but knew he had to let me go.

A man known in the business for his ruthless efficiency, had let me into his heart and I walked away when his heart was already shattering.

'Mr Boswell, he is in lounge, madam.' Pauletta peers at me. 'I send him away; you not see important man with tears in your eyes.'

I look up at Pauletta, would she understand? I struggle to stand. 'But I must see him, Pauletta. I put tears in his eyes, a long time ago.'

Pauletta rests her hand on my arm. 'Was a long time ago, madam. Do not keep troubles in your heart.'

I nod at her sage reply. 'But still, Pauletta, I need to see him.'

She shrugs and turns to leave. 'I tell him you will be moment or two.'

I glance at my reflection in the mirror, then at Scott's portrait and sadly smile. What a lover sees and a mirror reveal are two entirely different things.

I walk gingerly to the lounge, meeting Pauletta in the doorway. Her eyes are filled with concern. 'Madam.' She bobs and continues on her way.

Tim stands as I enter, his face creases into his familiar smile, his pale-blue eyes appear as perceptive as ever. 'Hello, Maddie.'

'Hello, Tim.' We stand awkwardly looking at each other. His sandy hair has thinned, the freckles on his arms have merged to give the illusion of a suntan, and he still boasts a lean figure in his casual slacks and open-neck shirt.

I start to reach out my hand, but I'm pulled into a mellow bearhug. His chin rests on the top of my head. Moments pass. I can feel the heat of his body beneath his cool, cotton shirt as my head rests on his chest. The steady beat of his heart. The security of his embrace. The smell of him. All the familiar triggers reminding me I am loved. Reminding me I'm worthy of being loved. I relax into his embrace, know that I am safe. Forgiven.

Again, my cheeks are wet with tears. 'Thank you,' I mumble. 'It's been a long time.'

'Yes, indeed.' Tim guides me to the sofa. 'A long time.' Unlike Scott, he's kept his crisp English accent, though it is at odds with his Californian lifestyle.

I raise my chin and look at him sat beside me. I can feel his gentle scrutiny smoothing away my name-sake, Madeline, and revealing Maddie. I nod. 'Can you see me now?'

'I see you, Maddie. A heart full of promise and pain. I see you.'

I look away, too soon to delve into the pit of pythons waiting to snap and snare my thoughts. 'I'm okay,' I assure him.

He turns my face to his. 'But cannot say it to my face...' He lets the observation roll towards me. 'I, however, am okay,' he says, looking into my eyes.

I nod. 'It's good to hear that, Tim, I've never thanked you for all you did for me.'

'Finding Madeline De-Muir propelled my career, as you know – we were a great team—'

'Until I left.' Again, I turn away.

Again, he turns my face to his. 'You came home for your daughter; you had already decided to before Tilly d—'

'I'm sorry.' A fresh batch of tears spring to my eyes, and I dab furiously with a tissue. Turmoil churns up within me, unsettling the uneasy peace I've managed to conjure over the years. Seeing Tim brings back all the old demons. 'I still feel like I abandoned you and the girls when you needed me.'

Tim lets out a heartfelt sigh. 'It was a difficult time, more so for Molly… Mia, she just seemed to accept it. But then, Mia is so very much like Tilly, scarily so, now she's a mom herself.'

Lucky, lucky Mia. But poor Molly, with her abrasive front to shelter her sensitive soul, of course she struggled. 'I didn't know. I haven't kept track… What about Molly, has she married, children?'

'Would you believe, she's a doctor. Married to the job, determined to save as many lives as she can. I don't think she ever got over losing her mother. She had counselling; we all did. Miriam – you remember Tilly's sister – she insisted on it.'

'I remember.' I remember being reminded I wasn't Tilly's family. 'She looked after you all. Good, I'm glad.' My voice sounds strained even to my own ears.

'In her way. She stayed for a while.' Tim shrugs. 'But the girls, they felt like she was trying to take the place of Tilly. In the end, I had to ask her to leave, give us space to learn how to be a family of three.'

Another wave of guilt washes over me, as I think of the three of them struggling to fill the void left by the loss of a wonderfully-complete human being. 'Nobody could ever replace Tilly,' I all but whisper. 'She was remarkable.'

'Nobody ever came close.' I can hear the loneliness of the years in his words. 'It would have been good to hear from you…'

The honesty of his admission catches me off guard. I gulp and swallow the lump in my throat. 'I couldn't, I felt… it was too painful, Tim.'

'It was painful for us too.'

I nod. 'But you were all family, I was just a house guest.' It feels strange even describing myself like that because I never felt like one. I glance away, know my words cut Tim as deep as they cut me.

'The girls loved you, you were one of the family, Tilly made sure of that.'

'I know, but in my head, I've always linked leaving with Tilly dying, and deep down, I'm sure you, Molly and Mia do too.'

Tim takes a deep breath and lets out another sigh. 'We do, of course we do. But we also remember you reading aloud to Tilly when she was too ill to concentrate herself. And the way you shielded the girls from the true horror of her illness. I'll never forget the last time the five of us went to the beach. You keep bashing the volley ball onto Tilly's blanket so she'd be included in the game. Every time the ball headed her way, her face lit up. Those are the things we remember.'

'I remember them too. She was so weak, but fiercely determined to fill every second. I'll always be grateful to you, Tim. You showed me how family should be. In a way, you spoiled me, my reality of family life has been… Let's just say disappointing, at best.'

Tim's supressed smile is filled with concern. 'That was one crazy stunt you pulled! Coming out as a single, teen mum, twenty-four years later by exhibiting your daughter's artwork.'

I shrug and roll my eyes. 'What can I say? It needed to be done. Christie is incredibly talented, and had zero expectation of ever having her work shown.'

'I'm glad you did it. It gave me the opportunity to track you down.'

A hurried knock on the door, and Pauletta appears. She bobs respectfully, though her fully-loaded utility belt is at odds with her apparent demure nature. 'Madam, is time for lunch. Dining room is all ready for you and vegetarian.' She gives Tim a modest smile.

'Thank you, Pauletta. We will be through presently.'

'Is my pleasure, madam.' Pauletta bobs from the room.

Tim's mouth curves into a grin, and he nods toward the door. 'Bit of a handful, is she?'

'How did you guess?'

He taps the side of his nose. 'Director's intuition.'

'Well, I hope you have a good sense of humour, because I have no idea what food we are about to suffer.'

He stands and holds out his hand to help me to my feet. 'Come on, only one way to find out.'

I lead Tim into the dining room, which is its usual pristine self. Scott's portrait is still propped up on one of the sofas. The table is set for two, all the cutlery and crockery immaculately placed with a large, covered serving platter to one side. An array of twigs, leaves and imposing sprigs from my prized magnolia tree have appeared centre stage. The impromptu floral display would kindly be described as eclectic –

unkindly, a dog's dinner – but that phrase I may need to save for the hidden food on the platter.

'This is all very Madeline,' observes Tim. 'I do, however, like it.'

'Thanks, I think!'

'Come on, Maddie, I just know you usually eat in the kitchen…' The twinkle in his eyes softens the blow of his perception. 'This room is to impress your guests.'

'I have no guests, usually. And frankly, Tim, coming from you, that is something to be reckoned with. Your home is a mansion compared to this little old place.'

He pulls out a chair for me to sit. 'Ah, but I am the all-powerful director. I need to impress and sometimes intimidate my guests. Whereas you, my petal, are a fallen star.'

The term of endearment allows me to almost forgive the slur. 'A fallen star, you say – I prefer reclusive icon. Only yesterday I met a—'

'Yawn, yawn, my dear girl. Let's face it, you've lost your lustre!' Tim sits opposite, the sporadic sprigs between us making eye contact impossible.

I reach out and push them to one side. 'Tim, I know you too well. I know exactly what you are doing, and I will not fall into that trap.'

'I have no idea what you are trying to imply.' He gestures to the platter. 'Are you doing the honours, or shall I?'

'I think I'll let you, I have no idea what Pauletta has prepared. She is an excellent cook; however, she also has a peculiar sense of humour.'

Tim stands and lifts the elaborately embossed top from the platter. I let out a silent sigh of relief as an array of beautifully prepared savouries entice. Along with Pauletta's famed stilton and spinach quiche, mini lattice cheese and onions flans and a tossed Greek salad, there is a selection of homemade dips. Indeed, she has pulled out all the stops to produce a light lunch any high-class establishment would be happy to serve.

'Maddie, this looks splendid. I suppose it's worth enduring her temperamental nature when she can produce food like this.'

I nod, and preen on Pauletta's behalf. Tim's complement will be passed on, knowing Tim though, he'll track Pauletta down and tell her himself. She'll be unbearably smug and an absolute nightmare for weeks! 'I'll pass on your compliments, but just wait until you taste it!'

We each make our choices and tuck into the delectable delicacies. The pastry is to die for. I can see the pleasure on Tim's face as he relishes the homecooked cuisine.

'This does taste as good as it looks - this is what I have been missing in my life, someone dedicated to looking after me.'

I raise my brows. 'You have a raft of staff at your beck and call, day and night... Or you always used to...'

'Ah, yes, the help. Running the house was always Tilly's department. I leave it to the housekeeper now, I don't take much interest I'm afraid. Tilly had them all eating out of her hand.'

'And you?'

'They tolerate me. I'm out early and home late. Sometimes away for weeks on end if I've location shoots or a reclusive icon to tempt back into the business.'

I glance away for a second or two. 'Reclusive icons are a tricky breed, you know.'

'I do, but sometimes it's worth the time invested to return a star to their rightful sphere.'

'Maybe they don't want to be returned.'

'And that's where I come in, to remind them of the adulation they once took for granted—'

'The 5am starts.'

'The creative process of developing a character—'

'The hours spent in makeup being treated like a slab of meat.'

'The premiers and after-party parties—'

'The paparazzi.'

'The accolades, awards and Oscars…'

I look away, unable to meet his eyes. Know how hard it must have been for him to go up onto the stage to collect mine in my place. His first award ceremony without Tilly – I watched on the TV. He was sat flanked either side by his daughters, both beautifully poised with an ethereal aura of tranquil acceptance. Their mother's death gave them a gravitas that raised them above the grasping celebrity and insincerity of the night's proceedings.

A spree of goosebumps shimmies through me as I recall sitting in my PJs crying, watching the three of them. I was so proud of them. I felt alone, not only bereft of losing Tilly, but of losing the three of them in my life.

Tim touches my hand across the table. 'I still have it.'

I nod, sure he's seen the tears back in my eyes. 'Thank you. I was numb, it was nothing to me.'

'You *earned* it!'

'You dragged it out of me… Syllable by syllable, shot after shot, scene by scene. It was my life for months…'

'Mine too.'

I look into his eyes. 'We were both so absorbed in Rose, that we didn't notice the life ebbing away before us. I didn't put in the performance of a lifetime, Tilly did, pretending she was…' I drop my head into my hands as shame and guilt prompt my tears again.

Tim is beside me in seconds, his beefy hand on my shoulder, his forehead resting close to mine. 'Now listen here, Harris.' The soft English accent is at odds with his words. 'Tilly did what she did to protect us, and all this self-serving sobbing is not what she'd expect from any of her girls – and she was so very proud of you, of all you'd accomplished and all you'd overcome.'

I turn to him, rest my head on his shoulder, unable to look into his eyes. 'You told her about Christie?'

'I told her everything, everything about—'

'I wish I'd known.' I bite my lip. 'I could have explained…'

Tim strokes my head. 'She didn't need your explanation. She knew, and made me promise not to keep you.' Tim passes me a napkin from the table. 'Please rescue my shirt,' he says.

I hold it to my face. 'Why did she make you promise? Did she want me to leave?' I try to catch the sob as the pain in my throat becomes too much. The thought of Tilly wanting me out of her home a torment more than I can handle.

'She knew I'd want you to stay. She knew, we both knew what an extra-ordinary talent you are. And she knew I'd want to keep you under my wing...' He raises my chin and looks into my eyes. 'But Tilly said I had to let you fly to find your own way... She said you'd fly back to me in your own time... I've been waiting a long time, Harris, and I want you back.'

Backstory

He kneels in front of me

'You didn't tell me your Scott is the famous Scott Scobie.' Tim continues to scrutinise my portrait.

'He wasn't the famous Scott Scobie when I knew him. He was just an art student from the local college. I stumbled across him one dark and rainy night.'

Tim nods. 'You only stumbled across him once?'

'Yep – every other time I was drawn to him like molten metal to a magnet.' I shrug. 'Like an addiction, I had no control and no explanation as to why him. He was hardly the charismatic character he is now. He was a lanky teenager who liked to paint. End of.'

'And now?'

I run my fingers through my hair, leave them resting around my neck, remember Scott's arm loosely draped there last night. 'I can't contain or control how I feel. The chords that bind us are beyond my comprehension. Honestly, I'm afraid.' I glance away. 'I'm afraid of what our future can be… I've only just reconciled with Christie; I can't walk away from her again. And yet Scott is the part of me that's been missing for a lifetime.'

Tim squats in front of my portrait. 'I've seen his work before, and it's good, it's very good, but this is by far the most exceptional piece I've seen. He's captured the being inside the beauty.'

'I hope *that* is a compliment, Tim, you know how fragile my ego is.'

'It is a compliment. However, I'm still going to need to push you for an answer.'

'I don't know. Like I said, I can't walk out on Christie, and I have no crystal ball to see what the future holds for me and Scott.'

Tim takes my hand. 'Come on, show me your fabulous garden again.' He leads me out through the kitchen.

I'm hoping Terry is distracted by his ball as easily as last time, he's far less territorial out in the garden than inside the house – a lesson learned the hard way by Scott. Terry – tail wagging frantically – bounds towards Tim and drops his ball ready to play.

Tim picks it up and throws it the length of the garden. 'Fetch.' There was no need for the command, Terry is off like a torpedo, his tail a streak of white froth. So, it's game on.

'How can I even think about leaving Terry, never mind Christie?' I say, as the soggy ball is dropped at my feet. I pick it up and throw, but nowhere near the distance Tim managed.

'There are such things as kennels.' The ball is dropped at his feet.

'I hope that was a joke! I'd never leave him with strangers, he'd pine, besides, he'd eat them.'

'I'm sure you'd be able to entice someone to house-and-dog-sit – the charming Pauletta, perhaps? Anyway, I don't want excuses for why not. This is a prime opportunity to garner the limelight *and* remind the public why they adore you!'

'I don't think they adore me now, after my baby abandoning admission.'

Tim chuckles as he throws the ball again. 'Either way, they will be chomping at the bit to get a glimpse of you in action again.'

'And confirm, I only outed Christie for my own gain.'

Terry starts snuffling in the borders, I hope Pixi isn't about. I wander over to the outside tap and rinse my hands, shaking them dry. Tim follows suit.

'Either way, petal – damned if you do…'

'I know, but I hate being second-guessed, we reclusive icons do, you know.'

'Don't let what other people think, control who you are. I know you. I see you. And if anyone was put on this earth to act, it's you.'

'I haven't been on a set for years! I'm scared, Tim. You can understand?' I walk midway down the garden and sit on the bench by the pond. The sound of the trickling water from the little waterfall usually soothes my mood, but today it's just noise. 'I'm not sure I can deal with anymore negativity. The details of my life, rehashed, repackaged and rammed down my throat, publicly.' I cover my face with my hands. 'I can't endure that, Tim.'

The bench creaks. Tim puts his arm over my shoulder and pulls me close. I've seen him do it hundreds of times with his girls, Tilly, Molly, Mia – never me, until now. I sag against him, accept the security of his platonic embrace.

'I will protect you.'

I let his words sink into me, and nod.

'I remember meeting a girl called Madeline De-Muir, such a grand name for the scraggy offering she appeared to be. I expected little, rather like Simon Cowell with Susan Boyle. But, by God, when Madeline acted, she was like a lioness, fiercely in control of every aspect of the performance. She commanded everyone's attention. More than that, she became alive. I had to have her.'

I lift my head and let the heat of the sun seep into my soul.

'The girl – that's all she was, a girl – she had issues. She had a physical scar that could expose a secret from her past. She had a void inside her psyche, which had never been filled with anything of any value. But still, I had to have her.'

I peel my hands away from my face, the sunlight is still too bright for my eyes. Even with my eyes closed the light permeates through my eyelids.

'I made a vow to myself, I shared it with no one but my wife. I promised myself, that if I was the one exposing her to the world, then I would be the one to protect her. Always.'

I nod as a single tear escapes, I let it charter its path unchallenged, I have no need to hide myself from Tim.

'I've kept her secret even though she walked away from me. I've kept her secret for years, until she was ready, strong enough to tell it herself. And even now, when the whole world knows her secret, I will never disclose anything about that secret to anybody. It is still her secret, and it is still my job to protect her.'

The bench groans as Tim stands. I feel his shadow fall over me and open my eyes.

He kneels in front of me and takes my hands in his. 'I will always protect you, Maddie.'

I nod, know the truth of his words.

'Have no fear. Do not let fear be the reason for not doing what you were born to do.'

'I know you'll look after me, Tim, but I don't want to lose them again. I have only begun the journey to reconciliation with Christie, I've a long way to go... And Scott...'

Tim sits back beside me. 'I'm not asking you to choose. You can have both. The rule of life is to bring the important people with you on your journey.'

'Christie won't come to LA.'

'She doesn't need to come physically, but metaphorically...' Tim shrugs. 'Tilly never once stepped foot on set, but she was with me every day, she still is. I tell her everything.' He taps his head. 'In here, I talk to her all the time, I imagine the tone of her voice, the advice she'd give, the admonishments she'd dole out.'

Like every imaginary conversation I've had with Scott and Christie over the years. I haven't the heart to tell Tim the reality nowhere near marries up, instead I say, 'It stops you moving on, Tim.'

'Ah Maddie, my girl, why would I want to? I'd just be constantly comparing whoever with Tilly, and I'm fairly sure nobody would measure up.'

'You never know until you try,' I say, but deep down I know he's right. Nobody ever came close to Scott.

'Nice try, Harris, this isn't about me. And I've already told you, you'd be away no more than a week, with three, four days max filming. Christie would probably be glad to have you off her back. And, a plus, you'd get to stay with me.' He grins.

'Now you put it like that—'

'You'll do it?'

'I'll do it, but keep the press out of it until after I've left!'

'Deal.' We shake on it. 'Great, I'll just get on to the screenwriter. I know exactly how I want you to play it.'

'The part doesn't exist!'

'Backstory, it exists in my head. This is going to be out of this world.'

Terry's Torment

I am not stupid, madam

'Like I said, Maddie, I'm surprised,' says Miles. 'It's a huge step, a step into the lion's den.'

I hold the mobile close to my ear, and try to stop the tremor from sounding in my voice. 'Yes, it is stepping into the lion's den, I know… But I'll have Tim the lion tamer with me.'

'Are you ready for this?' I can hear the concern in his voice.

I sigh. 'If not now, then when? Seeing Tim, and remembering that time of my life… I was alive.'

'And Christie?'

'I'll be away for about a week, and if she wants to, she can come with me. Tim has invited her to stay at his home too.'

'So, I'll be all alone—'

'Miles, I don't know! Tim has only just left, and you're the first person I've told. It would have been nice to have a bit of moral support.' I always feel like adding, after everything I've done for you, when we have these little spats – but I never do.

'Like I already said, I'm shocked.'

'You said, surprised. But you must have guessed this visit wasn't simply going to be a social call.'

Miles sighs. 'But you've been so adamant in the past, about never going back…'

'I know. There is an awful lot of things I've never told you, Miles, and over the phone is not the way to do it. Suffice to say, I owe Tim, big time.'

'Shall I come round? This is a big deal.'

I inwardly groan. I want a couple of hours on my own. It's going to be Scott's last night, and I want it to be perfect. 'Maybe tomorrow.'

'Of course, you'll be entertaining Scott later.' His tone is neutral.

'Does Christie know about us?'

'I haven't told her, if that's what you mean.'

'Good, we plan to do it together.'

'Right, I'll get on, I'm still sifting through this insurance policy. I'm sure we can claim for loss of revenue.'

'Thanks, Miles. Bye.' I look at my mobile, he's already disconnected the call. The last thing I need is a Miles strop, on top of everything else. His allegiances are already shifting towards Christie, I knew they would.

The trouble is, Miles has been the only man in my life for years, and I've been the focus of all his time and attention. I suppose it's only natural for me to feel pushed out now he has Christie, and for him to feel pushed out with Scott.

Somehow, we need to both come to terms with the new situation. I hit Call on my mobile. Miles lets it ring five times before answering.

'Maddie?'

'Just a thought, Miles, how about you and Christie joining us here tonight? Pauletta will rustle up something simple and tasty.'

'With you and Scott?'

'Y-e-e-s, you and Christie can tell Scott about your relationship, me and Scott can tell Christie about ours.'

'I'll say yes, but if Christie has a wobble…'

'Great, I'll let Pauletta know. Let's say 7 for 7.30. Any change, let me know as soon as.'

'Will do, bye!'

I shuffle out of the snug to track down Pauletta. She's probably outside having a crafty smoke. I'll let her off, she *has* been on her best behaviour for Tim's visit, even doing the floral display. I wander through the dining room, the table has been cleared, and reset for two. The floral display is nowhere to be seen, clearly deemed too grand for Scott.

The kitchen is immaculate, no signs of any food preparation or Pauletta. I open the larder fridge, a smattering of random salad, cheese and quiche. Nothing likely to have the makings of an evening meal.

I step outside, smile to myself.

Pauletta is sat in the middle of the lawn with Terry sprawled on her lap. 'Is this crazy dog! He will not let me help.'

I notice Pauletta is clutching Terry's paw. 'What's happened?' I hurry to them and crouch down.

'Is something nasty stuck in his feet, but is too far for me to get.' She lifts his paw level with her nose, going cross-eyed in the process.

'Hey, Terry,' I sooth. 'Let me see.' I run my forefinger over his pad. Terry whimpers and tries to pull his leg away. Pauletta is right, I can feel something. 'I can feel it. Are you any good with tweezers?'

'Is not a safe thing to ask me!' she says. 'He needs animal doctor before whole foot goes bad.'

'Should we try bathing it?' I suggest.

'I tried everything. He needs animal doctor now.'

I pull out my phone and call the vet's.

Terry is sat in the window seat making a bigger fuss over his lampshade head, than his bandaged paw. Having the pride of place has done nothing to relieve his irritation. On the plus side, the veterinary nurse who attended him still has all her fingers – Terry didn't like the muzzle.

My plan for an elegant, evening dinner has fallen very much by the wayside. Pauletta announced she had no time to prepare now, and it would be something out of the freezer with rice or a takeaway…

Oh, how I love being the mistress of my own destiny!

Pauletta steps out of the kitchen, her apron swivelled round, and flapping over her bum. 'Poor, poor baby.' She kneels down in front of Terry and ruffles the fur beneath his cone. 'Is this what bad lady do to my little friend.'

Terry looks pitifully back at her, and lets out a whimper.

'I'm sure he'll be fine,' I say, more harshly than I intended. 'The antibiotics will make sure there's no infection.'

'Is good job I find him in agony, while you see one of your men.'

'It was a thorn, Pauletta.' I'm tempted to add, not a three-inch shard of glass, but I'm mindful I need her.

'Yes, yes, madam.' She turns back to Terry. 'You will soon be better, Pauletta will take good care for you.'

'Is everything under control in the kitchen?' I ask, well aware there is not a whiff of food.

'Is all under control, will be magnificent, as usual.' She turns and looks me up and down. 'Is time for you to get ready for party.'

'It is, but it's hardly a party.'

'You said dinner party.'

'Yes, Pauletta.' There is no point correcting her. 'I'm getting ready now.'

'I will take Terry to my home later, so you can have nice party and no worry,' announces Pauletta, leaving the room.

My plan for a lovely long soak has evaporated, a shower is all I have time for.

'Is all I am can do, with dog in agony, needing me, and no time.'

'I'm sure it will be wonderful, as always.'

Pauletta gives me a sideways look. 'Dishes are in oven keeping warm. Salad in fridge,' she says, pointing to the kitchen appliance she is talking about. 'Paella not in wok, moved to steady oven.' – Slow cooker – 'Messy Eton all in bits in fridge.'

'I love your Eton Mess, Pauletta, thank you.'

'It is not messy yet! Meringue on baking tray.' She points to the fridge, and I nod obligingly. 'Strawberries choppied and sugared in tupwear. Cream, whippied in tupwear and choppy-strawberry, green tops to twinkle on the top after you make messy swirl.'

I press my lips together to hold in my frustration at Pauletta's laborious explanation of such a simple task. 'I think I will manage.'

'Is two bottles of Chardonnay.' She gives me one of her critical looks. 'Is more in your hidie, bedroom fridge—'

'Thank you. But I think Scott and I will be drinking soft drinks tonight, and neither Miles or Christie drink much.'

Pauletta nods. 'Is good boy, Miles. Now I will get poor Terry to take home. Goodybye, have a happy party.'

She scurries from the kitchen before I've chance to reply. I step into the dining room. The floral arrangement is back, and the table is set to Pauletta's exacting standards. She has used a medium-sized cruet for the olive oil, so I will assume we have an extra bowl of olives with the salad. So far, I cannot fault her hasty preparations, though I notice the napkin rings are the ones embossed with the comedy and tragedy motif. I hope that isn't an omen.

She's moved my portrait, it is now propped up on a side chair, leaving the two matching sofas free for us having our coffees later… If we last that long.

I catch a glimpse of movement outside. I turn in time to see Pauletta scurrying past the back window carrying Terry, in what looks like a pink blanket. I only just caught sight of them, but Terry has a look of terror in his eyes, as his cone swings perilously back and forth.

I move to the front of the house, surely, she isn't planning on carrying him all the way home, it's above a mile!

I tap on the window and open it as she comes up level. 'Pauletta, there's no need to carry Terry, I'll call a taxi. It will only be maybe ten minutes or so.'

'Is no need. I have no time for taxi men. Terry will be happy bunny on my bicycle.'

An image of Terry strapped to Pauletta's back flashes into my mind. I shake my head. 'I'm not really sure how you're going to manage keeping hold of Terry all that way.'

Pauletta gives me a withering look. 'I am not stupid, madam. Terry is going in basket.'

As far as I recall, Pauletta's 1970s, top of the range, girls, red Raleigh bicycle, has no basket. 'Has your bike got a basket? I can't remember.'

Pauletta smiles smugly. 'It has now. Very kind lady in village shop let me borrow wire shopping basket – one night only, I promise. I fasten it with strong wire from shed. Is perfect.'

'Oh.' Poor Terry, he may never be the same again. 'Hold on a minute, I'll come outside and check—'

'Is no need, is perfect.'

'But still.'

I make my way to the front door and step out onto the steps. Pauletta's bike is propped, ready for action, against the wall. The wire shopping basket is not only securely fastened to the handlebars, but also to the brakes by copious amounts of thick, hedging wire.

'See, is perfect.' She holds the handlebars with one hand and lets Terry slide down her body into the basket. The pink blanket offers him some comfort and also ensures he is unable to wriggle free as Pauletta wraps his lead around the handle of the basket. She chuckles Terry under his chin. 'Is happy, little bunny, snug as rug and bug.'

Terry raises his chin and looks pitifully at me. He tries to rest his head down and lets out a whimper as his lampshade cone jars against the handlebars.

Pauletta tuts. 'Will have you home in jiffy.'

I look at my watch, Scott will be here any time soon, so will Miles and Christie. I really could do without this. 'Pauletta, I do think a taxi is a better option. It's not too late for me to call one.'

She holds the bike still and manoeuvres herself into position, one foot on the ground, one on a pedal and her bum poised ready to drop onto the seat. 'We are on our way.'

And off she rides. The front wheel wobbles, Terry's head sways from side to side, but Pauletta remains solidly in her seat. I watch as she makes her way steadily down the driveway. I wait and listen as she curves out of sight towards the wrought iron gates. The tell-tale clang as the automated gates open confirms she's well on her way.

I turn and go back inside.

Undertones

You left me

Miles stops with his fork midway to his mouth, returns it to his plate as he's overcome by another burst of laughter.

'It isn't funny, Miles,' I repeat.

He shakes his head. 'Poor Terry, his head in that cone—'

I raise my hand. 'Please… I did my best to stop her.'

Christie shrugs. 'I don't understand why she had to ride her bike home when you'd offered to get her a taxi.'

'This is Pauletta,' I say. 'She has a very loose grasp of what is accepted as normal behaviour.'

Miles laughs again. 'Oh, Maddie, I think she knows exactly what she's doing. She thoroughly enjoys winding you up.'

I can feel both Scott and Christie watching me from across the table. I resist the urge to look their way, instead I look back at Miles by my side. 'It's just her way, I really hope they both got home in one piece. That shopping basket was secured to the brakes.'

Miles grins. 'I hope she hasn't been stopped by the police! Could you imagine Pauletta being interrogated?'

I laugh. 'Is not for me to say!' I notice Scott and Christie exchanging confused looks. 'It's Pauletta's catchphrase, "Is not for me to say", and sort of an in-joke Miles shares with me.'

Miles nods. 'Every time Pauletta disapproves of something, "Is not for me to say!". You should have tried it on her before she left, Maddie.'

'Not a chance, I'm already the lowest of the low for having a party while Terry is so-o-o critically ill.'

'I hope we aren't celebrating my leaving?' says Scott.

I'm certain they'll all be able to notice the swell of tears in my eyes. 'Not at all, I'm sure we are all going to miss you.'

I spot the brief exchange of glances between Miles and Christie sat across from each other. They're probably playing footsie under the table.

Miles clears his throat. 'Actually, there is something I'd like to discuss with you before you leave.'

Scott leans back in his chair, his legs sprawl under the table, his boots nudge my toes. Though his posture is relaxed, by the set of his jaw I can tell he's on full alert. He looks directly at Miles. 'Fire away, Miles.'

Miles straightens, his fingers are loosely linked on the table and I note Christie offers a discrete, reassuring nod. I have rarely seen Miles so ill at ease. Though the top half of him is totally still, I can perceive the slight twitch in his leg confirming his anxiety. 'As you know, Scott, I have been working with Maddie for a long time. Many years. Actually, all my adult life.' He looks at Christie, then back to Scott. 'Christie has played a big part in my life, although until several weeks ago, we had scarcely met—'

'We had met a few times, briefly at Mum and Dad's,' says Christie.

Kathleen Clunan

Miles smiles at her. 'We had. I already knew Christie was a talented artist because of the work she did for Maddie. But getting to know her over the last few weeks has… It's been a pleasure.' – I can see his eyes shining – 'And we have become close.'

Scott sits up. 'So, Miles, what exactly are you saying—'

'He is saying,' says Christie, her voice matter-of-fact. 'We are dating. Not that he, or we, owe you any explanation. We just wanted you to known as a matter of courtesy.'

'Well, thank you kindly,' says Scott, doing little to disguise his irritation. 'I appreciate your candour.'

Miles shuffles. 'I don't want you to think I'm coming between—'

Scott stands. 'I don't, but this is my last night in the UK and I kind of wanted it to be more about solidifying my relationship with Christie. If you'll excuse me, I'm going for a breath of air.'

I catch his eye as he strides past. In that instant I can see his hurt, understand that he wanted to enjoy Christie as his daughter before having to share her with a significant other. I can tell that Scott knows Miles is most certainly Christie's significant other.

I look across at Christie, and know my brows are raised. The actress in me knows I should keep them under control. The diplomat in me knows it will muddy the water. But the mother in me says Christie ought to know I'm not pleased.

Christie raises her brows in return. 'I think that went as well as can be expected.'

'Really?' I question. 'I think you could have been more thoughtful.'

Christie shrugs. 'Maddie, Scott's only just met me, he hardly knows me.'

'Exactly. He's only just met you, and, I think he would have appreciated more time to get to know you without having to share you—'

'Well, I'm not in the habit of half-truths and smokescreens, they only store up trouble for the future.' – I accept the brutal accuracy of her insinuation – 'And I'm sure Scott is resilient enough to stand my honesty.'

Again, the jibe hits hard.

I place my napkin on the table, and ready myself to stand. I lock eyes with Christie and shake my head. 'The expression on his face as he left would suggest otherwise.' I stand.

Miles catches my hand. 'I think it would be better if Christie went to him.'

I look from Miles to Christie.

She rolls her eyes and gets up. 'Fine. I'll go and talk to him. But I think you are all being melodramatic about something as mundane as me dating a guy.' She reaches out and catches Miles' hand as she passes. 'Back soon.'

Miles turns and watches her leave. 'Should I go with her?'

'I wouldn't.'

Miles lets out a breath and rests back in his chair. I can tell he's eager to smooth the way between Christie and Scott, it is one of his skills. But they have to sort this out between them, and how they prioritise each other is for the two of them to decide.

I place my hand on top of Miles'. 'I know you want to help, but that's the point. They need to be left to sort it themselves.'

'I do want to help. Christie is still getting to grips with all these changes, and I'm not 100% sure she's grasped the fact that Scott is in the same position she's in.'

'Quite. But to be fair, she's had a double whammy. Scott, being older, has more experience at dealing with tricky situations.'

Miles leaves the table and starts pacing. 'But I like the guy, and Christie can be… less than sympathetic.'

'Don't I know it,' I mutter. 'Anyway, they are both adults, and whatever *they* decide to do, *we* are both going to have to live with it.'

Miles settles in front of my portrait, bends to take a closer look. 'He is very talented.' Miles looks back at me. 'Clearly Christie has inherited her artistic streak from him.'

'She's also inherited his stubborn streak.'

Miles follows a brush stroke with his finger. 'But isn't that what makes them constantly hone their skills, their perseverance?'

I wander over and stand next to Miles. In all departments, Scott has most certainly honed his skills. His portrait of me is translucent, the skin tones positively glow and the fluidity and texture of the sundress almost palpable.

I nod. 'It is, but Scott is far more intuitive. Christie has a lot to learn, and the first thing is tact. She ploughed in telling Scott about the two of you without any consideration to how it would affect him. Tonight, *is* his last night with Christie.'

Miles turns to me. 'And his last night with you.'

I turn away not wanting Miles to see the sudden swell of tears in my eyes. 'Come on, make yourself useful, I need help clearing the table and piecing together the dessert.' I head off to the kitchen hoping he'll bring the pots through to the dishwasher.

I lift out all the containers Pauletta has neatly stacked in order of use, and line them up on the counter. Light streams in from the huge, picture-frame window. Glistening in the amber, evening sunlight are four, vintage, cut-glass dessert bowls and several tablespoons ready for dishing out the various sweet ingredients. I send a silent thank you to Pauletta. To deem the occasion worthy of the vintage glass, is something akin to a miracle, knowing her feelings towards Christie and Scott – the interlopers – maybe she's softening.

I absently peel the lids off the containers as I look outside to where Scott and Christie are sat by the garden pond. Scott with his legs stretched out and crossed at the ankle, Christie turned towards him, her legs tucked under the bench. Both have heads bowed, but I notice Christie's hands are animated. Scott nods occasionally.

Carefully, I scoop a layer of strawberries – succulent with sweetened juices – into each of the bowls. 'Miles, do you want to casually wander over and see how long they're planning on staying out there?' I smile hopefully, as I send him into the lion's den.

'Sure.' He goes out, leaving me the chatter of evening birdsong from the open door for companionship. He raises a hand. 'How's it going?' he calls out, almost as you would an old acquaintance.

I marvel at his ability to adapt himself and his attitude to suit his audience. I can only do it with an actual audience. Reality is too scary, yep, too real.

Christie meets him halfway. I notice she slips her hand into his as if it belongs there. Scott ambles towards them and nods in the direction of the terrace. All three of them head that way.

I'm still craning my neck to see what they are up to when Miles dashes in from the dining room.

I drop the strawberry spoon; the clatter and splatter of syrup add to my edginess. 'Miles!' I look down at the mess, at least it hasn't gone on my clothes.

'Sorry.' He starts swabbing the counter with kitchen roll.

'Well? Are you going to fill me in on what's going on?'

'I think there's a truce. They were chatting about Christie going to visit at the start of the school holidays when she has more free time.'

'She might have a new exhibition venue by then to promote.' I shrug. 'Or not.'

'Like you said, we have to go with the flow with the two of them, and follow their lead. We've done our best.'

I roughly crack the meringue with the end of the rolling pin and scoop spoonfuls into each of the dishes. Then add a dollop of whipped, fresh cream and Pauletta's secret ingredient – all I know is it involves a vanilla pod – then I add another layer of each. Finally, I give a swirl through with a chopstick and sprinkle the chopped strawberry leaves.

I've got to hand it to Pauletta, even at short notice and under pressure, she knows how to deliver.

'So,' I say, turning to Miles as I nimbly restack all the containers back into the fridge – a midnight snack for later, maybe, 'are they on their way back in?'

'Scott thought it would be nice to sit on the terrace and watch the sun going down on his last night.'

I let out a silent sigh and look at the vintage, cut-glass bowls Pauletta guards with her life. 'We could have eaten dessert first.'

'They're already out there, and yes, I know Pauletta will kill us both if anything happens to those bowls, so I'll bring them back in as soon as we have all finished eating.'

'Thank you, I'll go and get the cutlery—'

'And I will carry out the desserts…' He grins. 'Just like in the olden days—'

'When we used to have picnics in the garden.' I smile at the memory. 'Yep, I've always been such a high-end diva.'

'Not,' confirms Miles, as he sets off with the first two precious bowls of Eton mess.

In the dining room I gather up the dessert spoons. The eclectic floral arrangement looks forlorn, left centre stage with no audience in sight. I know exactly how it feels, not that I crave an audience, it's the process I miss. The eking out of a character from a writer's vision, building on the director's ideas, and all for the audiences' pleasure.

The three of them are sat in the recliners on the terrace, each nursing one of the precious bowls on their laps… Mine is placed safely on the wrought iron table, the table I expected them to be sitting at! I dart an irritated look at Miles, he returns it with an almost undetectable look of helplessness.

'Here we go.' I smile as I hand out the spoons and dessert forks. 'I hope you like it, it's one of Pauletta's specials.'

A jolt of recognition shoots through me as Scott catches my hand for a split second. 'Thanks, honey,' he says under his breath.

I fire him a quirky, silencing look, with pursed lips and crossed eyes. Miles and Christie are already bent towards each other, deep in conversation as they eat the delicacy with scant reverence for Pauletta's culinary skills, and quite oblivious to the world around them.

I sit close to Scott and nod towards the two of them. 'Oh, to be young and in love,' I mutter, so only Scott can hear.

'Hey, we aren't doing so bad ourselves,' comes his husky reply. 'And this is mighty fine food, compliments to the chef,' he says much louder.

Miles looks up. 'It is, I'm sure Pauletta will be pleased to hear she has hit the mark for a second time today.'

Christie sits up a bit straighter and leans forward to look at me. 'Are we the second sitting, then?'

I laugh, hope it doesn't sound forced. 'Not at all, I had a visit from an old friend of mine. We had a light lunch.'

'Ah, yeah!' says Scott. 'The esteemed Tim Boswell, how'd it go?'

I shrug and smile at the same time. 'It was emotional, for both of us – it's been a long time...' I notice Christie passing her bowl to Miles and resting back in her seat. Miles places his and hers on the table – two safe. 'And it was cathartic, after all these years to put some demons to rest.' I look past the three of them into the middle distance, focus on nothing but the memory of those early days. 'I suppose he felt the same.'

'From what I recall,' Scott starts, 'finding you was his big break.'

I look back at Scott. 'He was already on his way, but you're right, he took a huge gamble on me... And it paid off, in one respect...'

Scott makes to put his bowl on the floor beside him, Miles intervenes. 'I'll take that in for you,' he says, and collects the other two from the table.

'Thank you, kindly.' He nods at Miles, then looks back to me. 'So, it was just a social call? Yeah?'

I watch Miles retreating into the kitchen just as I need an ally. I shift in my seat, and reach out, placing my half-eaten dessert onto the table out of harm's way. 'It was a little more than a catch-up. We talked for much of the time about Tilly, Tim's wife... She died just before I came home to England.' I feel my voice crack and clear my throat to cover the raw pain of loss.

Scott places his hand on mine, his expression filled with concern. 'I take it, you were close?'

I nod, look away clamping my lips together. Already the tautness in my cheeks causing a familiar ache. My life with Tim feels like a lifetime ago, but hurts as deeply as yesterday. I clear my throat. 'I lived with Tim's family. Tilly made me belong... After we lost her...' Miles is stood listening from a little way away, giving me time to order my thoughts. 'It was tough, I'd already committed to coming home to England...'

I can feel Christie watching me, taking in the unspoken message.

Scott squeezes my hand. 'The year you won the Golden Globe for best actress.'

'Yes.' I nod.

'Yeah, the only year I watched it live, to catch a sight of you,' says Scott.

I smile a painful smile. 'I'd been back months by then.' I look across at Christie. 'I was lucky enough to have started seeing Christie again – remember, I used to take you to the ice-cream parlour and fill you full of either chocolate chip or honeycomb flavour.' A shard of ice shoots through me as I take in Christie's lack of emotion.

'I remember "Auntie Maddie". But Mum still made me eat my tea when I got home.'

'Well, she would,' I say, trying to coax another response. She remains unmoved, unwilling to enter into joint remembrances with me. I look away from her, allowing the topic to be closed without further humiliation.

I bristle at the pity I see in Scott's eyes.

'So, I guess you had a good deal to catch up on,' he says, obviously keen to help dig me out of my misery.

'We talked about working together, and we talked a lot about Tilly and the girls – both grown up now. He told me things about Tilly that reminded me just how brilliant she was, and how much I still miss her.' The lapping waves of grief wash over me. There's always a ripple somewhere, waiting for the tide to change and drag me under with their unpredictable currents.

I'm aware Miles has sat next to Christie, is holding her hand. He clears his throat. 'I don't remember you ever talking about her – or Tim, for that matter.'

I look at Miles, surely, he of all people knows about not going back. 'I had no need to. Tim and Tilly were part of a life I'd left behind. It was easier to blank out that whole episode of my life, than deal with the guilt of leaving Tim and the girls.'

Christie sits upright. 'You left me!'

'But I came back for you. I left Tim grieving along with Molly and Mia – their girls – after all they'd done for me. However, Tim knew why I needed to come home, he didn't try to stop me, even though I was the only shoulder he had to cry on.'

Scott nods. 'He's got that tough reputation of his to hold on to. I guess they had therapy.'

'I'm sure.' I smile at Scott's easy reference to using a therapist to help the grieving process. I marvel at how far behind we Brits are, with our stiff upper lips.

'I guess it's all good between you now?'

'It is… Better than good. Actually, I've some exciting news.' Already I'm beginning to feel the wonderfully-scary fizz start to bubble and build in anticipation and fright at the thought of being on set, amidst all the action. Closing my eyes I recall the heat of the lights, the intimacy of the lens and how much leverage I wangle out of the lines.

I can feel all their eyes on me. It's been a long time. Inhaling deeply, I let my eyes flutter half open, savour the command of being the centre of attention, if only in this select group. Oh, how I've missed this.

'Are you going to tell us, or do we have to drag it out of you?'

'Yes, Maddie, do tell!'

My eyes flash open at the curtness of Christie's tone. I look from Christie to Miles, then back to Christie. 'Well…' I straighten the hem of my blouse and gently thread my fingers together – an act of supreme control, allowing me time to garner my thoughts. 'Tim reminded me of all the time and effort he invested in my career – like I don't feel guilty enough – he's *begged* me to play a part in the movie he's direc—'

'And you said yes!' Christie is up on her feet.

I reach out my hand towards her. 'It's only a small part, a couple of days film—'

'I knew it. All of this—' Christie tosses her arms in the air. Her voice is taut, low and controlled, the fury only a pulse beneath the surface. 'All of this – outing me as your beloved daughter, launching my career, turning my whole life upside down… It's all been about the fabulous Madeline De-Muir—'

'No, Christie, this came as a total surprise to me.' I can feel the quiver in my voice.

'So why didn't you tell him, no?'

Scott leans forward out of his chair, an elbow resting on each of his knees, hands outstretched. 'I think your tone towards Maddie is unwarranted, young lady—'

'Unwarranted…' she shakes her head. 'You know what, I'm done with the pair of you. Come on, Miles, we're leaving.'

`

Release

An involutory sigh escapes

The, "I'll sort this" face Miles bestows on me as he follows Christie through the French doors, does little to ease my concerns. I turn to watch Scott, who's already paced the length of the terrace. Embers of a thousand bonfires ignite the cold chill of fear, transforming it into white-hot sparks flicking at my skin.

'I'm kinda shocked, I thought Miles was your right-hand guy.'

'He is.'

'Looks more like Christie's stooge, to me.'

'Maybe I should have kept it to myself.' As I say the words, the flames scorch my skin. I can feel the veil of self-respect falling, falling, falling away.

'You think?'

'Oh, I don't know. Whatever I do, she's… It's been an eventful
few weeks… Who can blame her?' I keep pushing the fireball in my chest down deeper and deeper, try to quash its raging destruction.

Control.

Control.

Control.

I try to tame the quiver in my hands, I feel them curl into fists by my side.

'I guess, but you know, this isn't going to sort itself.'

Maybe Scott's right, but I'm sick of fighting a battle I'm never going to win. I stand and reach for the glass bowl. I can feel Scott's eyes on me, I turn and meet his expectant expression with no answers. I carry the bowl inside, place it alongside the rest on the counter.

Scott follows, stands with his hands planted low on his hips. 'Haven't you got something to say?'

'I've said enough.'

'We need to go and sort this. Tonight.'

I shake my head. 'No, Scott. Like Christie, I'm done.'

'What the hell happened to you, Maddie Harris? The girl who could blaze through the town setting every tongue on fire with expectations.'

'She fell asleep, and when she awoke the will to fight had dissolved and turned into an ever-growing pit of despair.'

He stalks over to the door. 'Well, I'm not leaving it like this. Are you coming with me?'

I drive back the tears, refuse their solace. So many tears, to little avail. 'No, Scott.'

'Well, I've got to.' He pulls me into an embrace, runs his fingers round the back of my neck, holds my head to his chest.

I can feel, hear the strong beat of his heart and my blood runs cold. I pull away, smile. 'Off you go, Scott.'

He turns and leaves, only looking over his shoulder once to give a half-hearted salute.

As I hear the front door slam shut, I clutch my belly as my insides crumble. Closing my eyes, head bowed I let out a silent, tearless sob. The tightness of my throat strangles my jaw and pain shoots upward to my ears. I stand cowering at the mercy of my own misery as the last licks of sunlight cast their glorious best into my home.

Motionless, I wait until dusk has finally settled and all the birdsong has ceased. A coldness creeps into my soul. In the semi-darkness each breath becomes deeper, stronger. Slowly, slowly, I unfurl, strengthen my resolve.

I will not follow that path again; it only leads to darkness, more pain.

I will not.

I will not.

Drawing my shoulders back, I roll them, taking deep, cleansing lungfuls of air. Each gasp bringing me further away from the daunting edge of self-destruction.

I open my eyes. The moon is low-slung and full – a night for madness – it radiates caressing beams into the still kitchen. I'm drawn to the cut-glass bowls reflecting jagged prisms of light onto the counter. I pick one up, hold it high, turning it, squinting my eyes at the dazzling colours. The temptation taunts me. Carefully, I place it back onto the counter. I nudge each of the bowls close to the edge of the counter. Pauletta's pride in these salvaged heirlooms niggles at my conscience.

I open the dishwasher, lift out a dinnerplate, am pleased to see Miles has rinsed it before slotting it in. I lift each one out in turn to check, stacking them carefully as I do. I push closed the dishwasher. I lift the pile of plates high above my head and toss them to the ground.

The thunder of shattering china, pierces the silence, setting me free from the bonds of expectation.

'I'm back.'

*

I lift my head on hearing the chime of the doorbell. I look at the hall clock and calculate. For 1 hour, 47 minutes the house has been silent, waiting for his return. So, I wait, not willing to be summoned so easily. The comfort of the chair not nearly as appealing as Scott's embrace.

The doorbell rings again, followed by rapid knocks. 'Hey, Maddie.'

I take my time to open the door, time to enjoy the sparks of recognition, time to get them back under control. 'You're back.' I keep my tone and expression blank.

The portico lighting casts weary shadows. Scott stands, his face haunted, his arms hung loose by his side. 'It's our last night, Maddie. I can't leave you like this.'

'But you did leave me.'

'To quote a famous actress, I came back for you. Can I come in? Please.' I open the door a tad wider to let him enter. 'Thank you.'

We stand, maybe a yard apart. The urge to shake this man has never been stronger. 'Well?'

'Do you want the long version or the short version?'

'I don't care, any.'

'In the doorway?' Scott nods in the direction of the kitchen. 'A cup of English tea would be nice.'

'Okay, why not.' I lead the way through the dining room and on into the kitchen, flick the light switch. Shattered plates glisten in the warm white of the LED spotlights – the china is a visually-spectacular display of my dysfunctional life.

Scott lets out a low whistle. 'Did you have a private party after I left?'

'You asked what happened to Maddie Harris.' I place my hand on my chest. 'She's here, every day, screaming to be let out. Some days, I let her. Today was one of those days.'

'Is she always so… messy?'

I laugh. 'No, sometimes she fancies herself as an actress. She really misses being an actress – life got in the way.'

I walk around the shards, and click on the kettle.

Scott pokes his head into the utility room. 'I guess the broom's in here.'

By the time a pot of tea is brewed, the floor has been swept clear. We sit at the breakfast bar in silence. I look into my mug – the rich, amber tea, strong and still, has no answers. I can feel Scott's eyes on me.

I look up. 'How did you get on with Christie?'

'It was kinda tough, you know. Yeah, she didn't want to lose face by backing down. We agreed to take it slow and steady.'

I nod, note there was no mention of me. 'And she still thinks I used her to get back into the spotlight.'

Scott looks away from me. 'I guess.' He puts a hand on my shoulder, and looks me in the eye. 'You got to give her time, she'll come round.'

I let out a snort. 'The thing nobody seems to get, is that I've been turning down parts, cameos and guest appearances for years.' I click my well-manicured fingers. 'I could have got a part like that!'

'Yeah, I believe you could.'

The boulder of dual grief hardens in my chest, pushes down on my heart. I lost my daughter and my identity. 'I'm a fool for turning them down. I could have been someone.'

'You are someone.'

Recognition flows like lava through my body as Scott envelops me in his embrace. The heat of his breath on my neck sends a sensual shimmy of shivers down my spine. I rest my head on his shoulder and our bodies melt together. Closing my eyes, an involuntary sigh escapes. He scoops me up into his arms.

'Where are you taking me?'

'To the place I can remind you who you are.'

Loyalties

Nuzzling the sensitive skin

'What's Scott doing here? It is his car in the drive, isn't it?'

I pull my robe tighter around my body. 'It's very early, Trudy. Far too early for a social visit, is there a problem?'

She lets out a loud sigh and plops down on the sofa arm. 'Christie and Miles had a quarrel. Miles left – I thought he might have come here.'

'Not very likely, because—'

'He knew you had other plans.'

'It's not like Miles to be like that, impulsive.'

'Yes, well, Christie *was* very upset.'

'All the more reason he'd stay.'

'He didn't go back to his place, we checked, and his phone is off.'

'He does that sometimes. He must need to think things through. Is Christie here?'

'She's waiting in the car. Why would she want to come in when Scott's car is blatantly parked in the drive? It's humiliating enough.'

'I don't see why.'

Trudy stands, the hem of her shift dress drops down to a decent length again. Like a boxed beetle, she skirts around the edge of the lounge. 'Your home is very beautiful.'

'Yes.'

'And Miles used to live here with you.'

'I'm not sure what you are implying, Trudy.'

'I'm not implying anything, but why was he here in the first place, and why did he move out?'

'You know, Trudy, that is absolutely nothing to do with you. But if you want to know, why not ask the man himself?'

'I would, if I could find him. Christie is stressed out, and she knows she can't compete with you. Whatever hold you have over him. it isn't natural.'

I run my hands over my face, stroke my tired eyes. 'I have no hold over Miles.'

'But I bet you know where he's gone.'

'I've an idea.' I remember the first time I saw him, cowering in the church porch, half-starved and far from clean. He's come a long way from that pitiful youth. I look at Trudy, do I trust her with that sacred piece of the jigsaw? 'He might be at the Church just up the road from here, St Mary's.'

'I didn't know he's religious.'

'He's not. Let Christie go to him, she'll understand why he's there.'

'Morning, ladies.' Scott is fully dressed in yesterday's clothes and has a day's worth of stubble.

'Hardly. Miles is missing,' snaps Trudy.

'I'm sure he'll turn up,' he returns without missing a beat.

'Haven't you a plane to catch, or are you planning on staying here with the delightful Miss De-Muir.'

'Appealing as that sounds…' His lips curve into a luscious grin. 'I've only a few hours to go before I leave. I was planning on swinging by to see Christie.'

'Whatev's.' She turns to me. 'Right or left?'

'Pardon?'

'At the end of the drive, do I turn right or left to find the church?'

'Right, it's a couple of hundred yards, and it's on the right.'

'Bye, then. I'll see myself out.' She sidles from the room like a cat on a tightrope, all the while eyes flicking between me and Scott.

'Remember, let Christie go to him.' I hear the door slam.

The look of amusement on Scott's face is filled with mischief. 'I kinda like her. She'd make an interesting study to paint.'

'She's certainly interesting, but I think you'd have to fight Christie for that pleasure.'

'It might be worth the fight.' Scott sits beside me. 'So, what's this with Miles?'

'They've had a row, and he's gone off. I'm more concerned about Christie. Miles, he just needs a bit of space to sort things out. Christie…'

He holds both my hands. 'Christie? You've got to give me more than that.'

I turn to look at him, let out a deep sigh. 'I just want her to be okay.' I shrug. 'With me. With us.'

I remember Christie's letter tucked in the drawer in the snug. She said she wants to love me. I close my eyes. Panic pulses through my veins. Have I forfeited the love of my daughter for the love of Scott? Opening my eyes, I look at Scott. Slowly I pull my hands from his as icicles spear my heart. I will not lose her again. I will not.

'Hey, I'm sure Christie will be fine.'

I stand and smile. 'Breakfast?'

*

It was hardly fit for a king, but the croissants and orange juice were as much as either of us could face, for wildly different reasons.

Scott reaches for my hand across the table, our fingers link. I remember the strength of his hands, the sensitivity of his touch. All the trappings of being in love and all the heartbreak of saying goodbye are etched into the expression on his face.

The yearning, desire, regret, the hope.

I try to smile, but the shattered fragments of my dreams pierce my soul, allowing the remaining glimmers of hope for a future with Scott to seep to their grave. I look away.

He squeezes my fingers. 'Hey, it's not that bad.'

I look back at him, force my smile. 'I know.'

'Yeah, I can clear some time in a couple of weeks if you want to come over.'

'I'm coming over to LA for the filming. I need to check with Tim on the scheduling. It makes sense to try and synchronise the visits.'

He lets out a low whistle. 'I kinda thought that could be months away. I'm not sure I wanna wait that long. Do you?'

'He's wanting the publicity shots to include me, so it will be no more than six week—'

'Six weeks. I'm struggling to think about the next six hours.'

'Once you get back, you'll hardly—'

'Are you running out on me again?' Scott stands, towers over me with the exact same expression he had just one week ago.

'Scott, please understand, I've got to sort things out with Christie before I can even think about—'

'Forget it. I'll see myself out.'

Waiting to hear the door slam for the second time this morning, I drop my head into my hands. I clench my jaw, eyes screwed up determined to hold back the amazon of tears until he's gone. Losing him the first time nearly killed me, but I survived. This time can be no worse. The metallic taste of blood prompts me to stop biting down on the tender flesh of my lips.

I hear movement in the room. I can't let him see me broken. I keep my head down, face covered. 'Just leave Scott, there's nothing here for you.'

'Is me, madam. I let him out.'

The softly spoken words trigger tears to squeeze from my eyes. I catch a sob in my throat. The crushing pain in my chest intensifies. I try to hold back the devouring claws of the black hole, already scraping at the boundary of my sanity.

She rests her hand on my shoulder. 'I take care of you now.'

I open my eyes as I hear a thud against the table leg accompanied by a pitiful whine. Blearily, I look at Terry, who looks woefully back up at me, his paw raised for added affect. I drop my hand to his head and scrunch his fur beneath the lampshade cone. 'Hey, Terry…'

'I take care of two of you. Is time for strong tea and doggy treat.'

Pauletta takes herself off to the kitchen, Terry does his best to rest his head on my lap. I concentrate my attention on the soft fur behind is ears. He's survived the adventure of a basket-bike ride better than I've survived my adventure with Scott.

I scrape the chair back and hoist Terry onto my knee, hold him close. The cone scrapes over my face as he tries to rest his head on my shoulder. I can feel his fast heartbeat pounding against my chest, sure it's synchronising with mine. The hollow of my belly feels taut against the yielding mass of his fur. I hold on to the innocent devotion of my dog.

'Is taking advantage of your soft nature.'

'I let him leave.'

'I talking about Terry.'

'Ah.'

She holds a dog treat under his nose, totally oblivious to the irony of the situation. 'He knows only allowed on chairs in snug.'

'You are right.' Can she not see I'm holding on for my life while she's only holding onto my china mug?

'Is time for decision.'

I close my eyes and draw in a lungful of air. 'I've made up my mind already.'

Her eyes narrow. 'It is?'

'I let him leave, Pauletta.' My tears roll unwittingly down my cheeks. 'I let him leave, I need to…'

'Yes, yes, madam. But tea in here or in snug?'

'The snug.'

I ease Terry to the ground as Pauletta leads the way. Terry follows, the temptation of doggy treats is enough to banish all thoughts of his sore paw altogether. In the snug, he settles himself in his usual spot next to mine.

Pauletta plumps up the cushions behind me and passes me my tea. She perches her skinny bum on the edge of the coffee table. 'Now, madam, tell me all about trouble.'

I let out a half sob. 'I think I've made a terrible mistake.'

'Is correct.' She nods solemnly, with only a hint of superiority.

'It should never have happened.'

'I agree, but is not for me to say.'

'If Trudy hadn't turned up this morning, I would never have…'

Pauletta frowns. 'I do not know *this* Trudy. Is she one more of his women?'

'Oh, no. She is Christie's friend.'

Pauletta grunts.

'Christie and Miles have quarrelled.'

Pauletta's expression brightens. 'Is no problem. Miles can come back here until he is well again. I build him up.'

'I'd been worried about Christie finding out about me and Scott. And now she does…'

'I do not understand this problem. These people cause you many tears, and again today. She not grateful and he not good for you. But is not for me to say.'

Pauletta stands and heads for the door shaking her head.

'But he is good for me,' I mutter, as the door closes behind her, 'and she is trying.'

I cling to the hot mug as the familiar shudders begin to take hold of my body. I manage to get it to the coffee table before my convulsions become too erratic to control. Drawing my legs to my body, I clamp my arms around them sinking into a tight ball on the sofa.

Terry's nose somehow manages to find the nape of my neck, nuzzling the sensitive skin, giving me all the permission I need to let out the anguish.

Silent screams fill the sanctuary of my snug, echoing back my grief a million times greater than I can ever recall in the past. The years of yearning for my daughter are now fully entwined and embedded in the loss of Scott.

The truths of Christie's letter taunt me from the safety of their nesting place in the drawers across the room. I know all I have done. I know all the reasons behind my decisions. Like the ball in a pinball game being flung from one ping to the next before falling into the abyss, spent and worthless.

I drag the corner of the throw to still the fresh surge of tears, pushing it into my screwed-up eyes and holding it over my face. Slowly, slowly the sobs subside. I'm left rocking, holding the remainder of my grief as one would a new baby – just getting a feel for how we are going to get along, how we are going to learn from each other. A painful process of trial and error. One I am so very tired of.

I reach out for Terry, fiddle blindly with his neck cone and release him from its confines. He snuggles in closer to me. My comfort. He always seems to understand what I need, better than I do myself. The luxury of unquestioning love and loyalty can only be guaranteed if your best friend has four legs.

And calm settles in my bones. I can feel the trauma leaving me now, like a mist over a meadow on an autumn morn, clearing so my view is panoramic. I can see all the paths ahead of me leading off in various directions, all with differing destinations and individual closures. If I turn round, I see all the paths I've already taken leading me to this place of trouble.

And now, I can see clearly. The only way forward, is back.

Repercussions

Trudy appears unmoved

'Let her in.'

'Is not good to let people see you like…'

I thread my fingers together and rest back on the sofa. Terry pushes his nose under my hands. The damp edge of the throw drapes down, revealing the threadbare upholstery beneath.

'I show her into lounge.'

'In here, Pauletta.'

She glances round the snug. 'Is very uppy young lady, madam.'

'Exactly.'

Pauletta picks up my cold mug of tea. 'Is not for me to say.' She leaves, head bowed and muttering.

I run my fingers over my eyes and know for sure they are still puffy and red. I flatten my hair and tuck it behind my ears. The cream linen of my trousers is creased beyond repair, my pink toenails peeping out profess a degree of elegance, which is more than lacking. My blouse is relatively neat despite the ministrations of Terry.

A sharp knock at the door announces Pauletta. 'Madam, a Miss Drummond to see you.' She ushers Trudy into the snug.

'Hello again, Trudy.'

She shifts from one slender limb to the other. 'Maddie.'

'Forgive me for not standing, I'm still nursing my ankle.'

She straightens. 'If it isn't convenient—'

'Oh, it's not a problem at all, please,' I say, outstretching my arm, 'make yourself at home.'

Trudy eyes the mismatched armchairs and threadbare chaise with a degree of disdain one would normally reserve for a rat-infested hostelry. She finally perches on the edge of the chaise. The hem of her shift dress rises to within inches of her underwear. Her perfectly toned, caramel legs come to an abrupt end with a pair of designer, flat pumps, tucked neatly under her chair.

She flicks her hair over her shoulder and settles her gaze on me. 'Thank you.'

'Would you care for a drink?'

'It's a little early, but—'

'I make tea, coffee or juice,' says Pauletta, from the doorway.

'Coffee. A coffee should do the trick.'

'I'll have a pot of tea please, Pauletta. And please bring a cafetiere of coffee for Miss Drummond.'

Pauletta nods, and closes the door behind her.

'So, Trudy, I'm feeling honoured, two visits in one morning.'

She clears her throat. 'I called to apologise if I appeared rude this morning.' She runs her hands over the remains of her vanishing skirt.

'Apology accepted. I understand you must have been more focused on finding Miles than your manners.'

Trudy's eyes widen. 'Quite. Christie was already distressed, and seeing Scott's car here added insult to injury.'

'I don't see how… We are both consenting adults.'

Trudy stands. 'I can see you are going to make this as awkward as possible for me. This isn't easy, you know.'

I allow myself an inward smile. 'I know. Interesting, isn't it?'

'Pardon?'

'It's interesting how far we are prepared to go for the people we love. I mean, turning up on my doorstep at silly o'clock in the morning, hardly your thing at all.'

'Christie needed to find Miles.'

'And did she?'

'Yes.'

'And was that not the most important thing to tell me, that Miles is safe and well?'

'I was getting to that.'

'Ah, please do.'

Trudy shuffles, eager to be gone, but is trapped by good manners now I've called her out on her behaviour of this morning. 'As soon as I mentioned the church, Christie knew you were right.'

'You found him there.'

'I let Christie go to him, like you said.'

'And they have reconciled?'

Trudy sits back down on the chaise. 'I think so. I left them there together, and went home. They arrived back just as Scott arrived to say his goodbyes.'

'Ah…'

'I thought it best I give them some privacy.'

'And so, here you are gracing me with your presence.'

A swift knocking and Pauletta is in, a laden tray held aloft in one hand. 'Madam, is it for me to pour?'

'Thank you, but I think we can manage.'

The tray is placed on the coffee table, and Pauletta bobs her way out of the room. Along with our drinks, the tray has a selection of biscuits and buttered scones.

'Please, help yourself.'

Trudy busies herself with her coffee and selects a scone. 'Thank you. Good help is hard to find.' She takes a tentative bite, closes her eyes and groans in pleasure. 'These are divine, still warm.'

I pour my tea, and add lots of milk and a mound of sugar. 'She is a gem.'

'Yes.'

'So, everybody is happy, and we have touched on the subject of good help... But, really, Trudy, I have no idea why you are here.'

'And you are determined to make it difficult.'

'You can take it.' I smile.

'I think I have underestimated you.'

'Ah...'

'All the things you have done regarding Christie – which I might add, I totally disagree with – have been for her.'

'Absolutely.'

'In your own way, I think you believe you've done the right thing—'

I laugh out loud, throwing my head back. 'Oh, no, no, no, no, no. I've done everything wrong from the day I left Scott. But no matter what I do, I can't go back in time and put it right.'

'But you want to.'

I shrug. 'What does it matter to you?'

'Because Christie matters. And that is why I underestimated you. You are prepared to do anything for Christie, and Christie is my best friend.'

I nod slowly, I love this girl.

'So,' Trudy continues, 'that means we are on the same team.'

'It does.' I feel tears well up in my eyes, and know now isn't the time to let them fall.

Trudy smiles for the first time *ever* in my presence. 'Congratulations,' she says, and offers her hand to shake mine.

I take her hand and shake it. 'Congratulations to you too.'

'You look like shit, by the way.'

'Thanks.'

'And, you of all people should know, going into battle you should always look your best.'

'Perhaps.'

'Scott looks like shit too.'

'Really?'

'Almost worse than you.'

'Was Lola-May with him?'

'She didn't come in. You've met her?'

'A lovely girl, I think she's going to do well.'

'So, what's the story between you and Scott?'

I place my cup back on the table and draw my legs back beneath me. Terry repositions himself back on my lap. I begin scrunching his fur behind his ears, grateful for the monotony of the soothing gesture. I know he has one eye on the plate of biscuits, but I'll forgive him.

My body has reset itself to this new norm of heightened distress. The constant feeling that the worst is about to happen, it is somehow a comfort when it does.

The slight shimmy of fission between reality and my connection with it, acts as a buffer for my delicate emotional state. I'm in a bubble, nothing can touch me, so any move is safe, until the bubble bursts.

'I never got over him.'

'But this morning it looked like…'

'Yes, it did. We were. But then you turned up.'

'Meaning?'

'I have spent years waiting to build a relationship with Christie. Waiting in the background, watching from the wings. She's grown up without me, and I can hardly blame her for not wanting me now. But there's a part of me that knows deep down we have a connection, whether we want it or not. I'm the one who pushed her to paint, to follow her dream.'

'She always prattled on about her marvellous Auntie Maddie. I was actually jealous.'

'All those years of writing to each other. She must know who I am,' I say, touching my chest, 'in here.'

Trudy nods, in a noncommittal kind of way. 'And Scott?'

'I didn't intend to let him back into my heart, but he was already there. And when you turned up this morning, it reminded me of everything I've sacrificed to get Christie back. And I needed to make a choice, Christie or Scott.'

'And you chose Christie.'

'Correct.'

While my insides churn, Trudy appears unmoved.

She selects another buttered scone, and takes a delicate bite, catching a wayward crumb with her manicured finger. 'Maddie, has anybody ever told you, you can have your cake *and* eat it?'

'I've a feeling you are about to.'

'Hell, yes.'

Threads

An echo of my past

I tuck my mobile under the cushion as she enters the snug.

Pauletta narrows her eyes. 'I see what you do.'

I choose not to respond to her speculation, though in truth, she knows me too well.

'Is one week now, madam.'

'Thank you. I think I'll go and sit in the garden a while.'

'Is raining.'

'Then I'll sit in the summerhouse.'

'Is time for lunch.'

I slip my mobile back into my pocket as I stand. 'Maybe later.'

Terry follows me to the backdoor, ball in mouth. I slip off my sandals before I step outside. Terry turns, not willing to wet his paws.

Rain-soaked grass tickles my feet and nudges between my toes. I look up at the monotonous sky promising a day as uneventful as I deserve. Delicate drizzle torments my face, my arms, my legs as I stride towards my sanctuary at the end of the garden. Proof I'm still mortal.

Pauletta will leave me to lick my wounds. Like Terry, the rain will keep her away.

I pause with my fingers on the handles before swinging open both doors. I close my eyes as my mind is saturated with memories of my time here with Scott. I will not allow them to wash over me. I need to unpack them one by one. I need to give each the full consideration of my reflections. Recall each moment we spent together.

And then I can put them away, for another rainy day.

I squint, tolerating enough vision to find a lounger. Disregarding the drenching I've had, I lay back, letting the mish-mash of cushions absorb some of the rainwater.

A shiver courses through me and I wrap my arms tight about my body, draw up my knees and turn onto my side. Head bowed I hold myself safe against the hammering certainty of a future without Scott.

I drag the throw over me keeping the chill at bay.

But no tears, they've all been spent, rendering my face puffy and red for days on end. I'm left with reality. A hard, unyielding conviction. A life sentence enduring a loveless existence.

I will smile. I will chat. I will laugh. I may even dance. But they will all be on the surface of my being. Like the mighty river Niagara, vast and serene on the surface, yet hiding a myriad of traumas beneath, while she forever gracefully hurtles towards an almighty fall. All that goes before leads to that crescendo, yet nothing can stop it other than a dry riverbed.

I know this is how I must protect myself from another mighty fall. I must render my heart barren, lifeless. I must still the flow of passion, allow its heat to scorch any pockets of resistance, evaporate any fertile thoughts.

The moment I saw him again, I knew. I knew nothing could stop the overriding momentum of my desire to delve back into his life. Every innocent touch, every nuance of my demeanour radiated reverberations of the love we once shared so nonchalantly. A love that never had the opportunity to fully develop and realise the joy of simply dwelling.

I hold the throw to my face, breathe in its scent. Slight echoes of my past life are somehow captured and retained for all time in the decades-old fabric. Only now do I recognise the hours of dedication revealed in my mother's gift. All the time I thought myself adrift from the restrictions of her love, she was channelling her love into making these patchwork throws. How often must she have held the remains of my old clothes to her face to breathe in the memories, to garner a nugget of comfort, to feel a bond. Those little threads of my life bound together to create an eclectic semblance of unity. If only I could do the same with the tattered remains of myself.

I'd spent hours getting ready for the sitting with Scott. Wanted him to be drawn back to a time when we were young, carefree. But it went far deeper than a re-enactment of the past.

From the moment Scott traced my scar, it was a new beginning, I was forgiven. I knew it. I believed it. I felt it.

His embrace, and his alone, has the power to piece all my fractured fragments together, and make me whole, worthy, loved.

And yet, I cannot accept this gift of renewal.

I must not.

Though the sacrifices I have already made pale into insignificance at the loss of Scott, I have no choice but continue on, until Christie lets me back into her life.

As Auntie Maddie, I held the privileged position of being Christie's confidant. I witnessed the dramas from a place of safety, cocooned from the fallouts and disappointments of everyday life. But her successes and highs became part of my life. Every room here was graced with a selection of her paintings, bringing my home to life, bringing Christie closer to me.

As good as it was, it wasn't enough.

I wanted more.

Needed more.

And by exhibiting all Christie's work and revealing our true relationship I forced the issue. And I knew, I knew there would be a pile of problems to sort out, but I was prepared.

But I blew it when Scott turned up. And now I've got to get back on track. Start again to build trust with Christie.

I wrap the throw more tightly as skirmishes of goosebumps assault my whole body. The thought of being banished from Christie's life is too painful to contemplate.

I have lived without the love of Scott for so much of my life, surely what remains is tolerable.

But Christie... I've become accustomed to the cherished position I held in her heart. The loss is like a black hole sucking the pleasure from everything I see and do.

At least Miles is keeping me updated, and Christie has spoken to me a couple of stilted times on the mobile.

My breathing is steady and the shivers have stopped but the jagged spikes of uncertainty continue to jab. The constant unrest is exhausting, I have no energy left to fight and no zest to enjoy the beauty of my existence.

I've turned the portrait Scott did of me round. The ethereal image is nothing but a fleeting beat of a blissful heart. I cannot bare to witness the beauty he saw in me. All that is left of me is a shell, like the ones at the beach – as you hold them to your ear and hear the echo of the ocean – so all you see of me is an echo of my past.

I groan as I hear the summerhouse door open, know it can only be Pauletta. 'Leave me alone.'

'Is what I wish. But uppy lady is back, and tapping her foot.' I raise my head, peer out from under the throw. Pauletta is stood arms clamped across her middle. 'I try to send her away, but is very uppy.'

I heave a sigh and drop my head back onto the cushions. 'I'm really not in the mood.'

'This is what I say, but she not listen. She point her finger at me.'

I roll my lips to halt the smile desperate to escape. I doubt anyone has ever risked pointing at her before, I daren't look. Suddenly I'm overcome with the urge to giggle, try to cover it with a cough. Histeria is a heartbeat away.

'Is nothing to be funny about. I not going back without you. My life, it does not deserve this.'

But still, a bubble of laughter escapes. 'I'm sorry.'

She lets out a deep sigh and plants her hands just above her utility belt. 'I happy to wait.' Her foot begins a frantic tapping.

There is no point trying to best her. Sitting up, I swing my legs down, but hold the throw partially covering my face and the smile reluctant to leave. I look past her through the open door. 'Is it still raining?'

'Is a little, but is time to go.'

I turn and rearrange the throw, squint my eyes. The random fabrics blur into one crazy abstract puzzle. One that cannot be fathomed.

I follow Pauletta from the summerhouse and she closes the doors firmly behind us. No going back. I must suffer the confidence of Trudy.

I scrunch my toes into the wet grass as I make my way back to the house. The smell of damp earth and peonies fills me with the twin sense of needing to stay absolutely grounded but also to seek out whatever delicately-exquisite distractions I dare.

Trudy is balanced on a breakfast stool examining her fingernails, she glances up and smiles. 'Thanks for making the time.'

'Hello, Trudy.' I attempt to dry my feet, but the doormat is rough and unyielding offering little help. 'Let's go through to the lounge. Pauletta, can you organise a pitcher of orange juice?'

'Yes, madam.' Her tone says no.

Trudy stands, amazingly there is still three miles of perfectly honey-toned thigh on display. 'Lead the way.'

For the first time in days pain shoots from my ankle down into my foot. I grimace, but do my best not to hobble. 'So, how are things at Rose Cottage?'

'Changeable.' The click from Trudy's sandals echoes through the hallway emphasising her stark reply.

'How so?'

'For starters, Miles is constantly sneaking off to see you.'

We step into the lounge. Trudy sighs. Without looking at her, I know she'll be evaluating every detail, pricing and number crunching. I turn towards the large bay window and gesture to the oversized sofa. 'Please, take a seat.'

'Thanks.' Trudy rests back, her legs fully on display, knees together, ankles crossed. She threads her fingers through her hair drawing out her silky mane and lets it fall to her shoulders. 'She isn't jealous.'

'Sorry?'

'Of you and Miles.'

I nod. 'So, it's changeable at Rose Cottage, you say.'

'Christie is feeling… deflated. All your attention—'

'Which she rejected—'

'All the media interest—'

'Which she hated—'

'Will you just listen?'

'I am, but I'm pointing out the relevant facts.'

'What do facts have to do with emotions?'

'Good question.'

'I'm trying to help, Maddie.'

'I know.' I sigh. 'But I think I will just have to wait this one out—'

'No. You need to step up!'

I admire her conviction. Wish I had half of it. But then, she's had a life blessed with an easy road – paved with gold and excellent connections. 'Look at me, I'm tired of fighting. Christie will come round in time.'

Trudy stands, begins to pace. 'I thought you had balls. I was wrong.'

'Maybe they got crushed.'

'She needs you now. She needs to know you'll stick your neck out for her—'

'I allowed myself to be outed on national TV.' My voice is hushed, barely audible to my own ears.

'You threw Christie to the lions—'

'No.' I sigh. 'I've spent my life watching my parents bringing her up to be strong and resilient. I knew she'd cope.'

'You aren't.'

'I never really have.'

'Bullshit.' She raises an eyebrow and tosses out a wrist pointing loosely around the room. 'Ta-dah. Where'd all this come from?'

'I was an actress—'

'Another thing Christie is upset about, your new movie deal.'

I shrug. 'Hardly that, helping out an old friend. A bit part, nothing more.' The buzz in my belly blasts through my body. Even the thought of being on set fills me with an instant intensity. A focus of emotion. I crave the vibrancy and clarity needed for a successful character. I raise my chin, and look Trudy in the eye. 'I'm a damn fine actress, actually.'

'You need to be. You've a daughter to win back.'

'I know.'

'Oh, and a lover.'

Setups and Upsets

Perhaps I should leave

'Leave it,' she snaps.

'It's too much.'

'No.'

'It's very—'

'It's everything you are. It's everything, and a little bit more.'

'Exactly. I don't want my *little bit more* on display.'

'In your own dining room? It's hardly a sin.'

'It's vain.'

'No, it's justified.'

I look at my portrait and at Trudy. Know I've met my match. These last three weeks have been a hectic schedule of self-promotion. Mum and Dad have been keeping me up-to-date with snippets of feedback from Christie. And to be fair, Trudy's, "Operation: Impress-the-hell-out-of-her" seems to be working.

I've paraded the Keep-a-Key kids for the tabloids.

I took afternoon tea with Christie's headmaster and Slimy Sloan.

Twice.

I've done improvisation with Year 7s.

Macbeth with Year 8s.

An *English Rose* with Year 9s.

Romeo and Juliet with Year 10s.

And a Q&A with Year 11s.

All this has resulted in a very strained relationship with Pauletta, who has been burdened with ball throwing for Terry. Quite frankly, I'm ready to snap.

I don't remember working being this much hard work. I practically fall asleep in my soup – the only thing I can force down because my nerves are that frayed – and another reason for Pauletta's wrath.

And now Trudy is redoubling her efforts for reconciliation because Tim wants me in LA next week for promo filming. Trudy sees this as an ideal joint venture with Christie…

Christie is bobbing round to see me after work, and Trudy is making sure the "ambiance" is just right.

Trudy's insistence of my portrait being the focal point of the dining room, positioned over the mantlepiece, is making me nervous. Even Pauletta's latest floral arrangement – strangely incorporating Terry's discarded neck cone and random twigs – cannot compete.

'The idea is, Christie will take a selfie of the two of you in front of it.'

'Yes, I understand that bit.' Ha, not going to happen in a thousand years.

'Then when she comes home, I'll get her to send it to Scott.'

'My focus is on building a relationship with Christie.'

Trudy flings her arms in the air. 'I know! When Scott sees how well you are getting on, he'll invite you *both* over together.'

'But I'm already going.'

Trudy closes her eyes and draws her fingers through the length of her hair, stopping midway to scrunch the back of her head. She opens her eyes and settles her scary scrutiny on me.

The metallic taste of blood prompts me to stop biting the insides of my lips. The rollercoaster in my belly has come to a shaky standstill, but now a stampede of buffalo is making their way around my intestines.

I cover my face with my hands. 'This isn't going to work.'

'Not with you looking like a neurotic has-been.'

'Just what I needed to hear. Thanks.'

'Look at yourself. I'm beginning to think all your *heartbreak* over Scott was a huge act, cos you are making no effort—'

'I am making a tremendous effort and I am exhausted! But like I keep saying, Christie is my focus.'

'Oh, come off it. You want Scott too, and as I keep saying, you can have your cake and eat it.'

'Maybe I don't deserve it,' I whisper.

Her arms wrap around me, her hand cradles my head to her shoulder. I hold myself rigid in this unexpected embrace. Her fingers stroke my hair and suddenly my guard falls away and my body sags against hers as I simply absorb the support she's giving.

'Of course, you deserve it.'

She strokes my hair over and over, her fingers doing fluttery things with the tangled strands. All the months of tension drain away and a sense of peace and wellbeing washes over me.

Maybe I do deserve it. Maybe now it's time for me. I feel tears on my face, but I'm not crying. The tears are leaving me, I don't need them anymore. I don't need to hold them in, or pour them out. I just need to hold onto this feeling I have right now. An overwhelming certainty that everything's going to be all right.

'Thank you.'

'You're welcome. Now get your soggy face off my designer frock, and get your skinny arse into gear.'

'I have no idea how you do that every day. I'm exhausted.'

'I love it. The kids are great. But we all have our off days, I suppose.'

'And it's your last week before the summer holidays.'

'Yep, and we are so ready for a break.'

'Have you any plans?'

Christie shrugs. 'Nothing definite. Miles is tied up with the gallery insurance claim, as you know…'

'I did offer to help—'

'He's got it under control, he says.'

'He's very thorough.'

Christie offers a meagre smile and looks away in the direction of my portrait. She clears her throat.

'Is here now. I have spinach and stilton quiche and strawberries later.' Pauletta ushers us from the window seat to the table by wafting a wooden, salad fork.

We both sit, and help ourselves under Pauletta's watchful gaze. Satisfied, she leaves us to eat our food.

'Thank you for coming, I wanted you to hear from me rather than from Miles…'

Christie stills her fork midway to her mouth, places it back onto her plate.

'I'm going out to LA next week. Tim has set up promo shots for the movie.'

She picks up her fork and continues eating.

'I haven't even done any filming yet,' I blunder on.

'What's the film about?'

'It's about a group of small-town folks preparing to welcome home a prom queen years after she left to seek her fortune…'

'How sweet,' she says, sarcasm oozing from every syllable. 'I take it you're the prom queen.'

'Originally she was a no-show. But Tim couldn't resist a subtle twist.'

'I bet.'

'Christie, what is the problem? I'm doing my best here. I'm being open about this, trying to engage. I had no idea about this until Tim turned up on my doorstep, at the insistence of Miles, I might add.'

'Did you sleep with him?

'Pardon!'

'Tim. Did you sleep with him?'

'Why on earth would you think that?'

'It didn't take you long to lure Scott back into your bed.'

A feeling of nausea hurtles from my belly to my hand at my throat. The quiver in my legs and the sweat on my brow gives me a moment's notice as to what is to follow. My chair crashes to the ground as I dash from the room. I make it just in time to get my head over the basin in the cloakroom. While I'm doubled up on my knees my stomach turns itself inside out. My body convulses until nothing but bile is left.

I rock back, resting my haunches on my heels and steady my breath. The grip of control my quaking stomach claimed, is slowly broken as I take shaky lungfuls of air. Breath by breath I settle myself. The tremors ease, but I still feel panicky, my fingers like frozen stalagmites clutch my chest.

I feel cold. Clammy. I stand up and swill my face with lukewarm water. Looking in the mirror, a ghost of the woman I used to be stares back, emotionless and drained.

I have spent over twenty years skulking about in the shadows fearing the day I would be exposed.

That day has been and gone.

I roll back my shoulders, pinch my cheeks to add some colour, take a deep breath and walk back into the lion's den.

Christie stands as I enter. My chair has been righted and my plate put to one side.

'Perhaps I should leave, if you are unwell…'

'Perhaps.' I cross the room to the window seat. 'I've told you about LA. I was going to invite you along, but now I understand that would have been a mistake.'

She nods and looks away. Embarrassed perhaps. She gestures to my portrait. 'He is a skilled artist.'

'He is.'

'I suppose you'll be going to see him… in LA.'

'I very much doubt that—'

'But you were back together.'

'Yes, we were. But I had a choice to make, and I chose you.'

'I don't understand.'

I smile the smile I've worn for the last two decades. 'No, Christie, you don't.'

In the Nick of Time

It's going to be a long flight

'Is not my place to say.'

'Pauletta! Now is not the time.'

My stomach feels like a washing machine filled with forks on a spin cycle, my head, a scout's jamboree and my nerves a shattered chandelier.

I have packed and unpacked six times, started to phone Tim twice to cancel and sobbed while pouring my heart out to Terry – probably the only one who'll truly miss me.

I can't blame Christie, and Miles was only doing what I asked. But Sod's Law, a new venue for *Evolution* is only available for three weeks starting this weekend, so, tomorrow the paintings need to be taken out of storage and transported to… I don't even know where!

Of course, Miles is going to manage the whole caboodle, he did last time.

Christie at least had the grace to look sheepish when they arrived to tell me yesterday. She wished me well, even gave me a stilted hug. Miles insisted it was still going to be a huge adventure for me.

He knows my nature too well. In the same breath as withdrawing his support, he gifted Pauletta his flight, knowing darn well I wouldn't… couldn't deny her the opportunity of seeing Hollywood. So, now I'm going to be besieged with the ever- critical, pseudo-humble Pauletta for the duration.

And to put my mind at rest – not likely – tyrannical Trudy is taking up residence here to take care of Terry and Pixi. She has already selected her bedroom. Pauletta has taken it upon herself to explain the finer details of poop-scooping after Terry. Also, the day the bins and recycle go out, and to Trudy's horror, the correct procedure for the disposal of female sanitary products.

It was a very one-sided conversation.

I look at Pauletta's sturdy holdall propped up besides my trio of Louis Vuitton luggage, and cringe. I have no idea what the VIP shuttle service Miles has organised will make of *that* combo. At least the two of us will be ushered into a private lounge before boarding.

'Towels'

'Pardon?'

'We need towels.'

'No, Pauletta. Everything we want, could possibly need, will be already there.' Give me strength.

'Is rude to expect.'

'Tim has house guests all the time, his staff will ensure we are well cared for.' I glance at the clock, a whole ten minutes before we are being picked up. My stomach rolls.

Pauletta is sat on the bottom step by the cases like a displaced person. She refuses to sit by my side on the chaise with her typical, "Is not my place".

Trudy wanders in from the back of the house. Her Jimmy Choo's have been replaced by hiking boots – it's 24°outside – her trademark shift dress is still eight inches shorter than it need be. Terry is tucked under her arm like a designer clutch.

'Still here? I don't want poor Terry-werry getting all upsetty-wetty, do I my little buddy-woody.'

Terry looks at me with his help-me eyes. 'I'm sure you are going to take excellent care of him.' I pat the seat beside me. 'Come on, Terry.'

Terry makes scrabbling movements with his paws and Trudy lets him down. 'Off you go to mummy, one last time.'

Terry jumps up next to me.

'Is not allowed on furniture.'

I ignore Pauletta and snuggle up to Terry. His warm belly presses to mine as he tucks his head on my shoulder, one paw either side of my neck. The only true hug I've had in weeks. I wrap my arms fully around his skinny torso, and scratch the pink flesh of his belly. He settles his snuffling nose in my hairline.

A piercing yap sears through my skull as he scrambles off my lap. At the door he repeatedly bounds up, letting out the same high-pitched bark as he reaches the pinnacle of his leap.

Pauletta dashes to the door and scoops him up. 'Will be car.' She turns, and hands Terry – legs dangling and tail wagging furiously – to Trudy. 'Boot room, quick.'

Trudy takes the pooch and pops him in his safe place, away from excitement and intruders. Pauletta turns as the door swings open.

'Phew, we caught you!' says a beaming Miles.

Christie follows him in. 'Hi.'

'This is a pleasant surprise.' I stand as Miles bends to kiss my cheek.

He turns to look over his shoulder. 'Christie wanted a word before you left.' He ushers her towards me.

She shrugs. 'In private, if we can.'

I nod, my legs like spun glass – ready to snap at any moment – walk me into the snug. The comfort of my familiar furniture, my old friends. I glance at the sideboard, know exactly which drawer holds her letter. I clasp my hands too tightly, loosen them as I gesture for Christie to sit. I perch on the opposite sofa, and wait for whatever Christie feels fit to level at me.

She sits, her eyes darting around the room, her legs crossed, but her right foot frantically flapping. Finally, she settles her attention on me. 'This is you, isn't it?'

I allow myself to sag. 'It is.'

She waves her arm in the direction of the hallway. 'And the rest?'

'Is who the world expects me to be.'

'You don't let the world in.'

I snort. 'But I feel I owe it to them to live up to their expectations, after all, they made me.'

'And what about me, what do I deserve?'

'You deserve this. After all the pretence, you deserve the truth. And this is it, the true me. The me others don't see, don't want to see. People prefer the illusion.'

I walk over to the sideboard. I open each drawer, from the bottom to the top, like stepping stones to the temple of truth. 'Take a look at my life.'

Christie looks sceptically at the open drawers as I return to the sofa. My stomach feels like it's about to revolt as I wait. After what seems like minutes, but is likely only a few seconds she reluctantly goes over and looks into the top two drawers. Her hand sifting through the pile of baby photos, scarce few of them with the two of us together. Those are the ones I never look at, the reminder of a time too painful to embrace.

Yet, just my luck, she holds one up. 'You look like a child.' Her voice is strained, I can hear the bottleneck of tears held in check by the tightness of her throat.

'I was.'

'And lost.'

'I'd been lost a long time, a long time before I even met Scott.' I look away. 'But you'll see, until the bottom drawer, it's all you, Christie. All of it. I've always loved you, I just needed time to grow up.'

Her hand rests on the letter she sent me only weeks ago. 'Me too, I suppose.'

'I am sorry for the hurt, it was never my—'

'I get it, Maddie. And Scott—'

'I know it's not going to be a happily ever after.'

'Can I take this?' She holds up the old photo.

'Take any you like.'

She nods. 'I'd like this one. Did you show these to him?'

I bite my lip. 'A few. The ones of you.' I drop my chin, focus on my hands. 'Not me.' I want to say more, want to say that girl was the one he loved. That girl was the one who loved him. I look back at her. 'He wanted to see all the photos of you, it was you he came for.'

'And, I want you to know—'

The door is flung open. 'Is here! Big car to take us to airport.'

'In a moment, Pauletta.'

'Is now, must be quick.' She is waving her arms like a French Police officer in charge of the traffic around the Eiffel Tower. 'We will miss it.'

'I'll be one minute.' She darts from the room and I turn to my daughter. 'You wanted to say something.'

She waves the photo. 'Thank you for this. I want to understand the girl you were, Maddie, and this reminds me how young you were making the decisions you made.'

'I hope so, and Scott, he was young too.'

'Yes.' She looks away.

'It wasn't some casual hook-up, we both… I don't know, we expected it to last, ironic as that sounds.'

She half nods, her eyes challenge me. 'And what is it now? You knew he was only here for a week.'

I snort. 'Christie, I can't explain why, but again, it was no casual hook-up. And again, ironic as it sounds, we both expected it to last. Shame it hasn't.'

'What do you mean? I know he stayed here that last night.'

I sigh, remember his caresses, close my eyes and draw in a deep breath. 'Trudy turning up, you staying in the car, too angry with Scott. Too upset to even face me.' I offer a sad smile, open my eyes. 'If a choice is to be made between you and Scott, I will always choose you.'

She steeples her hands, just like Dad does. Her eyes fixed on my face. 'And what if I say,' she shrugs, 'that I'm cool with the two of you?'

'Is that a trick question?'

'No, it's a deadly serious question.'

I swallow, take a moment to gather my thoughts, rub my palms over my thighs. 'If you were *cool*, genuinely, I hope I'd be brave enough to tell him. Yeah, I'd want to tell him I still love him.'

Pauletta bursts into the room. 'Madam! We are ready!'

Christie and I stand at the same time. She steps forward and holds me in an awkward embrace lasting nanoseconds. Her tight-lipped smile does little to subdue the somersaulting pickaxes in my belly. I run my hands over the cool linen of my travel trousers.

'I think you should meet up with Scott, in LA. Tell him, you know. I'm a big girl, I can handle it.'

My heart pounds. 'Really?'

'Really. Trudy gave me an earbashing. Seems you've made a friend.'

'Thank you, all I need now is nerves of steel.'

'You've got them.'

'And I so hope your exhibition relaunch goes well.'

'Thanks. I'm sure Miles will pull out all the stops.' She looks towards the open doorway – to her escape route. 'I hope you find everything you want in LA, Maddie.'

I can see Pauletta from the doorway. She has strapped on her extra-large bumbag, in place of her utility belt, and is taking charge of the luggage loading, as if the chauffeur has never handled baggage before.

I look heavenward and Miles stifles a laugh. 'Good luck.'

'Thanks, I'm going to need it.' I pick up my handbag, have a quick shifty through it. Passport, mobile, purse, tissues, lippy. I look at Miles and Christie, side by side, not holding hands, but fingertips grazing. 'I'll see you both when I get back. I hope the exhibition is successful.'

'It will be.' Miles grins. 'Sarah McBride has taken it upon herself to make sure of it.'

Trudy places her hands on my shoulders, and bestows air kisses. 'Have a great trip,' she chirps. Leaning in close she whispers, 'Everything sorted?'

I nod and pull away, and give her a confident smile. Stepping away, I pat Miles' arm and Christie moves closer to him. They look perfectly at one with each other – the one I gave away and the one I found.

I let out a sigh. 'I'll phone when we get to Tim's. See you when we get back.'

Trudy joins them in the doorway as I glide into the plush interior of the car and sit beside a fussing Pauletta.

'Just sit down and stop making a big deal out of it,' I grind out.

She shoots me a mutinous look. 'In the bin, they throw it all away.'

'You are not allowed scissors on flights.'

'Is little sewing kit.'

Our hostess hovers closer. 'Would you like any assistance?'

I smile at the pristine thirty-something. 'No thank you, we are fine.'

She gestures to Pauletta's bumbag. 'Shall I put your bag in the locker for you.'

Pauletta grips her bumbag tightly to her. 'No. Thank you. Is safe here.'

'We will be taking off shortly…'

'I will sort it out.' I smile. 'She's a little nervous.'

The hostess returns my smile and moves on.

'I am not.'

'Look around – we are in the most expensive first-class seats, with every possible comfort, and you are clutching your bumbag! Stop drawing attention to us. Put it in the locker and get your seatbelt fastened.'

I can see the shock and hurt on her face as she unclips her bag and stashes it in the compartment by her side. She pulls her seatbelt across and secures it over her waist and shoulder – one of the advantages of first class, a seatbelt that doesn't snap your spine.

'The shoulder strap will adjust, you know,' I point out. At the moment it is perilously close to throttling her, and to be honest, I'm very close to letting it.

I make eye contact with the air hostess, who promptly comes over.

'May I help?' she asks.

Pauletta nods slowly, eyes dark. The hostess readapts the buckles so that they are safe. She then checks mine. 'Those are fine, I'll take your drinks order now and bring them round after takeoff.'

Pauletta perks right up. 'Vodka and orange juice, please.'

I close my eyes. It's going to be a long flight.

Home

I see what I've lost

My body tells me it's nearly midnight, but as soon as I step out of the airport, a wall of energy-sapping, jetlag-inducing, mid-afternoon heat hits me. LAX airport, USA. I can feel the heat through my sandals radiating from the concrete pavement, and beads of sweat rolling down my back. I'm almost blinded by the sunlight and my eyeballs are practically melting.

Pauletta is still clutching the luggage trolly for support, her bumbag hanging, clipped around her neck. After several vodka and oranges, a three-course meal and ten minutes, apparently trapped in the loo, she was escorted back to her seat by the charming stewardess. Smoking in the toilets, I was informed, is still very much frowned upon even in first class.

Irritation, already festering, bubbled to the surface and I hissed at her to stay in her seat for the rest of the flight. It was like taking an unruly teenager on a field trip to Buckingham Palace.

I could have shrugged and made excuses, I could have said she had an addictive nature or mental health issues. Maybe she had been overcome with anxiety because it was so out of character…

I'm not happy with the way I spoke to her. Normally, I would have shielded Pauletta from the demeaning attitude of the hostess, would not have been so crass as to hiss at an already intimidated soul.

But really, she's got herself a free all-inclusive trip to Hollywood, and she's behaving like a spoilt brat.

She slept for the rest of the flight.

I did not.

I lived every minute of it, as I'm sure my face can confirm. After giving myself a good talking to, I tried swotting up on what Tim has been up to career wise for the last twenty years. Accolade after accolade, award after award. I feel swamped and out of my depth. I'm not sure I can live up to his expectation of perfection and dedication, not with Scott taking centre stage in my thoughts.

I know for sure I have to see him. Can't be so close, without reaching out and baring my soul before him again. A flutter in my belly awakens me to the prospect of what the future may hold for us, if only I am brave enough to reach out and lunge for it.

One thing I know, there is no safety net. If he walks away, I'm on my own, for life.

The chauffeur guides us to the limo and stands holding the door open. 'Miss De-Muir,' he says.

'Thank you. Pauletta, if you can manage a few steps…'

She starts moving my way, one hand with splayed fingers covering her eyes, the other reaching towards me. The chauffeur helps her in then walks round to the other side and opens the door for me. I nod my thanks.

Pauletta half covers her mouth. 'Is not what I expected.'

I look at her wan face. 'It isn't what I expected either. Simply because you may drink as much as you like, does not mean you should. And smoking in the toilets.'

'I do not feel well, madam.'

As the car rolls forward, so does my stomach. What have I got myself into? 'As soon as we get to Mr Boswell's home, you may excuse yourself, and sleep it off.'

She lowers her head. 'Who will take care of you?'

'I am quite capable of looking after myself.'

Encouraged by the weight of the day and the gentle undulation of the car I let my eyes close, and simply accept the awkwardness of the situation. No doubt tomorrow Pauletta will be horrified by her behaviour and doubly eager to please. Not.

'Is impossible, madam. I will help.'

I let out a deep sigh. 'For now, I just want to rest my eyes.'

'I understand.'

'And my brain.'

'I understand.'

'And relax.'

'Is good idea.'

The cool of the aircon is a welcome contrast to the heat of the day, maybe a little too keen after the comfort of the flight. The car makes smooth progress away from the airport, and soon enough we are heading towards Santa Monica.

I hear her heavy breathing and open my eyes to confirm she's back asleep. The road is wide and sprawling with low-slung buildings either side, a backdrop of skyscrapers and a peppering of palm trees. The huge billboards, overhead powerlines and overhung traffic lights are all symptoms of urban city life. Pauletta isn't missing much, it isn't beautiful, that will be later.

I sit upright, crane my neck to see the first views of the ocean, vast and forever, the craggy rocks daring to encroach on its majesty. Soon the miles of beach and pier, I feel the excitement bubble up, just like the first time I laid eyes on them all those years ago. A magical, perfect dreamland, sprinkled with beautiful people and oiled with unspoken wealth.

I loll back in my seat and let the views unroll.

Away from the commonly rich, the wrought-iron gates peel open and perfectly manicured gardens caress the sweeping driveway. The house stands back, almost in awe of itself, a little embarrassed by the opulence it has to offer. Not quite apologising, but certainly not boasting either.

'Pauletta, we are arriving.'

She makes chomping sounds and scrubs her hands over her eyes. 'I must have been sleeping.' Opening her eyes fully, she stretches her mouth into a perfect "O".

'This is Mr Boswell's home. I did tell you he was a very important man – you can close your mouth now.'

'Is vegetarian.'

'Yes, he's a vegetarian, but I'm sure we will be able to eat whatever we like.'

The car slows to a stop in front of the house, Tim is stood on the steps. Dressed in casual slacks, open-neck shirt and his customary hot-weather trilby. His hands are clasped behind his back and he is totally still, waiting.

I can't wait. I push open my door and rush towards him flinging my arms around his neck. His arms wrap around me and he's spinning me. Like a child after the first day of school, at last, I am home. I can feel his smile against my cheek. I clasp my hand over my mouth, hold in the sob desperate to escape, contain the manic laughter bubbling inside.

'What took you so long, Harris?'

The spinning stops, and my toes take my weight again. Shaking my head, unable to speak, I absorb the strength and security his embrace affords me. I ease my arms down his shoulders and rest my head on his chest. 'I have no idea.'

I breathe in the fresh cotton scent, feel the warmth of the sun on me, and know I'm home. I step away from him and look into his eyes, and know he knows me well. 'Thank you.'

I turn, remembering I've left Pauletta in the car. My luggage is stacked up, while a tug-of-war is developing between Pauletta and one of Tim's staff over the ruck-sack.

'It's okay, Pauletta, people are here to help.' She lets go, and walks slowly towards us.

'Tim. I'm sure you remember Pauletta.'

'Sure, I especially remember the lovely meal she made us. Welcome to my home.'

She bobs her head. 'Thank you, Mr Boswell.'

'My pleasure.' He turns to me. 'I do have an unexpected surprise.' He nods towards the doorway.

Out of the shadows steps a tall, slim, young woman. Delicate features framed by a harsh, blonde bob, a rigid stance and clasped hands. 'Hey there, Maddie.' The honeyed Californian lilt could only belong to one person.

'Molly!' I hurry towards her, embrace her as Tim had embraced me – with total openness and an outpouring of love – no spinning, she's too tall.

Her stance softens slightly, but she still maintains her posture. I reach up and cup her cheek. 'I've missed you. Oh, look at me, I'm off again!' I brush the tears from my face.

'It's been a long time.' She smiles. It's a sad smile, one that doesn't quite reach her eyes. 'I had to see for myself. When Dad told me, I didn't believe him.' She looks at Tim, and I sense unspoken messages between them.

'I'm here.' I link my arm through hers. 'Come on, show me to my room and fill me in on all the gossip.'

I feel Tim's eyes on me as I leave. My gut instinct tells me, I need to be with Molly.

'But you told me to guard my heart, and I believed you.'

'I was wrong, I've been wrong all my life. What is the point of living, if not to love, and love without any boundaries?'

'Dad loved Mum like that, but she died.'

'He was lucky to have loved her. He was lucky to have had her love.'

Molly closes her eyes. 'We all died a little with her.'

'But she'd filled us to the brim with love, so we survived.'

'I don't think I'm brave enough to let go so completely.'

'I hope I am.'

I stand on the balcony of my bedroom, still feels like mine after all these years. The breeze from the Pacific Ocean is acting as a truth drug, filtering through my flawed core beliefs, forcing me to tell the world, starting with Molly.

I can't believe I've been so wrong, for so long. And it took someone most people think shallow and flippant to bring me to my senses.

One line, one sentence has been gnawing away at me for weeks. One which she stands by, lives by, preaches.

"You can have your cake and eat it."

Trudy Drummond has opened my eyes and expectations to a whole new level of credibility.

I'm glad I followed my dreams, but…

I should never have let Scott go.

I should never have left Christie behind.

I should have fought like a warrior to have it all.

But filled with fear of what everyone would think of me, I lost myself. Or, more likely, at sixteen, I didn't know my worth, my strength, my enduring ability to overcome.

I've acted for such a long time I don't know how to be me. Don't know if people will like me if they see the real me…

But Scott did, Scott does. He knows the worst of me, and still, he actually loves me. And fool that I've been, I pushed him away.

Christie, what of her? No matter what I do, I will always have done her wrong. I can't force her to like me, forgive me, love me. Those things are for her, and her alone to fathom. All I can do is wait for the verdict and accept it when it comes.

I'm here, that's all I can be. Giving up on any form of fulfilment to atone for the past is simply throwing away my future.

Molly stands beside me on the balcony, her hands resting on the cool, marble parapet. She leans out with her chin raised and eyes closed, straining towards the vastness of the open sky. 'I wish I could be that sure.'

'What is there to lose?'

She lets out an ironic laugh. 'My sanity. The passion I have for my work and the comfort of independence keep me sane.'

'They fill your days so you don't need to feel.'

'I do feel.' Her hair is swept back, made fluid by the breeze, her skin clear and free of makeup, looking like this she could be fifteen or thirty-five. I place my hand on top of hers, and she turns to me.

'I know you feel, you feel too deeply, you always did. And because you feel too deeply you shield yourself from the pain you know comes from loving.'

She looks away. 'I still feel her, here.' She places a hand on her heart. 'I wish I was more like Mum and maybe more like Mia.'

'But you're Molly. Your mum always said you'd change the world, and you have. Being a doctor, saving lives. She would have been so very proud of you, but she would have wanted you to be happy too.'

'I am.'

'I thought I was. But these last few weeks… I fooled myself into believing I was happy, all the while I was simply existing.'

She turns to me, looks into my eyes, searching, maybe? 'What changed?'

I laugh. 'What didn't? I'd thought having Christie back in my life would change everything, it just brought another raft of problems. And Scott, it brought Scott back to me, and your dad with an opportunity to act again, and now you.'

'Ahhh.'

'Indeed. My passion for acting and all the people I loved in the past, pushed under my nose like an enormous banquet set before me, reminding me of what I turned away from. What I gave up. And why?

For Christie. I never got Christie. Never could. She's her own woman now, it's up to her. But I see what I've lost, what I've missed and I'm not going to lose anyone I love again without putting up a darn good fight. After I'm done filming, I'm going to see Scott.'

Safe Hands

I was part of his family

6:45 am. Already 79°. The buzz of activity, a given. And today is a quiet day. Tim wanted to ease me in gently, but I'm fired up and ready to go.

Back story. Small town preparing to welcome back one of their old prom queens, allowing her to save face after a miserable existence in the big, wide world. Her former sweetheart vowing to win back her heart.

The original script had only the speculation of the townsfolk as to the whereabouts and fortunes of their lost beauty. However, Tim – seeing an apt little cameo for me – has arranged an ever-demeaning line-up of failed careers for me to act out. Starting with prospective starlet and ending with pot washer with all sorts in-between.

'Welcome home, Maddie.' Tim is standing, arms clamped across his chest as he surveys his domain.

I take a deep breath, the air is filled with the clutter of familiar aromas, coffee, makeup and sweat. Familiar sights, lighting, reflectors, mics. The familiar sound of equipment being positioned, the shouts, the welcome drone of the aircon. Faces change, scripts change, sets change but the essence of moviemaking remains the same – the relentless money-making machine of the studios – an enduring accolade to the almighty dollar.

'Feels like I've never been away.'

'Come on, the costume department awaits.' As we walk, respectful nods from various members of the crew, a reminder and indication of his status. 'Rhona can't wait to get her hands on you.'

'I hope she's gentle.'

He laughs. 'She's a whizz, and you'll look the part… at what cost, I'm not at liberty to say.'

'Thanks.'

He nods towards a youth leaning against a wall, one foot casually slung across the other, sporting well-worn trainers. The branded shorts, and LA Dodgers baseball top and cap, mark her out as a fan. 'Rhona,' he whispers.

'She looks about twelve.'

'Showing your age, petal.'

'Acting the part, Mr Boswell.'

The banter stops as she pushes herself off the wall, and steps towards us. 'Mr Boswell.'

'Miss De-Muir, this is Rhona.' We exchange smiles of acknowledgment. 'Rhona is well acquainted with the script, knows the itinerary and tone of the movie. I'm more than comfortable to leave you in her capable hands.'

'Thank you, I'm sure we will get along just fine.'

She smiles, turns and swings open the door and vanishes inside. 'Keep up, time is money,' she chimes.

Tim grins, and waves me in. I roll my eyes.

The cavernous room is well lit. Rail upon rail, from front to back and side to side, are all covered with the mandatory dust sheets, each has a clipboard with an actor's name, a list of costumes and scene numbers.

She leads me to the far side and nods towards a screen. 'I'm happy to take your measurements as you are, but you'll get a better fit if you strip to your undergarments.'

'Of course.' I step behind the screen. A full-length mirror and a wooden chair are provided for my comfort. I slide off my sandals, the cool floor a welcome bonus. My fingers tremble as I slip open the buttons of my blouse. Taking it off, I drape it over the chair. Unzipping my skirt, I let it pool around my ankles and scoop it up, folding it neatly. I tuck my sandals under the chair.

I push back the whisps of hair stuck to my clammy forehead. I dare to look at my reflection. My underwear is modest, built for ease and a smooth line, no thong or balconette bra for this old girl. I look flushed and a wave of nausea hits me, I steady myself, holding onto the back of the chair. I look again in the mirror, but noticing a heat rash spreading across my chest, I look away.

I sit, drop my head into my hands and start sucking in great gulps of air. I cannot be sick. The excitement and anticipation have got the better of me. Jetlag and the soaring heat aren't helping. All the romance and nostalgia of being on set has been replaced by the cold reality of the film industry.

Again, that feeling of being nothing more than a slab of meat, to be prodded, poked and primed ready for action, seeps into my soul.

No. I am more.

Breathe, breathe, breathe.

I am a vessel. I hold within me a performance to stir and entertain my audience. I am preparing to pour out the essence of a character they will believe in.

I can do this.

But first, I've got to let Rhona view my quivering body.

I stroke away the pearls of perspiration from my brow and under my eyes while still taking deep breaths. I stand and step from behind the screen. Raising my chin, I place my hands resting on my hipbones and look directly at Rhona. 'Ready.'

'Let's get to it.' She pulls off her cap, and from the lining pulls out a tightly rolled tape measure and a tiny notepad and pencil. She flicks out the measure like a whip, and slots the pencil over her ear. The pad is tucked in the waistband of her shorts.

Her hands and tape flash over my body like an electric eel over coral. Nape to waist, shoulder to nape, waist to knee, waist to ankle. Things get interesting. Calf and thigh. Hips, waist and boobs. From the top of my sternum to my navel.

She drops the tape, and starts writing frantically in the pad, head tilting from side to side as she bites her lip with a concentrated look on her face. She returns the pencil to atop her ear and slots the pad back in the cap. 'Getting there.'

She places one hand in the hollow of my back and cups my tummy with the other. She pulls a face which is neither critical nor encouraging, merely confusing.

'I'm forty,' I say, as a way of defence.

'I didn't ask.'

'But you looked…'

'Makes no matter to me, I've seen all shapes and sizes. I've just got to dress you.'

'Thank you.'

'It's my pleasure, but for the record, Mr Boswell has a skewed sense of fun, so don't blame me.'

Mr Boswell's sense of fun extended to me missing lunch and being speed-read through my script – such as it was – by someone called Geoff who had no hair and a blue beard.

Tim had called ahead from the car to make sure a meal was ready for our return. After a quick wash I hurried to the dining room. Pauletta was sat like a statue, hands folded on her lap, waiting. She looks up as I approach. 'Madam, how is your day?'

I sit beside her, leaving the place set opposite for Tim. 'It is long! And I am starving since I missed lunch.'

Pauletta scowls. 'Is not good. I will make you lunch to go tomorrow.'

'It's fine, I'll make sure I get something to take with me.'

'I go now.' She starts to get up, I place my hand on hers.

'Mr Boswell will be here in a moment, it would be very rude to leave the table now.'

'Is very rude to leave you with no lunch.' She pulls her hand away. 'Is not good for you.' She steps away from the table.

'Pauletta,' I hiss under my breath, 'sit down.' She turns to look at me, I can see the shock in her face. I eye her seat. 'Sit.'

She returns to her place, but pointedly looks away.

'We are guests in somebody's home. Good manners dictate we accept what we are offered, and deal with what we are not.'

She turns her head to give me the full benefit of her distain. 'Is not for me to say.'

'It is not,' I say, to my surprise. A brief surge of power pulses through me but is cut short by Pauletta's look of distress.

She doesn't know the Maddie I am in LA. The Maddie who grew to love herself. I came here with a hope for stardom. I left with something more precious. I left knowing I belonged to Tim's family. I left knowing I could come back anytime I liked, and would be welcomed with open arms. I left with a taste of stardom, but knowing I could do better than that. I left knowing I had to do everything in my power to make things right with my family, because it turns out I am good enough.

But Pauletta knows the UK Maddie. The me everyone in the UK sees, and more. She knows my secrets and my pain. She understands my longing to make amends with Christie. She knows the lengths I've gone to, to try and fix it. If she's read the letter Christie sent me, and she probably has, she knows I'm not there yet. And it hurts.

But here in this beautiful house, I am more at home than in my own house. The very first time I stepped into the grand hallway with its marble pillars and sparkling chandeliers, I felt like Cinderella at the ball. Now I feel its embrace, its warmth, its acceptance. It's the keeper of precious memories. And I can be me. I don't want Pauletta to snap me back to reality. Not yet.

I place my hand on hers. 'I'm sorry, but please understand, Tim has been very kind to me.'

'I understand. Important man.' She looks down.

'No, a kind man, and I don't want him to be upset. I was part of his family… like you are part of mine.'

A shy smile transforms her face. 'But I am cleaner.'

'Oh, Pauletta, you are so much more than that! How many cleaners are treated to this?' I gesture around the opulent dining room.

She shrugs. 'Is not for me to say.'

Butterflies

I lean in to kiss his cheek

It comes back to me. At night. When I should be sleeping. When my body is exhausted from a day's filming. When my mind has been busy. It comes back. And it taunts me.

I want to have my cake and eat it.

I want Christie, I read and reread her letter over and over. I trace my scar, the proof she came from me… and then I remember Scott. I remember his gentle kisses of forgiveness.

I want to have my cake and eat it.

I want Scott. The measure of his love was matched by the gift of his forgiveness. And again, I failed him, pushed him away, but that was before.

Before I knew I could have my cake and eat it.

I'm leaving tomorrow, should be. Trudy has decided she will collect me and Pauletta from the airport. She says Terry can't wait to see us. She says she has been working on Christie. She asked how my cake was coming along.

I have a secret. I'm going to see Scott today. Tim knows. Tim guessed. Molly absolutely knows, she would of course. Admitting my mistakes to her, instantly redeemed the friendship of our youth.

The truth does that. It sets you free. It also hurts, a lot. Realising how much energy and time I've wasted in pursuit of something beyond my control is a stinker. So now, it's truth time.

I'm going to say it as it is. God help me. I've never been as terrified in my life. I've only got today to get it right. Otherwise, I'd be doing it tomorrow, or the day after, or maybe I'd never get another chance.

Tim's gifted me today. He made everyone stay at the studio last night until all my takes were done. He was not popular, neither was I. He's sorted out the car. He's sorted out a reservation on the terrace at *Chateau Marmont* overlooking *Sunset Boulevard* – "Obviously, I have connections, Harris. And if it goes well…" – he'd smiled, alluding to the private bungalows in the grounds.

Despite the lack of sleep, I'm alert. Need to be. Pauletta is buzzing round me like a buzzard round a bone. Peck, peck, peck.

My words last week were harsh, too harsh for someone as fragile and stubborn as her. Since then, she has been on her best behaviour, has been a delight, fussing, but a delight.

'Is a little bit white.'

'Yes.'

'But is white.'

'My sandals are golden.'

'And is floaty.'

'I prefer dreamlike.'

'Is very—'

'After being squeezed into twelve costumes this week, I want to feel special.'

'Is special, is very white.'

'It's symbolic.'

'This is very nice "go-to-get-him" dress.' She eagerly holds up a close-fitting power dress.

A wave of uncertainty washes over me. 'I might not get him.'

There is a fleeting look of concern in her eyes as she pats my arm. 'I think you beautiful today. Even more beautiful than painting. You will get him.'

I caress a fold of delicate fabric between my fingers. 'But I'm wearing white.'

'Is symbolic.'

I don't want to do this. I can't. It's a stupid idea. Selfish. Interrupting his busy schedule. He only agreed because Tim contacted him. I'm going to make an absolute fool of myself. Throw myself at his mercy. Then walk away. With dignity when he rejects me? I should just fly home. Leave him be. But I have to give it a go. I have to know.

'Is a new bag?'

I eye the small, quilted, patent leather bag. The stitching makes small pillows of white. The buckle and sleek chain – both gold-plated – elevate the unspoken elegance of the ridiculously priced accessory. 'Yes.'

'Is very small.'

'It's big enough for my phone and cards.'

'And tissue?'

'And tissues.' Will I cry? I think not. My days of crying are over. I scoop my gold bangles up my arm, touch the droplet solitaire at my throat and lick my lips. 'I won't need them.'

'Because he cannot resist. You beautiful.'

'No. Because, if he doesn't want me, I'll just have to suck it up.'

Her face shrivels as she draws her chin back. 'What is this suck it up? Is disgusting.'

'Deal with it, it means deal with it.'

'He will not.'

I wish I had her confidence.

The journey lasts 45 minutes. 45 minutes to ask the driver to turn around and take me back. The novelty of my surroundings, celebrated on my arrival only a week ago, pass me by.

Soon enough, the view familiar to film buffs the world over is before me. The shabby chic Chateau Marmont rises from a sea of green, a picturesque paradise overlooking mile after mile of golden sand. Legends, secrets and scandals as flamboyant as the building itself shroud the sight before me.

My hands are trembling as they did at my first visit all those years ago. This is a place history is made. A place where icons idle, stars shine and discretion is demanded. A place steeped in its own notoriety, arrogantly proud of the role it has played in the fortunes and falls of its famous guests.

My driver drops me at the inauspicious doorway, a foil for what lies beyond. The discernment of the maitre'd is as legendary as the stars themselves. The opulence and presence encapsulated by the grace, elegance and old-style grandeur is breath-taking. I'm guided between the tables and on through the impressive archways. I let my fingers trail over the ferns and foliage of the tropical plants, as much a part of these surroundings as the dated decor.

The high, vaulted ceilings, lush with lavish embellishments give the authority of a cathedral. Indeed, to many in the industry, it is just that. A place to marvel at beauty, worship their gods and demonstrate their piety to the art of their craft.

I look out to the terrace beyond, maybe the place I make my own history with Scott. The magnificence of my surroundings has momentarily mesmerised me with all thoughts of Scott suspended. My skin prickles, and I run my hands over my arms.

A gnarled hand catches my wrist. 'De-Muir, is that you, girl?'

I turn and look into a startlingly youthful face. Her eyes dance with merriment, but the rest of her face is expressionless. I nod, feel like a first-year student sneaking into the prefect's lounge. 'I'm meeting… a friend.'

'Sure you are. Wanted you to know, what you did back in little old England was a brave move.' She gives my wrist a gentle shake. 'I wish more folks would own their mistakes,'

Mistakes, my life is littered with them. 'I wasn't brave. I had no choice.'

'Either way, it kept us entertained a while. You've still got it, girl, so you'd best use it.'

I laugh out loud. 'Thank you. I needed to hear that today.'

'My pleasure. Now off you trot, don't let me break your stride.' She releases my wrist.

I tilt my head and place my hand gently on her shoulder. 'Thank you. You are very kind.'

As I leave to make my way further out onto the terrace, I hear her mutter, 'Nobody called me that before.' I smile, I've made one person happy today. Result.

The smile freezes on my face. I thought I'd have some time to compose myself. He's already here, sat at a table in the far corner beneath the shade of a palm.

Our eyes lock. He stands and waits for me to reach him.

Jeans and cowboy boots, cornflower-blue shirt open at the neck, sleeves folded up a couple of turns, thumbs hooked into belt loops. I'm struck by déjà vu. His face is unreadable, and still, he's 100% the man I've wanted all my life.

I feel like I'm in one of those cartoons with my heart pounding out of my chest, butterflies in my belly and sparkles around my eyes. I want to run to him. Fling my arms around his neck. Feel his body wrapped around mine. Instead, I try to look relaxed, in control.

'Maddie.' He inclines his head and holds a chair for me to sit. He gives no opportunity for me to launch myself into an embrace, or even a handshake.

'Scott, thank you for agreeing to meet—'

'Your friend was very persuasive.'

'He can be.'

'He said you'd be heading back.'

'Tomorrow.'

'You've been here over a week and made no effort to see me.'

'I've been busy, I wanted to—'

'Sure.'

'I've been filming every day without any let-up.'

He shrugs, pulls a face. 'And it didn't occur to you, to, I don't know, phone?'

'I phoned hundreds of times after you left.'

'I was busy.'

'Sure.' A waiter places drinks before us. 'Oh, thanks. Could I have a tonic water, too?'

'Certainly.' He bobs away.

I look at the cocktail glass before me. Recognisable instantly by the golden flake and overriding aromas of cinnamon and vanilla. Chateau Marmont's famed *Butterfly's Kiss* used to be my favourite, back in the day. The paper butterflies dancing on the ceiling of the bar, plush surroundings and dim lighting always made this feel like a magical place. A place of fantasy. A place of escape.

No escape now.

I push the glass away.

'I thought it was your favourite.'

'It was, but not today. How did you know?'

'Your friend told me.'

'Tim?'

'Who else?'

Trust Tim to try and force the issue, words will be spoken! 'He also knows I like to order my own drink.' I notice a slight flicker of amusement in Scott's eyes.

'He set me up.'

'He set us both up.' My drink arrives. A skinny, frosted glass has chilled tonic water poured before me. 'Thank you.'

'Strange he'd do that after the lengths he went to to get me here.'

'He knew I wanted to see you, he made it happen.'

'The kind of friend to have.'

'Yes.'

'How good a friend is he?'

'The best I've ever had.'

'Any point me being here?' He takes a sip of his juice.

'Tim made my career. He and his whole family took me in.' I look at the ferns, how the breeze catches them. Fixed in a beautiful place, but at the mercy of their surroundings. Tim's family were my beautiful place, and he shielded me from the murky reality of what some young wannabes have to endure. What some have endured in this very place. 'They looked after me when I needed it.'

'You didn't give me the chance.'

'Have you heard from Christie?'

'We talk on the cell most days.'

'Good. That's good.' The elephant in the room is now sat on my chest, squeezing the breath from me, crushing my bones.

'How are things…'

'We've talked. She sent me a letter. Did she say?'

'No. She sent me a photo, of the two of you.'

'I don't remember us having—'

The old snapshot Christie took from me only a week ago, is pushed across the table. The one she'd asked to keep. The one with us together when she was only a baby. I don't touch it. Can't. I fold my hands together on my lap and swallow back the tears. No tears today, I told Pauletta.

'I remember it.' It was taken on one of those rare days I'd managed to get dressed. Mum helped. She'd ushered me into the garden and nestled Christie into my arms. I'd been numb, but obliged. Beneath the cover of the table, I draw my hand to my abdomen, trace my scar with my finger, rest my palm over it. 'She asked to keep it.'

He takes the photo back. 'You just don't care, do you?'

'Things aren't always as they seem, Scott.'

'I would of looked after you.'

'We've been through this.'

'I'd have looked after you and painted you every day of our lives, if you'd let me.'

I place my hand on the table, close to where his rests with the photo. 'And now?'

'We've been through that too. Christie has to come first. Your choice. Not mine.'

'And if I told you I'd made a mistake? If I told you I want you back, I love yo—'

'Don't.' His eyes flash, his jaw sets and his knuckles whiten as his fingers tighten on the photo.

'Scott, please.'

He tosses the photo towards me, stops it with a jabbing finger stabbing at my image. 'This girl here broke my heart when she vanished from my life.'

'I'm sor—'

'She didn't just steal herself away, oh no, she stole my daughter, too.' His voice is hushed and deathly controlled. His face contorted with the anguish of his loss.

I look down at my hands, the tremor visible to my own sight. 'I'm sorry.'

'How many lives have you messed up, Maddie? Christie's, mine, let's not forget the poor Rev and your mum!'

'I didn't do it on purpose, it just turned out that way.'

'I was sorted, happy with my life. Then BAM.' He slaps his hand down on the table.

The hum of conversations from the other tables stop, and I'm aware of everyone's attention turning to us. I lower my eyes and turn my head away from them. I can feel the heat of my flush speeding up my neck, burning my cheeks. 'Scott, please,' I mutter. 'Not here.'

'You've been back in my life a few weeks and I'm back feeling like that jilted kid all those years ago. Not knowing what to think, I'm not sleeping. I lay in bed trying to make sense of everything that went on between us.' He shakes his head, looks away from me.

I reach out, place my hand on his, he snatches it away as if scalded and turns his glare back on me.

I swallow. 'I know, I feel the same. I knew as soon as you left, I'd made a mistake.'

'Why did you do it, I told you how I felt.'

'For Christie. I didn't want to lose her again.'

'I suggest you best get back to her then, 'cos there's nothing here for you.'

Our eyes lock, his defiant, mine pleading. I try to search his soul for any glimmer of compassion, but he is closed to me. I hold my breath a second or two. Give him chance to change his mind. I let out a controlled sigh. I have my answer. I feel my heart shrink and put it back in its desolate dungeon of acceptance.

I stand, gather up my elegant purse, settle the dainty gold chain on my shoulder.

'Go ahead, scurry on back to Tim Boswell, the man who made you.'

'Thanks for sparing the time.' I lean in to kiss his cheek.

'Don't.'

The harshness of his tone slams into my heart delivering the death knell to any hope of reconciliation. I shrivel away from him. 'See you, then.' I turn to leave.

He catches my hand. 'Is that all you got to say? Tim will be disappointed. No Oscar-nominated performance. No snivelling declarations.'

'What good is there?' I raise a brow and wait. Nothing. The point of no return. 'Goodbye, Scott.'

As I walk away, I feel the flutter of a butterfly.

Encore

Is not for me to say

Tim's waiting. He's sat in the elaborate, high-backed armchair – the one Tilly bought him, with piano keys swirling high. He stands and walks over to me as I enter the drawing room. My face tells him all he needs to know. His arms fit around me like a goalkeeper's gloves making a sure save.

Cocooned in his embrace, I give way to the shuddering waves of grief I've been keeping in check. Pauletta must not know, she would never be able to forgive Scott.

Tim strokes my hair. I can feel his breathing… slow… steady… sedative. The rise and fall of his chest. His heartbeat. His aroma. The warmth of his body. No words… No action… Simply being. For as long as I need… For as long as I need. My rock, holding me together, while I tumble apart.

I ease away. Keep my eyes closed. I don't want to see the pity in his. He's lost far more than I, and with far more dignity.

'I didn't beg.'

'You shouldn't have to.'

I half open my eyes. 'I told him I loved him. I hoped that would have been enough.'

'You told him—'

'I love him. True love conquers all, right?'

'Aw, Maddie, only in fairy tales and Hollywood films.'

'Surely you get it? Only the fairy tale will do, nothing less.'

'What are you going to do?'

'What I always do. My best.'

He kisses the top of my head. 'You are a remarkable woman, Maddie. You don't have to be alone, you're always welcome here with me.'

'I think I'm destined always to be alone. Alone, I set up the Keep-a-Key charity, and everyone sat back and waited for it to fail – it hasn't, it's transformed the lives of Frankie and Micky and scores of others. I can do good things, on my own.'

'He might have a change of heart—'

I place my forefinger on his lips, shake my head. 'No.' The hope for reconciliation has been snuffed out in the pyroclastic ash from my imploding dreams. I dare not risk hope. I don't want pity. I need to be strong. I look up at Tim, pull further away from his embrace, his support. 'I've got this.'

'And what of Scott?'

I let out a sigh I feel like I've held in for a lifetime. 'I will always love him, mourn the loss of him.' I blow out a breath. 'But it's his choice. I've got to do this on my own. I'm stronger than I've ever been. Allowing the whole world to know the worst thing about me has freed me from the weight of their expectations. I'm me, it's all I can be. It has to be enough.'

'It's going to be tough.'

'I know, but I'm ready for it this time.'

'I'm proud of you… as proud as if you were my own daughter. I'm always here for you, Harris. I always have been.'

'I know, I know. Walking away from Scott is turning into a cliché, but I couldn't tell him. I want him to want me for me.'

He reaches out, pushes my hair off my face, pulls me in close and kisses my forehead. 'I understand, petal.'

'Thanks. I hope everyone else is as understanding.' I laugh. 'Be careful what you wish for…'

'You *are* going to tell him, because otherwise…' He lets out a long, toneless whistle.

'I'm going to tell Christie first. After all, it's not every day you get to tell your grown-up daughter she's going to be a big sister.'

I look at the muesli and yogurt. It is too much. Too much grain. Too much fruit. Too much yogurt. The smell of sliced banana sticks in the back of my throat. I push the bowl away.

'Is going to be a long day.' Pauletta doesn't know, but as usual is being a mother hen with a brood of one.

I nod. My cases are stacked in the hallway, while her rucksack is by her feet. With little interest I reach for a croissant. 'I'll have this.' I pick it apart on my plate, pop a small fragment in my mouth and chew, it sticks to the top of my mouth. I take a sip of orange juice and swallow. And again. And again. I continue until only the flaky crumbs remain.

I smile across at Tim, who's been watching my progress more keenly even than Pauletta. 'Thank you, Tim. I can't tell you how much this visit means to me.'

'Thank you! I've managed to drag the elusive Madeline De-Muir out of her self-imposed exile.'

'You've done more than that. And I want you to know, I've always been grateful for everything you did for me. I was just too scared to come back.'

'I leave you old friends to say goody-bye.' Pauletta stands and hoists her rucksack onto her back. 'Mr Boswell, is very kind to let me be here in your beautiful, big house with madam. Very kind.'

'It has been my pleasure, Pauletta.'

She bobs her head and turns to me. 'Madam, you are my family, I always try to do my best.' She walks towards the hallway.

I shake my head. 'Sounds ominous, I'm hoping the journey home is going to be less eventful than our journey here.'

'And I'm hoping you'll be coming over to see me as often as you can.'

'I will, maybe you'll even get to meet Christie.'

'I'd like that, very much.' Tim looks at his watch. 'But for now, if you're going to arrive in good time at the airport, you'll have to make a move. I've never known anyone take so long over a croissant.'

We both stand and Tim slings his arm casually over my shoulder as we head to the waiting limousine. 'I'm going to miss you, Harris.'

'Me too.' My throat feels tight with emotion.

'And yes, the filming. It was all a bit frantic, sorry.'

'Couldn't be helped.'

'I'll be in touch after the rushes, I can iron out any issues.'

I stroke my hand over my almost flat tummy.

'And that, my dear girl, is as much as anybody can wish for.' He squeezes me closer then lets me go.

Pauletta is stood with her hands propped on her hips looking out across the expanse of perfectly manicured lawns.

'Come on, Pauletta, time to go home.'

'I did a bad thing.'

'It doesn't matter, as long as you remember no smoking—'

'Is not that.' She turns to look at me under her lashes, her head hung low. 'Is much worse.'

'I very much doubt that.'

'Is true. You will see.'

'We need to—'

A motorcycle roars up the drive drowning out my words and halting with a screech of rubber on the tarmac. The rider launches himself off the bike and yanks off his helmet as he strides towards me.

Scott!

My entire body is electric with sparks zapping all over my skin, a tingle of anticipation is building up inside me. 'Pauletta, what – have – you – done?'

She shrugs. 'I remind him he never see you again. And here he is.'

Tim lets his hands drop from my shoulder and steps forward blocking Scott's advance. 'Can I help?'

'Yeah, step aside and let me speak to Maddie.'

'Maddie has a flight to catch, she's about to leave.' Tim's elegant English is a stark contrast to Scott's ragged Scottish/Californian drawl.

'She's not going nowhere before I speak to her.'

Scott tries to peer round Tim, but Tim puffs out his chest and plants his hands on his hips to continue blocking Scott's view of me, and my view of Scott.

'That is entirely up to the lady herself.' Tim looks over his shoulder to me, his expression loaded with dramatic overtones. 'Madeline, my little petal, can you spare the time to speak with Mr Scobie?'

I roll my lips, clear my throat. 'I suppose I can spare a moment or two.'

Tim tilts his head, offers a sage nod and steps to one side.

Scott steps towards me, still ruggedly beautiful in a more rugged way than usual. 'Maddie.' His voice is strained, the set of his jaw beneath the stubble, taut. Even so, just to hear him say my name is music to my soul.

'Scott.'

He glares at Tim. 'Can we get a bit of privacy?'

'Whatever you have to say, I'm happy for Tim and Pauletta to hear.'

Tim smiles, Pauletta raises herself up to her full 4ft 11 and threequarters. I wait. All eyes on Scott, I hear him curse under his breath.

'You aren't going to make this easy for me, are you?'

I remember how I felt walking away from him less than 24 hours ago at the Chateau Marmont and push away the urge to fling myself at him. 'Oh, no. I made it easy yesterday. Today is your own doing.' I take hold of Tim's wrist, turn it to look at his watch. I raise my brow.

Scott turns away from me, stomps back to his motorcycle. He balances his helmet on the handlebars, places both hands on the saddle and drops his head.

My whole body is screaming for him, the aching in my chest unbearable, tears prick my eyes as I swallow back my pain. So close. So close. I look at Tim and know I can't make a step towards Scott. I know I need to stand firm. Tim catches my hand and gives it a gentle squeeze. He mouths, "well done". I shrug and look at Pauletta who is scowling at Scott, looking like she has murder on her mind.

Adrenaline is surging through my body. My skin tingles with every remembrance of rejection I've ever known, each jabbing for my attention. All my life, behind every perceived success is the agony of rejection, spurring me on to strive harder, be more than I'm capable of being. My mouth is dry and my clenched jaw is making that drone kind of hum inside my head.

After what seems like an entire four seasons of *Killing Eve* – aka killing Maddie – he turns and walks towards me.

He stops within an arm's length of me.

'I can't do it, Maddie.' He scrapes both his hands down over the day's growth he's sporting. 'I thought I could watch you walk away and put you right out of my mind. But you're just as big a part of my life as my own arms. Hell, if my arms aren't for wrapping around you, there is no point to them at all. I'm not stupid enough to let you go again. I want you to stay here, with me now. Don't go, please…' He waves his arm towards Tim's house. 'I can't compete with what he has to offer you.'

Tim shakes his head. 'It's not a competition, son. This is down to you, so, get on with it!'

Scott lets out a deep sigh. 'I've never stopped falling for you since that first day, you with streaks of mascara down your face, and me splattered in mud. We've got history, and that history hurts. But I'm interested in your future, our future. They say lightning never strikes twice in the same place, but when all the elements are right, that's one hell of an electrical storm. You're my electrical storm, Maddie. I love you, it's as simple and complex as that. And it doesn't matter how many shocks you give me, I'm going to keep coming back for more.'

I look into the tsunami of emotions laid bare in his eyes. The pain. The love. The longing. I feel the flutter in my belly reminding me I am not alone in this decision.

'Scott, I have responsibilities.' I look at Pauletta.

She raises her arms. 'No, madam. Is not for me to say.'

'There's something you need to know.' I take a gulp of air, bite my lip. I take his hand, place it on the unperceivable curve of my abdomen. 'That night,' my words flutter, only audible to Scott, 'when you traced my scar, you kissed away my guilt—'

'Maddie, I—'

I place my finger over his lips, shake my head. I look into his eyes, lose myself in the love reflected in them. 'It was the most precious gift I could have ever imagined. For the first time in forever, I believed my life was worth living. I thought we could rewind time and start again.'

He raises his hand to cup my face. 'We can start right now, if you'll have me.'

'I want it more than you know, believe me, but there's something you need to know first before—'

'Whatever you throw at me, I'm ready.'

I take his hand from my face and place it back on my belly. 'We are having a baby.'

His eyes, clear and blue, widen. 'This isn't the life I planned, Maddie.'

His words hit me like a physical blow. I step back, accept the security of Tim's outstretched hand for support, sag against his body. Sucking in the warm Californian air, desperately fill my lungs with enough breath to scream. The scream never comes. It never does.

Scott steps towards me. 'No, Maddie.' He peels my hand away from Tim's, takes hold of my other hand too. 'I'm trying to tell you. I never believed I'd ever have a child of my own to love, then along comes Christie—'

'I'm sorry,' the words slip automatically from my lips.

He turns over my hand, traces the heart line on my palm. 'She was a gift, and now you are giving me the gift of the life I always dreamed of having with you. You are giving me my life back, Maddie.'

I swallow, try to make sense of his words. 'So…'

Scott pulls me into a loose embrace. 'I'm trying to say, in my usual clumsy way, I love you. And if you'll have me, I want to be by your side forever, whatever forever holds.'

'I'm scared, what if I blow it again?'

He drops his head to my shoulder. 'Darn you, Maddie, just say yes, I think I'm going to explode. Just say yes and stay.'

My body feels like electric, my skin tingles with anticipation of what our futures hold. 'Scott Scobie, yes.'

My feet are lifted off the ground as I'm pulled fully into his arms. His lips on mine endorse our union, the course stubble at odds with the tenderness of his embrace.

He eases me back down, eyes locked with mine. 'Thank you, I won't let you down.' He places his hand back to my tummy. 'I won't let either of you down.'

I reach up and draw my fingers over his rough cheek. 'I know. This is our time. At last, it's our time.' I ease away, seek out the pixie-like figure of Pauletta. 'This is down to you. What do you have to say about me staying here with Scott?'

'Madam, he is fool to say these things to you. A crazy fool. He must be big fool in love. But is not for me to say.'

Maddie's Men

Kathleen Clunan

Acknowledgements

A debt of gratitude is offered to everyone who has supported me with my writing. I would like to thank specifically, my good friend, Margaret Leak, who gave me the confidence to keep on writing, many times over. Without her support, I doubt I would have continued my writing.

Many thanks to the members of Chorley and District Writers' Circle for their advice, support, and friendship – a wonderful collection of talented, kind souls who are always willing to go above and beyond to support each other.

Thanks also to Matt Kenyon of Fertile Frog, who has helped develop my vision for both the *Christie & Co* and *Maddie's Men* cover.

And finally, Dr Greg Hall, who has worked tirelessly in helping get this book to publication. Again, without his expertise and dedication, I would not have the pleasure of seeing my novel in print. Thank you one and all.

Book 3: Trudy's Tryst

Yes, yes, I know you are desperate for more of The Harris Connection. Next, we join Trudy, in *Trudy's Tryst* as her exquisitely crafted life is snatched away in seconds. Her only connection from her past life, Pauletta. Trudy is desperate to redeem her father's reputation and restore her lavish lifestyle. Her new-found status throws up some uncomfortable home truths, which Pauletta is more than happy to point out. Turn over the page for a sneak preview of what is in store for Trudy.

Kathleen Clunan

A stranger and a sight

Keep up, princess

'Trudy Drummond?'

'Who's asking?'

'I'll take that as a yes. I'm going to need your mobile, cards and keys.'

I smile, if this pretty boy thinks he can take me, he's in for a shocker. 'Look, if this is some kind of scam, sweetie pie, I suggest you run along home.' I look across to the scrum of passengers leaving the terminal building. No sign of her yet. It's one thing taking care of a dog for a week or two, but I can't believe I let Maddie inflict her cleaner on me. Pauletta's a liability, she's probably been pulled by security. Again.

'No scam. I need you to do as I say. People are looking for you.'

'Look, buddy, I'm here to collect someone. I don't know what your problem is, but I do know it has nothing to do with me.'

He licks his bottom lip, casts a downward glance then darts intense eyes at mine. 'I didn't want to tell you like this.' He lets out a huff of air. 'Your father has been arrested. The police have impounded the—'

'Don't be ridiculous!'

He pulls out a mobile from his jeans, scrolls and hits play.

"Trudy," Dad's solemn voice breaks, "I expect you are wondering what the hell is going on. Well, you are going to have to sit tight and trust me on this one. You can rely on Ben. He's going to get you out of the way until things have settled down. Do not go back to Rose Cottage or contact anyone. Go through Ben, he's a good guy. Hope to see you soon, princess. It's not going to be easy for you, but you need to do as you are told!"

A surge of nausea smacks me in my stomach filling the space between my ribs and hipbones. I clutch at my bag to disguise the tremble of my hands. 'I don't understand.'

'You don't need to, yet.'

'You're Ben.'

'At your service.' He inclines his head and holds out his hand. 'Keys, cards, mobile and let's get out of here,'

I look round. No Pauletta. People are moving about quite normally, pulling suitcases, chatting, clambering into taxis. 'I need to find Pauletta, and I've left Terry in the car.'

'They'd be in the way. I need to get you out of here as fast as I can. People are look—'

'Well, I'm not leaving Terry in a hot car! He'll die.'

'Ah, your dog.'

'Duh. Obviously. And Pauletta is...' Much as I loathe the woman, I can't just leave her. I spot her coming out of the terminal, and nod in her direction. 'Pauletta is hardly a risk.' I start walking towards her raising my hand.

Ben grabs it. 'If she sees us, she will have to come with us. Do you understand. No loose ends.' He doesn't let go.

I glance across at Pauletta who's frantically looking for me. 'I can't just leave her. Look at her!

Her bumbag is hanging from her neck and random clumps of hair are fastened by a luminous purple scrunchy on the top of her head. Her clothes drape from her body almost ashamed to belong to her. She's swaying as the weight of her backpack – worn over her front – pulls her body forward, every few seconds she straightens up again.

'That's her?'

My insides crumble, what I've committed myself to? 'Yes.'

He lets out a long breath. 'She'll have to stay with you. Wait here.' He raises his hand and walks across to Pauletta. He nods over to me, Pauletta scowls. He eases the backpack from her shoulders and slings it effortlessly over one of his. Placing a hand in the small of her back he leads her to me.

'Miss Drummond,' she says. I can feel the contempt oozing from each of her pores.

'Pauletta, how lovely to see you.'

'Is not the same for me.'